JUL -- 2020

P9-DOF-019

WITHDRAWN

THE PRETTIEST STAR

The Prettiest Star

Carter Sickels

Mount Laurel Library
100 Walt Whitman Avenue
Mount Laurel, NJ 08054-9539
856-234-7319
www.mountlaurellibrary.org

HUB CITY PRESS
SPARTANBURG, SC

Copyright © 2020
Carter Sickels

All rights reserved. No part of this book may
be reproduced in any form or by any electronic
means, including information storage and
retrieval systems, without permission in writing
from the publisher, except by a reviewer, who
may quote brief passages in a review.

Cover Design: Luke Bird
Interior Book design: Meg Reid
Front cover image © Roberta Lo Schiavo /
Millennium Images, UK
Author photograph © Amie LeeKing
Proofreaders: Kalee Lineberger, Ryan Kaune

Library of Congress
Cataloging-in-Publication Data

Names: Sickels, Carter, author.
Title: The prettiest star / Carter Sickels.
Description: Spartanburg, SC : Hub City Press, 2020
Identifiers: LCCN 2019046338
ISBN 9781938235627 (hardback)
ISBN 9781938235634 (epub)
Subjects: LCSH: AIDS (Disease)—Patients—
United States—Fiction.
GSAFD: Historical fiction.
Classification: LCC PS3619.I27 P74 2020
DDC 813/.6—dc23

LC record available at https://lccn.loc.gov/2019046338

This book is a work of fiction. References to real people, events, establishments, organizations,
or locales are intended only to provide a sense of authenticity, and are used fictitiously. All other
characters, and all incidents and dialogue, are drawn from the author's imagination
and are not to be construed as real.

Hub City Press gratefully acknowledges support from the National Endowment for the Arts,
the Amazon Literary Partnership, South Carolina Arts Commission, and
Chapman Cultural Center in Spartanburg, South Carolina.

Manufactured in the United States of America
First Edition

HUB CITY PRESS
186 W. Main Street
Spartanburg, SC 29306
864.577.9349 | www.hubcity.org

for José

Hello, Mother.
Your son is dying. You knew—no, don't hang up.
Your son is dying.

—Karen Finley, "A Certain Level of Denial"

Home is the place where, when you have to go there,
They have to take you in.

—Robert Frost, "The Death of a Hired Man"

*H*e went out with his camcorder. The sun was just beginning to rise. He left his place on Fourth Street, between A and B, and walked west, passing the park and empty lots and boarded-up buildings with broken windows and graffiti-sprayed storefront metal gates. Sidewalks were littered with city souvenirs: an empty Coke can, a greasy paper plate, crack vials with balloon-colored tops—red, green, yellow, purple. Hardly anybody was up this early on a Sunday. An old man swept church steps. A wino dug through a trashcan, and a sturdy mule-faced woman with a floral-print kerchief tied over curlers walked her little dog. Crackheads huddled in a doorway. Two pretty guys in jeans and leather jackets and boots crossed the street, chirping like excited birds. Probably still coked up from a night out, bodies exhausted, alive.

Record everything, Shawn told him. Even my death, he said, especially my death.

He saw the city through the eye of his video camera. The new morning light exposed the grime, the gum-stained sidewalks, garbage cans spilling over. But the city was hushed and golden as prayer. As the sky behind him turned pink, he walked toward a silvery blue.

He didn't know the last time he was up so early. Or walked so far. When he first came to New York, he barely slept, too worried he'd miss something. He walked everywhere then—too scared to ride the subway and too broke for cabs. He wanted to understand how the city was laid out in a way only a real New Yorker could. He wanted to know where he was. To feel like he belonged.

It was 1980 when he arrived. He rode a Greyhound from the hills of Ohio, and all he brought with him were a couple of changes of clothes, a few cassette tapes, and three hundred bucks. He was eighteen. Now he's twenty-four. In AIDS years, does age even matter? Before New York the only funeral he'd ever been to was his grandfather's, a man he hardly knew. In the last two years he's been to nine—all men between twenty-five and forty-five. How many others does he know who are sick? They don't always tell each other. He doesn't want to go to any more funerals.

It was a ridiculously long walk, but he didn't care—he needed to make the journey. The camera was heavy, and a dull pain rippled down his shoulder and spine. He took breaks, stopping along the way to rest his legs and catch his breath, sitting on stoops or leaning against bus stops. A lifetime ago, he played baseball. Shortstop. His body was invincible. All he knew of pain then were aches from pulling a muscle or something equally inconsequential. Now his body was no longer his own, taken over by various ailments: shortness of breath, sudden aches, blisters in his mouth. He shouldn't complain. He's been spared, so far, of the Kaposi sarcoma lesions. He's not going blind. Not losing his mind. He wakes in the mornings and gets out of bed and his legs work and his heart beats. But he knows how things go, how quickly they shift, take you away.

A couple months ago, a fever consumed him, a crackling in his lungs. When Annie took him to the hospital, he thought he wouldn't come back out. The doctor barely spoke to him—another faggot taking up bed space.

He stopped in Washington Square Park. A few dealers were already lurking around the perimeters. He sat on a bench, looking up at the park's marble arch, where pigeons perched. Hundreds or thousands of birds. The arch looked grand and beautiful against the brightening blue sky. This was New York. Suddenly, the pigeons lifted into the air at once, a dance of gray and white beating wings. They soared overhead, across the park, and then changed direction and came back, together. They landed on the arch, and stood still again. It was like they'd never left.

He crossed Sixth Avenue and headed into the winding web of the West Village, where they'd lived together. The last of the darkness had lifted and the city was awake, awash in sunlight. The sidewalks squirmed with people. Taxis and graffiti-bombed delivery trucks rumbled by. A woman wearing too many coats talked on a pay phone and gestured wildly, holding an urgent conversation—but was there anyone else on the line?

He wandered the crooked streets like a tourist, walking by brownstones and shops—a hat shop, a frame shop, a pet shop with puppies in the window. He recorded all of it. He stopped outside their old apartment building on Charles Street. He never felt like he belonged in the Village, where the gays with money lived. Shawn didn't have money either, but he'd landed in a rent-control apartment a dozen years ago. They were together two and a half years. They lived on the second floor, a corner apartment. Their bright pink curtains had been replaced by industrial beige Venetian blinds blocking the windows like prison bars. Everything in this city reminded him of Shawn. It was too much.

The West Village used to be where you went to see manicured, muscular, moneyed men. Now, it was turning into a hospital, a graveyard. Ghosts glided beside him. He passed one ghost pushing another ghost in a wheelchair, probably neither over forty, but their sunken faces and shriveled bodies were that of very sick, ancient octogenarians. The one in the wheelchair had glassy, sightless eyes, his head tilted toward the treetops, and his companion, who was pushing the wheelchair, looked out from a face ravaged by a hideous map of purple-black lesions. Another emaciated ghost-man leaned on a cane. Two others held hands, their eyes big and dull and resigned. City of ashes, city of bones.

Record everything.

When he reached the West Side piers, he sat on a ledge, and gave his shoulder a break from the camera. A pigeon flapped its wings but didn't fly away. It stood its ground and stared at him with unsettling orange eyes. His first couple of years in New York, this was a different landscape—crowded with men sunbathing, shaking their hips to Donna Summer, writing poetry, checking each other out, finding dates and lovers and quick fucks down by the decaying edges of the docks. Not many guys came here now. Too afraid. A couple of boys turning tricks planted themselves and waited; others headed up to Eleventh Avenue. The sunlight reflected on the water, and the current lapped against the piers and over the wooden posts sticking up like submerged trees, reminders of another time.

The last two weeks of Shawn's life were a blur, but also creaked by painfully. He'd lapsed into demented babbling. He had a tube shoved down his throat. He died in the hospital, alone. At the moment of Shawn's death, instead of being at his boyfriend's side, he was standing in the hallway staring at a vending machine, waiting for a paper cup to fill with thin bitter coffee.

He no longer went out, not even for work. He'd lost his job. Nobody would hire him now; they'd see his sickness; they'd know. Annie, his roommate and best friend, said she would help with rent and take care of him, but he didn't want that. He wanted…to leave.

For a long time, he sat there watching young guys, many of them already infected, hustling for johns, as tugboats and barges moved like giant fish across the Hudson. He thought about Shawn and the other men he'd loved. The morning gave way to early afternoon, and the cool air warmed until the sun felt hot on his face. The video camera sat on his lap, turned off. Nobody knew he was here. Nobody glanced his way. He was already turning into one of the thousands of ghosts. It wouldn't have been so hard to finish things off.

He'd heard about others going this way, taking control before the virus did. He read the headlines, heard the whispers. They leaped off the Brooklyn Bridge, or swallowed pills, or used a rope. If you waited too late, like Shawn, then nothing could be done—you suffer in a hospital bed, die alone.

But now the urgency wasn't there, or, a different kind of urgency had taken hold. The drop off the pier wasn't going to kill him, although who knew what sharp objects lay beneath the surface. Maybe the current would sweep him under. The contaminated, filthy water might kill him, but that would take too long. Anyway, he was already contaminated. He could swim along the river, floating, buoyant. Or dive down and force himself to hold his breath. But he knew how the body would fight, do everything it could to survive.

The water looked frozen. Seagulls screamed and circled. Behind him the constant hum of traffic. A couple of kids walked by, one carrying a boombox on his skinny shoulders, and the beats rippled out across the afternoon. He was thinking of the place he left behind. His grand-mother, his little sister. He was thinking of green hills and the clean smell of baseball fields and the light-filled woods on a summer day. His mother. His father, who he had not spoken to in years. For the first time in a long time, he wasn't afraid. He walked to the edge of the piers and looked to where the tiny green lady rose from the water like Jesus, holding up her flame, welcoming the poor and the tired. He couldn't jump. He couldn't let go.

Life on Mars?

Sharon

On Sunday we go to church, like we do every Sunday. Like every Sunday, my husband sits beside me. We're in our usual spot—five rows back, center aisle. Our daughter Jess sits in the row behind us next to my mother-in-law Lettie, who never misses a service.

The church is small and old. Behind the pulpit and on either side of the building, stained glass windows fracture the morning sun into shards across the dark walnut pews and the maroon carpet, reflecting in the gold plates where we drop checks and dollar bills.

"Look around! God's light shines." Reverend Clay reads his part from the bulletin. He stands in the same place where my father used to.

We dutifully respond: "The darkness disappears and gives way to light."

The congregation is sparse, glaring gaps of emptiness. This is how it will be through spring and summer. Now that Easter's over, people have absorbed enough religion to carry them through to Christmas. Birth, death, resurrection. Those are the days people remember.

Reverend Clay lifts his arms and we rise as one. The old widow Anita Brewer plays the opening chords to "How Great Thou Art" with great passion, her eyes squeezed shut like she's in pain. It's one of Lettie's favorite hymns, and I hear her from behind us, drowning out everyone within a three-row radius. She is off-key, practically shouting, *Then sings my soul, my Savior God to thee.* Travis glances over, the edges of his bristled mustache curling up, his eyes saying, *That's just how my mother is, what can you do?* I try returning his smile, but my mouth feels stiff, like my jaw is wired shut. A son's first love is always for his mother, that's what they say isn't it?

Travis rests his hand in the middle of my back. He smells clean and minty like mouthwash. Sundays are the only days I see him dressed up. For him, this is just like any other Sunday. He doesn't know about the letter from our son. Back at the house, folded up in my jewelry box, it is my secret, my cross to bear.

When the hymn ends we stay standing, except for Anita, who remains seated at the organ, her twiggy fingers now still. Someone coughs, then the crinkling of a wrapper. The reverend holds out his cupped hands in supplication and looks up: *Let us go forth in peace, may God be with you.* He sounds muffled and far away, like I'm sinking underwater. The letter came on Friday. After I read it, I wept. I prayed to God to give me an answer.

We bow our heads. I keep my eyes open. The faded, thinning carpet. My navy flats, Travis's dress shoes with the tassels. His hand still on my back. He stands close to me, breathes easily. A soft, sad silence thumps in my head. I will have to tell him. When? There will never be a right time. Reverend Clay says, *Amen.*

Unlike most of the congregation, I'm not a native to Chester or even to Boone County. I grew up in Columbus, the state capital. After it seemed like the last of the cancer had been removed from my mother's body, my father asked the Methodist bishop for a new appointment, some place away from the city, some place rural, small, quaint, and when a position opened up in Chester, my father moved us, believing southeast Ohio was close enough to the Appalachian mountains, where my mother grew up, that she would finally be happy. I was fifteen.

On the way to our new home, Father had to pull over for me twice. Embarrassed, I hunched like a dog by the trees and vomited, not used to the winding roads and lurching hills. As we got closer, there were fewer and fewer houses. No more blocks of apartment buildings or clusters of stores. Instead: stretches of cornfields and hilly green pastures where rust-colored cows stood and watched us drive by. I felt displaced but not uneasy. I was eager for change, for a new start. My father drove with both hands on the wheel, and looked freer and more at ease than I'd ever seen him. He wore sunglasses, tan slacks, and a canary yellow short-sleeve shirt with blue diamonds across the front linked like paper dolls, and he pointed out a river that ran alongside the road, a hawk soaring over a barn, trees spangled with pink and white flowers. My mother looked out the window and did not speak.

Chester United Methodist Church welcomed us with open arms. My father, a kind but aloof man, delivered positive, uncontroversial sermons. He did not preach fire-and-brimstone or talk politics from the pulpit. Small town ways of life were new to him, and he enjoyed them. We lived in a house owned by the church, and my father built birdfeeders and took up gardening. And, like the lilies and hyacinth he planted, his child also blossomed. Back in Columbus, I'd been timid, easily lost among the many hundreds of students, a lonely child, but at Chester High, I was the new kid, the minister's daughter, a city girl. I quickly found a place. Cheerleader, choir, yearbook staff, prom committee. I did it all, and I was happy.

My mother did not find happiness as my father had hoped, and a year after we moved to Chester, the cancer returned. When members of the church found out, they descended upon us, kindly but with purpose, the women especially, an army of angels. My mother had not befriended these women, though, Lord knows, they had tried. Now she was too weak to shoo them away: they fluttered in to clean, do our laundry, and feed us, especially to feed us.

I was not there for her last breath or for much of her dying, which at first was slow. The cancer had been hiding in her for months, years, then returned suddenly, ferociously. Church members attended the funeral, and for a long time after, the church ladies continued to bring us casseroles and homemade bread, pies and cakes. Leading the army of angels was Lettie. She often sent food over with Travis, her youngest son. From the beginning, Lettie showed me the kind of love my own mother couldn't, or wouldn't.

After I graduated from high school, Father moved back to Columbus. For him, Chester was just a few years of his life, a time overshadowed by pain and loss. For me, Chester is my home—a home built out of family, friends, church, community. I believed for so long it could not be broken.

President Reagan makes a stop in Hawaii. Maria Shriver and Arnold Schwarzenegger get married. A clothing line embraces basics: stone-wash jeans, Bermuda shorts, madras shirts. As I flip the newspaper pages, the printed words blur, jump, blur again. Since church this morning, I've been trying to stay busy—I've mopped the kitchen floor, dusted and vacuumed the living room. I thought reading the paper would distract me, but my mind buzzes, a beehive of worry.

Jess doesn't respond. I knock again, then open the door. She's stretched out on the floor with a book—she's a reader, just like my mother—and she looks up and scowls. Sadie, curled up next to her, thumps her tail.

"I told you to take your laundry downstairs," I say over the blaring rock music. "Can you turn it down?"

"Wait, it's number three on the countdown. I bet it'll be Prince again," she says. She's changed out of her church clothes into her favorite attire, gym shorts and a T-shirt.

I maneuver my way over to the boombox and turn the dial. In the last year, my daughter's room has morphed from a child's room of innocent stuffed animals and Smurf figurines to a fourteen-year-old's den of clothes, cassette tapes, secrets. On the walls, posters of rock singers wearing too much makeup—both women and men—have joined the whales and underwater scenes of rainbow fish and coral and other strange creatures.

"Jess, come on."

She sighs dramatically and moves in slow motion, tossing her clothes into the wicker hamper. She's tall for her age and starting to develop, but still hasn't shed her baby fat. It's the junk food. I don't dare say anything, just like I don't tell her she needs a haircut and a perm—she's too sensitive, easily wounded.

"You should be washing your own clothes," I say. "I'm not your maid."

She rolls her eyes. With Travis, she doesn't complain as much, and their relationship is easygoing and gentle. Doesn't work for us. I've tried. When she told me she started her period, for example, I wanted to celebrate. I drove us all the way to Columbus, where we went to the mall and out to lunch. I offered to buy her a new outfit—a skirt, or a nice sweater—but she hated everything I picked out. All she wanted was a cassette tape and a poster.

The utility room is downstairs in the finished basement, next to the family room where Jess and Travis like to watch TV. I pull tangled sheets out of the washing machine and move them to the dryer. Darks, whites, delicates. How many loads of laundry have I done over the years? It's strange to think about, how we spend our lives.

Travis's muddy boots sit next to the door to the garage. He's out working on his Chevy with Gus, our nephew. Tools clanking, the sputtering of an engine, cussing. Noise carries easily room to room, upstairs, downstairs. We bought the house after Travis came back from Vietnam. It's a split level with a two-car garage, blue-gray siding on the top and the lower half brick veneer, with a small font porch Travis built. It sits on an acre of land, which makes it feel like we're in the country instead of town. Back then the house felt a dream—not huge, but more than enough room to start a family, and nicer and newer than Travis's brothers' houses. Twenty years later, it feels old and cramped, and yet a part of us, an extension of our bodies.

Brian's bedroom is also in the basement. Travis started building it for him when Brian was fourteen—it was maybe one of the last times they worked on something together. Brian helped Travis frame the walls and lay down the carpet. It's been six years since I saw my son. I reach for the knob. The cheap, hollow-core door sticks. I pull harder and fling it open, and the room's cold stale air smacks my face.

It took us a while—months, years—to realize he wasn't coming back. It's difficult to remember the anxiety of those first few months, which gave way to a dull yearning, sadness, and everyday sorrow. There were times when the pain came on hard and unexpected, like a sudden, sharp gasp. But you can't live like that. We had another child to raise. You have to go on. We didn't forget him, but we let him slip under the surface, drift away. Travis and I stopped talking about him, and after a while, Jess, who used to follow her brother everywhere, stopped asking for him.

His room became a place to put things—no reason to treat it like a shrine, he wasn't dead. *He's not dead.* A black-and-white TV. An exercise bike turned into a clothes rack. Collapsing cardboard boxes packed with Christmas decorations and old magazines. *National Geographic, Handyman, Children's Highlights.* Some of Brian's old rock posters still plaster the wood-paneled walls, the corners torn and peeling, the air-brushed faces fading. Those tight pants, the lipstick. Should I have known he was *that way* by the music he listened to? But he was captain of the baseball team. His trophies still line the shelves, golden men and baseballs lacquered in dust.

I don't know what I'm looking for. Even as I open drawers, I already know his clothes aren't here. We packed them up a couple years ago, donating some to a church rummage sale and storing the rest in plastic bins in the garage. Now the dresser drawers nest Travis's folded T-shirts and socks and workpants. He uses the room as a second closet—maybe his excuse to come in here to think about the son he never talks about.

I slide open the closet door, unleashing the lonely smell of mothballs and must. Travis's winter sweaters and a couple of old suit jackets drape from wire hangers, and I push them away, and under the dim light, I spot a triangle of purple fabric and give a tug. It's one of Brian's old sweatshirts. The cold, wrinkled material unfurls, and I press my nose to it, but nothing—his scent faded years ago.

"What are you doing?"

Travis's voice startles me. I shove the sweatshirt back in its place and step out of the closet.

"I was just looking for something."

He stands in the doorway, arms crossed. After Brian left, Travis didn't say much, but whenever he'd come upon me crying, he'd tell me, "He'll be back," always with conviction. As time passed, he stopped saying those words and pretended not to see my tears. I don't know if he ever cried when he was alone. He grieved silently, and did not let me in.

"When do you want to go over to Mom's?" Travis asks. His silver hair, speckled with brown, is combed back with a little bit of an Elvis curve, and he's been growing his sideburns long again, like he used to wear them in the '70s.

"Pretty soon." I cannot stay in the room, in the house, for another second. "We're out of milk," I blurt. "I need to run to the store."

"It's Sunday, the store's closed." Travis gives me a funny look. "Just borrow some from Mom."

I tell him I also need to get gas, and I'll buy milk at the filling station. Travis doesn't argue—he wants to get away too. As I slam the door behind us, the flimsy wall trembles.

Outside, Travis's weekend project, a broken-down '67 Chevy pickup, rests on blocks in the front yard, making us look like our trashy next-door neighbors, the Dennisons, with their busted bicycles, broken toys, a half-standing chicken coop. On the other side of us live the Rollinses, strict Pentecostals who keep to themselves. Across the street Jean and Victor O'Malley, a quiet, kind couple in their fifties—Baptists—preside over a neat, tidy yard. They've been our neighbors for over twenty years, and bring us plates of buckeyes and sugar cookies every Christmas.

As Travis fishes in his toolbox, Gus raises up from under the hood. "Hey, Aunt Sharon."

"Got it running?" I ask.

"Well, I wouldn't say that exactly. Not yet." Gus breaks into a dumb, sweet grin. He slouches when he stands, but can't hide his towering height—six four or six five. He's big all around, used to play football. Gus and Brian were born just two months apart, and although Gus loomed over him, Brian ran the show.

"We'll get her running one of these days, won't we?" Travis claps Gus on the shoulder. "This boy can fix anything."

I tell them I'll be back shortly. My car, an olive-green Citation hatch-back, is parked on the street. Behind the wheel, I glance in the rearview mirror and catch the reflection of my own frightened eyes. Behind me, Gus and Travis laugh about something. The sight of them, my nephew standing where my son should be, makes my throat catch. I turn the key.

It was not supposed to turn out like this.

That's the angry, lonely thought thundering in my head as I drive through town, past Dot's Diner, the credit union, Mitchell's Funeral Home, and the dentist office where I've been Dave's secretary for eighteen years. *It shouldn't be like this.* And, yet, here I am, trying to get away from my family. Driving around. Where am I going? My son isn't here. He's long gone. Far away. He turned his back on his family to live a life of sin and he's sick because of it. He's dying.

On the outskirts of town, I turn in to a filling station. Milk, I think. I'm not running away, I'm buying milk. I pull up to a pump, and an overweight boy of about sixteen ambles out of the store. I ask him to put in ten dollars.

The store is dimly lit and too warm, and has the feeling of worn, grubby dollar bills. A few plywood shelves, raised by cinder blocks, display a hodgepodge of items: toilet paper rolls, hotdog buns, a can of baked beans, blue windshield wiper fluid. A beat-up boombox plays a slow country song—it's Reba McEntire, wondering which of them should leave the marriage. In the back a refrigerator holds a few cans of Pepsi and Dr. Pepper, and a single quart of milk that expires tomorrow.

An old woman with big but thinning hair sits on a stool behind the counter, hunched over a *People* magazine. She taps the page with her pruned twig of a finger.

"I tell you what, the carrying on that goes on between these movie stars. This one here, she's on her third husband." The wrinkles around her mouth tighten sharply in a prim, prudish way, but then she lets out a loud, rusty cackle, revealing dark gaps where teeth should be. "I'm still on my first, but, honey, I wouldn't mind being on my third."

I laugh along, but I'm looking at the cigarettes behind her. Something stirs inside me. I haven't smoked in fourteen years. My cheeks flush like I'm sixteen again.

"And a pack of Marlboros, please."

"Lights or regular or Reds, hon?"

"Regular."

With surprising agility, the old woman climbs up on the stool, and her hemmed slacks hitch as she reaches for the cigarettes, revealing bony white ankles.

"Just the one pack?"

I say yes. "And matches, please."

She climbs back down and slides over a ceramic cookie jar in the shape of a smiling orange cat. The lid is its head. Instead of cookies, it's stuffed with matchbooks from different bars and restaurants around the county. "Get you one or two," she says.

On the way back I drive past the cemetery. Green hills rolling with headstones and white crosses that sprout like terrible trees. I would like to just keep driving, past the county line, maybe the state line. When I was a girl, we would go on family drives on Sundays after church. My mother was happiest then, not saying much, content with the breeze on her face, in motion and leaving.

I grew up comfortably. We lived in a modest house the church provided, and the ladies in the congregation made sure we had plenty to eat. People did things for Father for free—car repairs, plumbing, house painting. I used to sew my own dresses and occasionally Mother would make me an outfit. I owned store clothes too, but not the way kids do today, all this brand-name stuff they can't afford. Things were different then—people didn't need or want as much.

But Chester was not exactly the quaint town my father had been expecting. Rural and small, yes, but no gleaming white picket fences. It's a hardscrabble, forgotten place in the foothills of the Appalachians, about eighty miles from Columbus. The nearest big town is Madison, the county seat, where we do most of our shopping. All of Boone County is rundown and forgotten. Used to be different, Lettie tells me, when there was coal in the hills and money in the railroad, before all the good jobs went elsewhere and the companies took the money and ran. Since I've lived here, I've watched businesses disappear, homes dilapidate.

Not everyone is poor, but nobody is rich either. Every year there are fewer and fewer jobs. Travis is lucky to have a steady, good-paying one. He works for the electric company, and I work full-time too. Unlike most people around here, we manage our money well.

I drive past the Green Valley Trailer Park, the shuttered library, the beer carryout, and the town's pride, the Chester swimming pool. Built in the '20s by a rich railroad family, it closed in the '60s, and then a dozen years ago, the county, using taxpayer money, renovated it and reopened it to the public. Brian used to go every day in the summers— so at ease and graceful in the water, just like he was on the baseball field.

Clusters of white flowers burst from craggy cherry trees and irises shoot up from the sides of the road like yellow-tipped purple paintbrushes. The sky is turquoise, cloudless, a perfect spring day. At the old drive-in, the marquee still stands, dusty yellow with faded blue script, SUNSET DRIVE-IN. I pull in.

The drive-in didn't fare as well as the swimming pool. When Brian was little, the place was always crowded with families, couples, and teenagers, and we'd sit on lawn chairs, eat popcorn and drink pop, and wander between cars, talk to friends, the screen alive and glowing against the darkness. Brian would sit on my or Travis's lap, or alone in a lawn chair positioned between us, looking up, rapt. He never fell asleep during the movie, but on the short drive home, as soon as Travis started the engine, he'd be out like a light. Body limp, stale popcorn breath. Travis would pick him up, even after Brian was getting too big, and carry him inside.

In his letter, he said he'd been in the hospital. Why didn't anyone call me? I'm his mother. If I'd known, I would have boarded a plane, nursed him back to health. I've never been on a plane.

I light my first cigarette in years. The smoke comes in and goes out, smooth and easy, quieting the drumming in my chest. After a few drags, I feel a little dizzy, but calm, clear-headed, settled. I turn the car back toward home. I'll tell Travis about the letter tomorrow. What does it matter, one more day?

"Well, it's about time," Lettie says. "Get you something to eat."

She's set out cold cuts, potato salad, and a cherry pie.

Travis and Jess act like they're starving and pile up their plates, then go out to the backyard to join the others. I linger in the kitchen, and Lettie studies me.

"You okay?"

"Yeah, why?"

"You look a little peaked."

"I'm fine," I say.

She makes a dismissive clucking sound, meaning she doesn't believe me, and lights a menthol. Lettie's a stout, strong woman who raised three sons mostly on her own, and now she's a grandmother and great-grandmother. Her bouffant black hair and dark, penciled eyebrows make her blue eyes look even more striking, but the caked-on makeup gives her the look of a washed-up Grand Ole Opry star. She's traded her church dress for knit slacks and a short-sleeved pink blouse that shows off her pale freckled arms. Gaudy fake rubies—clip-ons—sparkle from her ears, and her thick fingers are studded with rings.

"Last night I had a dream about him," she says in a low, secretive voice, and every receptor in my skin rises like a thousand candlewicks suddenly alight and burning. Nobody else in the family ever mentions Brian, only Lettie—and whenever she says his name, a thin, delicate fissure cracks my chest, bones splintering like dry wood.

For a second, I wonder if Brian also sent Lettie a letter, but, no, she would have told me—Lettie can't keep a secret. She's described her dreams to me before, the signs that tell her Brian's okay and he'll be coming home. I've always ignored her premonitions, but now I want to know.

"What happened?" I ask.

"It's fuzzy." She draws on the cigarette. "He was a little boy, and he was telling me some story, you know the way he used to do, laughing and his hands flying around." She stops. "Well, I don't remember. Sometimes he just comes into my mind."

"I know," I say.

"It's been so long since we heard anything."

I pinch the insides of my crossed arms so hard I wanted to cry out. "I'm sure he's fine," I say. "He just lives a busy life."

My voice sounds strange and hollow like someone else is speaking through me. Lettie takes another drag and sets the cigarette down on a glass ashtray.

"I better go on out there. You coming?"

"In a minute."

After the screen door swings shut, I pick up the burning cigarette and taste the sourness of Lettie's lipstick, probably one of the many tubes leftover from her Avon days. When Brian was little, she used to take him along with her to sell makeup and creams and perfumes. Maybe he spent too much time with her. She was too soft with him, Travis said, loved on him too much.

The backyard buzzes with conversation and laughter. I settle into a green and white striped lawn chair between Liz and Carol, my sisters-in-law, and as we catch up, Jess, who is much younger than her cousins, plants herself on a quilt, cooing over Allie, Gus and Pam's six-month-old. Travis talks to Paul and Wayne about work, and my nephews Matthew and Kyle toss a green foam football with their sons, while their wives, Sherri and Lisa, also Chester natives, smoke cigarettes and complain. I always thought Kyle in particular would end up dead or in jail by twenty-five, as wild as he used to be, but here he is: a father and husband, alive and healthy.

It was the bigness of the Jacksons that drew me to them. They took me in without hesitation, sweeping me in as easily as a river would a leaf or a twig. Everything about their way of living was new to me. I grew up in a house of quiet. Mother in her room or at the kitchen table, reading historical novels. Father busy at church, writing sermons or ministering to his wife. At the Jackson house, the TV or record player or radio was always on, sometimes all three at once. Lettie raised her three sons on her own, after her husband died in a car accident when Travis was three years old. Lettie doesn't say much about him, just that he was a good man. She never remarried, never even dated again, as far as I know.

Everyone in the family lives nearby. Carol and Wayne in a little brick ranch on the outskirts of town, and Paul and Liz in a double-wide. Travis and his brothers, and his brothers' sons, all work at P.T. Gas & Electric, the same place where their father once worked. After their father died, Wayne and Paul helped take care of Travis, and he credits them for teaching him how to be a man.

After a while, Wayne's voice dominates, as usual, demanding everyone's undivided attention. My neck stiffens, preparing myself for his vulgarities—Travis is always quick to defend him, says he doesn't know any better—but today Wayne just tells a tedious story about a boss who gave him trouble (he claims) because Wayne knew more than he did, one we've all heard before.

"Yes, he treated you bad," Lettie says. "I remember."

Lettie is one of the kindest souls I know, but when someone does her or her family wrong, she doesn't hold back. Even a minor slight by a store clerk can set her off. She doesn't yell or throw a fit, but she'll say what's on her mind. She holds grudges.

"Told that son-of-a-bitch to stick that pipe where the sun don't shine." Wayne smiles in his surprisingly charming way. The oldest brother, he has black hair and deep-set dark eyes that make him look like he's always a little bit hungry. He's strong with wiry muscles, and rides a motorcycle, and, like most of the men around Chester, he's rough around the edges.

Carol smiles at Wayne, bored—she's heard the story a hundred times. Back in high school, Carol used to be wild: cutting classes, smoking in the bathroom, nipping whiskey out of a flask. But over the years as a mother and now a grandmother, the wildness has disappeared like muscles lost under the folds of flesh. She's put on at least twenty pounds in the last two years.

"I remember him, he wasn't from around here," Paul says. "Didn't stay either." The middle son, chubby, with shaggy hair and thick eyeglasses, Paul is the most easygoing of the three. He reaches into the cooler and hands Liz a beer. "Here you go you, baby," he says. After all these years, they still hold hands.

Travis pulls down his baseball hat to shade his eyes. My husband was different from his big brothers, had ambition. While they skipped classes and smoked cigarettes and drank too much, Travis made good grades, and played baseball and basketball. He was a clean-cut, all-American kid. But after the war, he stopped talking about going to college or trying to work his way up to foreman. He didn't say much about Vietnam, except, *It's hell over there.* I used to watch the nightly news with Lettie, both of us quietly terrified as Walter Cronkite gave his report. The number of the dead rising and rising, and no end in sight.

"Sharon, we ought to go on a girls' shopping trip soon," Liz says. "Lettie, you want to come with us?"

"You know me," she says. "Shop till you drop."

Conversations float in and out like too many different radio stations playing at once. The sun is beginning to set, and I feel chilled. From the center of town, a passing coal train blasts its horn.

Lettie mentions Wayne's upcoming birthday, and the attention swerves back to him. "Fifty," Paul says. "Brother, you're getting old."

"Hell, I'm still not as gray as Travis," Wayne says.

"I don't know about that," Travis says. "Mom, you think you ought to take him to the beauty shop with you?"

"Well, Annette sure knows how to hide the gray," Lettie says.

"Should I get a perm too?" Wayne pretends to fluff his hair. "Won't that look good?" he says in a falsetto.

Everyone laughs, and, encouraged, Wayne keeps going, talking about getting his nails done, looking pretty. His pretend lisp gets louder, as if he's shouting into my ear, and everything turns too bright—the green lawn, the black of Lettie's hair. Jess doubles over with laughter.

"Wayne, you seem a little too comfortable, if you know what I mean," Travis jokes.

I don't know if I'm angrier at Wayne or at my son for putting me in this situation. The flash of brightness fades and the voices start to sound normal again. But my heart races, my mouth tastes strangely of blood. This wasn't supposed to happen. *They* were the ones with the troubled kids: teen pregnancy, jail, school suspension. Travis and I were different from his brothers and their families, and so were our children, who we believed would go to college and find good jobs, get married and give us grandchildren, and live close by. They'd live happy lives like the kind you see on television. We felt protected from tragedy and looked forward to the future, a glistening river of possibilities.

✳

Once you know something, you can't un-know it.

I first heard about the disease two or three years ago, mentioned on the news, and I remember seeing it come up on a TV show, some hospital drama that Lettie had on. I still remember how I felt when they said the character was gay: everything in me went still and I started chattering, it didn't matter what came out of my mouth, I just needed to talk over the TV, block it out, cover it up. Since then, of course, you can't escape hearing about the gays or the disease, especially after Rock Hudson died last year. The preachers say it's a punishment from God.

Now I have this letter, a half page written on yellow legal pad paper. He said in the first line, *There is something I need to tell you.* The word AIDS printed carefully in capital letters. He's been in the hospital already. Didn't want to worry us. He's doing all right, he says, he feels stronger. The letter was shockingly direct, but also vague. *It's been a while, and I was thinking maybe I'd come home to see everyone. I'd like to see the family. How is Sadie doing? I wonder if she'll remember me.* His phone number was written below his signature. He was waiting for us to call.

A few years ago, Brian sent a picture of himself with a man. They had their arms around each other. Brian looked healthy, handsome, strong. Hair curled around his ears, crooked teeth, blue eyes. Head tilted to the side. His smile was big. Then, this man. Older than him. Tall, muscular. *Black.* Later, Brian told me that his friend was dead. Didn't tell me how he died, but now I know. It was him. He infected my son.

Alone in the kitchen, I hear my husband and daughter upstairs, the creaking of the floorboards. I'll tell Travis about the letter tomorrow. Let us have one more night where nothing is changed.

But when I walk in the bedroom and close the door behind me, I can't hold onto it any longer. Travis pulls on a pair of blue plaid pajama pants, his T-shirt crumpled in a ball on the floor.

"I have to tell you something."

He raises his eyebrows. Pants on, no shirt. His chest hair curly and thick, silver as pencil shavings. "What's wrong?"

I open the jewelry box, which used to belong to my mother. It sits on top of the dresser like a white cake. I open the lid. Inside, pink silk lining, the faint scent of stale perfume. There are two layers, and the letter rests on the bottom, folded in thirds. I take it out. Hand it to him. His face wrinkles with confusion. He opens it, barely glances at the writing, and closes it. Doesn't read it, doesn't want to know. There is a tremor in his voice.

"What is this?"

He holds up the folded letter away from him, a piece of evidence he doesn't want to see. But I want him to read it: why do *I* have to explain? As I glance away, I catch sight of our reflections in the mirror, our drawn, worried faces, how naked and vulnerable they look, and I quickly turn, don't want to see. The light is low in the room, a dull yellow, and everything seems old and worn: the pale blue carpet, the beige bedspread with peach and blue flowers. I hear Jess, opening the bathroom door, closing it.

"It's from Brian," I say.

Travis holds the letter towards me, wanting me to take it back, but I don't.

"He's sick," I say, and as soon as the words leave my mouth, as soon as I let them go, my bones turn to mush, I have to sit. My legs fold, the mattress holds me up. "He has AIDS."

Travis is standing in front of me, so I have to look up to see his face. The skin around his eyes crinkles, as if he is staring into the sun. His eyes are light blue, like glass canning jars. He cocks his head like he misheard.

"He has what?"

His tone is incredulous and sharp, like he thinks I have everything wrong, and a rush of anger spreads through me like a fever, gives me the strength to stand back up.

"AIDS," I say, then say it again, louder, getting myself used to the word. "He has AIDS."

Travis doesn't understand. Staring blankly. Of course, he knows about it—he's heard Wayne's jokes, he's read the newspaper articles, heard the preachers and politicians. But, like me, he has ignored, deflected, refused. He drops the letter on the bed. Still, disbelieving. An accusatory tone of voice: "What does that mean?"

His pajama pants hang low on his hips and he is wearing white tube socks, and now I wish I told him before he started getting dressed for bed. The anger dissipates from my body like a dying light. He looks old and childish at the same time. He looks scared.

"Brian's sick," I say. "He could die."

Could die, would die. The words swell inside me like a bruise. A disease of the blood, a disease that people catch. People die from it. People, what kind of people. He doesn't ask, I don't say. It is quiet except for the ticking of the alarm clock, but outside these walls, the noise is normal and good. Jess running water. Jess brushing her teeth. The lid of the toilet. Bathroom door, bedroom door. Jess climbing into bed, pulling up the covers, closing her eyes. Her heart beating. Healthy, alive.

"He wants to come home," I say.

For a moment, a band of light, hope, twitches across Travis's face: his son is coming home. The son he loves, the son he carried in his arms. Then he remembers. Shaking his head, he takes a step back, further away from me, in the shadows, the way he used to disappear after he came back from Vietnam. He was the same man, a good man, except quieter—sometimes he vanished from conversation, eyes fevered with memories he wouldn't share.

"Is that even safe?" he asks. "For him to be here?"

He crosses his arms over his chest, letting go of nothing, making me do all the work.

"It's not contagious," I say. "Not by touching." Stop. Don't want to think about the ways it is spread.

Travis rubs his jaw, thinking. His eyes hooded, protected, downcast. He is studying his socks. How clean, how white.

"They don't know for sure," he says. "There's a lot about this they don't know."

He wants me to agree with him, to take everything back, to apologize, to keep things from changing. I am close enough to touch him, but I don't. I hold my arms at my sides, heavy and dense like they've been packed with mud. My legs still feel rubbery, and my feet are weak, useless things.

"He wants to come home," I say.

The pause of silence that follows is not quiet but hot and panting.

Travis looks up. "So he only wants to come home when something's wrong," he says, his voice swollen with anger and hurt and guilt and accusation. All of the same feelings in me. He is hurting, I am hurting.

Travis goes over to his side of the bed. Him on one side, me on the other. The bed a mountain between us.

"How sick is he? Does he just want to come here for a little bit, or stay here until…" He trails off.

"I don't know." My voice is sharp and prickly. But I understand: we've already been through so much. Travis, sighing, sits heavily on the bed, his back to me. I return the letter to the jewelry box, close the lid. I don't know how to fix any of this.

I change into my nightgown, and get into bed. Travis lies on his back, staring at the ceiling. His chest is wide and strong, and I remember when we were young, how easy it was to sleep with my head right there, to curl into him, holding on until we grew into a single body. But now to slide up beside him like that feels awkward and forced. I stay on my side. Why is it up to me to do the talking?

"We need to tell him something," I finally say.

He turns toward me, his face sad and scared and pale, and I feel sorry for him, sorry for us. When Brian left, Travis said it was his choice—we were not the guilty ones, it wasn't our fault. He was strong then, maybe too strong. He made me believe everything would be okay, and I want that again, for Travis to take charge, to do the right thing: I will stand by him.

"I don't know what to do," he says.

I hold my breath as he reaches over and turns out the light. He rolls on his side, away from me. In the dark, where he now feels safe to tell me his fears, his voice sounds husky, strange.

"If he comes back," he starts, and I stay as still as possible, hollowness thudding through me. "What will people—"

I force myself to speak, just to stop him from talking. "He's our son," I say. It is the right thing, but even as I say the words, they sound easy, rehearsed, false.

Travis says nothing else. Neither do I. But the decision has been made. We have to let him come back home and I must bury the unspeakable thought: I wish I'd never even opened the letter. I lie next to Travis for what seems like hours, until finally his body softens, his breathing slows. He's been awake all this time. Both of us staring into the dark, not touching, not talking. When his breaths turn to snores, quietly, I get out of bed, go downstairs. I shuffle my into my tennis shoes, dig the cigarettes out of my purse. I'm a smoker again.

I walk into the backyard. The wet grass brushes against my bare ankles like pieces of velvet and soaks through my tennis shoes. The Dennisons' hound is quiet, but the night insects sing and hum, calling each other. The moon is almost full and the sky is clear and everything glows under the silver light: the towers of trees, protecting our still house.

Travis's words, spoken in the dark, ring in my head as I strike the match. He asked the same question six years ago when Brian left this family and all he knew. This isn't supposed to happen, we raised our kids right, we weren't perfect but we were good, and now here I am sneaking out in the middle of the night and our son, five hundred miles away, is dying from what is in his blood, dying because of what he did, dying because of what he calls himself, and what if he comes back here and what if people find out the truth, then what will happen to us? *What will people think?*

Jess

The killer whales are the most misunderstood of the whales. To begin with, although everyone calls them whales, they're actually dolphins. For hundreds of years, people believed killer whales were man-eaters. It's not true. They don't attack humans. Killer whales travel in pods, and hunt, play, and rest together. In the wild, the females can live up to a hundred years. A mother's offspring stays with her for life. They mourn their dead.

My mother fakes interest. Something is wrong. She hardly ever comes downstairs except to do laundry, and she's not much of a TV watcher.

"Would you look at that?" she says, eyes on the screen. "How can that be real?"

The show has moved on to blue whales, the biggest mammal on earth. One parts the ocean like a giant submarine. A close-up shows its enormous battle-scarred body, all the nicks and healed-over cuts and scrapes, cement-colored barnacles clinging to it like clusters of dead flowers. Bigger than any of the dinosaurs, the man says in his calm voice. Its heart is the size of a Volkswagen Bug. Facts I already know. When I was little, I poured over the pictures in *The Sea*, part of a collection of books from the Life Nature Library my grandmother gave me and my brother one Christmas. We also had *Early Man, The Mammals, The Universe.* I saw my first episode of *The Undersea World of Jacques Cousteau* when I was four or five, and after that, I was hooked. I want to be a marine biologist, but I live in Ohio. I've never even been to the ocean.

I reach into the box of Cheez-Its.

"You're going to ruin your supper," my mother says.

My mother doesn't eat junk food and she's always on a diet, even though she isn't fat, not like my aunts. I'm not either, but I'm plump— that was what one of my Sunday school teachers said about me. Plump is a horrible word. Like chunky. My mother is pretty, everyone thinks so. She looks like a movie star in one of those old black-and-white movies that run on Saturday afternoons, when nothing else is on except baseball or kung-fu.

"Jess, honey, there's something I need to tell you."

This was what she sounded like the day she told me about sex. When a man and woman love each other, when they're *married*, she'd started, using the same teacher-voice she's using now, and I wanted to die, hearing my mother say the word penis.

"What?" I ask. The orange crackers are the size of postage stamps and I drop them one at a time in my mouth, splintering and crushing them with my teeth.

The corners of her lips lift, but they are pressed too tightly to turn into a smile. She's still wearing her work clothes—ironed tan slacks, a navy blouse with a scooped neck—and her makeup is soft around the eyes. Unlike my grandmother, my mother believes makeup shouldn't call attention to itself, but only be used to "enhance" natural beauty. When I turned fourteen, she told me I was allowed to wear blush and lip gloss, but I hardly ever put it on—I don't look right in it, not like the girls at school.

"It's about your brother," she says.

"Brian?" I ask stupidly, as if I have more than one.

"He's coming home."

My mother's eyes, a light brown like watered-down Pepsi, the same color as mine, glisten, but no tears fall. She tells me he'll be here this weekend.

"To visit?" I ask. "To stay?"

A little sigh escapes, her shoulders sink. "We don't know yet."

I have a million questions and she says we'll talk more during supper, after my father gets home. She needs to check on the meatloaf, she says. She kisses me on the forehead, and the fruity, soapy scent of Charlie, her work perfume, lingers after she's gone.

The invisible man on TV, in his trusting, all-knowing voice, explains they still don't know where the blue whales go to breed, somewhere deep in the ocean that scientists can't pinpoint. As a marine biologist, I will work for *National Geographic* or *NOVA*. I'll go out on a boat in the middle of the ocean, no sign of land for miles. Blue, more blue. Brian and I used to watch Jacques Cousteau together. One time he brought home the record *Songs of the Humpback Whale,* and we listened to it stretched out on our backs across the carpet, pretending we were floating in the sea.

I dust off my hands. My mouth tastes salty and dry. A sperm whale lifts its gigantic, wrinkled head out of the dark water, and then the screen goes to static. The tape ran out before the show ended. I curl my knees up to my chest, wrap my arms around them. Suddenly, I feel very small. I haven't seen my brother since I was eight years old.

Sometimes Brian would let me come in his room and we'd listen to records and play Go Fish. Candles dripping wax. David Bowie singing about moonage daydreams and outer space and a starman. Thick, flowery scent of incense. Brian blew cigarette smoke out the cracked windows, talked about California, New York. Dream states, he said, where people went to be free.

After he left, my parents told me he was away at college. I didn't know anyone who'd gone to college, and I believed them for a couple years—until my grandmother told me the truth: he'd gone to New York, which to most people in Chester made about as much sense as saying you were going to live on Mars. If you left, you'd meet the same fate as Major Tom in his tin can. There are other stories about him too.

When I was younger, I told kids at school about the movie stars and rock singers he hung out with, the parties, the money. I never knew any of this. I made up a life for him. I had to. Because he just disappeared. Like those missing kids on milk cartons. But nobody kidnapped him. He just went. My parents, except for those early lies about college, don't talk about him. Nobody does except for my grandmother. She tells me stories about my brother and has never doubted one day he'd come back home.

The kitchen smells disgusting: baking meat and green beans boiled with onions and hambone. My mother stands at the counter tearing pale lettuce and dropping the pieces into a plastic bowl. She asks me to set the table and I get out plates for three. This is how it's been for years, like I'm an only child, just like my mother.

We eat in the dining room, a little alcove outside the kitchen that opens into the living room. Sadie follows me around the table, tags jingling. She's a mix of some kind of terrier and who-knows-what. The scruffy fur under her chin and belly has turned milk-white. I wonder if she'll remember Brian. She used to be his dog, now she's mine.

The front door opens and my father walks in. "How are my two favorite gals?" he says, which is what he always says when he gets home from work. Sometimes he sings, badly, lines from weird oldies, to make me laugh. "The Purple People Eater." "Blue Suede Shoes."

"It'll be ready in about ten minutes," my mother calls from the kitchen.

Because of my father's silver hair, he looks older than my mother, but they were born the same year. He likes to joke that he started to go gray after meeting her. His mustache lifts as he smiles at me, and for a second, I wonder if she hasn't told him. Then he asks, in a too soft voice, "How are you, hon?"

He knows.

"Fine," I say.

He bends to remove his muddy boots and socks. Against the mossy green carpet, his bare feet look extra white, like thin loaves of bread. He wears dark blue pants and a matching shirt with his name stitched in red on the front pocket, a white T-shirt underneath. My uncles and cousins wear the same uniform. My brother probably would have worked for the electric company too, if he hadn't escaped.

"You all right?"

"Yeah," I say.

After my brother left, my father told me he'd be back soon. I think he believed this, for a while.

Occasionally, Brian would call, and make promises about visiting. But he never came back, not once. He forgets my birthday every year. The last time I talked to him was a couple of years ago, and it was weird, like talking to a distant relative I'd never met. Last year after his birthday, which my parents didn't mention, I asked my cousin Gus if he thought Brian was dead.

A tremor in Gus's soft round face. "What a question, Jess. No, he's fine."

I wanted to know how he knew. Gus hem and hawed, his face turning crimson, then he finally admitted he'd heard from Brian.

"He calls you?"

His eyes darted. "It's been a while."

"So he could be dead."

"He's not dead."

"How do you know?"

"I just know." He held his eyes steady. "Jess, you'd know if he was dead."

"How?"

"You just would. You'd feel it."

All I felt was a dull hammering in my chest that grew fainter and fainter as time went by. How could I feel him when he was dead if I couldn't even feel him when he was alive?

My parents sit at either end of the table, across from each other, and I'm between them, facing the side window. Brian used to sit across from me. When he first went away my mother would sometimes forget and set his place, and the plate and silverware would just sit there all through dinner, like she'd left a place at the table for a ghost, and nobody would say a word about it. As time went by, I stopped noticing the empty chair. But today I can't stop staring. Today Brian's chair grows big as a sycamore tree.

"When did you find out he was coming back?" I ask.

My parents exchange a look.

"I talked to him," my mother says evasively. "Not too long ago."

My father reaches for the salt shaker and shakes it over his plate, and when he sets it down, he isn't smiling, isn't frowning either. More like his whole face forms into a tight question mark.

"We haven't told anyone yet," he says.

I ask if we should throw a party. I remember a movie about a long-lost brother who comes back home and his family and friends show up, laughing, crying, shouting, *Welcome home, brother.* Maybe he came back from a war, I can't remember. What sticks out in my mind is the reunion scene, the movie star's face wet with tears, his family forming a tight circle around him. His father tells him he thought about him every day, my son, my dear, dear son.

"I don't think a party is a good idea," my father says. He sets down his glass of milk, his face stiff with concentration, the way he looks when he is watching a close ballgame on TV, that and some other expression I don't know.

"We want to keep this news to ourselves for now," he says.

"Why?"

"Well, we just want to wait until he gets here. We want to be sure."

"Because he might not come back?"

"He will. We're just being cautious," my mother says. "I didn't want to keep any of this from you," she adds, like she's done me a big favor.

"What about Mamaw?"

"You know how she is," my father says. "She'll get too worked up. Let's just wait to tell her after he gets here. Okay?"

My parents look at me with worried smiles. They want this to stay a secret. Just like when he left.

"Yeah, whatever." I look down at my plate, the soggy, watery beans, the thick ketchup smeared over a gray slab of meat. "Can I be excused?"

"You've hardly eaten a bite." My mother doesn't like when she slaves over a meal all day and I don't eat it, she tells me all the time.

"I'm not hungry."

"What did I tell you? No snacks before supper."

My father spears his fork into the little hill of green beans on his plate. "Let her go." He presses his lips together, forces a smile. "It's going to be okay, hon."

I carry my plate into the kitchen. Without making any noise, I open the cupboard where my mother hides junk food and slide a Twinkie into the front pouch of my sweatshirt. The setting sun turns the trees in the woods behind our house a bright, spooky orange. My brother and I used to play in the woods. He built me a fort out of old tree limbs and scrap wood. He taught me how to skip rocks. He told me about the places in the world he wanted to go. I would have followed him anywhere.

I walk home the long way, listening to a mix tape on my Walkman, old and new stuff. "Live to Tell," "Hold Me Now," "What Have You Done Me Lately," "I Would Die 4 U." When I'm wearing the soft foam headphones over my ears, the voices carry me outside of dinky, dead-end Chester, outside of myself to some better place that's big and goes on forever, like the ocean.

On the bridge I stop and look over. Five feet below Buckeye Creek cuts a jagged line through Chester, but it's easy to forget it's even here—it's like a country road or the train tracks, the same old thing you see every day. Nothing ever happens in Chester. The dark greenish water sweeps twigs and a dented Pepsi can downstream.

"What are you doing?"

Brandy White and two girls who never talk to me cross the street. I press pause.

"Nothing," I say, hoping they didn't see me spit over the ledge like a boy. I feel self-conscious in my gray sweatpants. "I just had softball practice," I explain.

The only reason I joined the team was to make my father happy. I used to do okay when I played summer league—nobody hit very well, and it didn't matter if we won or not, the coaches always took us out for ice cream after. But in high school the girls play fast-pitch and they're scary-serious. I rarely even swing, and if I do, I usually just smack air.

"Oh, that," Brandy says.

Brandy is a cheerleader, not a jock. She wears tight icy-blue jeans, a turquoise shirt with the collar popped, ankle-high black boots. She's with Steph Patterson and Angie Ray, juniors, who looked totally bored, like if I were to fall over the side into the creek they wouldn't bat an eye. Brandy White and I used to be friends. She's a couple years older than me, but that never mattered until high school.

Brandy isn't pretty—pug nose, thin lips—but she's skinny and has big boobs and a loud, teasing laugh that calls the boys to her. Her hair is big too, reddish-blond, like a lion's mane. She paints her nails dark cherry, and wears hoops the size of shower curtain rings in her ears. Her purple purse, with a bow tie on the front, looks new. I know it holds cigarettes and cinnamon gum and teal-colored mascara and tampons and notes from friends and notes from boys.

"We're going to Rudy's," Brandy says. Then she surprises me. "Want to come?"

I should say yes, grateful she's inviting me, but I know they are not going to Rudy's to eat pizza—they're going to meet up with boys, and they'll joke and flirt in some language I don't know how to speak.

"I can't," I say.

A horn beeps and we all turn, them with eager, flirty smiles, expecting a carload of boys. But it just happens to be my grandmother in her butterscotch Crown Victoria. The Queen's Ship, my father calls it.

"Hey, girls." She leans out the open window, cracking her gum. Her puffy, hard black hair sparkles in the sunlight. "How are you, Miss Brandy?"

"Good," Brandy says, her face turning up in a big smile that might be real, or maybe not. Brandy's aunt used to live next door to my grandmother, and whenever Brandy's mother went on a tear—going out to a bar to look for a man, according to Mamaw—then Brandy would stay at her aunt's, and come over to my grandmother's to play. We'd read supermarket tabloids and try on Avon eye shadow and lipstick samples. Brandy wanted to be a model. The next Christy Brinkley.

"You girls want a ride?"

Brandy says no thanks, they'll walk. She catches up to her friends, and I toss my duffle bag in the backseat and dust off the bottoms of my tennis shoes before I get in. My grandmother does not allow eating or drinking in the Ship, but she does allow herself to smoke. The inside smells just like her, cigarettes and hairspray and whatever Avon perfume she is wearing. They all have different names—Timeless, Candid, Here's My Heart, Moonwind, Sweet Honesty—but smell about the same, so strong that if you stand too close when she sprays her neck, your eyes will water.

She's wearing slacks and a pleated blouse, and clip-ons that look like big teardrops. I glance down at the navy one-inch heels, her going-out shoes.

"Why are you all dressed up?"

"Oh, I drove Helen over to Madison for her doctor appointment, and then we had lunch at this new Mexican place. Helen had never had Mexican before and she didn't know what in the world to make of it. But she ate every bite. We had ourselves a big time."

My grandmother is always chauffeuring somebody around, one of her church or bingo friends. She has never lacked for friends. I wonder if she was popular in high school, like Brandy White. Or like my mother, who was also a cheerleader.

"Honey, you could have gone with those girls," she says.

"We're not really friends."

She clucks her tongue. "Why, I thought you was."

"No, not really. Not anymore."

I only have a few friends. They're benchwarmers, same as me. We aren't popular but we don't get picked on either—nobody notices us, thank God. We eat lunch together and sometimes hang out after school, but we don't trust each other with secrets the way best friends do. Today, I almost made the mistake of telling Molly Williams about my brother coming back, but then Coach Feldon hit a fly ball that went sailing over my head and that broke the spell.

"Well, it's probably better you're not friends. That Brandy always has been wild. Gets it from her mother." Wrapped over the steering wheel, Mamaw's fingers glitter, a rainbow of gems and stones. She says she feels naked without her rings, like going out without her face on. "Why don't you come over to my house? I made coffee cake."

I'm nervous I'll spill the secret, but I can't think of a good excuse. Plus, once my grandmother gets her mind set on something, there's no changing it.

We sit in front of the TV with squares of coffee cake. My grand-mother watches more TV than any grownup I know. She was one of the first in Chester to get a satellite dish, and the first in the family to own a VCR.

As she flips channels, I look through her most recent *National Enquirer*. She's been buying these for years. Brian used to read them aloud to me in a dramatic storytelling voice, weaving tales of plastic surgery, drug addiction, and divorce.

"Oh, goody, it's almost time for Naomi," my grandmother says, and turns to channel 7.

On Location With Naomi is one of our favorite shows. It's a talk show, like *Sally Jessie Rafael* or *Phil Donahue*, except that Naomi Cook travels to different places around Ohio to talk to people with a good tear-jerker story to tell, like women who finally broke free of abusive husbands, kids with brain tumors, or criminals who turned their lives around. My grandmother says one day the show will go national. "She's going to be big," she says. "Just you wait."

Naomi, who my grandmother says must use good moisturizer because she is almost fifty and doesn't have any wrinkles, always begins the show at the studio. She stands in the center of a stage wearing a milk-white double-breasted jacket with square shoulders, and matching pleated pants with a wide wrap belt. Her red hair lifts a few inches off her head and frames her face like a fluffy cat.

"Today, we talk to a mother of three who lost practically every-thing. She was a Girl Scout troop leader, a PTA member. And she was addicted to barbiturates." Naomi raises her eyebrows. "What hap-pened? Where will she go from here?"

"Ooh, this makes me think of that Rutherford woman up in Clark County. Naomi ought to do that story. I'm going to tell her about it." Mamaw calls Naomi's "Do You Have a Story to Tell" line regularly, but Naomi so far hasn't taken any of her tips.

"Jess, did you hear a word I just said?"

"What? Yeah."

"You're acting funny."

I can't stop thinking about Brian. His picture on the mantle looks right at me, like he's trying to tell me something. Mamaw has family pictures all over—my aunts and uncles, and tons of cousins and second cousins, and old people I can't tell apart. But this one of Brian, stuck in a fussy gold frame, is front and center. Mamaw has never said Brian is her favorite grandchild, but we all knew. Here, he looks like a movie star from the '70s. Jean jacket, big-collar shirt with the top three buttons undone, and long feathered hair that he and my dad used to fight about. Brian inherited our parents' good traits—our father's blue eyes, our mother's high cheekbones. A thin silver chain hits his bare chest where his shirt opens in a V. I wonder what he looks like now.

Friends of the drug-addicted PTA mother tell Naomi they never would have expected this of her. "She's a good woman," they say. When Naomi interviews her, the woman dissolves into a crying mess. People always cry on her show.

As the credits roll, Mamaw suggests we sit on the porch to watch the world go by. There isn't much to see. Two shirtless guys bend over the hood of a red Trans Am, a cluster of empty beer cans at their feet, and a little boy with a dirty face rides a girl's bike up and down the sidewalk. Across the street, stooped, balding Betty Russell, in a housedress and slippers, sweeps her porch with a straw broom.

"How are you doing, Betty?" Mamaw calls.

"Can't complain," she hollers back. "What about you?"

"No worse for the wear," she says. My grandmother wouldn't ever go out in public if she were to go bald. Not without a wig or a scarf.

"There was one of them *NOVA* programs on the other night, did you see it?" she asks.

I tell her I taped it. She lights a cigarette. She doesn't know what to make of me, wanting to be a marine biologist. "Why in the world would you want to be down there with them sharks and such?" she says. "They'll eat you alive." She doesn't understand, but says she's proud. "You're smart, like your brother."

I used to think I'd get a job at SeaWorld, so I could train killer whales. There is a SeaWorld, if you can believe it, in Ohio—it's up north, near Cleveland. My parents and grandmother took me for my twelfth birthday. We sat three rows from the front, and when Shamu, a 5,300-pound killer whale, leapt out the water, Mamaw screamed. Water splashed all over us. I'd never seen anything so perfect. But something about it bothered me too—a whale confined to a pool, taught to do tricks. Mamaw tried to make feel better about it. She said the whales were well cared for.

"A whale needs to be in the ocean," I said. "There is no ocean in Ohio."

"Well, maybe no ocean," Mamaw said. "But they's Lake Erie."

We're not out here long before Edna Davis, my grandmother's next-door neighbor, comes over to gossip. My grandmother always has a story—so-and-so's husband is messing around, so-and-so's pregnant, so-and-so's lost his job—and the women in town flock to her for the latest information.

"Lotto's up to three million today," Edna says. "You better get you a ticket." Edna is wide and tall, and looks like she'd make a good wrestler on WWF. She has curly gray hair she fluffs with a pick, and wears velour jogging suits most of the time. She used to be one of my grandmother's most devoted Avon customers, and is still partial to shimmering electric blue eye shadow.

"I played the numbers this afternoon," Mamaw says. "Woo-wee, wouldn't that be something."

Edna's a better audience than I am, and Mamaw tells her the story about the woman in Clark County selling drugs.

I interrupt. "What kind of drugs?" In school we watch films about teenagers smoking angel dust, which makes them scratch their eyes out and leap from windows. Apparently, drugs are everywhere. I have never even been offered a joint.

Mamaw narrows her eyes. "Well, Jess, for land's sake, I don't know what all kinds of drugs. Probably marijuana."

"Cocaine," Edna says. "I heard tell it's spreading into small towns."

Car doors slam, screen doors rattle. People are getting home from work. They fuss in their yards or sit on their front steps with a cigarette and a beer. Tomorrow, my brother will be here. I look over at my grandmother, the secret like a grain of sugar on the tip of my tongue. She taps her cigarette against the green glass ashtray, sprinkling feathers of ash on the 7UP decal in the center, and shakes her head, still thinking about the drugs.

"I'll tell you what, sometimes I don't know what the world is coming to."

Killer whales use echolocation to communicate. They call out, and the time an echo takes to come back to them tells them how far away an object is. The echoes help them to navigate and hunt and find each other. Echolocation is like a sixth sense.

When I was little, I used to think that Brian and I could communicate telepathically, like the brother and sister in the movie *Escape to Witch Mountain*. I believed I could send him my thoughts, like whale signals, and he would hear them. I was just a dumb kid. At night, after I said my prayers, I would close my eyes and listen to the pulsing of the dark, but I never heard any voice, never received any message.

I'm in my room with the door cracked, Duran Duran on the boombox. Volume turned low, so I can still hear my mother moving around in the kitchen, putting away dishes, making herself a cup of hot tea. My father is out in the garage. We're hiding from each other, waiting. The house smells like the pot roast we had for supper. Hot, soft potatoes melting between my teeth, stringy beef like veins. I could only eat a few bites.

I stare at myself in the mirror. I don't look anything like Brian. I'm plain-faced with scattered freckles across my nose. Boring brown hair and boring brown eyes. I pull my hair back in a ponytail, then take it out again, and the ragged ends fall around my shoulders. My body looks soft and flat and weird. I've changed three times already. I'm wearing my only pair of Jordache jeans, a bright pink T-shirt, and my Reeboks, the coolest clothes I own. I don't look cool.

A muffler rumbles underneath the music. Gus's truck. I thought we'd all go to meet Brian at the bus stop, but my mother said Brian didn't want a big to-do. From downstairs, Sadie barks. I count to three, and then I go.

I'm the first one at the door. I stand still, watch the knob turn, like I'm one of those dumb girls in a horror movie, stuck in my tracks. Sadie is barking, wagging her tail. Gus steps in first. Rain trickles down the bill of his Chester Eagles hat and slides down his jacket. He wipes his boots on the welcome mat. He is carrying a big lime-green duffle bag.

"Hey, Jess," he says.

The door swings wider, and a man walks in, his face shadowed by a blue hooded sweatshirt. He's wearing a jean jacket, and black jeans, and Nikes with a red swoosh. He pulls down the hood. For a second, I don't think it's him. He's skinnier than I remember, and looks old, a grownup. His hair isn't as blond as it used to be. He wears it short on the sides and on top, longer in the back. His teeth are the color of tobacco juice, and his raggedy lips look dry and chapped. Stubble on his chin. He reminds me of the pictures I've seen of drug addicts. Maybe he's a junkie.

"Jess," he says, and his voice is the same, it's déjà vu, hearing him talk. "You've gotten so old. What are you, like thirty now?"

"Fourteen," I say.

He sets down a small silver suitcase and stands close enough to hug me, but doesn't. Keeps his bony hands at his sides, and I don't make a move toward him either. I don't know him, and feel shy. Sadie whines at his feet, pushes her muzzle into his legs, and he crouches down and digs his knobby fingers into her fur.

"You got old too, Sadie," Brian says.

When he stands, I see a little gold hoop in his right ear, delicate, the shape of a fingernail. I can't remember which one is the bad one to have pierced. Right or left, gay or straight.

The air shifts, thins out. It isn't just the three of us anymore. My father moves slowly up the stairs, and my mother comes out of the kitchen. They stand next to me, about three feet from Brian. Big Gus tries to scrunch himself into the corner of the doorway, tucking his fat chin, like he doesn't want anyone to see him.

"You must be hungry," my mother says.

"Run into any flooding?" asks my father.

Six years he's been gone and this is how they greet him, like he just went out to the store for cigarettes. We crowd in close, no one touching. My father looks at the grease rag in his hand like he has no idea how it got there, and balls it up and stuffs it in his hip pocket. "Glad you made it okay," he says.

He takes a step forward, standing a head taller than Brian, and clamps his hand on Brian's shoulder. Just as quickly as he touches him, my father reaches his hand back. But it's enough. Him touching Brian like that seems to break something in my mother, like she has just realized who this is, and she lets loose a quiet sigh, and goes to him with open arms. Brian, taller by a few inches, keeps his head lifted, looking behind her at the wall. My mother stands with her back straight, and her arms around him, holding him but not, uncomfortable, the way boys are when they slow-dance, all stiff. No boy has ever asked me to dance, but in gym class last year old Miss Prescott put us in pairs and made us learn the waltz. *One two three, one two three.*

"Where's Mamaw?" Brian asks, stepping back from our mother.

"We decided to wait and tell her tomorrow," she says. "So she'll be surprised."

Brian's disappointed. "I was expecting to see her."

Gus says he has to hit the road and slaps my brother on the back. I don't want Gus to go. His big, soft presence takes away some of the weirdness in the room.

The gold beam of headlights drizzles through the windows as Gus backs out of the driveway. Then it's quiet again. All of us still and standing in the same place until Brian walks around us and goes into the living room. He looks up and down and around.

"Nothing's changed," he says.

"I've got a pot roast warming in the crock pot," my mother says.

Brian sits at the table and our mother dishes an enormous helping of pot roast into a bowl and sets it in front of him. All of us in the kitchen together for the first time in six years. My parents are trying to make conversation and act like this is normal. The light over the stove gives off a yellow glow. We are in a dream. The three of us standing here watching him eat. The rain falling. The air heavy and fragile, like at a funeral. And, I guess that's what it is, in a way. Because I think, for just a split second, that my brother has come back home to die.

Brian

Hello.

Here I am in Chester, Ohio. My hometown.

I'm shooting this from my bedroom. Down in the basement. Got my own bathroom down here too. This used to be my sanctuary, where I'd go to listen to records, dream about New York. David Bowie's voice carrying me out of Chester into the starry sky. It's emptier now, but looks about the same. Wood paneling, shag blue carpet. A real '70s museum.

Here are all my baseball trophies—I used to be such a jock. And, here's my idol, with his blushed cheeks, feathered hair. Cigarette in hand, silver bracelet sparkling like a disco light. Space oddity, alien, freak. I'm surprised my mother didn't get rid of all my posters and records, a reminder of my weirdness, my queerness.

Here's my dog. Sadie, hey, Sadie, come here. I didn't know if she'd remember me, but she came right up and licked my hand, while my parents and Jess just stared at me, the bogeyman.

Obviously, I didn't jump into the Hudson. Didn't off myself. That day, when I was thinking about it, when I went to the piers for the last time, I knew I didn't really have it in me. Anyway, now I'm in this weird honeymoon spot—I feel stronger, healthier than I have in a long time. Like there's a little bit of hope.

Hope is a dangerous thing.

Instead of killing myself, I wrote my parents a letter. I didn't know what I was going to tell them. I've known guys who were sick and went back to small towns all over the country—upstate New York, Kansas, Florida, Kentucky—and never said a word about what was wrong. They went back to their hometowns and died from a mysterious illness.

I sat there for a long time, pen in hand, trying to figure out how to compose the letter. I thought about telling them I had cancer or something. Then I thought about Shawn, what he would do. I wrote the word to see it for myself.

Dear Mom and Dad,
There is something I need to tell you:
I'm sick.
I have HIV.
I have AIDS.

I wanted to give them the chance to tell me no, you can't come home again.

After I mailed the letter, I didn't know if I'd hear back. But my mother called. I held the phone to my ear like a fucking life line. *Come home*, she said. My dad didn't get on.

Truth is, I missed my family. And, I didn't know what else to do. I had to get out of New York. Everything reminded me of Shawn. And death. I saw my reflection in the ghosts of men I passed on the streets.

And here? In Chester?

My parents told me no one knows and they want to keep it that way. Jess doesn't know, my grandmother doesn't. The word AIDS will never be said. The word gay will never be said. We'll live happily ever after in denial. Denial has helped me along so far…

Except, look at me.

My symptoms started about year ago, maybe a year and a half, but I was pretty sure I had it even before I noticed anything. That's how it goes. For years the virus works on the inside, invading white blood cells that are supposed to defend the body against infections. Then, the monster really begins to show you what it can do. Night sweats, skin rashes, diarrhea. I came down with colds I couldn't shake. A few months ago, I went into the hospital, disgusting white thrush coating my tongue, bacteria in my lungs. I thought I wouldn't come back out. That's how it goes. A cough, a fever. *Pneumocystis carinii pneumonia.* You check into the ICU and come out in a body bag.

After I spent three weeks at Bellevue, I started to feel strangely better. It's not going away, I know that. Sometimes I wake up in the middle of the night with cold wet sheets tangled around my ankles like snakes. Sometimes herpes blisters flare up in my mouth. Oh, you pretty things.

Sharon

I call in sick and wait for him to wake up. Jess is at school, Travis at work. Earlier this morning, Travis and I went over to Lettie's to tell her Brian was home. She couldn't believe it. "My Lord," she kept saying. She had tears in her eyes, and Lettie isn't a crying kind of woman. Travis didn't want to tell her ahead of time, in case Brian didn't show up, he said, but I think he wanted to see what Brian looked like first. He's shockingly skinny. And yet. He doesn't look like the men I've seen on TV. What I was so afraid of, what Travis was afraid of. He's not completely wasted away in that way that makes them resemble concentration camp prisoners, doesn't have the cancerous splotches on his face or hands. People won't take one look at him and know.

Travis told Lettie a lie about Brian getting over a sickness. "Don't drink after him," he warned.

I've told him it's not contagious like that—I've read this, I'm sure, in the newspaper and in the magazines at the dentist office. Even Lettie's supermarket tabloids say as much. But Travis says there are no guarantees. Maybe he's right. When Brian walked in, at first I felt unsettled touching him—my own son—and hated myself for it.

Travis doesn't want anyone to know about Brian, not even Jess. If Lettie finds out, she would be devastated. If others find out, they'll run him out of town. It's happened other places. That little boy in Indiana who got it from a blood transfusion. I remember seeing him on the news, thin and sickly and pale. The interviews with angry parents who didn't want him in the same school as their children. I felt sorry for the boy—it wasn't his fault—but I also understood their side: I'd do anything to protect my kids.

I warned Lettie about Brian's thinness. "I'll fatten him up," she said. She wanted to come over right away, but I promised to call her as soon as he woke up.

It's all I can do not to go downstairs and wake him. My body jitters with disbelief: my son is home. All week I cleared the junk out of his room, trying to make it look like his again, but last night Brian just dropped his bag on the floor, unimpressed, and flopped on the bed with all his clothes on, even his dirty tennis shoes. I stood there waiting for something—a word or gesture, a truce of some kind. "See you in the morning," he mumbled. "I'm beat."

Around eleven he trudges upstairs, just like when he was a teenager, sleeping late and annoying Travis. I remember him as tall, but that was never true—he was one of the shorter players on the baseball team, and never caught up to Travis's six feet. His thinness makes him look even smaller, an undernourished waif. Sweatpants and a T-shirt hang loosely off his limbs, like he's wearing someone else's clothes.

He holds a movie camera on his shoulder.

"What's that for?"

"My camcorder," he says.

A red light blinks. When I try to move out of the way, he follows me. "Brian, please."

"Okay," he says. He presses a button and the red light disappears.

"I don't want to be in any video, thank you very much," I say. This past Christmas, Matthew and Sherri got a camcorder and recorded us opening presents at Lettie's, and then we had to sit there and watch ourselves do it all over again on TV. I don't see the sense in it.

Brian sits at the table and stretches out his legs and crosses his bare feet one over the other. No, he's not as sick-skinny as I was expecting, but it's still bad. His cheekbones are more pronounced, his forehead looms. He looks like he's been up all night, the skin under his eyes thin and smoky blue. Blond stubble shadows his upper lip and chin. Discolored teeth. Those teeth! I'll take him in to see Dave Green. As a teenager, Brian was striking—people commented all the time on his looks. I thought he would grow into a beautiful man.

"Did you sleep okay? Was the room warm enough? Do you need more covers?"

"Everything was fine, Mom."

But he's looking around like he doesn't know where he is. Not much has changed. The same harvest-gold refrigerator and stove, same wallpaper with its tiny bouquets of daisies, and a framed needlepoint that says "Home is Where the Heart is". I'm embarrassed by how old and dull everything looks.

"I've been wanting to get new wallpaper," I say.

"You got a microwave. That's new."

The sun coming through the side window turns his face a deep pink, like he's standing in front of a fire. I can't take my eyes off him. No, he's not strikingly beautiful anymore, but he's still handsome—in a worrisome way, like he's walked through dangerous land to get here, spent days without food, water, sunlight.

"Do you want coffee? Tea?"

"I'm usually a coffee drinker, but tea sounds good."

I fill the kettle and turn on the burner. "You used to drink it with me when you were little. Remember?"

"Yeah, Lipton. With lots of sugar."

"Now I use Sweet'N Low."

"That stuff will give you cancer," he says, and reaches up and runs both hands through the back of his hair like he's going to pull it into a ponytail. The little gold hoop in his ear catches the light. Last night I saw Travis staring, and I was worried he would start something. But then he looked up at the clock on the wall, maybe wishing he could turn the hands back.

Brian picks up the *Chester Times* and reads the headlines aloud in an exaggerated newscaster voice. "Church bake sale. High school girl to enter beauty pageant. Church fish fry." He raises his eyebrows. "Exciting stuff."

"Well, it's not New York."

I can't read his expression. Amusement? Resentment? He started talking about leaving Chester when he was a little kid. Wanted to be an actor, a singer, a famous writer, a famous something. Isn't that what all kids say? Even when things were at their worst between him and Travis, when Travis wanted him apply to colleges and talk to baseball scouts, and instead Brian took a job at the now closed IGA to save up money, I didn't believe he'd go. I never stopped thinking about him—every day I prayed for him to come home—but whenever I tried to picture New York, my mind drew a blank. Sometimes I made things up. I pretended he was away in the army and would come back home, just like Travis. Or, I imagined he was away at college on some pretty campus with ivy growing on brick buildings, like you see on television. I never once thought of him as anything but alive. I didn't grieve for him like he was dead. He was away, and one day he would come home.

The kettle whistles. I pour boiling water over the teabags, carry two steaming cups over to the table. Brian folds his bony fingers around the cup and blows on it, and the steam rises in a cloud between his face and my own.

"So, really, what is it for? The video camera."

"It's what I do."

"Make movies?"

"Sort of. I document stuff, like my friends, and just things I see. I've made a few videos, like video art. Stuff that's, like, in progress. I really want to get you on camera."

"I told you, I don't like to see myself on TV."

"You'll get used to it," Brian says.

Sadie comes up, tags jingling. "I missed you," Brian says, and kisses her between the ears.

All of those years, gone. Now, here. When he left, he was moody and handsome and funny, a know-it-all. He slurps the tea, and the intimate noise jolts my memory, nothing specific, but just a deep feeling of knowing—he made the same sounds as a boy. For so many years I recognized his every sigh, movement, flicker of the eyes. Then he left, turned into someone else.

My body feels like it's going to crack open. With fear or love, I don't know. "I'm glad you're home," I say.

"So sweet," he says. "The tea."

"Too much?"

"No, not too much." The corners of his mouth turn up into the smile that I know. He's the same person, he must be. The boy I raised, the baby who grew inside me. "I'm glad I'm here too," he says.

We look at each other with anticipation. The phone's shrill ring shatters the moment. "It'll be your grandma," I say. "She's been calling all morning."

"Tell her I'm still sleeping, and let's go over and surprise her. I can't wait to see her face."

Brian showers in the basement bathroom—designated as his, the one Travis wants him to use—and when he comes back up, he's changed into jeans and a long-sleeved shirt, his hair damp and shiny. He's got the movie camera with him.

"Can you go the long way? I want to see everything in the daylight."

He puts on red plastic sunglasses with mirrored lenses. I drive down our road and turn onto High Street, the main road in Chester. As he looks out the passenger window, I try to see the town through his eyes—the junked-up yards and closed-down stores, and a man digging a ditch, his camouflage pants sagging to reveal his crack. Hideous. I feel that same unnerving embarrassment that I did earlier in the kitchen. Brian doesn't say a word, but I know what he's thinking: *I got away from all this*.

"Probably doesn't look any different."

"Not really," he says. "The dime store closed."

"The drive-in too."

Brian mentions teammates and friends and teachers from high school. He wants to know who is still here, who left. "I didn't stay in touch with anyone," he says.

"Most people don't go anywhere," I say.

It's not entirely true. The town is small—around 1,200 last I heard—but it occasionally fluctuates. People go, people arrive. People die. They divorce. They move to nearby towns or across the county line. A few may go to other states—but never to New York City.

"I'm sure your grandma can fill you in on the gossip," I say.

"Oh, no doubt."

I park in front of the mint-green two story. The house is old and worn down, the paint chipping away and the once-bright shutters a dull dirty white. Travis and his brothers are always working on it—fixing the roof, replacing porch boards. Lettie will never leave. Red tulips line the walkway like hearts. Brian walks carefully up the slanted porch steps, not bounding them two at a time like he used to.

"Should I knock or just go on in?"

"If you knock she'll think it's a salesman or somebody collecting for something. It'll be more of a surprise that way."

"Why don't you knock, so I can get her reaction on camera?" he says.

His giddiness moves through me, but just as I raise my hand, the door flings open—she's heard us. Lettie stands there in her all her jewelry and makeup, her bright blue shirt and plum slacks and big eyeglasses, and looks like a winning contestant on a game show—disbelief, joy, and a kind of terror all working over her face at once.

"Hi, Mamaw," Brian says.

She lets out a whoop. "Is that thing on? My hair's a fright. For land's sake, put that down and give me some sugar."

Brian, grinning, hands the camera to me and tells me to look through the viewfinder. I put my eye against the rubber cup. At first they're fuzzy, but as I back up, they come into focus. Lettie envelops him in her fleshy arms, her plastic bracelets clicking. "Oh, goodness," she says, smashing him into her body, holding him there.

When she lets go, she looks him over, and for a second I think her eyes flash with terrible recognition—*she knows*—but probably I imagine it, because then she smiles, big and open, just like she held out her arms to him.

"Look how skinny you are. I'll take care of that. I've already baked a Texas sheet cake." She touches his face. "Don't you look handsome though." Points to the earring. "I bet your dad didn't like that."

"Well, he didn't say anything." Brian tilts his head, smiling, still the charmer. "What do you think?"

"Don't bother me none. That's the style, isn't it? What the rock 'n' rollers wear?"

Lettie ushers Brian inside, and he goes straight to the kitchen, commenting on how good it feels to be back in her house, and although I don't want to leave him, not even for a second, I can already see how it is between the two of them. There is no strangeness, no lost time. Lettie always had a soft spot for Brian, who reminded her of her younger brother killed in World War II. "He was artistic too," she'd say.

When Brian was born, I was terrified of turning into my mother—distant, sad, unreachable. So I showered him with affection. Travis did too. He was our bright-eyed boy. Talkative, smart, joyful. He was different from his cousins, I knew that right away—curious about the world in a way that they weren't. Even at a young age, he loved music, movies, and books. He played dress up. When he put on an apron or a pair of my high heels, I convinced Travis not to worry. He'll grow out of it, I said.

And he did—at least that's what we thought. We hoped. By five years old, he knew how to swing a bat and throw a baseball. All through Little League and high school, he was a wonder to watch—diving to stop a line drive, or sweeping up a grounder. His swing was sharp and clean, and he nearly always rocketed the ball far into the outfield. Travis was proud. Brian didn't want to go hunting or work on cars, but he and Travis could throw a baseball in the backyard or watch a game on TV together.

We had planned on having a big family, but after Brian, I had two miscarriages. The first one happened at eight weeks, the second at fourteen. After the second one, I couldn't let go of the pain, which I carried inside me like another pregnancy. I drifted dismally through the days like I was trapped in a grainy, fuzzy photograph. Travis took me to a doctor who prescribed pills but I didn't take them. Distant, lost, I was turning into my mother. I don't know what changed—there wasn't a single moment. But, slowly, I pushed up through the foggy gray clouds to the place where my son and my husband waited. I told Travis, No more. We had our son, our little prince. He was enough.

So years later when I found out I was pregnant, Travis watched me anxiously. But I felt her moving inside, and I knew she would be okay. Jess arrived, strong and healthy and perfect, and our family was complete. Brian adored his little sister. He played records for her, made up elaborate games. She was a quiet, observant child, but around him, she danced and dressed up and laughed hysterically. He taught her to swim and how to read. In some ways, she was his child as much as she was mine. For months after Brian left, Jess kept asking when he was coming home. Soon, I'd tell her. Soon, soon, soon. After a while, she stopped asking. Or, maybe I stopped listening.

We don't usually pray at meals except for holidays, but Lettie, who invited herself over for supper, wants to say grace. "Lord Jesus, thank you for bringing our family together, thank you, God, for bringing Brian back, we're just so thankful he's home and safe and healthy." My eyes flutter at the word healthy. Lettie finishes with a loud *amen*. "Let's eat," she says.

We pass and reach for food, and fill our plates. Travis wanted to give Brian a paper plate and plastic utensils. You'll make him feel like a leper, I said. We compromised. He will not eat off disposable plates, but he'll have his own special set of silverware and dishes, his own cup.

"Everyone's excited to see you," Lettie says. Travis should have known she wouldn't stay quiet. "Should we throw a party?"

"That's what I said," Jess says. "Dad doesn't want to." She's wearing the *I Love New York* T-shirt Brian gave her. Shy at first, Jess is starting to warm to him. It's different with siblings, maybe. Not as many expectations.

"He just got here, Mom," Travis says, talking about Brian in the third person. "Give him time to settle in."

Brian reaches for the salt shaker, and his sleeve rises, exposing a bluish-white bony wrist. He ignores his father. "Sure, why not? Let's have a party."

Travis starts to respond, but then just takes another bite, and looks away. I remember how they used to fight at the dinner table, especially those last couple of years. Brian slouching, hair too long. He stayed out late and came home smelling like cigarettes and beer. One time he put on my black eyeliner, imitating the rock singers he listened to, trying to provoke his father. It worked. Travis rarely cursed, but Brian knew how to push his buttons. *For God's sake, get that shit off your face.* The fights always ended with Brian stomping downstairs, more at home with his music than with us.

Lettie asks Brian what he wants to do. There's the shopping mall in Madison. They could take a day and go to Columbus. What about going to a movie? She carries the conversation easily. Although there is so much I don't know about the past six years, about his life in New York, I have no idea what to say.

Instead, I focus on his plate. Brian has only taken a few bites. Goulash used to be one of his favorite meals, but now I realize the canned tomatoes, ground beef, and macaroni are too simple, too Midwestern. "You don't like it?"

"I'm just not very hungry." He smiles. "But it's really good. It's been a long time since I've eaten anything homemade. I never cooked much. Neither did Annie."

He's told me about her before. They lived together, but she wasn't his girlfriend. I wished she was—that they were living in sin, but a different kind of sin, a normal sin.

"That's why you're so skinny," Lettie says. "What in the world did you eat?"

"Anything and everything. Indian, Chinese, Japanese."

"Raw fish?" Jess makes a face. "Gross."

"Sushi is delicious. You'd be surprised."

"I'm with Jess," Lettie says. "No sir."

Brian continues to talk about the food of the world in his know-it-all way. He's both the son I remember and someone I've never met. His words sound flatter, and he talks faster. City-slicker. But it's more than that, the way he enunciates and stresses words. *Effeminate.* The word lands hard in my throat.

Travis suddenly gets up and offers to take care of the dishes, which he never does. He clears all the plates except for Brian's—he'll come back for them later, to wash separately and scour in hot water. Brian looks at me, his blue eyes darkening.

"Living in New York made me hungry to see the rest of the world, so to speak." He tries hard to sound casual. "Shawn and I used to talk about traveling. We wanted to go backpacking across Europe. We wanted to go all over the world. Turkey, Thailand, Iceland."

His friend. The one in the picture, the one who died of the same disease. Brian holds my gaze, and the sickening thought raises up and catches in my throat. He will never go to Europe. He will never even go back to New York. I cough into my napkin.

"But you just got here, honey," Lettie says. "Please don't be planning any trips around the world, I'm not ready to say goodbye."

Brian

It's bizarre to be back.

Nothing has changed, everything has changed.

The town itself isn't much different, just more rundown. Businesses closed, and touches of the poor everywhere you look: tacky lawn decorations and sagging underwear pinned to clotheslines. American flags. Old Reagan signs still staked into the ground. The horror!

Yesterday, I went with my little sister to the old drive-in, to record what was left. The tattered screen, the ticket booth covered in vines. I hid the tears in my eyes. Man, I used to love going there when I was a kid—it didn't matter what was showing, I just wanted to be swallowed up by the famous faces in the sky.

Talking to the camera like this is a new thing for me. Back in New York, I was trying to capture everyone and everything else around me. But since there isn't anything to do in Chester, I thought I might as well set up my tripod and talk to you—whoever you are. I'm going to tell you about who I am, and tell you about my family. Record everything, Shawn said. For posterity. The camera will be my diary, my shrink.

Okay, so, there's my little sister Jess. When I left, she was a chubby kid with a loud laugh. She's still chubby, but no longer a kid. She's got these pretty, inquisitive, watchful eyes, and you hardly ever see her without her Walkman. Her music of choice is brainless pop—Madonna, Cyndi Lauper, Whitney Houston. I mean, I love my divas, too, but I don't want her to forget the tunes she cut her teeth on. Jess had to be the only seven-year-old in southern Ohio who knew the lyrics to "Space Oddity." Kid knows everything about whales. She took to them the way some girls take to horses. She dreams of the ocean.

My mother. I feel her eyes on me all the time—examining me, curious, like a doctor's, but scared. Her face is the same, older, of course, with more wrinkles, a neck that's a little looser, but she's still pretty—the small mouth and nose, the high cheekbones. The face from my childhood. I can't get used to her short hair though, the tight, severe curls. When I was a kid, she'd sit on the floor in front of me and I'd brush her hair until it shone like glass. I wanted to grow mine long too. She told me, Silly, boys don't have long hair.

Dad's gone silver. He stands back from me, talks about the Reds. Doesn't know else what to say.

My grandmother, on the other hand, wants to spend every minute with me. I go over to her house and we watch TV, like the old days. When I was a kid, we used to watch the afternoon movie together. *Now, Voyager, National Velvet, Roman Holiday*. I was crazy about all of them— Bette Davis, Elizabeth Taylor, Audrey Hepburn. Now it's all soaps and talk shows.

Mamaw used to tell me I was like her brother Albert, artistic and sensitive. Code words. From her, I learned all about makeup, which helped when I became friends with drag queens in the city. Not a single gray hair peeks through my grandmother's midnight-black dye. She smells like Avon perfume, like face powder and hard candy and roses.

Whenever I record her, she pretends she doesn't want me to. But she loves the attention. Jess has started to loosen up too. My mother goes stiff whenever she sees the red light, struck with stage fright or maybe just annoyed. I haven't tried to shoot my dad—he'll think it's a waste of time, just more arty fag stuff.

📟 May 16, 1986

Hello there.

Today Mamaw took me shopping with her to the Kroger in Colby, the next town over, since the IGA where I used to work apparently closed down a couple of years ago. My parents don't want anyone to know I'm back, but Mamaw doesn't see why she shouldn't share the news with the entire town. She tells everyone I'm her grandson from New York. A movie-maker, she says.

While we were in line, this girl I went to high school with, Kelli Carson, was behind us, her cart crammed with frozen dinners, ground beef, pork chops, giant bags of potato chips, gallon jug of milk. Her hair was pulled back in a messy ponytail, and she didn't have any makeup on. She was wearing a T-shirt and sweatpants, looked like she'd left her house in a hurry.

Kelli looked at me with these blank eyes, then recognition, then fear. I forget, sometimes, how I look. Not dreadful, but not good. She recovered quickly though, flashed a smile. Brian Jackson, she says. I heard you were back.

Already, people are talking. Just like when I left. The only stories I ever heard about people leaving Chester were bad ones—guys who went out into the sinful world and came back broken and repentant, or were never heard from again. Vanished into thin air. Poof.

Kelli used to sit in front of me in English class. She was a smart girl. A different time or place, she would have gone to college. She dated this kid John Rollins, the third baseman—dumb as rocks, like most of the guys on the team.

She told me they were married now. He works at a used car lot in Madison and she stays home with their two kids. The usual. Then she goes, So, what brought you back?

What could I say? I just smiled and told her I guess I missed the place. She said we'd have to get together. I won't hold my breath, but I said, Sure, I'll be here.

And I will.

Annie wants me to come back to New York. We've been talking on the phone here and there, but not too often—I know what my dad will say if I run up my parents' long-distance bill. Hey, Annie, you watching this? Nothing is private, hon.

She says she'll find us a different apartment, that I won't have to live in her six-floor walk up, where I moved after Shawn died. I was always out of breath, climbing those stairs. Annie helped pay my share of the rent after I lost my job waiting tables because they assumed I had *It*— that wasn't the reason they gave me, but I knew. I don't want her to have to take care of me, even though of course she would. I can't go back. If Shawn was still alive, then it would be a different story.

Let me tell you a little about Annie. When we met, which seems like a lifetime ago, she was still in art school. She dabbled in everything— painting, photography, sculpture. She's good at all of it, but best at singing. She has a killer voice. She's fronted a few punk bands, and always quits after a couple of months, too annoyed or bored. I was surprised to find out she was a dyke—at the time, I didn't know any lesbians and only a few gay men. Annie told me she felt like more of a gay man, anyway—I don't believe in monogamy, she said.

I was the oddball in Annie's group of friends. They all came from money, went to private schools. I didn't even know anyone who'd been to college. When we met, Annie was delighted by what she called my country accent. I never even knew I spoke differently. I hear it now that I'm back—the way people drop "-ings," or says things like, "The car needs washed," or use "they" instead of "there." Sometimes, I'd watch Annie throw down money for a cab or buy a forty-dollar meal, and feel torn up with guilt—how frivolous all this would seem to my people. But I also loved the waste, the freedom. No one was telling us how to live. We could do what we wanted.

Annie took me under her wing and showed me the city I'd been dreaming of—the queers, artists, weirdos. Her world ran hot, and I wanted to be as close as possible to the flames. You only get one life, she used to say, before all our friends started dying, so you better make it fucking count.

▦ May 17, 1986

I'm coming to you live from the Jacksons'. It's like I've got my own TV show. Except I'm the only audience. At least for now.

I've been here a couple of weeks. Things are going all right, I guess. My dad, he didn't come home for dinner tonight. He's avoiding me.

I ate off my special plate, used my special silverware, drank out of my special red cup. My mother hasn't said anything about it, but I know. She won't even mix my laundry with theirs.

I haven't told Annie this—sorry, Annie—because I know what she'll say: *They should know better.* Actually, this is more her: *They should fucking know better.* I mean, true, it's not 1983 when nobody knew anything about AIDS. It's 1986. We know it's caused by a virus, and we know how it's transmitted. Sex. Shared needles. Blood transfusion. But nobody wants to listen to reason or facts. They'd rather just blame the queers. The media and politicians and preachers have whipped up a crazy storm of fear, and people are afraid they'll get it if you so much as breathe on them.

Still, I've heard worse. Parents who refuse to touch their son, who make him eat in a separate room, who do not visit him on his death bed, who bleach whatever he touches, who do not claim his body from the morgue.

Could be worse.

Well, I'm still here. I survived Mamaw's big party. Wasn't so much a party, just a family get together. My parents were nervous for everyone to see me. To tell you the truth, I was too.

First of all, I spent a ridiculous amount of time getting ready, like I was going out on a date. Couldn't decide if should butch it up or go full-force nelly. I went for something in-between, a casual going-to-the-movies look—rolled-up jeans and a button-down shirt, which around here I guess means gay. I primped in the mirror, worrying about my fucked up teeth. My mother doesn't want to tell Dave Green about me, which I guess is understandable. Dentists all over America are refusing to treat us. We're bad for business. Well, at least I'm in good company—half the population of Chester, Ohio, has fucked up teeth.

At first, everyone seemed happy to see me—even Uncle Wayne shook my hand. Mamaw set out a giant spread of food. I met my cousins' kids and their spouses. I held Gus's baby. She cried in my arms, and I handed her back. When we were kids, I'd recruit Gus to put on variety shows with me—we'd perform for our grandmother and our mothers, but not our fathers. Gus would get so nervous he'd practically break into tears. He was dopey and sweet, and he'd do anything I wanted.

Except for Gus, my cousins are older than me. Mamaw's pet, they used to call me. I never quite fit in, especially when I was a kid. It wasn't just about being gay, which wasn't something I could admit to myself back then—even though maybe I stared for too long at my uncle's furry chest or my cousins' rock-hard arms. I just didn't care about the right things, daydreamed too much. It wasn't always bad. Sometimes my cousins let me tag along. We played football and baseball and smear the queer. But, whenever I could, I'd sneak into my cousin Lori's room to steal her latest issue of *Tiger Beat,* mooning in secret over Donny Osmond, David Cassidy, Leif Garrett.

At Mamaw's, I had my camera with me, and nobody was pleased. Back in the city, my friends—I guess they're all narcissists—loved the attention. Here, it's different—people duck, hide their faces. The camera is the elephant I'm trotting into the room. Or, maybe I'm the elephant.

Nobody said much about me being gone for six years. My aunts asked a few questions. Wanted to know if I'd seen any movie stars in New York or been to any musicals? Had I ever been mugged?

No, I said, but I've had friends who were.

Mamaw covered her ears. Oh, Lord, don't tell me such things!

Wayne had his ears perked, and I braced myself for whatever fucked up racist or homophobic thing he might say in response. He just stared at me. Arms flexed, sleeves rolled up. The same strong jawline and hooked nose as my father's. I remember being a teenager gabbing about New York, where all the artists and musicians lived, and Wayne said, You mean the *queers.*

As I started to walk past him, he stood in the doorway, working a toothpick around in his mouth. Then he moved a few inches, just enough room for me to squeeze by.

You know, you got something in your ear there, Brian.

His mouth smiling, but not his eyes. Nervous laughter all around. Fuck this, I thought. I'm not scared of him, he's scared of me.

It's called an earring. You want to try it on, Wayne?

His face went bright red, and he looked like he wanted to grab me by the throat. I heard Jess cracking up. Others were laughing too. Shawn would be proud, I thought. As I walked away, I made sure to add a little swish to my step.

▦ May 18, 1986

Tonight, I want to talk about Shawn. Sometimes, the ache comes out of nowhere, the tears. How much I miss him.

This is the picture I was looking for. This is my baby, before he was sick. Here he is, playing in the snow in Central Park. That smile. Shawn loved New York winters.

Here's another one I took one morning after he just woke up. Sleepy eyes, fluffed bed-head, delicious chest hair. Shawn Crosby. The love of my life.

We met at a party. I knew by the way he was looking at me we'd sleep together, I just didn't expect to fall for him, or him for me. Shawn was ten years older. His father was black, his mother white. He was an actor from California, but he'd been living in New York for a dozen years, and he carried the pulse of the city in him like his hot, quick breath. He spent the '70s having a lot of sex and partying. When I met him, he was acting in plays and commercials, and for his day job, he worked part-time as a security guard at the Museum of Natural History.

Shawn had dark skin and curly hair and light green eyes. He was tall and muscular and lithe, with the body of a ballet dancer. He was out and proud. When he walked down the street, he sashayed. He preferred skimpy mesh shirts, backwards baseball hats, tight pants. He had a pair of gold pants that he especially loved to wear dancing. The beautiful children, he'd say, talking about the gays. He had a group of admirers, boys who latched onto him. Sometimes, I was jealous. I heard how country I sounded. How stupid, how uneducated. He called me Country Boy.

We weren't monogamous. Nobody was. We had lovers and one-night stands, especially Shawn—it was easy for him. I was always a little shy. Shawn burst with energy whether he was performing on stage or dancing all night when we went out. But he also could be quiet and gentle and peaceful.

Like on Sunday mornings, after a late night, we'd sleep in, and he'd make us coffee and toast, or sometimes run out for éclairs. He was a bear without caffeine, but after a few sips of coffee, he'd sink into the sheets and laugh and reach for me. We'd spend the morning in bed, fucking, reading, sleeping, watching TV if there was an old movie on, especially one starring a favorite diva. Shawn was mesmerized by Joan Crawford; I preferred Bette. Ohio was so far away then. Shawn would run his fingers down my spine, and I'd rest my head against his arm, breathe in the ripe, earthy scent of him. The softness and fullness of Sunday mornings brought out the best in us. We'd tie back those pink curtains and open the windows and the sounds of the city would spiral up and around us, holding us, keeping us safe.

I get why my parents don't want anyone to know. In Chester, people think we don't deserve to live, but it's not just Chester that thinks this way—it's most of America. Even in New York you feel the disgust grinding you into the dirt. *God is taking care of the homosexuals.* On bad days, the worst days, you wonder if they're right. The politicians, the pundits, the preachers.

Tattoo them, quarantine them, let them die in the streets.

In America, 15,000 people have died of AIDS, and there are almost twice as many infected. President Reagan still has not uttered the word. Queers, drug addicts, Haitians—we're the expendable, the scourge. They want us gone. When we die, Christians and Republicans must go wild with applause—that's what it feels like.

Sometimes I burn with anger, and I want to fight, to be seen. But most of the time, I'm just scared or tired. On my worst days, I feel the shame most of the world wants me to feel.

I understand why my parents don't want people to know, but that doesn't mean it doesn't fucking hurt.

Jess

"Killer whales have their own language and culture. They speak in different dialects from each other," I explain.

"Oh, yeah?"

"They're smarter than humans. Their brains are bigger."

"That doesn't surprise me at all," Brian says, and aims the remote at the VCR. A single black leather rope, thin as a twist tie, loops around his dainty wrist like a whip of licorice. With the earring and the hardened, moussed hair—a few curls as crunchy as Corn Pops—he looks like he could be the lead singer of a new wave group. He's got that face, too, the sculpted but delicate features, and the right clothes: tight jeans and a T-shirt under a pale peach blazer.

"They're more emotionally complicated than humans."

"Huh," he says. "Okay, here we go."

On the screen, a close-up of my brother's face. Then, strangers stream by. Gray skies. Buildings, shops. Signs written in Chinese. The screen turns black. When the video starts again, there is a close-up of silvery water that Brian says is the Hudson, then a flock of pigeons. The scene switches to Brian, behind the camera, going down steps, calling after his friend Annie. She turns, laughing, and flips him off. Hurry, she calls. Doors open to a train car laced with spray-painted gang symbols, and they get on. The doors close. Brian presses stop.

"What do you think?"

"It's cool."

I thought when Brian said he made movies, he meant real ones with famous actors. But all the ones he's shown me look like this: pictures without any story, broken-up scenes of him and his friends. Men in skin-tight pants and boots and women in mini-skirts and off-the-shoulder shirts. Sometimes I catch him sitting up close to the TV, watching the life he used to live, wondering why he left.

"I'm interested in documenting but also in capturing how random things are, and you know, like, there's not one way of being," he says. "The camera is my other set of eyes."

I don't know what he's talking about, but I agree. Brian is the only person I know who talks like this. When I was little I thought he knew everything, that he understood the world and all its mysteries. He used to talk about dreams and outer space and the trippy world we lived in. He told me that one day I would swim with whales. I believed him.

He runs through the channels, bored. This is Brian's space now—my father doesn't come downstairs to watch TV anymore. Brian's video camera sits next to him on the couch. Sometimes he records me—not doing anything special, just talking to him or listening to music. When he plays back the video, I squirm at the sight of my giant face looming like a balloon and the sound of my idiotic voice, but still, my heart races with a weird joy too: that's me on the screen, talking and breathing and laughing.

Brian stops on the news. The president makes a joke, smiles in his gentle old man way. He wears a navy suit and red tie, and his slick hair shines like Mamaw's, black as crow feathers. Cameras flash and click. He's an old movie star. Next to me, Brian twitches, his body suddenly turning on, like a robot's.

"What do you think of Reagan?" he asks. "You like him?"

The kindness has left his voice, and I can tell by his tight, challenging tone what I'm supposed to say. My parents voted for Reagan twice. Mamaw thinks he is good-looking and funny, and she especially loves Nancy. "She's a nut," she says. "A real kook."

"He's okay, I guess."

"I hate that motherfucker."

I've never heard anyone say they hate the president. It's like saying you hate God. Brian looks over, his upper lip curled. He's waiting for me to say something, maybe to disagree. I'm not even old enough to vote. There are purple rings under his eyes. He always looks tired, but not the way my father looks after he's been working. My brother just looks wrong, too delicate. He wears out easily. My dad told me not to drink after him because he's been sick. With what? I asked. He's getting over something, he said. Brian hasn't said anything about it. I'm not supposed to ask questions.

"You know, you should be more informed about what's going on in the world," he says.

My face blazes—I'm just a kid, he's telling me, I'm stupid. Something is wrong with him and no one will tell me what it is. Probably drugs. We learned all the signs in school, and Brian fits the profile: he's moody, unpredictable, and hardly eats. He's tired all the time. Heroin, probably—he has those sad, haunted eyes I've seen in pictures.

He switches to MTV, and Tina Turner, wearing snaky black leather pants and high-heeled boots, prances on stage.

"Those legs," Brian says. He sings along, then looks over at me. We used to watch *American Bandstand* and *Soul Train* together. "Get your groove on," Brian would say, shaking his shoulders, shimmying his narrow hips. I keep my eyes on Tina bopping her head, her giant hair like a shaggy crown.

"Hey, I'm sorry, sis."

He sighs deeply, like an old man. Maybe it's not drugs. Maybe it's cancer. That's what my mother's mother died from, and Mamaw always seems to know somebody who's got it. I've watched Brian stop to catch his breath, winded from just walking across the backyard.

"I'm just in a mood." He squeezes my knee with his spidery hand. "You mad?"

I look over and he's smiling. It's impossible not to smile back. I shake my head.

"I'm not mad."

Now that school is out, softball is over too, thank God. My mother doesn't want me laying around the house. At her urging, I've joined the youth group at church. Reverend Clay's son, Josh Clay, who recently moved back to Chester, is our leader. He has a pretty wife named Jennifer and a baby named Bo. Next fall, he will be the guidance counselor at my high school. He told us to call him Josh, unless we see him at school. "Then it's Mr. Clay," he said.

Josh says it's important for us to have a teen-friendly space where we can hang out. "I remember what it's like being a teenager," he says. "Nobody understands how hard it is, not your teachers or your parents."

We meet in one of the Sunday school rooms, where pictures of blond, blue-eyed Jesuses, drawn by the first and second-graders, hang from the beige walls. I take a seat next to Josh.

"Hey, Jessie." Josh calls me Jessie instead of Jess. I don't correct him because coming from him, my name sounds special. "How's your brother?"

Everyone looks at me. They probably don't even know that I even have a brother.

"Fine," I say.

"Didn't he move to, oh—where was it, some place crazy, like New York or California or something?" he asks, followed by a big, loose smile. Josh's two front teeth are as square as Chiclets—he's not quite buck-toothed but almost. He's tall and muscular. His light brown hair is spiked, and he wears a navy shirt tucked into tan shorts with a braided belt. He's a prep.

"New York," I say, my cheeks burning. Brian and Josh were in school together, and both played baseball. After he graduated, Josh left Chester, too—he went to a Christian college in northern Ohio.

"Brian Jackson, big league baseball star," he says, and tilts back in his chair. "What was he doing in New York City?"

I shrug.

"He get married? Does he have kids?"

I shake my head, stifling the laughter—Brian with kids?

"Well, tell him I said hi."

Josh pulls up his bent leg to rest one foot on his opposite knee—he wears brown boat shoes with no socks—and says he wants to talk about temptations. Sex. Drugs. As he walks around the room, he occasionally pats a girl on the shoulders, like a grownup version of Duck Duck Goose. Of the fourteen of us, eleven are girls. Each week, more show up. I'm waiting for him to touch me.

"Guys are going to try to convince you to do things. You've got to stay pure. One day, you're going to meet the right man. You'll be a wife, and a mother."

He turns to the three guys in the room and asks if they have girlfriends. "Treat them right. Be gentlemen. Protect them." He grins slyly. "And stay away from the homos."

Everyone laughs, and Josh does too, but then he holds up his hand like a politician, serious. "You'd be surprised. Totally normal people will fall into bad things. They go gay. Turn to drugs. Become prostitutes." He tells us about a young woman he met when he was working at a soup kitchen. "She came from a good family. Then she started drinking, smoking pot. Pretty soon, she was selling herself."

Each week he tells us lurid stories about people who sinned, those who were redeemed and those who weren't. He tells us about people he's known who died or became alcoholics or had abortions. These stories are the best part of youth group.

At the end of the meeting, we stand in a circle and stick our right arms into the center and close our eyes. Another one of Josh's games designed to teach us trust and teamwork.

"Get close," he says. "Closer, closer." He tells us to find and grab onto a hand with our right hand, and then do the same with our left. "Don't peek," he instructs. "Just take a hand. Okay, now open your eyes."

We look at the hands we're holding. One of the ones around mine is small and sweaty; the other one squeezes too hard. My hands look too soft—fat girl hands. Our bodies squish up against each other, and the smells of various shampoos and deodorants and perfumes mingle, making me want to gag. We're supposed to untangle ourselves without letting go. Everyone is laughing and directing each other: *Go this way, turn to your left, walk over here.* Queasy, I just want to break free and run out the door. Brian would think this is so stupid. We twist and turn, and finally, after many tries, we've untangled ourselves, we're a circle again. Dainty, eager-to-please Missy Scott stands on one side of me, and Josh Clay is on the other, holding my hand in his. He doesn't let go.

"I haven't been swimming in so long," Brian says. "Sounds like a blast."

I worry he'll want to come with me, but he already made plans to go shopping with Mamaw. "Watch out for sharks," he calls.

Brian used to go swimming all the time. He was the one who taught me. Fearless, he'd jump, all arms and legs, off the high-dive, doing crazy flips and spinning in the air. He used to be the kind of guy that people were drawn to—I knew, even when I was little, how cool he looked. Now I'm not sure what people would think.

I lock my bike to the metal rack, next to bikes with banana seats, three-speeds, and beat up hand-me-downs. Mine is a cheap rusted blue ten-speed that my grandmother bought at a yard sale.

After I pay the girl at the counter, I go in through the girls' locker room, but I'm already wearing my suit underneath—nobody changes in the locker room, otherwise you're a lezzie. The rubber soles of my white Keds slap the puddles forming on the slick tiles. The toes are grass-stained, like a little kid's.

My mother has been hounding me to go. "You love to swim," she says, but that's not why she wants me to go. She wants me to have friends, wishes I was popular, like she was, like Brian was. I used to spend just about every day of the summer here, but things have changed, that's what she doesn't understand. Girls my age don't swim. They lay out and swelter in the sun, and wait to be noticed by boys.

I miss the old days, when my grandmother would take me and Brandy White, and we'd stay for hours. Mamaw never wanted to waste money at the concession stand; she'd bring a cooler with pop and sandwiches, and we'd eat greasy Fritos from a plastic baggie with a green twist tie.

Brandy White was also a good swimmer. We'd dive down to find coins at the bottom, or spin somersaults. Mamaw, who is scared of the water, would sit on the edge to wet her feet and gossip with friends and read the *National Enquirer*. When you're a kid, you don't have to worry as much about fitting in.

This is the only swimming pool in the county. Fights sometimes break out between town kids and the kids from the hollers, and it's always bad when football players from Fayetteville show up. But today it's fairly peaceful. Young mothers wade in the baby pool and dip their fat babies in the water and complain to each other. Junior high brats and little kids line up at the concession stand, clutching damp dollar bills.

Molly Williams and Carrie Driggs, two girls from the softball team, wave me over. They're spread out on a blanket and wearing high-cut bikinis. Molly's is light blue with white stripes; Carrie's is pink with spaghetti strings that tie around her neck. I peel off my T-shirt and new pair of Jams, and I'm already embarrassed. My faded one-piece is from last year, the elastic around the shoulder straps frayed and loose, the material pilled. Even though I'm *chunky*, my chest, unlike Molly's, who wears a C-cup, is flat as a kickboard. Carrie isn't stacked, but at least she needs something more than an A-cup.

"You been in?" I ask.

They shake their heads, like why in the world would they do that.

"The chlorine will dry out your hair," Molly says.

My hair is flat and stringy and it wouldn't matter if I got it wet or not. Sometimes I try to take a curling iron to it, but it never looks right. My mother wants me to get a perm like hers, but the one I had last year made me look like Little Orphan Annie.

"Guess who was here earlier?" Carrie asks in a teasing voice.

"I don't know."

"Josh Clay." She licks her lips. "He's hot."

Carrie's family only goes to church on Christmas Eve, but now she comes to youth group meetings to flirt. Even Molly, a Catholic, wants to join.

"I swear he was checking us out," Molly says. Her silver braces shine in the sunlight.

"He's married," I say.

"Duh," Carrie says.

Carrie and Molly crunch carrot sticks and drink Diet Pepsi and look through *Seventeen*, their shoulders touching. I brought a book about a girl who gets addicted to drugs and starts hearing voices, but I can see that was a mistake—nobody's reading except for a few old ladies with paperback romances propped on their wrinkled bent knees. I leave it in my bag.

"I'm so tired," Molly says dramatically.

"Me too. We shouldn't have stayed up so late."

"That movie freaked me out." Molly adds, "Carrie spent the night," as if I don't get the hint. I wasn't invited, but so what? The three of us hung out at school, but things have changed. Now it's the two of them.

"I need to go on a diet," Molly says, and pinches a sliver of skin under her arm. Molly is a Tinker Bell with a blond bob and a sweet smile, and she doesn't have a jiggle of fat anywhere on her.

"Me too," Carrie says, who is as just as skinny as Molly, but not as cute. Carrie has a flat face and no chin and razor thin lips. "I hate my thighs. Look at the dimples."

My own thighs spread and squish, loaves of uncooked dough. Plump, my Sunday school teacher said. My stomach growls, and I press my hands across it. I won't eat a single carrot stick.

They talk about their exercise routines and ask me what I'm going to do for the summer.

"What do you mean?"

"Like, aerobics, or running, or what?"

"I don't know."

"You better do something, you don't want to end up like Wendy the Walrus," Carrie says, and Molly giggles. They're talking about Wendy Rooper, the fattest girl in school. She sits by herself during lunch, and she's always the last one to get picked for teams in gym class. She's even worse than I am at sports. She has a baby-doll face and dimpled cheeks, and when she walks down the hallway, guys make mooing noises.

Carrie and Molly go back to their magazine, critiquing hairstyles and outfits, and skipping over the pages with too much writing.

I slather on suntan lotion and put on my sunglasses. Boys hurl themselves off the diving boards, trying to make the biggest cannonballs.
"Faggot," a boy yells, followed by laughter.

Nearby, Brandy White sits on her towel like a queen on her throne,
flanked by a group of girls with big fluffy hair they probably spent hours
blow drying and sculpting with a brush or curling iron. Brandy used to
do my hair for me—she'd braid it or feather it. You need to do *something*
with it, she'd say, sounding like my mother.

"Check out her awesome earrings," Molly says, talking about one of
the models in the magazine.

Molly and Carrie think they're cool, but they'll never be like Brandy
White, who doesn't even try. It just happened to her. We were best
friends all through elementary, but when she was in eighth grade, she
found a different set. Two years older than me, she'd look at me and
shake her head, disappointed. I was a kid and she wasn't.

I wish I could go over and talk to her. We could get in the pool and
make up a swim-ballet routine like we used to, or stand on our hands
with our legs shooting up out of the water. I used to tell her stories about
Brian. She never met him, but she drooled over his picture.

"Hey."

Two boys our age or maybe older stand near us, dripping water all
over my towel, until Molly and Carrie, nervous as hens, rearrange the
blanket to make room for them. One has dark red hair and freckles all
over his face and arms and legs. The other one is thin and gangly, with
a long brown rattail that curls to the bottom of his neck. They talk and
laugh and say stupid things, and I'm starting to wish I'd gone with my
brother and grandmother to the mall. Maybe we could go to a movie.
Not one of Brian's weird ones, but a real movie.

Brandy White walks by. Sunglasses pushed up on her head, she looks
around, bored. Then one of the lifeguards calls her name, and her face
opens up into a big smile as she turns, hand on hip. She makes flirting
look so easy.

The boys are from Fayetteville. They mostly just talk to each other,
making inside jokes and saying, Fuck you, and laughing. Carrie and
Molly giggle at every stupid thing they say. They tell us about a party

this weekend, and the redhead writes down his phone number on a corner of the magazine. Rattail turns to me.

"Are you deaf?"

"What?"

"You haven't said a word."

"You mean *mute*," I say.

"Huh?"

"I can talk. I just don't have anything to say to you."

He makes a sour face. "What's her problem?"

Molly tries to laugh it off, shrugging like she has no idea who I am, and Carrie just ignores me. She asks the redhead about the party.

"It'll be cool," he tells her. "You should come."

After a while, but not soon enough, the boys go back to the diving boards, cussing and shoving each other.

"Jess," Carrie says. "Why'd you act like such a bitch?"

"I didn't."

"You're never going to get a boyfriend," Molly says.

"They weren't even cute."

"Whatever," Carrie says, rolling her eyes.

The two of them start making plans about the party, how they'll get there and what lies they'll tell their parents. They're acting like they do this all the time. The sun bakes the top of my head. I look out at the pool. Kids splashing and guys springing off the high-dive. There is no place to go.

"I've got a headache," I say, and start gathering up my things.

"You're leaving?"

"I don't feel good."

"Are you on the rag?" Carrie just started her period a few months ago and it's all she wants to talk about. "I hate going swimming when I'm on the rag, it's so gross."

"Yep," I lie. "I've got PMS."

"That's why you were such a bitch," Carrie says, laughing. But they sympathize and forgive me for screwing up with the boys. PMS works every time.

On the way home, I ride past all the same houses I see every day.

Same lawns and same trees. Same tire swing. Same falling-down chicken coop. Same cars on blocks, same stupid lawn decorations. The wheels of my bike roll over the busted sidewalk, weeds shooting up from the cracks. Brian says that people in Chester don't know how to dream. He left all of this. He went to live on another planet, one that's burning bright, but now he's back—faded, broken, frail—and no one will tell me why.

Sharon

There are moments when I hear him downstairs watching TV, talking on the phone, listening to records, and I feel startled, then joyful: my son is home. We are a family again. The sounds give me hope, and for those few seconds, my mind and body are consumed with a feeling as natural as breath. It never lasts. It can't. Seconds later, a rush of sadness knocks me off my feet.

He's been home almost a month. We are figuring out how to be a family again. I hoped it would be easier, like he would simply step back into place. But I don't even know what that place is anymore—too much time has passed, too much lurks in the unknown. I find myself studying him, wanting to ask how sick he is, but unable to speak. He takes vitamins and other pills (I don't know what), and he doesn't drink or smoke. He takes care of himself. But sometimes his face clenches in pain. He is often tired, or doesn't want to eat. I don't know what to do. I can't take him to our family doctor.

Some days, it's like he's come back from war or the dead. Like he's missing a leg or an arm. I don't know how to be around him. How to look at him, how not to. You can't stop to think about it for too

long, you have to keep going, because the moment you stop, you see the
truth. There's nothing you can do, or there is so much you should have
already done.

"Morning, Sharon." Dave Green takes off his ivy cap and hangs it on
the coat rack. He pats his thinning hair, adjusts his tie.

"Morning, Dave."

Dave and I have been working together for eighteen years. I took
time off when I was pregnant and switched to part-time when the kids
were young, but I've never stopped completely. I'm good at my job. I
keep the office organized and running smoothly. The surface of my desk
shines, as do the keys on the electric typewriter. Files, stapler, paper-
clips. A cup of pencils and pens. Easy-listening Muzak pipes through the
speakers to make the patients feel relaxed.

"What do we have today?" Dave asks in a sing-songy voice. He is
generally cheery, especially in the mornings. About a decade older than
me, somewhere in his early fifties, he's a trim, neat man with a receding
hairline and a plain, average-looking face. There are never any surprises with Dave.

"Mostly just cleanings. A couple of fillings, one crown."

"Easy peasy," he says. "How is everything? How is Brian?"

"Good."

"Must be nice having him back." He reaches for a stack of files,
smothering me in a cloud of Aqua Velva. After Brian left for New York,
Dave didn't ask many questions—like most people, he tiptoed around
the topic.

I want to bring Brian in to get his teeth looked at, but then I would
have to tell Dave the truth. I've heard him and Marjorie, the technician,
say how glad they are they don't live in a big city where they could
catch AIDS. Still, they wear latex gloves now. Marjorie laughs about
it. "There could be somebody light in his loafers that we wouldn't ever
suspect, just like Rock Hudson had us all fooled," she says.

The door flies open, and Marjorie, breathing hard, comes in. "Lord,
that coffee smells good."

A big woman with short hair angled like wings around her face, Marjorie is good-natured and nothing rattles her. But she couldn't hide her shock when she found out Brian was back. "I didn't even know that you had a son," she exclaimed. I felt ashamed that I'd never mentioned Brian. I didn't even have a picture of him at my desk.

"Shew, those kids wear me out," Marjorie says, talking about her twin six-year-olds. "Getting them out the door just about kills me. You're lucky both of yours are old enough you don't have to bother with that anymore, Sharon."

I took Brian's picture down just before Marjorie started working here because I didn't want to have to talk about him, I didn't want to answer questions. But a few days ago, I put one back up, one of my favorites: he's five years old, mop of blond curls, face scrunched up and mouth wide open with laughter. My son is happy. He looks at me with love and trust.

"I wish my kids were still little," I say. "Things were easier then."

For three months, nothing. Then he sent postcards, made calls. Promised to come back for Thanksgiving, for Christmas. Never did. Sometimes I sent him cards with money or pictures of the family tucked inside. Maybe I should have been more demanding. Begged him. Gone after him. But I didn't know how to swim across the river between us. He drifted further and further away, and I let him go.

A few years after he'd been in New York, he sent a letter. In it, he said that he was gay. I wept. Before, he'd mentioned friends—mostly the names of men—but still, I never thought anything. Maybe I had a few suspicions, but Travis and I certainly never talked about it. I didn't—still don't—know any gay people, except the characters you see on TV, ridiculously feminine men. Brian didn't act like that.

I didn't tell Travis right away. I knew the words would break him. But the secret became too heavy for me to bear, and so one morning I left the letter (but not the photograph of Brian and the other man—his *friend*) on the bed. When I got home, the letter was gone. Travis didn't mention it. I finally asked if he read it.

"We should have gotten him help," he said.

That was it. He didn't want to talk about it. I knew he would never accept his son as gay and I couldn't either. The wrongness of what he was doing and what he called himself sunk deep inside me like a rock in a lake that would never surface. It was against everything we'd taught him. The word itself left a bad taste in our mouths, so we didn't say it, ever.

A few months went by before I heard from Brian again. He asked if I'd read the letter. He sounded nervous—his voice high-pitched, the words clipped.

"I read it," I said. That was it. I didn't tell Brian he *couldn't* visit, that he *couldn't* bring this man with him. But I refused to indulge. The anger was easier than the pain.

Brian stopped calling. I hid the picture in my jewelry box, never showed it to Travis. Then one day, out of the blue, Brian called and told me his friend was dead. I'm sorry, I said. He said, You have no idea what's going on.

After church, the crowd lingers. Talking weather, sports. Chester families that go back four or five generations. Heels clicking on cement, car doors opening and closing. Kids running across the lawn. The light smell of summer. And me, with this hollow ringing in my chest, watching my son chat with Josh Clay and pretending everything is fine.

Brian and Josh were in the same grade and played baseball together, but they weren't friends. They didn't run in the same circles. I don't think Josh had many friends, not like Brian. I remember him as an awkward teenager—every Sunday he would sit next to his mother in the front row, watching his father preach, looking sullen and uncomfortable, like he was wearing shoes that hurt his feet. But now, grownup, in gray dress pants and a shirt and tie, Josh looks professional, sharp. He's in good shape, tan and healthy. Next to him, Brian, in wrinkled slacks cinched with a braided belt, and a drooping pastel purple button-down shirt, looks like a wilted flower.

"It's so good to see Brian," Anita Brewer, the organist, says. "You must be so happy he's home."

My smile is automatic, a natural reflex. "We all are."

Neither Lettie nor Brian mentioned that he was coming to church with her today. Travis stiffened when he saw him walk in and shot me a look, as if I'm to blame. Brian sat with his grandmother and Jess, a hymnal in his hands. I'm surprised he didn't bring his video camera.

Reverend Clay, in a white robe and dark green stole, walks over with Janice, his perfect, always pleasant wife, to join Brian and Josh. Both Reverend Clay and Josh are tall with broad shoulders, clean-shaven faces and neatly clipped hair. They look like father and son.

After my father left Chester, the church went through a number of ministers, and then the Clays arrived. They came from somewhere out west, Montana or Wyoming, and they were a little odd and standoffish at first. Over time, although Dennis certainly never inspired anyone with his clunky sermonizing, the family settled in and became pillars of the community. Dennis joined the school board, and Janice ran various social groups for women, like Bible-study and knitting. After all these years, I still don't feel very close to them. That's probably more my fault than theirs—I could have invited them for dinner, I could have joined Janice's knitting club.

Now Dennis smiles at me—I must be staring—and for a moment, I imagine telling him about Brian, the two of us sitting in the hushed, dark church, where he could pray with me, help me wade through fear and shame, show me the light that I cannot yet see. But we do not have that kind of relationship. I could never tell him the truth.

As Anita chatters about her arthritis, the crowd around Brian grows— the return of the prodigal son. Lettie and Jess, and Josh's beautiful wife Jennifer, and Gus and Pam gather around. Travis stands off to the side, talking to Jim Drewer, wiping sweat from his neck. I suddenly feel like I need to get over there.

Anita pats my hand. "God answered your prayers," she says. "You got your boy back."

Brian's talking about New York, and as he talks, his hands flutter— wings that never stop moving. But his hair is stuck in place with hair-spray or gel or whatever he uses. That earring. Won't take it out, not even at church.

"I went one time a few years ago," Dennis interrupts. "I was there for a church conference. It was neat to see all the lights. But mostly what you see is a lot of garbage. A lot of suffering, too—street people, drug addicts, homeless. It's no place for . . . most people, I don't think. Definitely not for me."

"No, if you love living in Chester, Ohio, then New York's not for you," Brian says, and Dennis forces a smile—unsure if he's just been insulted.

Josh says he'd like to visit. "I mean, Dad, if that's where the suffering people are, isn't that where we should be?"

Dennis's uncertain smile stays frozen on his face as Josh, eyes bright, talks about saving lost souls. Jennifer stands quietly beside him, the sleeping baby in her arms.

"Well, there are plenty of lost souls here," Dennis says.

A scowl of irritation crosses Josh's face, then he turns to Brian. "You ever go to a Mets game? I'm not really a fan, but it would still be cool to see them play at Shea Stadium."

"No, but I went to a Yankees game once," Brian says.

"The Yankees?" Josh makes a sour face. "Why?"

"I went with a friend—he wanted to go." Brian looks extra tired. Pallid and gaunt, he folds his skinny arms over his chest. "My friend Shawn."

Heat rushes to my face. I watch Brian's mouth twist, like he's trying to speak but can't. He looks like he might cry.

"Shawn died," he says.

Silence—then a few murmurs, no real words. Everyone stares, then looks away. Not Lettie. She reaches for his arm.

"Oh, honey, I'm sorry," she exclaims. "What happened?"

I can't breathe. My heart flutters and I feel light-headed. Brian squints, staring into the sunlight. Suspended in silence, we wait. He could tell her, tell all of them. He cocks his hip, tilts his head. Girlish gestures. He must know how he looks. *Fairy, queer, faggot.* The cruel words drum against my chest.

"Pneumonia," he says. "He died of pneumonia."

Lettie, still touching his arm, tells him she is sorry, and Reverend Clay frowns. "That's a shame, I'm sorry," he says, but he doesn't look sorry, just annoyed. Josh studies Brian with piqued interest. Are they all wondering how a young man died of pneumonia? Are they wondering about this word "friend?"

"We should get going," I say.

Brian huddles under an old afghan of rainbow colors that Lettie made years ago, the television's blue light washing over him. He scrunches his legs to make room for me and I sit on the end of the couch. His socked feet don't quite touch my lap. He's drinking out of the red cup. Every time I see him with it, I feel pinched with shame.

He picks up the remote, runs through the channels, stops on a rerun of *M*A*S*H*. His video camera sits on the coffee table, a stack of VHS tapes next to it. He's shown me a few snippets of videos of New York. The city looks exactly like I picture it—dirty and dangerous. He says he has other videos, but I won't like them.

"I was recording Jess talking about Greenpeace," he says. "She's smart. I hope she goes to college."

"Me too."

"I hope she gets out of here," he says.

As Hot Lips and Radar argue, I remember Brian and Travis watching the show together, laughing. It wasn't always hard between them. When Brian was little, Travis would tuck him at night, and they'd pretend to be cowboys sleeping under the stars. They were buddies. They wore matching Cincinnati Reds hats. They were happy, once, weren't they? Father and son.

I have not asked hard questions, and Brian has not offered any answers. I won't be like Travis, I can't. I make myself speak.

"How are you feeling?" I ask. "I mean physically."

He looks over, surprised. "Fine. Considering."

Canned laughter from the TV. I force my mouth to move. The words come out in a rush.

"Is there anything you need? Medicine? Should we go to the doctor?" I stop, swallow. My voice sounds loud, strange, not my own. "It's just, we don't know what to do."

Brian pulls his feet in closer, the feet I should touch, massage, but my fingers curl into my palms.

"There's no cure," he says. Without emotion or inflection, matter-of-fact.

"Not yet," I say quickly. "There isn't yet—"

"There are experimental drugs if you have money, if you know the right people."

"You're not taking them? I mean, we could help."

"There's nothing you can do." He sighs. "Also, I'm broke. I mean, I can't pay you for rent or anything like that, I wish I could—"

"Of course, we don't want you to—"

"I get Social Security. Medicare. To help, you know, with costs. I probably should go to a doctor but I don't know where."

"Should I call some places?" I say. "Maybe in Columbus?"

"Columbus," he says. "Kind of far away. But I guess it's the only option, especially if you don't want anyone to know—"

"No, I just thought maybe the doctors will be more experienced there."

On TV Klinger pirouettes in a dress, pretending to be a homosexual, more laughter. Brian's sweatshirt hangs off him. Underneath, I could trace his ribs so easily. I can see beyond this, and yet I can't: I don't know how bad it's going to get, I don't want to know.

"New York's so different. Friends are sick. Dying. Dead. I had to get away. But now, I don't know." Brian looks at me, his eyes soft and sad. "I don't know why I'm here."

I reach for his hand. I want to tell him I'm sorry. I want to tell him things will be okay. I want to tell him to stay here with us, his family.

"I'm praying for you," I say, and immediately I know the words are wrong—it's not what I meant to say, but I can't take them back. Brian's face falls.

In the made-for-TV movies Lettie watches, if there is a struggle or an obstacle the mother faces, her love for her child always wins. I didn't realize I was unloved until I had children of my own. For so long, I thought something was wrong with me. Then, after I held my babies, I knew what maybe I should have known all long—it was my mother, not me. Something was wrong with her. I would not be that kind of mother.

"I'm tired." Brian stands up. "I'm going to bed."

A mother's love is unconditional. Trembling, I pull the soft, stretched-out afghan over me, and watch the actors on TV talk and joke and laugh as they heal the injured, and the war around them never stops.

I'm not outside for more than a few minutes when I hear the door. Afraid it's Jess, I stub out the cigarette. I don't want her to know I've started smoking.

But it's Travis. Still in his work clothes, smelling of cheap beer and sweat. He squints, sounds hurt. "You're smoking? Since when?"

"I don't remember. A month or two ago."

I relight the cigarette, and Travis lifts his eyebrows and makes a "sss" sound, surprised. He doesn't look good. Heavy eyes, the skin around them pinched. Gray-black stubble, thick mustache. He needs to shave. I don't know what I'm sorry for exactly, but I am. We have not made love since Brian's been home.

"I made you a plate," I say. "You want me to heat it up in the microwave?"

"No, I had a burger at the Refuge."

I can't force them to spend time together. I've mentioned to Travis that maybe they should go to a ballgame, but he just says, "We'll see." I've seen how Brian looks at him, the longing in his eyes.

The sun flattens into a thin red line. Next door the Pentecostal girls' prairie dresses hang limply from the clothesline like drabber versions of themselves. Travis comes closer, doesn't touch me. The evening light spreads cloud-like across the yard, turning trees into tall still shadows. I feel his body tense next to mine, the hushed silence. The weight of what he wants to say.

"Today at work, Wayne asked me what was wrong with Brian." Travis pauses. "Wanted to know what is *really* wrong with him."

He can't stand the thought of disappointing his big brother. Can't stand the thought of embarrassing—or disgracing—the family.

"Did you tell him?" I ask.

"Are you kidding? Do you know what he'd do, what he'd say?"

I remember not very long ago, Wayne said that people with AIDS should be sent to a far-away island, and every one of us, me, my husband, my nephews and nieces, we all agreed whole-heartedly. Protect the good from the bad, the normal from the abnormal, the innocent from the infected.

"They know something is going on, Travis. Maybe we should tell them."

He has not said the word yet. Maybe he never will, and I'll continue to go along with the charade, because what else can I do? My son is sick. My son is dying. No, no, no. If we don't say these words, they will not be true. But I can't keep hiding, not like this—

"No," Travis says with finality. "We can't tell them—nobody can know."

Brian

Shawn told me to document everything, the good and bad. He was scared our lives would be forgotten.

When he first gave me my first camcorder, I didn't know what to do with it. It was a hefty, bulky thing he got from a dying friend who was giving away all his possessions. At first I just recorded Shawn making funny faces, or Annie telling me about her latest lady crush. Then I started to fool around—teaching myself how to take different kinds of shots, about lighting and editing. Rewind, pause, record, like making a mix tape. I screwed up all the time, and still do—I'll forget to change out the tape and record over my footage, or I won't have enough tapes with me to last through the shoot, or I'll forget to label them. But, still, I'd found something I was pretty good at, or could be good at. I started thinking about art school. Thinking I had a future.

A lot of the videos I made in New York were documentation of my friends just living their lives. Talking, kissing, dancing, or flipping off the camera—always a favorite move. Footage from clubs and bars. Drag queens sashaying down the street. Glitter, rainbows, feathers. Nobody wanted to talk about AIDS or death, and I was relieved—I wanted to capture the joy, the life.

But, Shawn—he wanted me to document the harder stuff. Even wanted me to record him in the hospital, dying. I couldn't do it.

I didn't understand then, but I think I do now. The world is ignoring us. We've got to document, even if it's just me talking to the camera in my parents' basement. At least I'm here. A face, a voice. The world wants to silence and disappear us. Well, here I am. Look at me.

June 10, 1986

Look at them.

Jess was in here earlier and while we were listening to records, she kept staring at the pictures on my wall. Shawn, Alex Morales, John Ziegler, Troy Benton, Jason McDonald. We're all too young, don't you see?

She asked me who they were, and I said they were my friends. I wasn't going to say anything else, but then I don't know—I couldn't hold back.

I told her, They're all dead.

Her eyes went wide. She wanted to know how. Were they in a car crash or something? How did it happen?

It was a reasonable question. She looked shocked—and I remembered, before AIDS, when young, healthy, handsome men just didn't die. I remember—barely—a time when all of us weren't so sad or scared.

Different ways, I told her.

Jess, all quiet, sank into the beanbag chair. Maybe she could tell I was lying.

But "Rebel Rebel" came on, so I told her the story of buying my first Bowie record. I know I've probably told her before, but she listened patiently. I was twelve years old when I heard the song on the radio, and I begged Mamaw to take me to the record shop in Madison. They'd sold out of *Diamond Dogs*, but they had one copy of *Hunky Dory* left. I'd never heard anything so strange and perfect. Later, I saw Bowie on TV performing with Cher, the two of them singing a crazy medley of songs, from the Beatles to Bing Crosby, long-legged, feral creatures in white pants. I was rapt, my body burning, and the edges of Chester exploding: there was a bigger world and I wanted to see it, to be in it.

Bowie showed me that there was another way of being, you know? Like, he broke all the rules about gender, and just like life. I tried to explain all this to Jess.

She just stared at me. She was wearing a shirt that matched her Jams, pink with blue palm trees, and a pair of shades with mirror lenses pushed on top of her head, which killed me—trying so hard to look cool, but still such a nerdy kid. She's not like I was at her age; she doesn't skip classes, or smoke or drink. Lately though, she's starting to worry about what she eats, calories and grams of fat, all that—an inevitable teenage girl thing I guess.

She asked if I missed New York. Jess is the only one really wants to know about the city.

Of course, I told her. Here, everyone worries about what everyone else thinks. Once you escape that mentality, you don't ever want to go back.

But you did, Jess says, you came back. She's sharp.

Well, I said, sometimes you have to go back to the place you left.

She goes, Why?

Why, indeed? To understand who you've become. To reconcile. To say goodbye. I turned the record over. I don't know, I said.

June 13, 1986

I'm doing okay. The same, really. I'm still taking antibiotics the doctor prescribed after my bout with pneumonia. And, I've been able to eat without throwing up or endlessly shitting. Right now, I don't feel incredibly ill, and I certainly don't feel like I'm dying. But the body plays tricks. I'm feeling practically normal, except I don't remember what normal feels like.

I've had a few bad moments, nothing debilitating. Mostly, I just get so tired. I've thought about trying to find a doctor to do my blood work and check my CD4 count, but nobody in these parts will want to examine me. Does it really matter? Like I told my mom, there is no cure.

Yeah, there is always talk of possible breakthroughs—drug trials, new medications. AZT is the brass ring. Men with money and connections get the drugs first. I've heard about guys going to Mexico for new drugs that may or may not work. There are those who believe positive thinking will make them healthy. Whatever. Everyone's desperate for the pain and fear to go away. There's no cure now, but there has to be one one day, that's what we're all thinking. Because if not, then what? The other option is unthinkable. Death, death, and more death.

I know how ugly it gets, but I wasn't a caretaker, not really, not like Shawn. He nursed a few of his friends, sat with them on their deathbeds, wiped their brows with a cold washcloth, listened. He'd tell me about them as we were falling asleep, holding each other in the dark, believing—hoping—that it wouldn't happen to us.

Shawn died in a hospital with a tube shoved down his throat. I didn't want to die in New York— I didn't want to die in a hospital—

I don't want to die.

📼 June 15, 1986

I haven't seen as much of my cousin Gus as I thought I would. I thought he'd be around more, maybe make things easier between me and my dad. But he always has an excuse about work, or else it's something with his kid. But, today he came over to pick me up, and we went to the Dairy Freeze in Colby. Listen, I have to admit, I was thrilled. I've been feeling pretty desperate to get out of the house and be around someone my own age. When I left, there was no reason to stay in touch with anyone from high school, so I'm not surprised none of my old teammates have come by or called me up. The only one I've seen is preacher boy, Josh Clay. He and Gus are buddies now.

I asked Gus about that. I said, How the hell do you stand that guy?

Josh played for a couple of seasons. Benchwarmer and right-field. He never fit in. Probably didn't help that his dad was a minister. He was always trying too hard and wound tight, even when he was quiet—like he was keeping track of everything people said so he could use it against them. He'd get on his high horse in class, making simplistic arguments about the death penalty or abortion. I'm pretty sure he was the one who ratted out a few of us on the team for smoking pot.

Gus said their wives were close, and so the four of them get together to play cards or watch a ballgame on TV, their babies sleeping. Gus said Josh wasn't so bad. He's changed, Gus tried to tell me, he's a nice guy.

Well, Jess sure thinks the world of him, I said.

At church, I didn't like the way Josh kept smiling at her, reaching over to knead her neck or squeeze her shoulders, and her eating up his every word.

Anyway, we went to the Dairy Freeze, and sat at a table outside. The girl behind the counter called our number, and Gus went up to get our food. He's a big guy with thick, tree-stump legs and giant feet, a football player turned soft. I try to imagine him in New York, lumbering through crowds, stepping on feet, apologizing. He wouldn't last a day. Most people in Chester wouldn't.

As we ate, Gus talked nonstop about his wife and daughter and job. He's usually not much of a talker. Sometimes, I'd call him from New York, and he'd hardly say a word, but his silence was strangely comforting. Now, he didn't leave any room for me to say anything. I started to feel—sick to my stomach. Gus shoving in fries, talking with his mouth full. Telling me all this bullshit. Look, I wasn't planning on it. I just couldn't stop myself.

I said, I have something to tell you.

He'd just taken a bite of cheeseburger, and a trail of mustard ran down his double chin. I used to tell him about the guys I spent time with, the actors and artists, and I'm sure I mentioned, once or twice, that someone was gay. But I never came out to him. I have no idea what Gus knows. He's a nice guy, but not the brightest bulb. Sorry, Gus, if you're watching.

I told him I've been sick.

He set the burger down and dabbed at his chin with a paper napkin. He wanted me to shut up, I could see it in his eyes.

Gus, I said, I have AIDS.

He started to pick up the burger, then set it back down. I said it again. Not too loud, but loud enough. There was a table of teenage girls not too far from us, but they weren't paying any attention. You bitch, one kept saying to the other, all of them laughing. I wish I was young again.

Gus looked like he might cry. He wiped his eyes, his mouth working but no sound coming out. Then he goes, I heard my dad say something.

His dad?

I remember when we were little, playing Superman and Wonder Woman—guess which one of us was Wonder Woman—and Uncle Wayne walked in as I was twirling around in one of Mamaw's aprons. He didn't touch me, but he grabbed Gus by the back of the neck and told him if he ever caught him acting like a little girl, he'd whip him good.

Gus told me his dad didn't know anything for sure, he's just saying shit, making guesses about what's wrong with me.

Then Gus said, I won't tell anyone, except Pam. I can't lie to her.

I said that was fine with me, I'm sick of the lies.

Then Gus started grilling me. He was worried about Allie, his baby. You held her, he said, accusing me.

I had to talk to him like he was a small child and explain I'm not contagious. Nobody is going to get HIV from me, not unless I sleep with them or transfer my blood into their bodies. You can't get it from doorknobs, you know, I said. I tried to tell him that actually, I'm the susceptible one. I'm the one with the weakened immune system, and his baby is more dangerous to me than I am to her. I could tell he didn't believe me.

But when I got out of his truck, Gus leaned over and gave me a big hug. You'll be all right, right? he asked.

What could I say? Him looking at me like that, all teary-eyed. I said yes.

Uncle Wayne, what does he know? Maybe he figured out I was queer a long time ago, before I did. I didn't know how to say the words to myself until I was living far away from here. That was when I discovered another language, not my family's tongue, but one that was older and bigger. I found another home. Now that home is burning down and nobody wants to put out the fire.

Jess

I've never gone on a run like this, just on my own. At first it feels strange, like I don't know how to make my legs work. I conjure Rocky, jogging through the streets of Philadelphia. I think of Josh Clay, who goes on long runs, he told me, to clear his head. I picture Wendy Rooper, the fattest girl in school. I picture Brandy White, stretched out on her beach towel, surrounded by boys. I'm making changes. This summer, I'm going to lose weight. I'm going on a diet. I'm going to look different.

It's the middle of the day and Chester is a ghost town. My tennis shoes slap the sidewalk as I run by the dentist office where my mother works. She is probably on the phone or organizing files. I never want a job like that. People around here gravitate toward boredom.

My grandmother's car, the Queen's Ship, sits outside of Dot's Diner, and I turn off High Street, so she won't see me. She wanted me to go with her and Brian to lunch, but I told her I was meeting up with friends at the pool, even though I haven't been back since that day with Molly and Carrie.

I lied to her because I don't want to be seen with my brother. When he came to church with Mamaw, everyone stared. I run harder. Janet Jackson sings in my ears. I'm in control.

An old woman on her porch watches me go by. Then I see Principal Gleason in his yard watering flowers, wearing a T-shirt and shorts, and I cross the street, embarrassed by his pale hairless principal legs.

My breath moves up into my mouth, my heart drumming against my chest. As I pass the Green Valley Trailer Park, a guy in jeans and a black T-shirt walks out of a trailer. He sees me and waves and I slow down. I know him. Nick Marshall. He moved away a few years ago.

"Jess," he calls.

Pretending not to hear him, I run faster. Sweat trickles down my back. My legs and stomach jiggle, the fat burning away. My feet hit the ground again and again, and my hands clench into slick fists.

I cut across a field and run over to the old drive-in and collapse next to the concession stand, my heart thundering. The headphones slide off my ears and I close my eyes. My body feels heavy and light at the same time, and I wonder if this is how a whale feels. Only water can carry their immense weight.

A shadow dances across my eyes, and I open them with a start. A boy stands over me. I scramble up and he laughs.

"Scare you?"

"What did you do, follow me here, weirdo?"

"No." Nick Marshall's smile disappears. "I didn't follow you. This is just where I like to hang out."

He smashes a cigarette into the dirt with the heel of his boot. I've heard that he's a hood now, and that's exactly what he looks like. He's wearing a T-shirt with the name of a band I've never heard of printed in red slashed letters, jeans busted at the knees. Same little ferret face, but now he has a dark fuzzy smear of a mustache, a few zits on his chin. His hair is longer than most boys, tips tapping his shoulders.

"This is my spot." He points to the concession stand, and I see a little transistor radio, like my dad listens to when he's working on his truck, and a few empty beer cans. "You can stay if you want."

"Oh, wow, thanks."

Nick's cheeks redden. He takes a pack of cigarettes out of his hip pocket and fumbles to get one out. "I know you don't want one," he says.

"I'm in training," I say, hear how stupid it sounds.

Nick snorts. "For what? The Olympics?" He cups his hand when he lights his cigarette even though there is no breeze. His hands are small and dirty, fingertips smudged gray, like he's dipped them in ashes.

"I hate this place," he says. Nick's parents divorced a few years ago, and his mother took Nick with her to live in Madison. He was one of the first kids I knew whose parents were divorced.

He walks past the empty speaker poles over to the playground, and after a few seconds, I follow. I don't know why. Nick Marshall wasn't anyone I ever paid attention to. The other kids made fun of him because he was so poor—his jeans were too short, floods that hit above the ankle, and he gave off a sour, eggy odor. Whenever a teacher called on him, he never knew the right answer. But he was good at drawing, and probably the only kid in our grade who could solve the Rubik's Cube.

There isn't much left of the playground. A rotted teeter-totter. A swing set without swings—just a couple of rusty chains dangling. We sit on the weed-mauled merry-go-round and look up at the blank movie screen. The sunbaked metal burns my thighs, and I'm conscious of sweat dripping down my face. Do I stink? The summery smells of sweat and sunshine roll off Nick. A few years ago, he was a shrimpy, dirt-poor kid. He's still small, and probably still poor, but looks older than most of the boys in my grade—like he's been out in the world, like my brother, and seen things.

"Did you move back to Chester?" I ask.

"I'm just here for the summer. Living with my dad." Nick picks at a hangnail. "My mom got remarried. My stepdad is a dick. He's worse than my dad."

Nick holds the cigarette between his index and middle fingers, and takes a deep drag. I've been watching my grandmother and aunts and uncles smoke all my life. My brother started at thirteen, and my mother smokes too, but she doesn't know I know. Josh Clay warned us not to start down the wrong path. If he saw me here, he would be disappointed, even angry. There is something thrilling about this.

"Give me one."

"You sure?"

"Yeah."

Nick lights the cigarette for me and I inhale and get a mouthful of smoke and explode into a coughing fit. He doubles over laughing.

"Shut up," I say, and this makes him laugh harder. He's snorting, slapping his thigh.

The smoke tastes old and thick, like musty carpet or heavy old lady drapes, but I like how the cigarette looks in my hand.

He finally stops laughing, but I can tell he's holding back. He points to my Walkman. "What were you listening to?"

"It's a mix tape."

"Let me hear."

It's one that Brian made for me. Nick puts on the headphones for a few seconds, then hands them back. "What is this?"

I bring one of the foam circles to my ear. "Pet Shop Boys."

"It's kind of gay."

"No it's not."

Nick prefers metal and hard rock. "Ozzy Osborne is my favorite. Next is Ratt. Then Mötley Crüe."

This is the most we've ever talked. Nick tells me that his new school is better than Chester, but still sucks. He wants to leave Ohio.

"As soon as I get my driver's license, I'm busting out of this stupid state."

The cigarette combined with the running makes me light-headed. Words flutter out of my mouth like little moths before I can suck them back in.

"My brother used to live in New York. But he came back."

"Why?"

The cigarette burns between my fingers and the ashy tip flutters to the ground. "I don't know," I say.

The ground spins, but the merry-go-round, stiff with rust and choked by weeds, remains still. Nick stretches out on his back, and then I do too. Nobody knows we're here. We look up at the movie screen, at the drifting clouds, the electric blue sky. The tops of our sun-kissed heads touch. Everyone has secrets.

✳

I listen to *Horses* on my Walkman while everyone else is asleep. The red digital numbers on my alarm clock say 1:23. When Brian first played this tape for me, I wasn't sure if I even liked it. But now I close my eyes and pretend to be floating in the middle of the ocean, waves gently rocking me as whales glide beneath me. When a humpback whale sings, it sometimes hangs upside down, like a giant bat. Whale songs can travel thousands of miles across the ocean.

Patti Smith's voice gets bigger and bigger—angry, desperate, demanding. I cross my arms over my chest and shadows of purple darkness explode behind my eyes, and Patti's moaning gets louder, until I realize I'm not hearing the song but something else. I hit pause. The noise is coming from downstairs. I creep out of bed and out into the hallway where the nightlight plugged into the outlet turns the carpet a glowing amber. The moaning intensifies, and the back of my neck tingles.

Brian.

A light is on in the basement family room. From the top of the stairs, I can see my brother huddled on the couch under a pile of blankets. My mother sits next to him, rubbing his back. They don't notice me until I've come downstairs and I'm standing in front of them.

"What's wrong?"

"Just got a little sick," Brian says in a high voice. "Don't worry."

His face is as white as eggshells and slick with sweat. He moans, he shakes. His eyes are pink and swollen, like he's been crying.

"It's okay," my mother says. "Go back to bed."

"But—"

"Jess, go."

Neither of them will look at me, and rage blazes through me. Going back upstairs, I stomp. I make a lot of noise, my entire body burning, and expect my father to come out of my parents' bedroom, but he doesn't. Nobody comes after me.

I push the screen up and climb out my window onto the roof and look up at the stars pulsing through the darkness. People used to use the stars as a map, as a way to navigate the world, but now they're just something to look at. I find the bright points of the Big Dipper, curved over the woods like it's not very far away at all. It's the only constellation I know. I wouldn't know how to get anywhere.

At youth group, I still taste smoke in my mouth. I hung out with Nick Marshall earlier today. We smoked and talked and listened to music. It's easy to be around him. I don't feel worried that I'll say the wrong thing, the way I do around Carrie and Molly. But now guilt and shame beat like a drum inside me as Josh Clay looks at me from across the table, tears in his eyes.

He's telling a story about someone he knew in high school who had an abortion. "It's ruined her life," he says. "She won't ever forgive herself."

I told Brian about the stories Josh tells, and he says they're bullshit. He doesn't like Josh. "He was such a little rat," he says. "He was only on the team because of his dad. He couldn't field for shit."

"Not everyone's a jock like you," I said, and Brian rolled his eyes.

On my way out, Josh stops me. "Jessie, you want a ride?"

It's not a far walk, but I say okay. He smiles big. I don't care what Brian says. At least Josh isn't hiding anything, he isn't lying.

I get in the passenger seat of his Corolla. Josh doesn't turn on the radio, and I wonder what kind of music he likes. Not heavy metal. Not Bowie or Patti Smith. Amy Grant, probably. Christian music. A yellow teddy bear sits at my feet, and I pick it up.

"Is this yours?" I ask, trying to sound the way Brandy White does when she talks to boys. It works—Josh laughs, then I do too. We're flirting.

"It's my kid's," he says.

Josh lives on the other side of town, a few blocks from my grandmother. I wonder what his wife thinks of boring little Chester. Jennifer has long, full hair that cascades around her face like a model's and shiny teeth that my mother says she gets whitened. They met at the Christian college.

Josh pulls up in front of my house, and turns the key and the engine dies. "I was thinking of coming in to talk to Brian."

I picture my brother, lounged on the couch, watching MTV or one of his own weird videos. He'll say something embarrassing, do the wrong thing.

"Um, he's not here," I say. "I think he's at my grandma's."

Josh frowns. "I think Brian's avoiding me. I mean, we weren't close in high school or anything. To be honest, Jess, your brother was kind of a jerk—one of the popular kids, you know what I mean?"

I nod, not surprised.

"But now we're grownups, we're different people, and I'd like to talk to him. I feel like he wants to, like he needs to talk." As Josh chews his bottom lip, he looks shy and sweet. "Jessie, I need to ask you something. Is Brian okay?"

I'm squeezing the little yellow bear, practically strangling it. "Yeah. Why?"

"Well." Josh shifts in his seat, cracks his knuckles. "It seems like, I don't know, like he's been through a lot. He just looks a little...a little skinny, like maybe he's sick or something."

"He's fine. Um, I better go." I reach for the door handle and get out as quickly as I can, dropping the yellow bear on the seat. "Bye!" I call.

Like a gentleman, Josh waits until I get to the front door before he drives off. My heart is racing, but I'm not sure why. There's nothing wrong.

It's been raining all morning. Instead of going on a run, I put on my mother's Jane Fonda workout tape. Wearing a shiny leotard and matching blue wrist and ankle weights, Jane smiles and doesn't break a sweat. I lift my knees, swing my arms in and out from my chest, twist and turn. I do a set of leg lefts, sit ups. Sadie watches from the couch. I don't look any different, but the scale says I've lost three pounds. The hunger pains are sharp and satisfying. Today I've eaten only a banana and half a grapefruit. I'm wearing a new sports bra.

After the cool down, I eject the tape, and then pick up one labeled "Pyramid" from a stack of Brian's videos. At first there is nothing but darkness, then a few red lights reveal a crowd of people chattering and laughing. A tall black woman wearing a sparkling evening dress comes out on stage, and people cheer and clap as she begins to sing "Endless Love" by Diana Ross, as a solo instead of a duet, and for a second, I wonder if it's actually her. The camera moves to the crowd again—mostly men wearing skimpy shirts, tight pants, holding drinks, swaying, smiling, happy.

I hit eject and choose another tape. This one is labeled SHAWN, 1983. His friend. The one who died. His picture is up on Brian's wall, along with all the others. Brian says they're his family. All of them so handsome, even pretty. Like Shawn. Like my brother. They're all dead.

Shawn was an actor, but only in plays and a few experimental films, nothing I would have seen. Brian told me how funny and smart he was, how kind. Then he looked at me and said not to listen to the racist shit that I hear from Wayne or our father.

"Dad's not racist," I said.

"Just because Dad doesn't use the n-word doesn't mean he's not racist," Brian said. "Everyone in this town is, even Mamaw. I'm not saying they're meaning to be, but they are." He looked at me. "Have you ever had a black friend?"

"There aren't any black people in Chester."

"Yeah, why do you think that is?" Brian told me that he learned a lot when he moved to New York about his own racism. "It's way under your skin. We breathe racism." He told me, "You've got to be open-minded. It's the only way. You've got to be willing to see it."

In the video, Shawn stands in front of a vanity, his back to the camera. He's wearing little purple shorts, no shirt. "I told that queen to pull it together, and she told me to fuck off, so, like, whatever," he says, and turns, holding up a dangling blue feather earring. "What do you think? Oh, shit, are you shooting this? You," he says, and reaches for the camera. Brian laughs and then he comes into the picture too—they're facing each other, close, too close. Shawn kisses Brian on the cheek, and then his mouth moves toward his—and suddenly, everything in me turns too hot and flushed, like I've come down with a fever, I hit eject.

My muscles are trembling. I'm thirsty. I should leave, I should get a glass of water. But I pick up another tape. This one just lists a date. A recent date.

He's sitting on a bed, in front of the camera, and it takes me a few seconds before I realize he's here, in this house, in his room. His bed, his night stand, his shelf of trophies. David Bowie on the wall behind him. Brian wears a button-down shirt, his hair combed back. He smiles, frowns, smiles. Then he clears his throat. "Hello again. So, I'm thinking about how no one really knows. Sometimes, I don't want them to know. Other times, I want to shout it from the rooftops," he says. "I'm sick. I have—"

The front door, footsteps.

"Anyone home?" my brother calls.

Frantically, I eject the tape, turn off the TV, and hustle out the door to the garage, where it's dark and cool, like a cave. I'm trapped. I press the button on the wall, and as the garage door rattles and lifts, I duck under. Outside, the air smells like worms and dirt, and the sky is gloomy. The downstairs light comes on.

He said it aloud on the tape. I heard him. He said, I have AIDS.

I start to run.

My brother's red cup. Mom washing his laundry and dishes separately. His thinness, his frailty. The ocean of secrecy. The huffs of my breaths make beats like music. I run harder, my side screaming. Everything hurts. I want to feel the ache in my muscles, to hear the pounding of my heart. There is still too much of me. He said aloud what I knew and what I thought I didn't. I keep going and my muscles burn through fat, through the lies of our family.

Brian

Jess doesn't want to hang out with me anymore. She's gone all the time—
on runs, or hanging out with friends. I've smelled smoke on her, just like I
have with my mother. I started smoking when I was Jess's age, filching my
grandmother's menthols. I thought they were so fancy, the special green
and gold package. Maybe Jess is wilder than I thought. I don't blame her,
really, not wanting to talk to me. She knows something is going on.

My grandmother, on the other hand, is always hovering, asking if I'm
okay. She worries about my headaches, how tired I get, how thin I am.
I've lost five more pounds.

Today, I asked my mom what she thought about telling Jess and
Mamaw the truth. It gets exhausting, pretending you're someone you're
not.

Her shoulder blades tensed. She was at the stove, pushing around
pink clumps of beef with a spatula, furiously working her arm.

They're going to find out, Mom, and then what?

She clicked off the burner and turned around, her face rigid. I'll talk
to your father, she said. But I don't think he's going to change his mind.
He's trying to do what's right.

Right for who?

There were tears in her eyes. Maybe there were tears in mine too. I went outside with Sadie. We sat for a long time, the sun on our faces. My dad doesn't want anyone to know I have AIDS because he doesn't want anyone to know I'm gay.

June 27, 1986

Today, I was watching TV with my grandmother, and Tammy Faye Bakker was on, singing about Jesus, and Mamaw looked at me.

Honey, even if you don't go to church, God will listen to your prayers, she says.

Good Lord. Was she telling me to get right with God? Does she worry I'm heading to hell? Tammy Faye doesn't seem to believe in a punishing kind of God, and I don't think my grandmother does either. As Tammy Faye blinked her mascara-thick lashes, I was reminded of drag queens I knew in New York.

I wouldn't mind going to church with Tammy Faye, I said. Especially if she'd let me do her makeup.

Mamaw giggled. Big alligator tears started to run down Tammy Faye's glittery pink cheeks. Oh, there she goes! Anything can set her off, Mamaw said.

When I was little, on "Avon nights," we'd sit at the table, and Mamaw would make lists of what she sold and what she needed to reorder. I'd help organize everything, lining up mascara wands, tubes of lipstick, flat pressed squares of eye shadow. Moisturizer that smelled like flowers. Eye cream. I loved the dark green bottles of perfume, the elegant gold cases of rouge. My grandmother didn't care if my hands fluttered. She asked my opinions, she trusted my taste. I think Mamaw would love to see a drag queen.

Sometimes, I'd help friends with their makeup, but I only did drag a couple of times myself. I never performed or went out in public, didn't have the nerve or the courage. But, still, when I sat in front of a mirror and brushed on blush and eye shadow, glued on eyelashes, I felt a wild shock of delight.

Boys came to me because I had the right touch. A few of them are dead, others sick, others infected. They were thrilled to be wearing makeup and sparkling gowns and wigs, and to be free from their fathers' disappointment and shame.

They were so beautiful.

I want to tell you about my life in the Before. Before the ghosts. And how all that changed.

When I first got to New York, it took me a month or so to work up the courage to go to a gay bar. I was terrified, walking into that room of men. It didn't take long for one to come over—mustached, older, wearing a muscle shirt. He took me home. I had never even kissed a guy before. He treated me to breakfast the next day and said he'd call. He never did. It didn't matter.

New York was all dancing with shirts off, bare chests bumping. With music inside our hearts, we moved in ways that we had never been allowed to before. I had sex, I fell in love—with the city, with men. I met men who looked at me like nobody ever had before. Everything I used to dream about, but better.

Before we started dying, we were part of an electric dream. Alive and young, I danced and fucked and loved. Stayed out all night, snorting just one more line, ordering just one more round. Now, it's all vitamins and juices, pills and pretend treatments.

My first couple of years in the city, I heard rumors of something called GRID—gay cancer. But, even in New York, it seemed far away. Who got it? Older, rich gays who worked on Wall Street and spent their summers on Fire Island—worlds away from the poor artists and faggots of the East Village.

Then, a few weeks after I met Shawn, a friend of his died. Shawn told me things were going to get bad. I didn't understand, I don't think most of us did.

He was right, of course. More guys started getting sick. You'd see a guy at a party with horrific, purple, cancerous marks of KS all over his face, trying to make small talk and act normal. Emaciated guys limping along on walkers. I was scared, we all were. Afraid of someone sweating on you, touching you. That was before we know what we know now.

Before AIDS was on the news, in magazines like *Time* and *Newsweek*, on TV shows. Before it had become a regular part of our lives.

You started hearing things—who'd gone back to their families, who was in the hospital, who was dead. I had a friend, Troy Benton, who lost his mind—a twenty-seven-year-old turned into an old senile man. All these young men in the prime of their lives. You'd see a guy who looked fine, and run into him a few months later and he'd be puttering around on a cane. Or, someone would just drop out—you wouldn't see him anymore at the bars or the bath houses, or at art shows or dinners—and you knew he was sick or dead. It wasn't like someone would say, I have AIDS, or I have HIV. They'd just disappear.

When I finally went in for the test, I wasn't surprised. Still, you don't want to believe. Even after your brilliant beautiful boyfriend dies in a shitty hospital room, even after you've seen friends and lovers wasting away, you want to believe you're different.

It's impossible to understand or explain what it feels like when you're told you're going to die. Back in New York, some days I wanted to breathe in every single second. I'd notice little things—like a scrawny tree pushing up through the cement—and feel grateful I was a part of the city I loved. Other days I was a sobbing mess. Still, other times I burned up with anger toward everyone who was not me—because they were alive, living their goddamn lives, and, I was sick. And people knew it, especially other gays. I had that look—I know because I'd seen it in others: a haunted, hunted look. My body once turned men on, but now they turned away.

Now here I am. Alive, in Ohio, where we do not speak of the dead. Let us pretend. Where are all my beautiful men?

June 28, 1986

I haven't asked my father to sit down in front of the camera, but I've shot footage of his things. His work boots, his baseball cap that says P.T. GAS & ELECTRIC. In the garage, silver tools hang from pegs on a pegboard above his workbench. Screwdrivers, wrenches, pliers. Everything so neat and orderly. Hefty tool case with little compartments filled with screws and nails. I touch everything. The smell of motor oil makes me weak in the knees, that male smell, that father smell. The sunlight falling through the dirty windows turns the garage into a faded Polaroid from my child-hood, yellow and summery—from a time when he still liked me.

I wonder what goes through his mind when he thinks of me, his only son. His queer son. If he has imagined what I do. On my knees, a cock in my mouth. If he thinks of me at all.

This afternoon I was in the kitchen, and he walked in smelling like outside. He'd been mowing the grass, and there were green flecks on his neck, on his pants legs and in his hair. Silver mustache, stubble on his chin. His rolled-up sleeves showed off his muscles. Sometimes I hear him lifting weights in the garage—his grunts as he presses the barbell up off his chest, a weight none of us can touch, and then the thud and clatter when he drops it.

It's going to rain, he says.

I could hear thunder rumbling in the distance. On hot summer after-noons, when I was a kid, we used to sit on the porch watching the storms roll in.

He made himself a baloney sandwich. Then he looked up and asked if I wanted one.

The simple question cut me open. Yes, yes, I want my father to make me a sandwich. I want him to feed it to me with his fingers, bite by bite. Yes, please.

I told him no thanks, I wasn't hungry.

He says, The Reds are playing.

An invitation? I followed him into the front room. Maybe noticing my shivering, he turned off the A/C and cracked a window. Then the gray sky opened up and the rain started coming down. I breathed in the metallic smell of it hitting the mesh screen and the prickly scent of ozone. The room went dark, and my father turned on the lamp—the spotlight shining on him.

The announcers talked in low, intense voices. The sky on TV was blue and clear. When the Reds scored, my father looked over, forgetting for a moment his son's a faggot, and gave me a thumbs up. When I was little, prancing around to Dolly Parton, my grandmother egging me on as I flipped my pretend long, beautiful hair, I caught my father's embarrassment, how could I not? For him, I learned to speak the language of baseball.

The rain was starting to come in, gathering in small pools on the sill, but I didn't close the window. I liked the fresh air on my face. A sudden clap of thunder shook the house. I felt so alive, and safe.

June 30, 1986

Today Mamaw picked me up in her Crown Vic, tequila-gold shining in the sun, washed and waxed, and said we were going shopping. She loves to drive, always has. She used to drive all over the hills of Ohio, hawking her wares. It wasn't easy to sell beauty products in Appalachia, but my grandmother was a hell of a saleswoman. Usually, the lady of the house would invite us in, offer us a glass of Coke. If Mamaw ran into any trouble making a sell, then she'd get me to sing a Dolly Parton number. My cuteness usually nailed it.

You have a special way of seeing the world, she used to say. Like her brother, the one who was killed in the war. A young man who never had a girlfriend. Whenever she talks about him, she gets tears in her eyes. He was a good man, she says.

When I left Ohio, my grandmother understood. She told me to live my life, but I also saw the hurt in her eyes. I'm scared for you, she said. I told her I'd be back soon.

Now I want her to take care of me, but how can she if she doesn't know? When I was growing up, she laughed at jokes about homosexuals, we all did. Since I've been here, she hasn't said a word about gays or AIDS.

We went to the mall in Madison. She wanted to go in every store, stopping to look at all the window displays. Oh, look how cute, she'd say, pointing out ceramic puppies, a mug with a bunny on it, a pair of tiny red Dorothy slippers. She touched things. She picked up a container of potpourri, and gushed, Oh, don't this smell good.

After an hour or so, we took a break. Not for her. For me. She pretended she needed a rest too, but she wasn't winded at all. I hardly remember how things felt during the Before: when I never had to think about breathing or walking or running any more than I did about eating or sleeping. Those were just things the body did—without pain, without effort. Now the shortness of breath comes and goes. My body—I want the old one back.

We sat on a cement bench next to the center fountain, the bottom lined with pennies and nickels. I dipped my hand in. The water was cold and clear, smelled like metal.

When my grandmother saw a couple of ladies she knew, she waved big.

This is my grandson, Brian, she tells them. He's back from New York City.

New York! They shook their heads with wonder, eyes locked onto my earring. Both were squat, boxy, with short, styleless hair. Dykes, I thought, but of course, they had husbands at home, kids and grandkids. One wore a loose T-shirt with Mickey Mouse on the front, so long it fell almost to her knees, and the other had on a plain blue oxford worn out at the elbows. They've probably never been out of Ohio. They have everything they need here, why go anywhere else?

After they left us, Mamaw opened her change purse, the same one she's had for years, with the little copper clasp that fastens together. She handed me a penny and took one for herself.

Make you a wish, she said.

I flipped the penny in, and when I opened my eyes, it had already sunk and joined the hundreds of others, all those drowned wishes. I'm scared, Mamaw, I wanted to say. Make me better.

We went to Sears and walked through the ladies' section where a few women browsed the sale racks. Watching them, hearing the click of the plastic hangers, I felt nostalgic. When I was little, I used to crawl under the racks of clothes, slipping between dresses and slacks, as Mamaw read price tags aloud and touched the material to see if it was well-made or not.

We rode the escalator up to the men's department, even though I told her I didn't need anything.

It's my money, she says. Look here. They're having a sale on tops.

She sent me over to a table of shirts and told me to hold out my arms, and a salesman with puffy blond hair came over and asked if we needed any help. He was probably in his mid-thirties. Tiny lines around his eyes. He wore silver rings on his fingers and spoke with a predictable lisp. I gave him a smile of recognition. You can spot your own. This one, what a nelly.

I told him we were just looking.

If you need anything, just holler, he says, voice all bright and gay. He said his name was Andrew.

My grandmother, chatty, told him all about me—her grandson, home from New York City.

Andrew gave me the same knowing look I'd given him. As he hovered, jabbering about upcoming sales, I started to feel like I couldn't breathe. The factory smell of new clothes and cheap carpet, the swirl of cologne—I was suffocating. I needed to get the hell out of there.

That's a good color on you, he says, as my grandmother held up a blue shirt to me. She goes, Matches his eyes, doesn't it?

Then the phone rang, and Andrew excused himself. He touched my shoulder before he whirled away. I felt relieved to see him go. I can't explain it, really, the sudden, sticky shame—it wasn't about being queer, not exactly. I felt disappointed in myself. I left this town so I wouldn't have to live this way, and now here I was, back in the closet, walking around in skin that's not my own.

What a nice fella, my grandmother says.

Jess

My parents think I'm an idiot.

Like I never heard of Ryan White, the boy in Indiana not allowed to go to school. Or about Rock Hudson. I remember seeing the pictures of him in the *National Enquirer*, how old and skeletal and creepy he looked. Mamaw couldn't get over it. She loved Rock Hudson, and was tickled pink when he joined the cast of *Dynasty*. I watched that episode with her, the one when Rock Hudson kisses Linda Evans. That was before people knew. After they found out, they worried over that kiss. And, of course, I've seen the news—the men in San Francisco and New York City. At school, kids joke with each other: Eww, don't touch me, you'll give me AIDS. Uncle Wayne:

Do you know what *gay* stands for?

What?

Got AIDS yet?

Nobody ever told me Brian was a homo. I just figured it out, even though he doesn't act like the men you see flitting around on TV, not exactly. I guess Rock Hudson didn't act like that either. Once I asked Aunt Carol if she thought Brian ran off to get married, and she and

Aunt Liz just looked at each other trying to hide smiles. "Oh, I don't think that's the reason," Carol said, her voice heavy with scandal. My cousins talk in code: Well, Brian was always different, ha, ha, ha.

One time when I was little, I was with Mamaw at the beauty shop, and overheard one of the ladies talking about her cousin, a hairdresser living in the big city, *Queer as a three dollar bill,* and they all laughed, including my grandmother. Later I asked her what the word meant and she told me not to use such language. Then she said it meant "funny," like Richard Simmons is funny.

At school boys who aren't good at sports are faggots. Boys joke with each other: Stop being such a fag. Wayne teases me about the fairies I listen to. Boy George, The Cure, Prince, Michael Jackson. Most of the time he's laughing, but sometimes his voice goes thin and tight. Homos are sick, he says, and that's why God's getting rid of them.

My parents let Brian come back, but they don't want us to drink after him or eat off the same silverware. I've read you can't catch it that way, but what if? What if people find out—my friends, my teammates, kids at school?

My mother's at the kitchen table clipping coupons.

"Where's Dad?"

Snip, snip, snip. "Probably at the Refuge watching the Reds game."

He'd rather be anywhere but here, even sitting in a dark bar on a sunny day.

I pour myself a Diet Pepsi. Outside Sadie relaxes in the grass, soaking in the sun, her head rested on her paws, looking a little sad.

"Where's Brian?"

"Over at your grandmother's."

I thumb through the coupons. Seventy-five cents off orange juice. Buy two get one free diet frozen dinners. Coupons for chicken, a gallon of milk, fat-free chocolate cookies. Before Brian came back, whenever I'd go into a public bathroom, Mamaw would tell me to line the seat with toilet paper. *Don't touch the seat, you could catch AIDS!*

"Mom."

"Hmm?"

She's distracted, she's always distracted. She cuts a coupon for tropical punch-flavored Hi-C.

"Nothing," I say.

Later, when I'm in my room, I hear my dad come in. He doesn't sing oldies like he used to, doesn't call out to us when he gets home. He moves quietly through the house. For a moment, I consider going downstairs to ask him what he thinks of all this, what he knows. But I hear the door slam, then the rumble of the lawn mower. I push open my window and crawl out on the roof. My father perches on the riding mower, a baseball hat shading his face. The air smells like cut grass and light and summer. He goes up and down the lawn, making perfectly straight lines. I watch him but he doesn't see me. Metallic green swallows swoop down to eat up the bugs.

Killer whale societies are matriarchal. The pods are led by mothers and grandmothers. My grandmother is the matriarch, but she doesn't know the truth about her grandson. As she spoons out strawberries and Cool Whip, her doughy arms jiggle. It doesn't matter how much you weigh when you're old.

"I don't want any," I say.

"What's wrong?"

"Nothing. I'm just not hungry."

She studies me, hand on her hip. I never get her to myself anymore. "Well, okay then. More for me and Brian."

My brother makes a big deal about how good the strawberry shortcake is, smacking his lips and making noises of delight. I've been avoiding him as much as possible. I thought this would be the missing puzzle piece snapping into place, but it doesn't feel like that—I just have more questions and nowhere to turn. Sometimes I feel scared, like I've been left behind in a stranger's house. Other times, I'm enraged—at him, the lies, the illness. The anger is better—sharper, like a barbed wire wrapped around my hands. I try to hold on because it makes me stronger. But then he starts talking to me, and everything in me gets twisted up and confused. I wish I didn't feel anything at all.

"You sure you don't want just a little piece?" Mamaw asks.

I won't be tempted. When *Days of Our Lives* comes on, Mamaw and Brian hush up, then start gabbing at each other and at the TV. Mamaw says, "Look at her, that floozy's up to something." "I thought he was in a coma," Brian says. They especially like when a character does something bad or a villain ruins a happy moment. I can't keep track of who's in love with who, who's betrayed who.

"I'm going on a jog," I say.

"A jog," Mamaw says, like she's hearing the word for the first time. "What in the world for?"

"I just want to."

"Are you going to be back in time for our show?" she asks, talking about *On Location With Naomi.*

My grandmother doesn't have a clue. I run as hard as I can. It's not enough.

Nick passes me a can of Pabst Blue Ribbon he stole from his father's supply. It's a hot, sticky day. The treetops drum and whine with cicadas, but the birds remain quiet, nowhere to be seen. We're sitting in what is left of the old concession stand, and the lean-to roof keeps the sun off our faces. Mud daubers bump stupidly into the rafters.

When Led Zeppelin's "Stairway to Heaven" comes on, Nick turns it up. The warm, bitter beer makes me shudder, but I drink it anyway. We see each other a few times a week now. Nick doesn't have any friends in Chester, and I don't either—I haven't hung out with Carrie or Molly since that day at the pool.

The song gets Nick thinking of death, and he asks if I know anyone who's died.

"My grandpa," I say. "A couple of great-aunts, but I didn't know them."

"My cousin Max died last year." Nick lights a cigarette, hands me one. "He was six."

I've only known old people to die, but in the made-for-TV movies there is always some kid with ivory skin and feathery hair and big eyes like a Precious Moments figurine dying of leukemia. I ask Nick if that's what his cousin had.

"No. He was stung by bees. He was allergic."

"Do you know anyone who died from a disease?" I ask.

"My grandpa had cancer."

I pick my fingernails. It would be so easy to tell him, but impossible at the same time.

"What if you found out you were dying and you got one last wish?" I add, "It could be anything," even though the dying kids I read about in Mamaw's magazines only ever want to go to Disney World, or else some movie star nobody has ever heard of visits them in the hospital and gives the kid an autographed picture.

"That's bullshit," Nick says. "Nobody gets a last wish."

"But, like, just say you could. What would it be?"

"I don't know. Maybe I'd ride across the country on a Harley." Even in this heat, Nick wears jeans and a black T-shirt. I've never seen his bare legs. I tell him my uncle Wayne has a motorcycle. A Honda. Nick says if it's not a Harley, he's not interested.

"What's yours?" he asks.

"I'd go out to the Antarctic Ocean to see pods of killer whales. Sometimes there are fifty of them together."

"They'd eat you."

"No, they wouldn't. Anyway, who cares? If I was going to die anyway."

"True." He spits. "Well, I don't think we're going to get a disease, so don't get your hopes up."

"People get diseases all the time." I hesitate. "Like AIDS."

"Only fags get that," he says.

I smoke my cigarette. I've said too much. One time I heard Mr. Trumble, the science teacher, talking to Mr. Michaels, our vice-principal, about AIDS, and he said it's a part of God's plan, to make homosexuals pay for their sins. I want someone to tell me differently. I don't want my brother to burn in hell.

The song gathers steam, all guitars and yelling. A staircase to heaven. Why do people always think heaven is in the sky? Why can't it be in the ocean? Most of the ocean is still a mystery, like outer space. I've watched the videos of the bright, spindly stars of coral and the spikey fish and ghostly glowing deep sea creatures on *NOVA*, but there is so much that is invisible to our eyes, a world nobody has ever seen.

Nick crushes the empty beer can and tosses it against what's left of the old popcorn machine—most of the glass is busted out, cobwebs matted over the kettle. I don't know if my brother has any last wishes. My mouth feels loose, I might say anything. But I can't. Nobody can know. Or know that I know.

Nick opens his notebook to show me his latest drawings, and we leaf through the pages, our heads bent close together. Monsters, spaceships, motorcycles. As I turn another page, Nick daintily strokes the top of my hand with his smudged fingertip. A yellow jacket buzzes around the crushed beer can. A tiny insect can kill a person.

Nick moves closer. His lips are warm and thin and hard. I know about French kissing. Still, it's a surprise when Nick's tongue darts into my mouth. The soft thin hairs of his mustache tickle my skin. After a few more seconds of wiggling around, Nick pulls his tongue out, leaving my lips feeling giant and empty and exposed. Embarrassed, I wipe my mouth with the back of my hand. My heart pounds hard and fast. What is naked to the eye can kill a person. Maybe the disease is inside me too, lingering in my saliva, poisoning me, and now poisoning Nick, who grins foolishly.

When I take another drag off the cigarette, the ground softens, tilts underneath me. The beer and cigarettes have left me feeling wobbly and thick-headed. When I tell Nick I have to go, he doesn't try to kiss me again. I walk away, carefully. The sun beats against my skull. One step at a time. When I'm far enough away that he can't see or hear me, I huddle behind a line of scraggly bushes and throw up.

"He has AIDS," Josh Clay says.

His tone is remorseful and hushed, but when he says the word, it's like he's let a rabid bat into the room, swooping and fluttering wildly over our heads. Collective groans, faces of disgust. "Gross," someone says.

This man, he explains, is someone he knows. "He left his family, went far away," he says. "He lived a homosexual lifestyle."

I'm sitting as still as possible, trying not to breathe, but my muscles in my face still contract and expand. The hurt hits my eyes like I'm staring into a bright light bulb and can't look away. The others in youth group are wide-eyed and innocent, as weightless as kites. I taste smoke in my mouth. Jesus loves you, Josh tells us. I want to be filled with the light Josh carries around. To feel safe. To be born again.

"He's in Chester," Josh says. He stares at each of us, emphasizing how wrong this is. "He's *here*, walking around with this disease."

The room spins. I hold very still. Josh never uses real names in his stories, but what if the others figure it out?

After the meeting, he offers me a ride. I don't want to go, but he insists.

At first, he makes dumb jokes and talks like everything is normal, but when he pulls in front of my house, he turns off the engine, and my stomach twists into knots. I feel exposed, like he's been in my room, touched all of my things, my underwear and bras. Josh opens a plastic container the size of a lighter and taps three Tic Tacs into my cupped hand. He pops one in his mouth, and for a second, I see it there, a bright green button on his tongue, and I wonder what it would be like to kiss him.

He reaches his hand out and touches my knee, and it makes me anxious, his skin on my skin. Thank God I shaved this morning. I've lost weight, but still I don't like how my legs look, too soft, wide. I crack my knuckles, then, embarrassed, shove my hands under my thighs. Josh's cologne overpowers the air like an ad in a magazine, tickling my nose. I want to hear the voice of God. I want to tell Josh everything. I want to talk to him about whales. About Brian. Nick.

"Jessie, are you okay?"

Maybe he knows about the beer, the cigarette, the kiss. Puking in the bushes. I'm a sinner, like my brother. I'm a fake, a liar.

"You know who I was talking about, right?" he asks.

The knot in my throat expands, a hard lump, like I've swallowed a buckeye. Josh's fingers tap softly on my knee.

"Your brother's sick, isn't he?"

One time I went with Molly to a Catholic mass, and felt swept up by the strangeness and mystery: the choir's low chants, burning incense, all the kneeling. I wanted to be Catholic too—to go to the confession booth and talk into the little square window to a hidden priest, and click rosary beads between my fingers and make the sign of the cross, the way athletes do on TV. Be forgiven.

"Jessie, look at me."

I feel him waiting—and his waiting, his expectation, is a ticking clock. The car feels too small. I raise my lowered eyes. Josh looking at me with concern.

"Jessie, does Brian have AIDS?"

I can't look at him. I suddenly feel cold. My voice sounds very far away.

"No. Who told you that?"

Josh brings his face closer, like he's going to kiss me, and this time I don't look away. I can see the dirt-brown stubble on his cheeks and chin. His lips are thick and pouty. I want to scoot closer, to press my lips to his.

"My wife heard it from someone in your family, I can't say who." His knowing eyes move over me, stop on mine. "People are talking. It's true, Jessie, isn't it?"

I'm looking at Josh but thinking of Nick, the bump of his Adam's apple, his smoker's smell, and hard little mouth. We're in the confession booth, no wall between us. It's a relief to finally say the truth.

"Yes," I say. "Yes."

Josh puts his arm around me and draws me in, the softness of his shirt pressed to my face, his spicy, musky scent enveloping me. "It's okay," he keeps saying. I crunch the mint between my teeth, and it's too clean and cool. I want my mouth to burn, to taste my own blood.

I walk through the front door. My parents sit side by side on the love seat, and Brian perches on the edge of the armchair. Weirdos all looking at me.

"What's going on?"

"You're late," my mother says.

"Youth group ran over," I say. The upstairs toilet flushes, the bathroom door opens. "Who's here?"

A woman wearing denim shorts, a black tank top with fringes, and anklet boots flounces down the stairs. Her hair is platinum-blond, like Madonna's, and short—buzzed close to the nape and on the sides, but bigger on top, like a pile of stiff feathers. Thick black pencil outlines her eyes and peach eye shadow curves up to her dark eyebrows.

"Jess! I've heard so much about you," she exclaims, and before I can say anything, she pulls me into a bear hug. My brother's friend. Annie.

"I didn't know you were coming," I say stupidly.

"Nobody did, not even Brian. Surprise!" She talks fast, hurtling over her words, interrupting herself. "I have a car now—it's so stupid, who needs a car in New York? But I have one. I took some time off—I'm an artist assistant for this tyrannical bitch—I mean, woman—and I never take time off. But I thought, it's time. Why not get out of New York and visit Brian? The drive took forever. All those cows and cornfields. It's another planet."

"Welcome to Ohio," Brian says. I haven't seen him look this happy since he's been home. My mother forces a stiff smile—she hates surprises—and my father shifts, uncomfortable, looking around like he isn't sure he's in the right house.

When Brian and Annie go downstairs, I follow them—I don't want be stuck here with my zombie parents. I can still smell traces of Josh's cologne. He held me for a while longer, then he turned the key. "You did the right thing," he said, but the softness had left his voice.

I stand in the doorway, a traitor, unsure if I'm invited in. Brian puts on a Diana Ross record as Annie wanders around the room touching things, not at all afraid of germs. She's a little taller than me, probably around five seven, with more curves and powerful legs—not fat but strong, like she could walk a hundred miles without getting tired.

"You didn't tell me they put you in the basement," she says, raising an eyebrow.

"It's not like that. It used to be my room."

Annie doesn't look convinced, but she holds back her comments, tightening her lips. She picks up one of Brian's baseball trophies and studies it like it's some kind of ancient artifact. "God, you really were a jock," she says. "I still find that hard to believe."

She stares at the wall of photographs, and touches one of Shawn. "I miss him."

"Me too," Brian says.

Annie sinks on the bed and Brian scoots over, fist propped under his chin, staring at her like he's in love. But he was in love with Shawn.

"Where'd you get the car?"

"Donny. He left it to me, of all people. I don't know why. I'm an awful driver."

"Donny? When?"

"Last week."

Brian sighs. They're quiet, looking at each other. Everyone who gets it dies. As I start to leave, Annie calls after me.

"Jess, you're just as adorable as Brian said you were. Come here," she says.

The beanbag chair shudders as I draw my knees up to my chest. I try not to stare at Annie. Upside down, Diana Ross sings. I can't look at my brother either. He didn't do anything wrong. Guilt expands in my throat. When I find myself gazing again at Annie, she smiles.

"Brian told me you're crazy about whales." Annie doesn't laugh or look at me with condescension, the way most grownups do. "That's so fucking cool."

Brian

Hello. Can't sleep. Annie's snoring on the couch, but I'm not complaining—it's a nice sound. She won't take the upstairs bedroom my mother offered her—she wants to stay close to me. I think she wants my parents to see you can't get it by touching. She's always grabbing me, hugging me, kissing my face. It's been a long time since anyone has held me so close. She's irate my parents won't tell anyone. She's irate about a lot of things.

It's been refreshing to have someone around to talk politics. Someone to rage against Reagan, or *Bowers* v. *Hardwick*—a homophobic sodomy law upheld by the Supreme Court that barely made the news here. Annie fumed, It's about criminalizing gays, taking away our rights. She says my parents' silence toward me comes from the same place—fear and maybe even hatred. God, I've missed her.

With Annie here, I don't feel as alone. We stay up late, talking about the city, looking at pictures and reminiscing about Shawn and our friends. When that hurts too much, we swerve back to politics. Annie says something will change—it's starting to feel different now in the city, all the queers on edge. Maybe all the sadness will build into a tsunami of rage.

Annie and my grandmother have hit it off splendidly, just like I figured they would. This afternoon we sat on the porch sweating in the disgusting humidity because Mamaw does not have central air, and bald Betty Russell came over to get a closer look at Annie—her punk hair and bangles and low-cut shirts turn heads around here. Betty studied Annie's glittery fingernail polish. Lord, ain't that something, she said, and Annie busted up. Jess also couldn't stop laughing. For weeks now, Jess has been avoiding me, but now that Annie is here, she follows us around like a little stray cat, ears perked.

My parents don't know what to make of Annie. Tonight she offered to cook dinner because she's horrified by my mother's meals—Hamburger Helper, chipped beef on toast. Annie's no cook, let me tell you (sorry, hon), but she can throw a few basics together. I knew it killed my mother to give up control of her kitchen, but she was polite enough about it. Annie cooked a macrobiotic meal of grains and greens. My father said he wasn't hungry. My grandmother kept saying, Isn't this interesting? Jess pretended to like it, just to impress Annie. Dinner conversation started and stopped. Me eating off my special plates. Annie shooting me looks. I was nervous she'd say something.

When my mother asked her how she slept, Annie said not very well. It's the quiet, she says. I'm a city girl. I need sirens, horns, people arguing. Then she says, It's loud here in a different way. What's all that noise at night?

This cracked Jess up. You mean crickets?

Annie doesn't know much about kids or about the way this family operates. She says too much around Jess—about gays, or guys who are sick. Ignoring the looks I give her. She talks about her girlfriends—she has a new one, a butch artist, a redhead named Patty—but Jess thinks she's using the word girlfriend the way straight ladies do.

Jess doesn't know I'm gay, I keep reminding Annie. Or, that I have HIV.

Well, she should know, she says. It's fucked up, your parents not telling her.

I don't know why I defend them, but I do. They're scared, I say. It's complicated.

Annie keeps asking me about my plan. She's worried about the monster waking back up. I keep telling her I feel fine. It's a lie, and she knows it. Last night a blinding headache shook me awake, and the sight of food this morning made my stomach turn. I have moments where I forget. Until my body reminds me—and, like an eclipse, everything darkens.

Annie wants me to go to the doctor. I told her there is nowhere to go. She picked up the Boone County phone book, started making calls. She talked to every doctor's office in Madison. Not one will see me. Annie slammed down the receiver, almost in tears. Fuck this place, she said, just fuck it.

📼 July 8, 1986

It's late, but I can't sleep, as usual. This is my comfort, talking to you, whoever you are. Even with Annie here, I need this—the click of the tape in the camera, the red light. I mean, look, I know I'm probably saying too much—about my family, about private stuff. But I can't stop. Maybe, one day, Annie will edit these for me. Though I can't imagine she'll do much censoring.

Anyway, today was a bad day.

It started off okay. Annie and Jess and I decided to go to Madison. I've already shown Annie just about all there is of Chester. It's seriously like the 1950s here, she said.

We were planning to see *Labyrinth*, the new movie that stars David Bowie and a bunch of puppets. I also wanted to introduce Annie to Andrew, that gay salesman at Sears. I thought she'd get a kick out of his puffy hair and fake silk, but it was more than that—maybe I wanted to see him again.

After that day my grandmother and I went shopping, I couldn't stop thinking about Andrew, and I went back a few days later. A chubby girl with dimples told me he had the day off, and I wrote down my parents' number on a piece of register tape for her to give to him. He called the next day, said of course he remembered me. We've talked a few times on the phone. He keeps asking to meet up, but I always make an excuse.

So there we were, at the shopping mall. I'd been feeling a little queasy, but I thought I'd be okay. As soon as we sat down to eat, I knew I'd made a mistake.

I need to go to the bathroom, I said, trying not to yell. I'm sure I was yelling, I'm sure others noticed.

Annie stayed calm. Okay, honey, she said, and led me to the men's room. I pushed past her. I locked the stall door and sat on the toilet and sobbed as the shit came out of me.

It wouldn't stop.

What if it never stopped?

But it did. It eventually stopped.

After, I couldn't even look at my little sister.

We left the mall. We didn't see Andrew, didn't see Bowie on the big screen, didn't do a lick of shopping. On the way home, I rode in the back, windows rolled down and hot air blowing my clammy skin. Whatever Annie and Jess were talking about in the front, I couldn't hear them. My stomach clenched and flipped, but I made it home without any accidents.

Later, Annie told me not to be embarrassed.

You know shit doesn't bother me, she says. I mean, literally.

Her face was so serious that I cracked up, and then both of us were laughing and crying.

July 9, 1986

Today, Annie took me to the hospital in Madison, and she said we weren't leaving until we saw a doctor. The receptionist's face went green.

She goes, We can't treat that here.

Annie explained I needed something for my nausea. You can treat him, she says.

She asked—demanded—for a doctor who specialized in infectious diseases, and the woman kept trying to put us off but Annie wouldn't take no for an answer. We waited for three hours in the ER. I wanted to be angry, but I was embarrassed—the way the nurse looked at me, like I was filthy, like she didn't care if I took my last breath right there in the waiting room.

Finally, another nurse called me in. She was covered up head to toe, latex gloves and a mask. She didn't even take my temperature. She asked me what was wrong, and scribbled down a few things and left me there on the cold table. I waited another hour.

Finally, a small, brusque man came in, also suited up in a gown, gloves, and mask. Irritated, he said they only had one infectious disease specialist, who wasn't on duty today. He obviously didn't want to be in the room with me. I told him about my diarrhea, about my past battle with PCP. He checked my heart rate, gave my glands a quick pat. Then he wrote out prescriptions for Bactrim, sleep aids, anti-nausea meds. He didn't care about my CD4 count or medical history. I had AIDS, that's all he needed to know.

He begrudgingly told me the name of the infectious disease doctor. Dr. Patel. I said his name aloud, so I wouldn't forget.

There's nothing he can do for you either, the jerk says. You should contact hospice.

The disease can come for you in so many ways. Cancer, blindness, dementia, pneumonia, wasting. It's never pretty, never easy. How much time do I have?

Once, Annie and I talked about it—how many pills would a person need? Could she put a plastic bag over my head? We didn't make specific plans, but I told her, Do not let me suffer.

📷 July 10, 1986

Remember me talking about Josh Clay?

Well, today, I was sitting on the front porch when a tan Corolla pulled up. I didn't know who the hell it was. Nobody ever comes to visit.

A man got out. Thick neck, bulky arms, athletic legs, thin waist, the build of a dude who works out a lot. Spiked hair, an Izod shirt, boat shoes. A square. Yep. Fucking Josh Clay. He waved and bounded up the porch steps, smiling, eyes bright.

Hey, Brian. How are you?

He stood there, arms crossed, smiling, looking down at me. Smug, superior. I can't believe he's going to be a guidance counselor. Who would turn to him for guidance? He said he was just driving by, saw me sitting here, thought maybe I'd want to talk.

I patted the space next to me on the porch swing in a flirty way, and told him to take a seat. He smiled politely, stayed standing.

He asked how I liked being back in Chester.

When I told him it was fine, he looked disappointed with my answer. I lobbed the question back. What about you? I asked. Why'd you come back?

He seemed surprised—maybe nobody had ever asked him that—and for a moment, I saw him as he'd been as a boy, flushed cheeks, a wide open face. He told me he and his wife had liked Cleveland, but he was having trouble finding a job. It just kinda worked out. My dad told me the high school here was looking for a guidance counselor, he said. What I really I want is to be a minister.

I told him he'd make a good one.

Josh smiled, showing off his nice teeth. He said his father was old-fashioned and wouldn't listen to his ideas for building up the church—for TVs, a rock band. I was surprised by how open he was being, how talkative. He didn't want to be in Chester either. He had his own dreams. But the more he talked, the more preacher-like he sounded, and I was getting tired of it.

He took a step closer to me. He dropped his voice, like we were swapping secrets. Brian, can you tell me the truth? he says.

About what? I asked.

He says, There are rumors going around.

A whoosh of heat passed between my ears. I went deaf. Then, as quickly as it arrived, the hot wind disappeared. I heard a cardinal calling, and the squeak of the swing. Josh watching me. I just sat there swinging back and forth, back and forth.

About what? I repeated. I tried to appear bored, but my mind was racing—he knows, he knows, he knows. I shouldn't be surprised. I told Gus, and Gus told his wife, who is best friends with Josh's wife. Or maybe Gus himself told Josh. People were talking, speculating.

Is it true? he asked.

But he couldn't say the word, nobody can. Fuck it, I thought. I wanted to make him squirm, and I checked him out the way I might cruise a guy at a club, even though he's totally not my type. He blushed—it was getting to him.

Then he goes, I'm here to help you.

Help me?

He was wound up, his tan healthy face shining in the sun, giving me a look like he was waiting for me to confess. He says, God loves you. No matter what. If you repent, you can be saved. But, you have to come clean. It's not right, you not telling people. People have a right to know.

That's when Annie came out of the house. She called out to me, Honey, you want a milkshake? She was wearing very short cutoff jeans, a black T-shirt. No bra.

I introduced them. I said, This is Josh Clay, the minister's son.

Annie got my tone right away. She sat next to me on the swing, and put a protective hand on my knee, eyebrows raised, daring Josh.

He looked deflated. I remember him walking in to the locker room, Hey, guys, he'd call out, all cheery and hopeful, and the team would just ignore him or tell him to shut up, preacher boy. He had that same look of disappointment now. But he recovered quickly.

Come back to church, he said, flashing a snake-oil preacher smile. You're welcome too, Annie.

No thanks, she says. Church isn't my thing.

We watched him drive away, and then Annie asked what the hell was that about. Is he trying to save you? she asked.

Maybe, I said. Maybe he is.

Jess

Annie drives Brian and me around in the car she got from the friend who died, and she's right, she is an awful driver—she takes curves too fast, drifts too close to the center, and soars over hills. She plays tapes of punk bands with loud guitars and drums, and screaming vocals. Brian says she has an amazing voice, but Annie won't sing for me—it's the only time she's shy.

Outside of Colby, she pulls into the Dairy Freeze. "Look at this adorable place," she says. Annie is a city girl, and everything here is cute or hilarious or terrifying.

We walk up, and the girl behind the counter stares at Annie, who's wearing rainbow stripes of eye shadow. Then she sees Brian's video camera and puts her hand up in front of her face.

"What do you want, Jess?" Annie asks.

"Uh, nothing." My stomach grumbles. I haven't eaten anything today.

"Come on, you have to get something. You're too young for this diet bullshit."

She orders each of us a sundae—hot fudge for me, strawberry for Brian, and caramel for her.

"What happened to macrobiotics?" Brian asks.

"Dessert doesn't count."

Annie and Brian dip their spoons into each other's plastic bowls. I know you can't get it like that, but it still doesn't seem like a good idea.

"Shawn would have turned this place on its head," Annie says. "He'd be talking to everyone, queening it up."

Brian cuts eyes at her. "Anyway," he says, trying to change the subject. "We should get back. Mamaw wants us to come over."

Whenever Annie mentions Shawn, he gives her a look. They don't know I know about him. Or about Brian. Nobody does—except Josh Clay. I've been nervous that he'll tell Brian. Every time the phone rings I feel sick to my stomach. What would Annie think of me if she knew I told him? I can't ever go back to youth group. Not now. Not ever. If my parents make me go to church, I'll avoid Josh. I'll pretend to know nothing.

The sweetness of the sundae shoots through me, stopping the hunger pains. We climb into the car, Brian riding shotgun. Cassettes are scattered all over the backseat and the floor. My mouth tastes sweet, my lips are sticky. Annie blasts Bowie and we scream the words into the wind. My hair blows across my face. I scoot as close as I can to the front seat, leaning in between Annie and my brother. I don't want her to ever leave.

The downstairs has been transformed by Annie's skirts and tank tops and cut-up T-shirts thrown over the recliner and sofa, and exploding from her open suitcase like confetti. Everything Annie touches—even our dark, sad house—jolts to life.

"I have an idea," she says.

She goes down the hall to Brian's bathroom and comes back with her giant makeup bag, pink and gray leopard print, as big as a football.

"Let me do your face."

"No," I say, shy. "I don't—"

"Come on, it'll be fun."

Annie rummages through the bag and lines up several pencils and wands and square eye shadow cases. She holds my chin in one hand and tells me to look up. I hear her breathing as she brings her face closer to mine. She draws under my eyes with a pencil, and sweeps a brush lightly along my cheekbones. It tickles.

"Now for the best part." She turns the bottom of the silver tube of lipstick and the waxy stick rises, a little red flag. "Relax your mouth."

I try not to flinch, but it feels funny, her face so close to mine. Her eyes narrow with concentration. I look past the swirls of green and blue eye shadow, and teal-colored mascara, to her dark brown eyes with specks of green and two black watermelon seeds in the centers.

"Okay, go like this," she says, smacking her lips.

When I do, she laughs. "You look fabulous."

Brian says, "You're a rock star."

They tell me to check myself out in the mirror, and after a moment of hesitation, I go down the hallway. This is the first time I've been in Brian's bathroom. I don't touch anything except the light switch. Annie's skimpy underwear and a lacy blue bra, with saucer-size cups, hang from the shower rod, and I stare, then look away, embarrassed.

Stuff is scattered all over the sink. Annie's hair products and jewelry, Brian's hair products and jewelry. I stare at my reflection. Not me, but someone else: a girl with electric-blue eyelashes, rouged cheeks, and full, red, glistening lips. I look strange and new, and even pretty. For a few seconds, I don't recognize myself. Then, the moment passes, and I see myself underneath the makeup. You can disappear and never disappear. Heavy in your skin, but not here at all.

Tomorrow, Annie goes back to New York. She's changed the way things feel in this house, made them louder and happier. And, she's made my brother laugh.

"I guess it's supposed to look like the ocean in here, right?" Annie asks.

"I don't know," I lie, seeing how babyish my room must look to her.

My mother helped me design it when I was eight years old, choosing just the right shade of aqua blue for the walls and a sandy-brown carpet.

"It's cool." Annie points to a picture of a Greenpeace raft next to a gigantic whaling ship. "Would you ever want to do that?"

"Yes," I say, but I'm not that brave. We sit down on my bed, and I hear myself babbling to Annie about saving the whales. Annie nods.

"Yeah, like if we save the whales from extinction, we can save ourselves. Activists can change things," Annie says. "I believe that. I'm just not a very good one."

The clicking and buzzing of night insects come in through the open windows. Annie says she won't miss that noise.

"I wish I could go with you," I say.

"You can visit any time."

"Ohio sucks."

"Get through high school. Then you can get the hell out of here and never have to see any of these people again."

My muscles coil like springs. For Annie, telling the truth is the only way to live. She isn't like my family. Every word out of her mouth is hard and shining like her eyes. I've been thinking about what it means to be brave, and what it means to be weak. I don't want Annie to think I'm just some dumb kid.

"I know about Brian," I say.

She looks at me with surprise. "Know what?" she asks cautiously.

"He has AIDS."

Her puckered lips soften. It's the first time I've said it out loud. The crickets suddenly stop.

"Shit, kid. How long have you known?"

"I don't know. A few weeks."

She asks how I figured it out. "I just did," I say vaguely, and she squeezes the top of my thigh. Her nails are long and the color of a grape popsicle.

"I need a cigarette," she says.

I follow her over to the open window. The chirping starts up again, louder this time, like the crickets have found their way inside the house.

"I want one too," I say.

"Your mom would kill me." Annie takes the pack out of the rim of the waistband of her shorts, a lighter tucked inside. "You shouldn't smoke," she says. "But just this once."

We blow smoke through the screen. Ashes fall on the sill like tiny flakes of gray snow. Annie's staring ahead, and then she turns to me.

"Your mom washing the sheets separately, washing his dishes separately, that's fucked up. You know that, right?"

Her face is hard, angry, sad all at once. Maybe she is thinking of Brian, or all her other friends who have died.

"Your brother worries about you. I told him you're tough. You have to be. You have to be brave. You cannot care what people say." Annie holds her eyes on mine. "He's going to get sicker," she says. "It's going to get worse. Do you understand?"

I nod. She takes another drag, and then gives me a small, sad smile. What would she say if she knew about my betrayal?

Annie steps closer and leans her head on my shoulder, and for a moment I'm still as can be, as if a butterfly has landed on me and I'm trying my best not to startle it. Then, slowly, I raise my arm and put it around her, like a boy would, and we both look up at the night sky. I want to ask her if Brian is going to die, but I don't want to ruin this moment. Her hair smells like wildflowers, like the woods after a hard rain.

"Do you think there is life out there?" she asks. "On other planets. Other galaxies?"

I feel older, like I just added a decade. "Only if there is water," I say. "Water is the source of life."

Sharon

Finally, she's gone. I couldn't stand having her in my house. Her grating, know-it-all voice and the trampy way she looked—all that makeup, and her bra straps showing. She'd sit next to Brian on the sofa, one arm over his shoulders like she was guarding him. From who? My son, a pale and tiny mole. What happened to my beautiful son?

I check with Brian to see what he wants for supper. Now we can actually eat a meal that we all enjoy.

"I'm not hungry."

"Well, if you want, I can make—"

"I said I'm not hungry," he snaps.

The anger in his voice startles me. I know he's upset she's gone, and I start to say something, but what? My mouth moves, stops. I want to grab him by his skinny wrists and make him look at me. What have *I* done wrong?

The kitchen is a mess. The blender clotted with yellow-brown foam, along with a stack of dirty dishes. A blackening banana peel, an open jar of peanut butter. All week Annie blended protein shakes and cooked up tasteless grains that she brought from New York, and Brian thanked her, called her *a gem, a sweetheart, a savior.* Before she left, she wrote down the name of a doctor at the hospital in Madison. She put her hand on my shoulder: "Sharon, do you understand what is going to happen?" I hated her condescending attitude, the way she looked at me as if I was helpless. And, yet, look here—she left one last mess for me to clean up.

I leave it sit—let someone else clean up for a change—and get out a package of bacon. Nothing sounds appetizing to me either. But I'll make supper because that is what I do.

As I stand at the stove, watching the bacon sizzle and pop in the hot grease, the phone cuts into my thoughts. One, two, three rings. "Can someone get that?" I shout.

Nobody does, of course. I set down the spatula, and pick up the phone. "Hello?"

The intimate sound of another's breath—calm but loud, like a child breathing open-mouthed.

"Hello?" I say again.

His tone surprises me, how gentle: "We don't want no faggots here."

A click, followed by the flat droning dial tone. I stand still but feel as if I'm tilting. The receiver slips out of my hand. It stops before it hits the floor and dangles from the stretched, coiled cord. Something's burning. Smoke swirls from the frying pan. Shit.

Bile rising in my throat, I scrape the supper nobody wanted into the trash, still hearing the man's hateful words, his soft librarian-like voice. *People know.*

"What's wrong?"

Travis walks in, tracking dust onto the floor. He's spent the summer working outside, putting in extra hours, whatever he can do to stay away from us, and his face and arms are burned a pecan brown, but the pale skin around his eyes, protected by his sunglasses, makes him look wide-eyed, innocent.

I stand at the sink, turning my back to him, and spray the blender with hot water. Who am I kidding? If I don't clean up the mess, no one else will.

"Why is the phone off the hook?" he asks.

"Why do you think?" I switch off the faucet and turn around quickly, ready for a fight. But he's just standing there, stiff as a pole. He says he doesn't have any idea, and looking at him, I think maybe he really doesn't.

"Someone called and said things about Brian. Hateful things."

Realization dawns over his face. We stand like statues, saying nothing. Then, maybe to break the stillness, he walks over and puts the phone back on the wall. The air conditioner kicks on and cold air shoots from the vents. A few years ago Travis had central air put in. Used money we didn't have because he didn't want to feel suffocated anymore. His brothers never said anything, but I saw their looks—they thought we were being extravagant.

Travis rummages in the fridge, looking for a beer. He cracks open a can, holds it out to me. Exhausted, I take a sip. The air smells acrid and smoky. Open package of bacon on the counter. Supper in the trash. Suddenly, I miss my mother. That ghost of a woman. Occasionally, when she was well, she would cook a big dinner on Sundays: fried chicken, thick slices of tomatoes, corn on the cob, mashed potatoes. The times she did give me attention—played paper dolls or read to me—were brief and thrilling, like falling in love.

"You should talk to Brian," I say. "He needs to know…"

"Know what?" Travis covers his mouth with his hand, breathes into it. Grease-stained, callused. The other night, late, in the dark, he reached for me with those hands but I rolled away.

I try a different tactic. "We're going to have to tell them."

He tilts back the beer and swallows, holding onto words he won't say. When he sets the beer on the counter, it's half gone.

"Who?"

"Your mom. Your brothers."

He shakes his head.

"If we don't, they're going to hear it from strangers. People know, Travis."

The hardness in his eyes dims. He looks befuddled, too old and gray for his age. I see us twenty years down the road, in this kitchen, worn down and sad. Twenty years down the road—a strange, unexpected sound creaks out of my mouth—my son won't be here.

"You okay?"

I hold back a sob. Travis starts toward me, but the ringing startles both of us. We stand apart and watch the phone like it's something alive, something dangerous.

"Don't pick up," he says. "Let it go."

Brian has been home a little over two months. We haven't had any big talks about the future. There are moments, usually at night, when an image from the news or a magazine will haunt me—a man's face covered in hideous sores, a fragile thing of bones in a wheelchair. Then a terrifying urgency seizes me, like I've entered a cellar and the door closes behind me. I'm trapped under the dirt and darkness of my own thoughts and questions. I remember Rock Hudson's picture on the cover of supermarket tabloids, that gaunt face, terrified eyes. A few weeks later, he was dead. I try not to think about the future, or about how he got this disease, and most of the time I can keep the worst of these thoughts at bay. There's been no one to talk to about it because nobody knows. But now?

Travis has decided we'll tell the family that Brian has *cancer*—this will elicit sympathy and understanding, and kindness.

"The reason I asked you to come over to Mom's…" Travis starts, and his eyes dart around the dining room table. His older brothers, with their wives by their sides, sit across from us, and Lettie's at the head. When she reaches for a cigarette, the rings on her fingers glitter as if they are worth something.

Travis takes a deep breath. I reach under the table, squeeze his knee. I just want to get this over with, and I'm not the only one. Wayne leans back in the tall-backed chair, tipping the front legs off the floor, looking both bored and ready for a fight. On the front of his T-shirt a lone wolf bays at a purple moon.

"If you won't say it, then I will." Impatiently, Wayne brings the chair forward, all four legs on the floor. His top lip curls. "He's got the AIDS," he says.

The air sucks out of the room and Travis tenses and I move my hand away, feeling both sickened and relieved. The big brother Travis looked up to, seeking his approval, his camaraderie, glares at him. There will be no lie about cancer. Finally, someone has spoken, and the words burst our bubble. Wayne's been wanting to say this for a long time. The box fan rattles. No one at the table looks shocked.

"I've known for a while, and I'll tell you what—it makes me sick," Wayne continues. "Absolutely sick." Carol lifts her pudgy hand to pat his shoulder, like she's tempering a wild dog, but Wayne won't be quieted.

"You've been letting him come over here to Mom's, eating, using the toilet, spreading his germs. He could make all of us sick. He's been around my grandchildren."

"Wayne," Paul starts.

"You feel the same way, buddy. We've talked about this."

Travis's face falls—his brothers have been talking behind his back. Paul pushes his glasses up, sighs. Liz gently strokes his forearm, her long red nails gliding through the dark hair. Travis says nothing. My throat aches, I've swallowed a ball of fire. The sudden thought—*Why is my husband so weak*—startles me.

"Boys," Lettie says, "listen."

They turn to her obediently. Lettie and her sons: who can touch that kind of love? She sits there calmly smoking. All made-up, hair sprayed into place. All eyes on her, waiting.

"I already know," she says.

"Mom," Travis says, but she waves her hand, dismissing him. She doesn't have time for excuses. She doesn't want to be mollycoddled.

"Tell me. How bad is it?" she asks.

Travis opens his mouth, but no words come out. He looks at me for help. He has no idea how bad it is. He wants me to tell her everything is okay, to reassure her, to reassure him.

"We don't know, Lettie," I say. "We just don't know."

The wrinkles Lettie works so hard to hide suddenly let loose, the sad creases and lines and folds of skin, and Travis clenches his jaw, disappointed in me.

"Well, he might could get better. People will surprise you," Lettie says. "I seen it just the other day on TV. Doctors told a woman her son was in a coma, as good as dead. Wouldn't you know a couple days later, he woke up and first thing he said was he sure would like meatloaf for supper." Lettie sits up straighter, pleased. "There's miracles every day."

Liz and Carol look away, embarrassed, then meet their husbands' eyes. They're a team, the four of them. Their kids are healthy. They do not understand the ache, the fear in my heart. I hold back tears; I won't let them see me break down.

"Mom, people are going to talk—" Wayne starts.

"Let them," Lettie snaps.

Wayne takes a deep breath and blows it out through his puckered lips. He will not fight with his mother, but he won't stay here either wasting his time. So many years ago, Wayne welcomed me into this family. Threw his arm around me, told me I was too pretty for his little brother. Laughing, joking, kind. But he never liked Brian—I can say that now.

"You never should have let him come back," he says to Travis, to me. "You knew," he accuses.

He stands up, gives Travis one last long look, and then he heads to the door. It bangs behind him. Carol, flustered, struggles to get off the chair and gather her purse, but she's too fat to move quickly. "I'll call you later," she says.

Paul gazes out the window, and Liz fiddles with her cigarettes. Travis won't look at us. His head tilts down, a strange start of a smile on his face—because he's worried he'll weep, or because he thinks Wayne is right?

When he gets up, he mumbles something about how hot the house is and then he's out the front door too.

Liz makes an excuse about getting to one of their grandkids tee-ball games, smiling apologetically, and Paul follows her, waving goodbye. It's just me and Lettie.

My thighs stick to the seat. A car backfires. A dog barks. Lettie holds my gaze.

"Can I have one?" I ask.

She shakes out a menthol, doesn't bat an eye. Cigarette between my lips, I lean toward the flickering flame. She knew. All this time.

"It's going to get bad, Lettie."

She exhales a stream of smoke. "People can run their mouths all they want. We've got bigger things to worry about, don't we?"

Brian

Change of scenery. Here is the creek behind my parents' house. I used to spend hours out here, watching the minnows, the birds. This is an Osage orange tree. When you peel back the bark, it bleeds orange. Gus and I used to rub it on our faces, pretending to be warrior Indians.

Gus knows, Pam knows. Josh Clay. And my grandmother and Jess and uncles and aunts and cousins, all of them know. But nobody has said anything to me, except my grandmother, and only indirectly: You're going to be fine, she said. Everything will be okay.

When I was a kid, after a hard rain the creek would rise, and you could swim in it. I miss swimming. I was good at it. Jess, terrified, used to cling to me. Trust the water, I'd tell her. One day I let go of her and she floated out, paddling her hands and feet. You're swimming, I yelled. It was beautiful to watch.

In the city, I hardly ever swam, except for a few times we went to Coney Island, Shawn and Annie and me. It was dirty and polluted, but I didn't care. The first time waves knocked me over and then lifted me back up, I felt exalted to the point of tears. I always thought I'd be the one to take Jess to the ocean for the first time. I wanted to do that—give her that experience, that pure, animalistic joy.

Annie asked if I want to talk about It, but I don't—I can't. What are my wishes? How do I want to be buried? Goddamn it. These are not questions a twenty-four-year-old is supposed to ponder. In New York, the memorials and funerals never stopped. Ashes blowing into the East River and the Hudson, raining down from bridges. Am I supposed to imagine my dead body in the ground at the Chester Cemetery, where my grandfather is buried, a man I never met? Maybe they'll refuse to bury me. Why should I care what my funeral looks like?

I grew up believing in God—it wasn't something anyone ever questioned in Chester—but as a teenager, I started to have my doubts. I honestly don't know what I believe anymore. It's hard to believe when we're all dying and everyone's telling you this is part of God's plan. I prayed Shawn wouldn't die. I prayed I wasn't infected. It wasn't really prayer—just words, desperate hope.

I used to be scared I was going to hell. I'd have terrifying nightmares where I was screaming for help and my mother was sobbing and my father was walking away.

Shawn would gently shake me awake. You're tearing yourself up, baby, he'd say. You've got to let go of this shit or you'll never be free.

He didn't push me to come out to my parents. He'd seen too many times how families turned away from their sons and daughters. He knew how it felt. His parents kicked him out of the house when he was seventeen. They didn't want to see him even when he was dying.

But he worried about the silence between me and my parents.

Talk to them. What's the worst that could happen? he used to ask. You already left home.

Eventually, I sent the letter and a picture of us. The response? Silence. It didn't matter, I told myself. My life was in New York—I had a boyfriend and best friend, and friends who accepted and loved me.

But it wasn't like all that anxiety, sorrow, and guilt just disappeared. One time, during a fight with Shawn, I told him maybe it was better his parents had just cut him off. It was easier that way, at least he knew where he stood with them.

Hc was pissed. Don't say that, he said. You can still go home. That's not nothing. You can still fucking go home.

Shawn wanted me to bring him here, to show him the places that made me and undid me, the hills and trees and dirt. What would people have said? Would they have guessed we were boyfriends? I grew up not knowing a single gay person. I also didn't know anyone who wasn't white. I tried to explain this to Shawn, but he wasn't afraid. "What are they gonna do?" he asked. "Stare? Talk shit? Kill me? Well, I'm still not gonna hide."

What would it have been like, him and me in the woods? We'd fuck under the branches of a sweetgum, yellow stars falling around us. I'd make him a crown of bittersweet. His strong hands holding me down, his hot mouth on mine. All of it, happening out here, in the dirt and leaves of the place I tried so hard to escape.

July 19, 1986

Hello.

Just me at home. On a beautiful, sunny, hot as hell afternoon.

My parents and Jess went swimming. Without me. Weren't even going to tell me. But I saw my mother getting things together. Towels, a cooler. She told me it was a church thing. Then Jess went out the door, saying she was riding her bike and would see them there.

My father came downstairs wearing swim trunks, his legs pale and hairy. He looked at me, then at my mother. Asked if she was ready.

My mother told me I should go over to Mamaw's to keep her company. Trying to appease me. She offered to drop me off at Mamaw's house, but I asked her just to leave me her car.

I said, I could meet you there. I think I have a pair of swim trunks.

My mother was still. My father folded his arms over his chest.

He says, That's not a good idea.

I asked why not.

You're not feeling well, he says, a little too loudly.

My father, master of understatement. I wanted him to say it, but he never will. He grabbed the cooler and his car keys, and told my mother he'd be outside.

Dad, I called for him.

I didn't think he'd turn around, but he did. His eyes were hard, his face clenched. My father has not been able to look at me since I came home. He has not touched me. He can barely be in the same room as me. I wanted him to fucking apologize. My heart was beating like crazy.

You can't get it like that, I said.

Nothing. He just turned and went out the door. I stood at the window, like Sadie, like a dog, and watched him load the cooler in the back of his pickup—the one that runs—and my mother came up behind me and patted me on the shoulder.

She said she'd stay home with me. She started to make an excuse for him, but I cut her off. Just go, I told her. Go!

I thought I heard a sob, but I didn't turn around.

A few months ago, I sat staring at the Hudson. I didn't kill myself because I wanted to come back home. Now here I am. In my old room, me and my stupid baseball glove, all these trophies. Look—I'm shaking. With anger or fear, I don't know. I'm not a goddamn ghost. Not yet, anyway.

Jess

My mother wanted us to go as a family, to show the church we're still a part of things. I probably wouldn't have gone, but then Carrie Driggs, who is fighting with Molly, called and asked me to go, and it's the first time in a long time that I've hung out with anyone except Nick.

We ride our bikes—I refuse to go with my parents—and set up our towels away from the church members. The pool is open to the public, but our church has taken over one side—balloons tied to the backs of pool chairs, and dishes of fattening food spread across two picnic tables.

"So embarrassing," Carrie says, reading my mind.

It's weird seeing my parents here. My father talks to Reverend Clay under the shade of an umbrella, wearing dad-style Bermuda-print swim trunks—mortifying. My mother, in sunglasses and a floral blue one-piece, wades into the shallow end. My aunts and uncles are here too, and a few of my cousins. Mamaw made an excuse about cleaning up around her house, but I think she just wants to stay with Brian, who wasn't invited.

Everyone in the family knows about him now. My mother tried to have a talk with me about it. "I already knew," I snapped, and then I felt bad because she looked like she was going to burst into tears. "We're going to keep this in the family," she said. "It's going to be okay." My parents wanted us to come to this church pool party so that we'll look like a normal family. A family of three.

The heat wave has brought out a huge crowd. Kids swarm the concession stand and call out Marco Polo from the water, and long lines form at the diving boards. A few elderly women in ruffled swimsuits dip their pasty legs in the shallow end. I keep an eye out for Josh Clay, but don't see him. Carrie said she heard his wife is pregnant. Every day I hope he's miraculously forgotten what I told him.

Carrie turns the pages of *Seventeen* and checks out boys, and looks around for other girls she'd rather be hanging out with—I'm not her first choice. Sweat dampens my back, trickles down the sides of my face. It's 101 degrees, with high humidity. I sip my perspiring Diet Sprite, already warm, and tell Carrie I'm getting in.

"Whatever," she says, bored.

I slip in at the six feet marker, where a rope of floating giant blue beads separates the shallow from the deep end, and as soon as my body touches the water, the worry about my family melts away. I forgot how perfect this feels—underwater, I'm quick and slippery, but still too human. I wish I was a whale. My body shifts and turns and moves along with the water, not fighting it. Brian used to tell me that: *Don't fight it, kiddo, just go with it*. I dive down and open my eyes underwater—I've always been able to—and strangers' feet and legs kick and pedal around me. I hold my breath and sway in the silence as long as I can, and when I come up through the surface, the noise explodes around me. All I want is to go back down to the bottom.

Then a pair of wet hands cover my eyes. A voice, close to my ear. "Guess who?"

The hands lift. I blink a couple of times in the sunlight and turn, but I already know.

"Surprise," Josh Clay says, laughing. "Did I scare you?"

"I knew it was you."

He holds onto the wall with one hand as he bobs in the water just a few inches from me, showing off his bare chest and arms, the cut muscle.

"Race you to the other side," he says.

Josh doesn't put his face in, and his hands spastically stab the water. I give him a little bit of a head start, then easily glide by. Swimming is a different feeling than running—no struggle, no fighting for breath. But, like running, swimming makes me feel more awake and inside myself. I reach the other side, far ahead of Josh, and wait for him. He stops at the wall, sputtering, sucking air.

"Dang, you're good," he says, and spits water from his mouth back into the pool.

"I used to take lessons." I don't add that it was my brother who taught me.

Josh shakes water from his face like a dog and doesn't let go of the wall. I'm bicycle pedaling my legs, treading easily. All around us, people swim and play, and two kids throw a Nerf ball. Josh's breathing slows to normal. The water laps between us. Maybe things will be okay.

"I haven't seen you in a while," he says. "I've missed you."

Bristles of his hair shine almost red in the bright sunlight. Delicate droplets of water stuck in his eyelashes. He's not my priest, he never was, just like he was never my boyfriend. As we float next to each other, Josh rattles on about youth group. I promise I'll come back, but he must know I'm lying.

Then Josh stops talking. His smooth brow wrinkles. Looking toward the other side of the pool, he raises his hand over his eyes like a sailor scanning for land.

"Jessie, is that your brother?"

My body suddenly feels heavy and immovable, I'm sinking. I don't want to look, but I can't not. I follow Josh's gaze, past all the people in the pool, and I see him standing on the edge, around the four feet marker. It's him all right. He strips off his T-shirt, and the lines of his ribs press up like twigs under his skin. His scrawny pale legs poke out from a pair of faded black swim trunks he's had since high school, loose on his hips. He crouches down and dips his spindly old man legs in the water.

"He can't get in," Josh exclaims. He heaves himself over the edge, biceps and back flexing, before I can say anything.

I scan the crowd for my parents. My mother sits on a beach chair, flipping through *Good Housekeeping*, and my father stands on the lawn talking to Gus. They have no idea.

I dive under, darting around other swimmers, and when I come up, the world is hazy, blurry, fuzzy. Brian's no longer there. It wasn't him, I think—I hope.

Then I see him. He's floating about six feet from me, looking up at the cloudless sky, oblivious. He lifted his hands under my back, teaching me how to float. *I got you*, he'd say. *Just relax, enjoy it, I got you.*

How much time has passed? Five minutes? Fifteen? A lifeguard, Greg Kennedy, a popular senior, heads in our direction, and behind him is Wanda Spellman, the pool manager, all angles and sharp lines. Wanda's gray hair is short like a man's, and her skin is leathery and orange, like a worn out basketball. She wears old-lady knit shorts and a baggy pink T-shirt that says TGIF with a cat blowing a party horn. I float over toward the wall, my face poking out of the water.

"You need to get out," Wanda says. "Hey, you."

It takes her calling a few more times before Brian hears her or realizes she's talking to him. He holds his hand up over his eyes like a visor blocking the sun.

"You need to get out of the pool!"

I lift my head higher out of the water. A few people cluster behind Wanda, watching curiously. I find my father in the crowd. At first, he looks surprised, confused. And, then, a shadow crosses his face, like he's resigned himself to this: he waves his hand, motioning to my brother. I think of Shamu—the trainer giving hand signals, everyone watching with bated breath, waiting for the miraculous leap toward the sky.

There is a moment when I think maybe everything will be okay—all Brian has to do is swim over, climb out of the pool, and be on his way. No one will even know. But he doesn't do that. He's no longer floating on his back, just treading water. He raises his hands up, palms up.

"Why should I?" he challenges.

"I know who you are," Wanda says. "You can't be in there, infecting the water."

My father steps closer to the edge. He's still got that look of resignation, and something else—sadness or fear.

"Let's go, Brian," he calls.

Past my father, I see my mother get up from the reclining chair, then she stops, frozen in place. I hide against the wall, my heart racing. The smell of chlorine stings my nose. More people are looking over. I want to sink to the bottom and never come up.

"Don't you give me any trouble," Wanda warns. "The police are on their way. I already called them, in case you wouldn't leave."

The police? Brian swims over and reaches for the ladder and climbs out one step at a time. His swim trunks, heavy with water, cling to his bony legs, and his little chest sucks in and out. Wanda takes a step back like she's terrified he's going to wipe his germs all over her. Josh stands with his arms folded over his chest, straight back, watching. No one notices as I pull myself up over the edge.

My father stands just behind Wanda, barefoot and no shirt on, his gray chest hair exposed, and looks like he doesn't know if he should go to Brian or run the other way. But my mother has snapped to action—she rolls up the towels, and pulls a T-shirt and shorts over her swimsuit.

"You can't do this," Brian says.

"Just go," Wanda says. "Don't make trouble."

My brother huffily grabs his things and wraps a towel around his waist like a skirt, Wanda watching him the whole time like he's a criminal. More people are starting to gather around. My wet swimsuit sticks to me, and I feel the icky sensation of water dripping down my legs and between them, a small puddle blooming under me on the cement. I want to die.

As my brother walks in the direction of the exit, Wanda's at his heels, herding him out. I join the crowd that follows, pretending I don't know anything. My parents are ahead of me, walking quickly with their heads down, like movie stars ducking from the paparazzi.

Brian, wearing his towel-skirt, holds his head high. Everyone is watching, and as he passes by the concession stand, a crowd of senior boys start to laugh.

Brett Wilson, a pimple-faced, brawny football player who is always terrorizing freshmen, points at my brother. I get a horrible feeling. I'm watching it happen in slow motion.

"He's got the AIDS!" Brett yells.

Silence. Then, laughter. High fives. Gross-out squeals, gasps, giggles.

Brandy White stands behind Brett, and she's laughing too. The hate I feel is sudden and fierce. I hate all of them. Wanda Spellman and Brett Wilson and Brandy White. Josh Clay. My brother.

Brian heads toward the metal turnstile connected to the chain-link fence that leads into the parking lot, but stops when a patrol car pulls up, the red and blue lights swirling. Two cops get out—one my father's age, the other one closer to Brian's. Their faces are sweaty and pink, and they look tired.

Wanda lets them in a special side gate, next to the exit, and they approach my brother warily, don't get too close. He unties the towel from his waist and drapes it around his shoulders like a cape. My parents stand behind him, both of them shaken, not knowing what to do. My mother's face scrunches. She's going to cry.

"We're just leaving," my father says, trying to smooth everything over.

It's like Brian has just realized he's not alone. He turns and looks around. There's Uncle Wayne, Gus, cousin Matthew. Church members, and kids from school. Instead of trying to save face, instead of just leaving, he seems to gain confidence from the crowd.

Brian steps up to Wanda, and she takes two steps back. He's wearing red Wayfarers. His gold earring catches the light.

"Brian," my mother says.

He points his finger in Wanda's face. His words are measured and controlled. "I will sue you for every last penny, you ignorant bitch."

Wanda, stunned, sucks in her breath. Her eyes are wild. Speechless, furious, she waves her arms at the cops. "I want him arrested," she says.

"I went for a swim," Brian says. "Is that against the law?"

"He's got the AIDS," Wanda screeches.

The young cop looks at the older cop, like he's waiting for an order. The older one, sweat trickling down his gray sideburns, his face long like it's melted from the sun, looks at my father.

"Travis, just get him out of here."

"He's going," my father says. "He's going right now."

He motions for Brian. My mother has already exited and she's on the other side of the fence, her shoulders hunched, trying to hold back her sobs. They haven't seen me. They've forgotten all about me. I'm standing next to a woman I don't know, a couple of little kids. Invisible.

Brian walks through the revolving door, the towel still around him like a cape—a rejected, ruined superhero.

"Don't you come back here," Wanda calls in a mean, hateful voice.

As they cross the parking lot, I hear Wanda prattling on to one of the cops, asking if she should she close the pool, call the mayor. On and on. Voices and laughter tangle around me, and I don't know where to turn. My aunt Liz starts toward me, but I quickly head back to my towel.

"Your brother has *AIDS*?" Carrie moves back as if she's nervous I'm going to breathe on her. "That's disgusting."

Without saying a word, I pull on my shorts and Te-shirt, and step into my tennis shoes, tugging at the canvas with my fingers, squeezing my damp feet into them.

"I can't believe you sat here," Carrie accuses. She reaches for her towel and makes a show of covering herself. "You trying to give it to me?"

I walk one foot in front of the other, melting in the heat, and when I'm at the exit, Josh Clay reaches for my arm.

"Jessie, wait."

He explains this is for the best, it wasn't right to keep it a secret. People deserve to know, he says, so they can protect themselves. His lips move and move, but I stop listening. There is no way to get out except to slide around him. I push the revolving door, the metal bar hot on my fingers, and spin until I'm on the other side, alone.

Rebel Rebel

Brian

Still here.

The house is a bunker. Jess is in her room drowning in music. My mother cooking and cleaning. My dad hiding in the garage.

Last night, after a slew of hateful calls, my mother unplugged the phone. Anyone could be making them. Neighbors. Friends. Relatives.

The idiot mayor has closed the pool for a week, to drain and disinfect it. The town rallied behind him. Discrimination, Annie says.

I called her right after I left the pool. I was losing it. Why the hell did I get in? I asked.

Because it was fucking hot, she said. You didn't do anything wrong.

I did everything wrong. What is it I want? Acceptance? Forgiveness? I don't know why the fuck I came back here.

Annie wants me to sue—something I said to that bitch that now makes me laugh. It's against the law, Annie says. Not here it's not. Or if it is, it doesn't matter. She says it's like the 1950s, segregation all over again. Um, no, I said. It's not the same thing.

But, yeah, it still sucks.

What would be the point of suing? This town doesn't have any money. I don't know even how much time I have left. I don't want to spend it in courts, burying my family in paperwork and legal matters.

At least call all the papers, Annie urged. Don't worry, I told her. The news will spread.

And what do you know? This morning I opened the Columbus paper, which my parents get delivered on Sundays, and there it was: front page news. There were no pictures of me and they didn't print my name, but still—people know.

Stories from Boone County don't usually make it in unless it's something big, like a murder or major drug bust.

Or a man with AIDS descending into the town swimming pool.

July 21, 1986

In the darkest moments, it's hard not to blame past lovers. You want to lay blame. You want to feel innocent. I probably was infected one of the first times I had sex—maybe that first guy, even. There is no reason that explains AIDS, Shawn told me, You're not being punished. But it's a hard thing to let go—you hear all the shit people say, like Jerry Falwell gloating that homosexuals will be annihilated and there will be a celebration in heaven. I've heard, more times than once: AIDS is a cure for fags.

Guys try to go back home and their parents turn them away. Hospital beds hold skeletons of men who the nurses and doctors do not want to touch. Even after we die they don't want us. Bodies in morgues that parents will not claim. Bodies disposed of in garbage bags. People afraid our AIDS-bodies will contaminate the ground. I heard about a funeral where they sealed the body under glass. It's absurd, but still stings—they don't want to touch us when we're alive or when we're dead. "Dropping like flies" is an ugly expression I've heard more than once. All these young men dying, and nobody cares.

First guy I knew was Alex Morales, who shot these amazing weird photographs of potholes, crumbling buildings, trash. One night in 1983 we all went out and he said he was feeling funny, couldn't get his breath, his chest felt tight. Next night he was at the hospital. Two days later, he was dead. Pneumonia. He was thirty years old.

People think death is this peaceful glow, softness, dreamlike, but it's ugly, dirty, smelly, lonely, painful. I don't want to suffer, who does?

You hope it's painless—go quietly, die in your sleep during a dream, loved ones gathered around you, all reconcilement and forgiveness. But, the truth is, AIDS is never painless. And there is nothing profound or beautiful about death.

I can't picture my own. There is no way to understand how it will look or feel. I don't know how to imagine it because I'm still alive.

July 22, 1986

There is something hard and complicated between me and my sister now, a tangled knot of confusion. She knew all this time. Today, I was watching one of her ocean programs with her, like we used to, and I felt spacey and relaxed, even if Jess didn't want me there. Back when I was a teenager, I used to get stoned and watch hours of TV with her, and that's how I felt—my body slowed down and my mind opened to the dazzling images.

A man in scuba gear, looking like an alien, descended into turquoise waters, bubbles rising from his mask. Neon fish exploding around him like thousands of butterflies. A silver tuna, as long as the man, swam under him, disappearing into the dark.

You would want to do that? I asked, trying to get Jess to talk to me. If she hates me, I don't blame her—she's the one who has to go back to school and face these assholes every day.

She shrugged. Her chin jutting out slightly. She's got our mother's heart-shaped face. The slightly pointy chin, our father's full lips. She's growing her hair out, and when she wears it down, it hits just below shoulders—the way I used to wear mine, enraging my father.

I tried to talk to her, probably sounded like any adult, saying something like, Jess, I know this is hard.

I'm trying to watch this, she said.

And, that was that. Fine, we didn't talk. We watched the TV screen.

The camera switched to the ocean's surface. Blue and sunlight. A fin cutting the water. The shark, all muscle, zipping through, goes in for the kill. The narrator describing the scene in a calm, comforting voice, like he's telling a bedtime story.

As bad as it was, the humiliation, the embarrassment, there was also this: for the briefest, sweetest of moments, when I was floating on my back in that swimming pool, looking up at the perfect blue sky, my own heartbeat thudding in my ears, I was alive, and happy. Everything was quiet and light.

A panoramic view of a sparkling sea. Then a cloud of blood.

Jess

On the roof outside my window, I suck in the weedy backyard night smells, wishing the woman's voice would fade away, but I can still hear her.

"You'll pay for what you've done," she said.

I'm not supposed to answer the phone because of the prank calls. But I wanted to know what people were saying. I picked up on the first ring and was surprised to hear a woman's voice. I was expecting a man's. She didn't sound like an old lady, not a girl either. Someone my mother's age. Maybe a mother herself. "Sinner," she said.

Moonlight shivers on the silver leaves. I hear the squeak of the back door. My mother walks out to the middle of the backyard where it's flat and exposed. She's been doing this all summer, coming out to smoke when she thinks we're all asleep. The hem of her sleeveless nightgown touches her knees. She's barefoot, and she doesn't look anything like the mother I know. She's a wild woman who lives in the woods. She gazes up at the sky, then suddenly drops her head and hunches over. At first I think she's fallen or she's hurt, but then low guttural noises tumble across the night, and I remember Brian's moans echoing through the house. I feel a sudden rush of adrenaline and fear, catching my mother at this—alone and sobbing in the dark.

I don't know how much time goes by. Not much. She pulls herself together. When she stands up, a cigarette still burns in her hand. Clutching her side, like she has a runner's cramp, she walks back toward the house.

If Josh Clay hadn't been at the pool, would anyone have noticed Brian? It's my fault for telling. But other people already knew, like Brett Wilson. Now everyone knows. The woman's white-hot voice echoes in my ear. *Sinner.* When I try to imagine what she looks like, all I can see is an angry red mouth—lips curling, daggered teeth.

I close my eyes and wish I wasn't in Ohio but on a boat rocking on the ocean's waves, and that the noisy crickets were actually giant, ancient blue whales singing to each other for miles, moving underwater towards each other and coming for me.

Brian sits at the kitchen table with the paper spread open, like this is just any normal day. He looks rough, like one of the Dennisons next door—raggedy hair, and glassy eyes downcast and hooded like he's trying to hide something.

"Pool's back open," he says.

"Is that supposed to make me feel better?"

He knows as well as I do that things have changed for good. After I lace up my tennis shoes, I go out the front door, bracing myself—for what? A crowd? Reporters? Boys laughing? It's not like that. It's quiet, for now. The sky squats low—gray and thin, the air surprisingly cool. The pool opened back up but the heat wave is over. People will be pissed we took away their best swimming days.

I stretch in the front yard. My father has fallen behind on the mowing, and bees thread through the long grass, bumping into shoots of clover and dandelions. As I look up from touching my toes, the Pentecostal sisters walk out to their driveway. They don't pay me any mind—they've already decided I'm going to hell. Two of them stand at either end of a jump rope and turn it in big, lazy loops; the third girl jumps in. I haven't jumped rope since I was in elementary school. They're chanting, but I can't make out the words. Probably something religious. They wear long old-fashioned dresses, and colored pompom footies peek over the edges of their cheap white tennis shoes. At school nobody talks to them. The religious wackos. The rope snaps against the cement. They don't care about friends, they have God.

There is no way I can go back to school in the fall. And I'm the girl whose brother has AIDS. I can't go back. I won't.

I head in the direction of Buckeye Creek. I forgot my Walkman so I have to listen to myself breathing through my mouth. The short hot huffs make me sound like an animal—I am an animal—and the insides of my thighs burn. The pain feels good. I want to see Nick, but I'm scared of what he'll say.

At the high school, I run out to the baseball diamonds and across the yellowing field where we played softball. How many days did I stand out here missing ball after ball? My parents and grandmother, watching me strike out. I never want to play again. After, my father would buy me ice cream, no matter if we won or lost, like the coaches used to when I was a kid. "Next time," he'd say. I wish Annie was still here—she'd know what to do.

I collapse in the outfield. Stretched out on my back, I close my eyes and purple dots shoot behind my eyelids. It's hard to get my breath. It's the smoking. I could get lung cancer. Maybe I'm dying too.

Drops of warm rain land on my face. I fold my arms over my chest and try not to move. The tips of grass blades scratch my legs. If someone saw me out here alone in the field, in the rain, they might think I was dead. I remember my mother bringing home a magazine from the dentist office last year, *Time* or *Newsweek*, that had a story on AIDS—pictures of a ravaged man with tubes sticking out of his skeleton body, his face melted away to sharp, ugly bones. The article said nobody was safe.

The rain comes down harder, pinging against the roof of the dugout, and I scramble up and run back home.

My wet T-shirt and shorts cling, and my socks squish in my shoes. After I dry off my face with a dishtowel, I sit in Brian's chair and look at the funnies. *Garfield* and *Cathy* and *Family Circus* and *Blondie* and *Beetle Bailey*. He used to read them to me when I was little. The drawings and black ink blur as water drips. I touch the cup of cold tea. The saucer with half a piece of toast. You can only get it from sex or sharing needles. I take a sip of the tea, lips touching where his were. What if it's in our blood too—mine, my parents', my grandmother's? What if whatever made him gay is also in me?

The rain stops and the light suddenly shifts, cutting through white-gray sky. A lily pad of gold blooms under the kitchen table. When we were little, Brian would drape blankets and quilts over the chairs, then turn off the lights. After we were safe under the ceiling of blankets, warm like the skins of animals, he would flick on a flashlight and we'd pretend we were at the bottom of the sea.

"Jess. Can I come in?"

I put down my book and take off my headphones, and my mother walks in, still wearing her office clothes. She sits on the edge of my bed, stink of cigarette smoke rolling off her crumpled shirt. I think of her smoking under the stars. Her desperate sobs.

"Hey, kiddo." She wraps her fingers around my ankle. "Is there anything you want to ask me?"

"No."

My mother's face sags, especially her eyes, the skin underneath them puffy and pink. Most of the perm has gone out of her hair, so that it lays against her head like the feathery wings of a chicken, looking flat and puffy at the same time.

"Honey, I'm sorry that we didn't tell you. We just thought it was best."

It's hard to stay mad at someone who looks so weak.

"The talk will die down. People know us. They know what kind of family we are. We're not strangers," she says, and holds onto my ankle like she's anxious I'll float away.

"I want to move," I say. I lower my hand over hers, fitting our fingers together like Legos. Our bones know each other, they come from the same place.

✳

Darkness sinks over Chester, except for the yellow globed street lamps attracting fluttering moths to their deaths, and a few TVs flickering alien-blue lights. Parked pickups and cars sit along the streets like empty husks of some giant land animals. Nobody sees me—I'm a shadow cutting through the night.

When I get to the drive-in, I check the face of my glow-in-the-dark watch. Ten minutes past midnight. When I called earlier, he said he'd be here.

Then I hear footsteps and see the tip of his cigarette burning red bobbing in my direction. When he's standing in front of me—small ferret face, hair in his eyes—I want to crawl inside his clothes, feel him all around me. I'm surprised how much I've missed him.

"Hey," he says.

"Hey."

Nick opens his book bag and pulls out two cans of Pabst. We sit on the merry-go-ground and crack our beers under the starry sky and don't say anything for a while. I wasn't sure he'd want to see me. But he reaches over and holds my hand. His skin feels warm and clammy. Nick Marshall, the hood. Am I his girlfriend? With his other hand he fiddles with his cigarettes, and shakes one out and puts it between his lips. Casually flips his Zippo. The orange flame waves in his eyes.

"It was your brother, wasn't it?" Nick says, matter-of-fact. "The dude with AIDS."

I pretend not to know what he's talking about. "What?"

"My dad told me."

The beer leaves a sour, bitter taste in my mouth. I tell myself to just get up and walk away. But he's holding my hand.

"How does he know it's Brian?"

"Guess he heard it from someone."

A million lies buzz on my lips. "I should go."

"Wait." Nick's little teeth crowd together, some of them pointy like a dog's. "I know you can't get it by drinking after him or anything. Or swimming in the pool." He cracks his knuckles. "You don't have it. Do you?"

I can't tell if he's being serious or not. I shake my head. Nick guzzles the rest of his beer and tosses the can out into the field. Something rustles from the trees and I jump—has someone followed us? Nick assures me, "Probably a raccoon."

He stamps out his cigarette, then pulls me closer. His beer-tongue wiggles in my mouth as his hands search for a place to hold onto. I still have my cigarette, and I smash it out on the metal, so as not to burn either of us. Nick knocks over the last of my beer and it trickles down my knee. The merry-go-round moves a little, and I dig my shoes into the ground to hold us still. Then Nick is on top of me, his mouth and tongue everywhere at once, all over my face. His hand slides under my shirt, strokes my chest. My *boobs*. They're not big, but not so flat anymore either. I stay as still as possible. Animals rustle in the trees. A frog chirps. My heart beats.

Then, a sudden rush of warm air and a wide empty space as Nick lifts off of me. He heaves big breaths. I straighten my shirt. He sits down next to me and rests his hand, always gray with pencil marks, on my thigh and it perches there delicately, a little sparrow that any second might fly away.

"You're a virgin, aren't you?" he asks.

"So are you."

He spits between his teeth. "No, I'm not." He's lying, but I don't care. He unwraps a piece of Big Red. "Want one?"

I peel off the silver foil wrapper and fold the stick of gum in my mouth. I don't tell him how bad things are. The phone calls and newspaper articles. My brother getting thinner, sicker, weaker—dying. The old movie screen rises above us like a white whale in the sky, and the speaker poles glow under the moonlight like headstones.

"I hate Chester," I say.

Nick chews his gum hard, popping and cracking it. "We could go somewhere," he says. "We could leave, just like your brother did."

Sharon

I thought by now the gossip would have died down. It's been ten days. Just when it seems it's going to, there is something else in the paper. An article about how the swimming pool has lost business—people don't want to go anymore, anxious the water is contaminated. Stupid, scared letters to the editor, and nasty, hateful talk, lies spawning more lies. *He bled in the pool. Peed in the pool. He went swimming with an open cut. He wants to infect people, he wants to infect children. He uses public restrooms, handles food in the grocery store, spits in water fountains.*

Even though the newspapers haven't used his name, people know. At work, Marjorie, who was always so easygoing, hardly speaks to me, and she's started wearing latex gloves all the time around the office, even when she's not with a patient. Dave tries to act like everything is normal, but I see him watching me like I'm a stranger, a crazy woman pretending to be Sharon. No one drops by the house or calls. I saw Liz at the post office getting in her car and I started to say hello, then realized she'd already seen me and was pretending she hadn't.

Even church, once my solace, has become unbearable. This past Sunday Travis and I went with Lettie, and friends flashed fake smiles or avoided us. Still, Lettie was hopeful. She had met with Reverend Clay to tell him how bad the situation was getting. As the service went on, I started to feel hopeful too. Dennis talked about the sin of judgment. He denounced gossip as unchristian. He never mentioned Brian, of course, or the pool—but we all knew what he saying.

After the offering, he invited Josh up to the podium to announce that the youth group would be raising money to go to a national Christian youth conference in Washington, DC. Everyone applauded, but not Lettie—her hands stayed on her lap, her mouth pinched. My hands came together lightly. I remember seeing him that day at the pool, arms crossed, watching, judging. The look of superiority on his face. And then feeling startled by my own unforgivable wish, that he was our boy—wasn't his the life we had imagined for our son?

After Josh returned to his seat, Reverend Clay delivered a sermon about God's grace and forgiveness. It was all going fine until about half-way through. After a long pause, he said, "We should love the sinners, but that doesn't mean we accept the sin. Make no mistake, homosexuality is a sin." He looked sorry to be saying the words. "These men, that's why they're getting sick, you see."

As the church went silent—not a cough or a rustle of a bulletin—a shock of air lifted up under me, sweeping away the floor. Then Lettie slipped her hymnal in the slot on the back of the pew in front of her with a bang and fumbled for her pocketbook. She moved slowly, making a lot of noise. "Excuse me," she said loudly. We stood up to let her by. All eyes on her, she walked down the aisle, straight-backed and determined, and pushed open the double doors—a whoosh, then the outside light vanished and she was gone. Travis sat down and opened his hymnal, and I took my place next to my husband.

The umbrella I usually leave in the backseat is missing, so I make a run for it through the rain. The double automatic doors part, and I step into a world that is refreshingly clean and quiet and bright. I brush the rain off my shoulders, pat my hair. An instrumental song—the same Muzak we listen to at the office—pipes through the PA system, saxophone and strings coming from the ceiling, smoothing over everything like white frosting. I pull a cart free from the train of carts, flip down the red plastic flap. When he was little, Brian liked to sit here, his little legs dangling through the front slats. Shoppers would coo over him, and he made them laugh with his jabbering. He wasn't shy like Jess, never hid his face.

I start with the fruit and vegetables and make my way through the store aisle by aisle. Here, I feel better. Here, I could be anyone. The rows of canned vegetables, arranged like a colorful paint-by-number, relax my jittery mind. Yellow corn, green beans, dark green spinach. Everything neatly labeled, organized, ordered.

An older, hunched gray-haired woman stops her cart next to mine, and reaches for a can of creamed corn, the loose skin under her thin arms quivering. She's wearing blue jeans and tennis shoes. It always surprises me when I see an old woman wearing jeans.

"Morning," she says, then corrects herself. "Guess it ain't morning anymore, is it?"

She's missing a few teeth, and I can't help but think of Brian. He lost a bottom tooth—a central incisor. I offered him to take him in to see Dave, and Brian just shot me a look, embarrassed by my pathetic offer, which I know is coming too late.

"Feels like morning," I say. "It's the rain."

"Shew, I'm glad it's cooled off. I can't abide that heat."

She looks familiar, but I can't figure out where I've seen her. As I watch her go, a funny sadness comes over me. Granny Ada. My mother's mother. I met her only once. We visited her at her home in the mountains of West Virginia. She smoked a pipe and wore a flowered shapeless dress, and held me in her lap and told me stories about fairies and magical creatures. I remember her kindness and warmth, how different she was from my mother who spent most of the trip staring at the patches of sky, beautiful and distant.

I add things to the cart, cross them off my list. Lunchmeat for Travis, frozen dinners for Jess. For Brian, even though he hasn't been eating much, ingredients to make his favorite meals, and bananas and yogurt for his special protein shakes. I keep adding things to the cart. I don't want to leave.

But I can't stay here forever. I get in line behind the old woman who watches her items ring up, making sure she's not being cheated, and set my groceries onto the conveyor belt behind the red plastic divider. Another shopper pulls her cart up behind mine. She also looks familiar—petite and compact with wavy brown hair and a smooth face, younger and thinner than me. I can't think of her name, but she has a girl Jess's age. They played softball together. What's her friend's name—Mary, or Molly? We've sat next to each other at softball games. Rhonda, I remember now. Rhonda Williams, Molly's mother.

She returns my smile, then her pretty lips twitch. I watch it happen: her sinking face, the flare of recognition and disgust.

"Oh," she says.

That's it. She says nothing else, just backs up and switches to the other line. My face pulses.

As the old woman writes out a check, I pretend to be interested in the rack of magazines. Celebrities with perfect, dazzling smiles, whitened teeth—Elizabeth Taylor, Madonna, Michael J. Fox. Fashion tips, scandals, advertisements. A headline on one of the tabloids, even too trashy for Lettie, claims Jesus will return to Earth in a spaceship.

Some of the letters to the editor were written by people I know. They said they wanted to protect the town and the children from this wicked disease. They said he was flaunting his homosexuality. They said we should be held responsible. I read each one in a blur of tears. One was from Sandy Nelson, who lives down the street from us. She said that my son should be arrested and thrown in jail. Our Pentecostal neighbors left a note in our mailbox reassuring us that they are praying for us, and the O'Malleys, who have always been kind, wrote a letter to the editor saying they are scared they could be infected too—by the ground water or sharing the same air.

The clerk, chewing green gum, scans my groceries. The conveyor belt chugs along. "How are you, ma'am?"

"Fine," I say with a smile, and hand over a stack of coupons. "Just fine."

The rain has stopped and the parking lot glistens in the sun. A bag boy packs the last of the old woman's groceries in the trunk of her station wagon, and she sees me and waves me over. The boy gives the cart a running start then hops on and rides it across the parking lot.

"I know who you are now," she says. My body tenses. "You come into the filling station sometimes, over on 54?"

Confused, I nod.

"Marlboros, right?"

The tight wires in my neck uncoil, and I'm surprised by my laugh. "That's me."

"I'm Lucy Highsmith," she says.

She doesn't know who I am.

"Sarah," I say. "Sarah Johnson."

The stranger's name falls out of my mouth as easily as a recited prayer. The old woman's pruned lips turn up, the wrinkles spray in a big smile.

"Well, come by anytime, Sarah," she says.

For the first time in weeks, the aching stops. The buzzing quiets. I feel suddenly light, like I can walk away from all of this, that everything before this moment can be erased. I can be someone else.

"I will," I promise.

"Do you need help?" Brian asks.

"There are a couple more sacks, but I'll get them."

"I can do it," he says.

"Okay, thanks."

Brian carries a couple of the lighter grocery sacks into the kitchen, and then sits back down, already worn out. Lately, just walking up and down the stairs makes him short of breath.

"Are you hungry? Want me to make you something?"

He pushes his thinning hair out of his eyes. He needs a haircut, a shave. The gap in his mouth upsets me—he used to have such a pretty smile.

"Maybe just a piece of toast."

I ask where Jess is and he doesn't know—he thinks she went for a run, or maybe to hang out with friends. Does she have friends? I've tried to pry, but she doesn't say much. What will happen when school starts, what will the kids say? She wants to move. Could we? Uproot ourselves, start some place new? Become the Johnsons? I feel a stab of guilt. *Sarah Johnson*. It isn't telling a lie that stings, but the way it felt so right, so desirable to say a name that wasn't my own, to deny my son.

"I was thinking of making barbecue chicken for supper." I drop a slice of bread in the toaster. "How does that sound?"

"Whatever. I'm not really hungry."

In the last few months of my mother's life, the weight slid off her until she was nothing but delicate bone. I remember her sitting up in her bed, so thin and pale and quiet—a strange queen on her throne, as fragile as a moth. I didn't like to be near her. Even in her dying, she intimidated me with her austere silence.

"I saw today's letters to the editor," Brian says.

I get out the package of raw chicken, and feel suddenly queasy. Pale puckered flesh, the detached legs and wings laid out on a light blue Styrofoam container, sealed under plastic wrap.

"You shouldn't read them," I say.

Brian gazes out the window to the side yard where a robin stabs at the grass, lifts its head with a writhing worm pinched between its beak. "I didn't think it would turn into all this," he says.

The toast pops up golden and crisp with a tinge of brown, just the way he likes it. Is he apologizing? He makes jokes about how ignorant Chester is, but I've seen his face crumple when the news comes on, his shoulders tense when the phone rings. I spread margarine on the slice and cut it into two triangles, the way I used to do when he was little.

"You know how people are. They like to gossip." I set the toast in front of him. Sometimes I forget how young he is, and other times I still think of him as a child with the whole world ahead of him.

"I got a call today," he says.

"Brian, we've told you not to answer the phone."

"It wasn't one of those." He lifts one eyebrow. "It was *On Location With Naomi*."

I put my hand on my hip and look at him hard, thinking he's joking. "What?"

"You know, the TV show. Naomi wants to do a story about this."

"Honey, that was something pranking you." The sudden panic fades, and I reach over to stroke his hair. "A mean joke."

He moves away from my touch. "It's real. She wants to interview me," he says, furious. "She wants my side. *Our* side."

When Brian was little, before I started working for Dave Green, before I had Jess, we'd spend the days together, just the two of us. I'd bake chocolate chip cookies, we'd watch *Sesame Street*. He liked to build towers out of wooden blocks. He danced around the house, spinning circles and falling on the floor, laughing. I only ever wanted to protect him. I don't understand how things went so wrong. I lost him once, and now I'm going to lose him again.

"Don't you want this to go away?"

He takes a bite of toast, crumbs falling.

"That's what you and Dad want," he says. "What everybody wants—for *me* to go away."

"That's not what I said."

"Don't worry. I hear you loud and clear."

I snap on yellow cleaning gloves and flick the light switch. The room is dank, musty, empty. Brian went over to Lettie's to watch television, and he'll probably stay a few more hours. His safe place. As I turn the window crank, the pane of glass slowly pushes outward. On the wall behind Brian's bed hang the pictures of his friends, all men. Maybe they're all sick too, or maybe—the thought is a sliver of glass under my skin—they're all dead. I step around stacks of records to get a closer look of a snapshot of him with his friend standing on a city bridge, arms flung around each other, the sun setting behind them, a pink light. Two men, smiling. Happy. One black, one white. Only one alive.

I strip the bed and pick up a damp towel and clothes from a pile on the floor. Brian thinks I'm racist, but that's not it. Is it? I knew black people when we lived in Columbus. Kids in school, families in the neighborhood. It's not that he's black, but that *this*, all of this, was not what I ever imagined for my son. That's what I tell myself. But maybe Brian is right. I can't help but think that if Brian had never met him, he'd still be healthy, he'd be okay.

My hands sweat inside the rubber gloves. There are accidents, Travis says. Open sores, cuts. Better safe than sorry.

To tell his side on TV. Would people feel sympathetic? Would they think, *Yes, this is a young man, a son, a brother, a cousin, a neighbor?* The show is popular. Real stories, real lives. Lettie and Jess watch it religiously.

As I walk out of Brian's room, my face peeking over the bundle in my arms, Travis comes downstairs, heading out to the garage.

"You're home," I say.

"Sorry I'm late. I had some things to finish up at work."

I don't even know why he still bothers with the lies. Where does he go? Not to his favorite bar with his brothers. They are not speaking. He says the guys at work are talking, doesn't tell me what they say, what it's like for him. He drives around or goes to Madison, where there are more bars to choose from, where nobody knows him. Maybe he has also made up a name, an alias.

"I need to talk to you," I say.

He follows me into the utility room. Sometimes, I catch Brian looking at his father, longing for his attention, just like when he was little, but Travis can't see past his own hurt and guilt and sadness. He can't articulate any of those feelings to me, but I know, deep down, how much he loves his son—he must.

I pour out a cup of powdered detergent and tell him about the TV show. Travis stares at me like I've gone insane.

"What are you talking about?"

"Your mom watches it."

His face flattens. He doesn't want to be here anymore. Maybe it's not even about Brian. Maybe it's about me.

"That's a really bad idea."

"That's what I thought too," I said. "But I've been thinking. Maybe it could help." I want to believe, like Lettie, that people don't hate us, that one day they'll feel bad about what they've said and done. "Maybe it'll help put a stop all the ugliness."

Travis's mouth twists, his jaw pushes out. He's too tall for this small space, a hulking mass of muscle and fear.

"No," he snaps. "No way."

I close the washing machine lid, turn the dial. Click, click, click. We have hardly spoken of that day, but I'll never forget. My shivering son.

People staring. The laughter. The police. My hands can't breathe, too hot and slick in the gloves. We stood there, we did nothing.

"Tell him no," Travis says.

I tug at one of the gloves, the rubber clinging to my fingers. "I'm not wearing these things anymore. It's stupid. It makes him feel bad, and it's stupid."

"It was just a precaution," he says in a thin, tight voice.

"I knew it was wrong, but I went along with it."

I yank at the yellow fingers, and when I finally free my hands, I hurl the rolled up gloves onto the floor. Travis walks out, a door slams. My freed fingers look like pink, clammy worms. I pick up the towel, the sheets, and a wrinkled blue T-shirt and hold them in my bare hands. I remember the softness of his tiny head when he was born, his little feet and hands, how he clung to me. The faintest hint of cologne, the smell of bark and something spicy and male, but more than that—sickness. The smell of sickness that cannot be washed away.

Brian

So, I still haven't called back the producer, or the assistant, or whoever was calling on behalf of Naomi. I don't know how they tracked me down. When I told Mamaw, she gasped. You have to do it, she cried. My land, this is so exciting!

I told her it's not a good idea, which is what my mother told me.

My grandmother clucked her tongue. Naomi will tell the truth, and people will change their minds, she said. They'll see how they've been doing us wrong. Why, this could get the story all over America!

Just what my parents want. Not only will everyone know I have AIDS, but they'll know I'm gay too. Nobody wants to acknowledge I have AIDS because then they have to think about how it's transmitted. They have to think about body parts and sex. They have to think about men fucking men, men loving men.

My mother thinks, hopes, prays, or whatever, that if we hold our breaths this will pass over like a storm cloud. Meanwhile, letters to the editor. Prank calls. Last night a carload of teenage boys slowed down outside our house, screaming out the windows, maybe the same ones who were at the pool. *Faggot, AIDS, queer.* My mother washed dishes, ignoring them. Jess ran upstairs and locked herself in her room. My dad stayed in the garage, transistor radio tuned to a Reds game. Disembodied sports announcer voices murmuring through the walls. I used to be able to speak that language.

Maybe I still do. There were times in New York, especially after Shawn died, that I'd feel the pull, a forgotten part of me waking up, and I'd take the train out to Coney Island to the batting cages. My body remembered. The twist of my torso, the reach of my arms. The loose, strong swing of the bat, the satisfying thunk. Buzzing lights. The whoosh of the pitching machine. The net rising all around and above me, taking each hit. The repetition gave me some kind of peace.

The body remembers more than the heart.

Now, my body is weak and everything makes me tired. Even holding my camera is difficult. I mostly just use the tripod. My grandmother bought me a bunch of VHS tapes, so I don't have to worry about running out. I could sit here and just run my mouth for hours. Not censor a goddamn thing. Record myself looking worse and worse. Yesterday, I woke up flushed and feverish, and stayed in bed until the evening. My joints hurt. I try not to cry. I stay down here, hidden.

But look at me. Rotting from the inside. I lost a goddamn tooth, look. When I woke up, I tasted blood. It sat on my pillow, a brown, hideous kernel.

I need to get out. Do something normal. Go for a drink. Talk to someone. Who? Not a single teammate has looked me up. No classmates. Gus—nope. I had this stupid idea that when I came back, he would be my anchor. To think that he still might be hanging out with Josh Clay— it's a slap in the face. Fuck him, fuck everybody in this town.

You know who I'm going to call? Where is my little phonebook—here it is. A, A, A. There he is—Andrew. Why not? What do I have to lose?

▤ August 1, 1986

I've got a lot to tell you, dear old diary. Maybe I'm spilling too much. But, listen:

Today, I felt better than I have in weeks. I shaved, cleaned up my neck, trimmed my hair. I changed out of my sad sweatpants, and put on pressed jeans and a button-down shirt. Tried to look presentable.

My mother let me use her car. It felt good to get behind the wheel, driving away from Chester. On a straight patch of road I hit the gas, passing the homes of families I used to know. The late afternoon sun hung low in the sky, turning the fields a flat yellow.

I was right on time. Andrew walked out of the mall's revolving doors, looked around with irritation, like he'd been set up—it's happened to him before. Then he saw me. How I wished Annie could have met him. He looked like a Broadway queen. His blousy slacks, rayon shirt with different blocks of colors—purple, pink, brown, peacock blue. Puffy hair. A loud, gold-faced wristwatch with a bright pink band. Fairy, faggot, sissy. He's heard it all before, I'm sure.

Long day? I asked.

Didn't sell hardly a thing, the ladies around here are so cheap, he says. He cocked his hip. Want to get something to eat?

I told him I was thinking we could just drive around, and asked if he'd mind driving because I wanted to record.

He laughed. You making a movie of this dump?

Sort of, I told him.

Andrew got in the driver's seat, adjusted the rearview mirror, and smoothed the pleats in his pants. He smiled at me, and I felt instantly comforted. He's got nice teeth, something my mother would say. I felt even more self-conscious about mine.

He asked where I wanted to go. I told him, Anywhere.

He pulled out of the parking lot. Flowery cologne rolled off him, saturating my mother's car. Just as I suspected, Andrew wasn't at all bothered by the camera. He talked and talked—about his co-workers and god-awful customers. In a field, starlings rose in a single swoop, a funnel of feathers twisting in one direction, then another.

I asked him questions, and he rambled on and on, but I wanted to know more. What is it *really* like here?

He still didn't trust me. What do you mean? he says.

Being gay.

Andrew hesitated. Not used to saying the word out loud, probably.

But then he started to open up. He told me he'd never lived anywhere else, and so for a long time, this was all he knew. But when he was twenty years old, he went to a gay bar in Columbus for the first time. I saw what I'd been missing, he says.

He told me now he goes a few times a year to go dancing and meet guys. One day, he said, I'll move there.

One of the letters to the editor said I never should have left Chester. If you leave there will be temptations. There is a price to pay. If you love men, there is a price to pay. The mouths I've tasted, the beauty I've found in a neck, a crook of an elbow, a knee, a mouth. Balls cupped in my hand, the salty, floury taste of a cock. Could you find that here?

I kept digging at Andrew. I asked him if he's ever met anyone around here.

He goes, There are guys around, if you know where to look. Why, you looking?

Just curious, I said.

Andrew says, Word of mouth, I guess. They find me. Married men, straight men. Maybe they can tell by looking at me. Then he let out a high-pitched laugh. He says, I'm not some old lonely queen, if that's what you're asking.

He took us down back roads and told me more about his life. He lives with his mother. His dad walked out years ago. Meanwhile, the sky changed to warm amber, the color of the fancy imported ale that Shawn always preferred to my crappy watered-down beer. On one side of us, a forest, and the other, an empty pasture that stretched out like a river of green.

After a few more turns, Andrew came to a dead end, stopped at an old, dilapidated covered bridge. Red rust, web of honeysuckle. On the other side, more forest, a washed-out road.

He asked if I'd ever been there, and I said no. We got out of the car, me with my camera.

It's pretty, don't you think? Andrew asked me.

Yellow weeds and vines twisted up like long antennas from the slats under our feet. The metal work of the bridge, the dark creek running under us, splays of Queen Anne's lace. Canada geese flying in a V. It was pretty.

I noticed Andrew looking at me curiously, arms folded across his chest.

Your turn, he says.

I asked what he meant.

Tell me something about you.

What do you want to know? I asked.

Andrew was handsome, once you got past the silly hair and outfit. The flushed pink cheeks, small mouth. His gentle eyes, a light, coppery brown. I've got all of it on video. Him lighting a cigarette, a menthol, same brand as my grandmother's. Andrew isn't afraid. He doesn't care what people think.

It's you, isn't it? he says. The man in the pool?

I told him the truth. Yep, it's me.

He sucked on the cigarette, looking out toward the creek, his brow slightly furrowed. When he turned to face me, I was surprised to see he was grinning.

Shit. You went in the goddamn Chester pool. Why?

I was hot, I said.

He laughed, a girlish, obnoxious laugh that sounded sweet to my ears, and told me I was crazy. Maybe I am.

After Andrew caught his breath, he settled down and took another drag. He says, I know you can't get it like that. But these people around here, they're ignorant.

I asked if he knows anyone who has it.

He didn't. I know it's out there, he says, but I don't worry about it too much, not here.

He rubbed his arms like he caught a chill. Then he asked, How does it feel?

It was my turn to let out a laugh. Not very good, I said.

We watched the last of the light disappear. A few pinpricks of gold still blinked from the creeping darkness. A perfect summer night. I turned off the camera.

Andrew said he had better get going, his mother would worry.

This time, I got in the driver's seat, but didn't start the engine. In the dark, it felt easy to talk, to tell him things I can't say to anyone, except maybe to my camera. The guilt, the hurt, the shame. But, also, the joy.

All the men I touched, the ones I loved, the quick fucks, the strangers and boyfriends and Shawn: they knew me in ways no one else could.

Andrew was quiet. Crickets and frogs serenaded us. His hands shone in the dark like two pale slivers of the moon. His fingers long, elegant.

It's not right. How people are treating you. How any of us get treated, he says. It was a brave of you.

Brave, or stupid.

Andrew's face looked pretty in the dying light. Can I tell you the truth? He looked beautiful. Clean-shaven, smooth-skinned. His eyes shone. He moved closer, the fake leather squeaking. Andrew, with his ridiculous shirt, his gigantic hair, his suffocating, cheap cologne, he held me.

I was panicked, and at first, I tried to stop him.

He goes, You can't get it from hugging and kissing. Even I know that.

His hands glided around to my back and I was surprised by how strong they were. It was the first time in a year or maybe longer that I'd had another man's tongue in my mouth. He tasted like cigarettes, and something else—fried onions. His tongue was little and quick, flicked against my teeth. He kissed my neck, and his hands slid down along my thighs and I was getting hard and he rubbed my dick through my jeans.

I asked why he was doing this.

He unzipped me. His spidery hand, his slender fingers. Gold rings, pink wristwatch, blond hairs. His hand squeezing, moving up and down, and I breathed him in, all his funky and beautiful odors, his body pressing against mine. I came quickly. And when I came, what also left my body were sobs. Deep, scared sobs.

Andrew held me.

Shh, he whispered in my ear.

Well, the night didn't end there, I'm sorry to say. When I got home, my parents were sitting at the dining room table, waiting for me. I felt like I was sixteen.

I set the keys on the table. My father didn't look at me. Arms crossed, biceps bulging.

My mother held a cup of tea in both hands. She'd been crying. I remember one time, I was eight or nine, I caught her, teary-eyed, in the kitchen. I didn't know what was wrong, but I picked up a broom and held it like a microphone, singing along to Carole King's "I Feel The Earth Move," and my mother, her long shiny hair held back by a headband, laughed, and took me in her arms and we danced together.

Your mother was going out of her mind, my father says, not looking at me but at the beer in his hand. He was wearing a Reds hat, and I couldn't see his eyes.

I told them I'd lost track of time.

I was standing close enough that my father could have grabbed me, hit me, pushed me. We used to fight all the time. At least then he would look at me.

I said, Nobody saw me, if that's what you're worried about.

I had his attention now. He snapped at me. Don't be smart, he says.

A heat—a good heat—filled me, one I haven't felt in a long time. I'm sixteen again. I'm strong. Fearless. Like Andrew in his blousy shirt and cloying cologne.

I saw a friend, I said. A guy.

Oh, Brian. My mother was disappointed, but it was my father I wanted to shock. He took a drink of beer. Then looked at me.

I know about this TV show, he says. I told her not to call here again—she's harassing us. I don't want you talking to her. You understand?

So maybe this time Naomi herself, not an assistant, called the house.

I turned to my mother, I don't know why—for help, defense, support. She looked out the window—nothing there, a world of dark. She'll always choose him over me, just like all those years ago, when I told her I was leaving.

📼 August 2, 1986

Notice anything different?

It's done.

The first thing I did when I got out of bed this morning was get rid of them. I couldn't look at the cheap plastic trophies staring at me any longer, all these macho men I was supposed to be. They clattered against each other as I carried the box out to the garage. I shoved it in a dark cobwebby corner of my father's space.

Then I listened to my parents' answering machine, in case Naomi had left a message. If she had, it had already been erased. But I still had the number scrawled on a piece of scrap paper. I dialed, and the numbers clicked one at a time. A man picked up.

I told him, Okay.

He said Naomi would be delighted. He explained the plan, and I said yes. Before we hung up, I asked him why they were doing this—just for the ratings?

He admitted a controversial story like this one will get people talking. But that isn't the only reason, he said. He paused. I could hear voices in the background.

AIDS is a story of America, he said. It's a story that must be told.

Jess

A night breeze blows the curtains back and they flap lazily against the window's screen. With my bedroom door cracked, I can hear my parents downstairs, arguing about my brother and the TV show. Naomi Cook is coming to town. To Chester! I can never go back to school now.

Mamaw was the one broke the news to me. She came over while my mother was at work and told me she had a surprise. We sat around the kitchen table with glasses of flat Diet Pepsi. Brian petted Sadie while Mamaw talked—she was giddy.

I thought—I hoped—she was joking, until Brian looked at me.

"It's happening, kiddo," he said, eyes darting. Mamaw grinned from ear to ear. I felt like I was in a car that's spinning off the road, heading straight for a tree, no way to escape.

The voices get louder. My mother tells my father we can't spend the rest of our lives hiding. A door slams. Then another door.

I spread open the dusty atlas that I found in the garage yesterday and look again at the long route that leads from Ohio to Washington state. Nick and I are making plans.

I trace my finger along the outer perimeter of the western part of the country and along the blue that surrounds it, the blue of my dreams, where killer whales ride through the waters. I've never been outside of Ohio, except once when we went on a vacation to Mammoth Cave in Kentucky, but I was little and don't remember much about it. Nick and I are going to cross the country, go all the way to the San Juan Islands. There is even an island called Orcas Island.

Yesterday, after Mamaw told me, I called Nick. "It could be cool," he said. "I mean, you'd get to meet Naomi."

"Are you crazy? I don't want my family to go on TV."

Nick didn't say anything for a beat. Then he said, "We'll go soon. I'm figuring it out." I felt better just hearing his voice. He's the only one who listens to me and who cares what I think.

The house is empty now—my mother is outside smoking, my father drove off. Brian is over at Mamaw's. I don't have to see these things to know they're true. I lay face down on the floor, my ear pressed to the carpet like a medic listening for a heartbeat, but there's nothing, only silence.

Everyone in Dot's Diner looks up when we walk in, but it's the middle of the day and not very crowded, thank God. Just a few other customers, old people mostly. My grandmother ignores the stares, and we take a booth by a window. She and Brian sit on one side, and I sit across from them.

I can't believe we're here. I don't want to be seen in public with my brother, but I didn't know how to argue with Mamaw. "Let's get a bite to eat," she'd said, acting as if nothing at all was out of the ordinary. Brian, the only one she'll listen to, suggested we just stay home, but she said she wasn't going to be a prisoner in her own house. Still, I thought she'd take us to Madison, some place where people don't know us. When she pulled up to Dot's, Brian stood next to the Queen's Ship, his arms crossed, head down. "Mamaw, are you sure about this?" he asked.

"Of course I'm sure. Jack is an old friend. It'll be fine."

Naomi will be here in a few days. My grandmother thinks Naomi is going to change everyone's hearts. She refuses to admit the truth: the whole town hates us.

Dot's is the only sit-down restaurant in Chester. The dark wood walls and wall-to-wall dark green carpet, like felt on a pool table, make it seem like we're some place fancy, but the people who eat here are just regular Chester folks. Oldies play on the radio. Going to the chapel, and I'm going to get married. It smells like greasy hamburgers and cigarette smoke.

Mamaw slides the sticky laminated menus out from between the ketchup and mustard bottles, and hands them to me and Brian. But before we can even crack them open, a woman behind us says, "I think I'm going to be sick."

The prickly voice rises over the background music and chatter, loud enough that people stop eating to look over at her, and then at us. I don't know who she is. She's probably around forty or fifty. Old. Bitter face, thinning hair, a faded blue sweatshirt. I see her when I look over my grandmother's shoulder—she's staring at us with hateful eyes, while her husband, in a country shirt with the sleeves rolled up, keeps his eyes on his plate.

"I think I'm going to be sick," she says again, louder, as if everybody in the restaurant didn't hear her the first time.

"They've got real good cream corn—it's homemade," Mamaw says.

Brian sits very still. His shirt hangs off him three sizes too big. Bones jutting out, cracked lips, missing tooth.

The woman huffs and stands up and pushes in her chair. Maybe it's the same woman who called our house. *Sinner.* Her country husband hesitates, then he sets down his knife and fork, and follows her to the door.

"I don't want to catch AIDS," the woman says on her way out.

My grandmother's face flushes, but she just keeps studying the menu. I wonder if they left without paying.

"Mamaw, we should go," Brian says.

"This taco salad is new—it's real good, not too spicy," she says, and proceeds to go through the entire menu, telling us what is or isn't worth ordering. "The pork chops, last time I had them, were a little tough, and the mashed potatoes were okay but the gravy was runny. I reckon it was store-bought."

When the waitress comes over and sets down three glasses of water, she doesn't look any of us in the eye. She knows who we are. Everyone does.

She pulls out her tablet from the pocket of her apron and asks if we're ready to order. She is probably around my mother's age, with no neck and frizzy blond hair pulled back in a ponytail. She also looks mean and sour.

"Yes, I think so," Mamaw says. "Are there any specials?"

The waitress's slack mouth pulls downward. Nothing but hate in her eyes—lightless and mean. "Baked spaghetti," she snaps.

"Well, doesn't that sound good," Mamaw says.

I order a garden salad with Italian dressing. Brian asks for a bowl of chicken noodle soup. The waitress doesn't write any of it down. My grandmother still thinks people will do the right thing.

We sip our water. Around us, people mutter and murmur but don't get up to leave. Then Jack McCarthy, the owner, comes out from the kitchen. He and Dot went to my grandparents' wedding, I've seen the pictures. When I was little, Jack used to give me Tootsie Pops.

"Jack, how are you?" Mamaw asks, like there is nothing weird about this.

"All right," he says, but his bulldog face is extra flushed, sweaty. He wears his pants hitched too high, a gold short-sleeved shirt with the top two buttons undone, wiry gray hairs peeking out. Dark hair combed over to one side. "Why I don't get you something to go?"

"Jack—"

"I'll make you up a nice plate, and throw in some apple pie too." His fat fingers rest delicately on the edge of the table. All around us gray and bald heads, and wrinkled faces turn our way. Eyes peering through thick eyeglasses. This is their entertainment, better than TV. A new song comes on. My baby love, my baby love.

"We came here to eat lunch," Mamaw says.

"Lettie, I'll wrap everything up for you. It's on the house."

Brian wobbles when he stands, like an old man needing assistance. "Let's just go. I'm not hungry."

Mamaw slowly moves out from behind the booth, heaves her purse over her shoulder, and faces Jack.

"I won't forget this," she says. "Don't you think I'll forget."

My heart drums inside my chest. Here we are again, everyone staring.

Brian goes out the door first, followed by me, then Mamaw. Then the three of us are outside in the bright sunlight, blinking, like we've just walked out of a movie theater. The town looks small and rundown and pathetic. Soon, I'll be going to a place that is beautiful and free and wild, where you can't look out at the sky without seeing the ocean. I won't miss Chester at all. I'll forget everything and everyone as I smell the salty air and feel the cold spray of the waves.

"You want to go over to Madison? We could go to Wendy's for hamburgers and Frosties," Mamaw says. "You like Frosties."

"I'm tired," Brian says. "I just want to go home."

Mamaw looks disappointed, but she doesn't try to convince him. I'm relieved we're leaving. It's not just that it's embarrassing because somebody might say something or look at us funny, or storm out of a restaurant. It's that when I'm around Brian, everything feels sad and tense, like we're stuck wandering around in a glass house—one wrong move and the walls will shatter. I don't know how to make him feel better. I don't know what to say to him.

As we start to cross the street, a red pickup rolls up. The driver, probably around Brian's age, turns toward us. He's wearing an Eagles baseball hat and aviator sunglasses, and his buddy in the passenger seat says, "That's him."

"Hey, faggot!" The driver throws something out the window, and then takes off—tires squealing, wild laughter.

Brown cola and chips of ice run down my brother's face. He stands very still, with the weapon the man threw—a large paper cup, empty now of its contents—crumpled at his feet.

"Oh," Mamaw says. I've never seen her look like this. She looks as old as those dim, dusty people in Dot's. Her face trembles with what must be rage, but her voice sounds a thousand years old—faint, warbling, broken. "Oh, honey."

Brian wipes his face with his shirttail and doesn't say a word. He climbs in the backseat of the Queen's Ship, hunkered down so nobody can see him, and Mamaw starts the engine. I stare out the window at this town of strangers and don't feel anything at all.

＊

After everyone has gone to bed, I sneak out of the house. Nick is waiting for me by the concession stand. I'm not crying, but I know I look bad.

"What's wrong?" he asks, eyes big.

We sit down on the ground, next each other, and Nick hands me a cigarette. He patiently runs his hand up and down my leg, waiting for me to speak. After a few puffs, I catch a buzz, feel calmer. I tell him about this afternoon.

"Nobody has asked me what I think about my brother going on TV, and they don't listen to me when I tell them I want to leave," I say.

Nick rests his arm around me, and I breathe in his scent of smoke and boy-sweat. He tells me he's been pinching things from his father, things he'll never notice are gone—a couple of old watches, his wedding band. When the time is right, he'll take the roll of cash that his father hides under his mattress.

"What about you? Can you get anything?" he asks.

"I think so." It will be easy to steal from my grandmother, though the thought makes my neck hot. I do my best to ignore it. "When will we go?"

"Soon. A couple of weeks," he says.

"That's so far away."

"We need to have enough money, and it's gotta be a time when my old man isn't breathing down my neck. I could barely get out of the house tonight."

Nick says we'll take a Greyhound. Maybe we'll keep going, all the way up the Pacific coast line, until we're in Canada, another country.

"You'll finish high school," he says. "And I'll find a job."

"Doing what?"

"I'm good with motorcycles," he says.

Nick says he better get back—his dad has been on a warpath. He leaves me with a couple of cigarettes, kisses me softly, and then struts off into the night. I stretch out under the stars and practice blowing smoke rings. I'm not afraid anymore. We have a plan. I wonder how long it will take my parents to notice I'm gone, and what they'll do about it once they realize. Will they come after me, or forget about me, the way they did with Brian?

At SeaWorld, after the show, I waited in line to touch Shamu. Kid after kid petted her. But when it was my turn, the killer whale suddenly dove beneath the surface, out of reach. I knew the truth: she didn't want to be there, no matter how nice everyone was. The trainers, dressed in their tight wetsuits, swam with Shamu, they balanced on top of her head, they gave her kisses and hugs—they loved the whale, but they wouldn't let her go.

Sharon

"**A**re you sure you want to do this?" I ask.

Lettie and I sit across from each other at the kitchen table, light cigarettes. Sadie comes up and rests her head on Lettie's knee, and Lettie scratches her behind the ears.

"If you'd asked me this a few weeks ago, you probably could have convinced me not to. But things have changed." As Lettie reaches for the ashtray, her plastic bracelets rattle against the table top.

"You mean what happened at church?"

"All of it. The way people are acting, all this mudslinging," Lettie says. "Spreading stuff about us. Telling lies. Those people at Dot's. The nerve—"

"It'll calm down," I say, using Travis's words. "But this is going to stir everything up again."

Yesterday, Wayne came over to tell us to call it off, as if we have any say in it. He stood on our front porch—he wouldn't come in, didn't want to breathe the air in our house—and complained about the TV people calling him and everyone else in the family, trying to set up interviews. They've been calling here too. Travis warned us not to say a word to anyone.

"Don't let Mom go on that damn show," Wayne said.

"She won't," Travis said.

"The hell she won't."

Wayne's right, of course. Travis asked me to please talk to his mother one last time, but there is nothing I can say that will change her mind. The TV crew is supposed to arrive today. For everyone else, it's the most exciting thing that's happened in Chester since the football team went to the state championship in 1970. Not for us. Our house is a den of dread.

"I won't forget the people who have turned on me," Lettie says, excited. "The other night, I went to Bingo, and not a single one of them would sit with me. Not a single one!"

"You think going on TV is going to make things better?"

Lettie purses her lips in a grim line, like she shouldn't have to say a word, I should just understand. "I don't see how it could get any worse," she says. "I know it's not easy for you either. What people are saying."

Maybe she's right. It can't make things any worse. Can it? Today I called in sick because the office has become unbearable—Marjorie with her latex gloves, and Dave barely speaking to me. I finally asked him to look at Brian's teeth, to give him a partial denture. "I can't see him, you know that, Sharon," he said. "You know what our patients would say." Nobody needed to know, I argued, we could do it after hours. He said his hands were tied. Like everyone else, he's afraid of my son, but even more worried about what others will say. Patients stand back from my desk as if they're scared I'll breathe on them—people I've known for twenty years. I overheard Marjorie talking to a patient the other day, and she said, "I don't care how much they clean it, I wouldn't stick my big toe in that pool."

Lettie takes a long drag, and we both watch the cigarette smoke leave her mouth as if it holds the answers.

"Well, you might as well know. I'm the one who told her," Lettie says.

"Told who?"

"I called the number that's always on at the end of her show. I called her after that woman kicked him out of the pool." Lettie's voice warbles, like she's going to cry, but she's smiling. "Never thought they'd pick us. This is our chance, Sharon."

Chance for what? Brian looks worse each day. He's lost too much weight, and has trouble walking up and down the stairs. He says his legs hurt, but doesn't say much else—doesn't complain.

But Lettie looks at me with such hope that I find myself agreeing. I remember how I felt that day at the swimming pool, for just a moment: I saw my son floating on his back, and he looked so peaceful. For a few seconds, I didn't care what anyone else thought; I just wanted him to be happy.

I don't know what to do with myself. It's just me and Sadie. Travis is at work, and Jess, who barely speaks to any of us, went on a run. Brian is over at Lettie's.

When the phone rings again, I remember Travis's warning, but I don't care—I pick up.

"Sharon."

I freeze. It's her. She's left messages on the machine, but this is the first time we've spoken. Her voice is strangely familiar and intimate, a voice I only know from TV.

Naomi wants to interview me.

"I'm not interested." I add, "Please."

"If people see you with your son on TV, they'll think differently about all this, they really will."

I could sit down with her and spill all my feelings, just like people do on her show. Cry in front of the whole town. Why in the world would I subject myself to that? I hang up. When the phone rings again, I don't answer.

How quickly things can change, how fast the ground can shift.

The moon is a cool sliver. Behind me, the house is hemmed in by darkness. I've already said so many prayers. I walk among the dark trees. Look up at the late summer sky, the scattered points of light. The air feels too thick and heavy, the night loud with the drumming of insects, shattering any illusion of peace.

The talk was already there. We just pretended not to hear it.

And now?

Talk spreads fast.

The tip of my cigarette burns, a red eye in the dark.

The paper didn't print his name, but everyone knew. And now, the story will be on TV. Earlier, a TV van parked outside of our house. It's been spotted all around town. I grind out the last of the cigarette against the trunk of an old tree. A flimsy cloud slides over the gold moon. There is no quiet. Keening and clattering and buzzing.

Brian

Well, good morning. It's 7:30. Too damn early. I'm at my grand-mother's, upstairs in the spare room. Stayed here last night.

In a couple days, I'll sit down with Naomi.

I can't back out now. Mamaw is wound up. She's been cleaning the house for days. In fact, I bet she's already up, mopping floors. She wants this house to shine.

I probably shouldn't have called Naomi back. The last thing I want to do is get on TV to talk about AIDS. Of course, it's the last thing my parents want. And what will this to do Jess? She'll never forgive me.

Last night, Annie and I talked on the phone for a long time. She's proud of me. Said Shawn would be too.

You're getting your fifteen minutes of fame, better make them count, that's what Shawn would say.

Maybe things will get better, like my grandmother believes. Can they get any worse? Those fuckers throwing the Coke, the look on my grand-mother's face. I thought people were better than that—they might hurt me, but they wouldn't say anything in front of her. Now I know.

Yesterday, she drove us through town, on the hunt for the TV crew. Outside of Dot's, we saw a flash of big red hair. "She's here," Mamaw shouted. She wanted to pull over immediately, but I felt too anxious. Too many people. They probably wouldn't have said anything to me, not with Naomi around—she's like my protection, my bodyguard—but still I had no desire to go back there, not after what happened. We'll get our chance, I told her.

I can't believe I'm going on TV looking like this. I hate the way I look. My ass is nothing but bones and slack skin. I used to have a great ass. Look how pale I am. No matter how much makeup Naomi's people put on me, it won't hide the truth.

Fuck. I don't care. I'm tired. I'm just so fucking tired.

Earlier today, while Mamaw went to the grocery store—she's worried she won't have enough food for Naomi and her crew tomorrow, even though I tried to tell her it's not likely they'll stick around for supper— there was a knock at the front door. I was apprehensive to answer—this stupid town has me on edge. But it sounded too polite to be a threat. Maybe it was Naomi, showing up early.

I peeked through the curtain. Andrew stood there, grinning foolishly, his hair perfectly coiffed. I opened the door and asked what he was doing.

He said he was close by and wanted to check on me. He was lying. You're here because you want to meet Naomi, I said.

Well, she ought to interview me, he says.

You weren't even there, I told him. You don't even live in Chester.

He said that didn't matter, she should interview him because he was on my side. And, it would be good to get another gay on her show. Except he didn't say the word gay. Guys like us, he said.

Andrew fluttered around my grandmother's kitchen. He poured a glass of water, and asked if he could make me something to eat. I told him I wasn't hungry. So, he made himself a sandwich. As he spread peanut butter on a slice of bread, he nonchalantly asked me about Naomi's plans. He wanted to know if she was spending the night.

Although Mamaw of course had offered her house, Naomi and her crew were staying at a hotel in Madison.

You know which one? he asked.

I told him I didn't.

Must be the Day's Inn, he says. That's the only nice one we've got. Then he rested his hands on the table, his nails neatly trimmed and manicured, and I remembered his hand on my dick. A heat shot straight to my face, but nothing stirred in my jeans. I looked away.

When will it be on TV? Andrew asked.

I told him I didn't know. Probably it would air in a week or two.

Andrew sipped his water, lingering, maybe hoping Naomi Cook would show up early with her microphone. I noticed the puffiness under his eyes, the lines around his mouth. He's older than me by twelve years, but he still looks better—healthy, living. He caught me staring.

You okay, baby?

Him saying that word—it nearly broke me open. I heard Shawn. I heard Annie. I heard every man who ever kissed me. Andrew just smiled, as if I didn't look a bit hideous.

He asked if I needed anything.

I shook my head.

You know, if you ever need to go to the doctor or something, I can take you, he said.

I thanked him, but told him not to worry. He licked peanut butter from his fingers. I tried to explain: You don't want to get involved with this. Believe me. My boyfriend—Shawn—well, it's just hard.

He asked if I was with him when he died.

I said I was. Andrew looked like he wanted to ask more questions, but I didn't want to talk anymore about me or Shawn. I tried to turn the tables.

Tell me the truth, was it hard for you growing up around here? Is it hard now?

Andrew didn't laugh or make some sarcastic comment, like he's prone to doing. He pressed his perfectly manicured hand over mine, and answered me with just his eyes—wearied and pained, and a beautiful shade of brown.

It's not easy, you know that, he says. But we'll be okay.

※

Here I am, still at my grandmother's. Missing Annie. Missing Shawn. Missing New York, and the way things used to be. Purple light turning to night. The gloaming, the most beautiful and saddest part of the day.

Sometimes, during the thick, oppressive New York summers, my body would crave the sound of crickets, the smell of honeysuckle, the green hills. Homesickness for the place I thought I'd never see again. I'd stand at a window looking out at a city that was never dark, and then a man, Shawn, or a stranger, or a lover, would call me back to bed, and I could find home there: an earlobe, a crease in the stomach, a shiver of breath.

It feels like a dream, sometimes, the men I loved, and who loved me too.

This was always Shawn's favorite time of day. He was a night owl. He stayed up late and slept late. I'd make a good vampire, he used to say, baring his teeth. I wish he was one. He could have drank my blood. We could have lived forever.

When Shawn died, the grief stunned me. I'd never known death, not like that—someone so close to me, someone I'd had inside me. His tongue, his dick, his fingers. After he died, I spent days in a drunken, drugged haze, and then more days in bed, listless. We had our entire lives ahead of us. I thought we'd travel the world. I'd make movies, he'd act in them. Why shouldn't we have those things?

Listen, what I told Andrew, it's not true.

Shawn wanted me to record his death, but what he really wanted was for me to be there.

I wasn't.

At the ER, the white woman at the front desk would not check him in. He was burning up, sweating, sick. She said he had to wait, that there were others who were in line before him. She asked him how he would pay for it. She was judging him, I knew, because he was black, and poor, and gay. I waited with him in the hallway, hot with rage, but when finally they took him away, I left. I walked the city streets, smoking, scared.

The truth is, I hardly visited him. He was in the hospital for two weeks. He had a lot of visitors. His friends and lovers and ex-boyfriends, and Annie, and all his admirers. I went a few times, but I couldn't bear to look at him. It terrified me, how sick he looked, the tubes and the beeping machines and the stink of death in the air.

I stayed out of the room as much as possible. I was getting a goddamn coffee when he took his last breath.

He must have been so scared.

The truth is, it isn't just that I couldn't look at him. I hated how the doctors and nurses looked at *me*. I was ashamed—ashamed to be gay. I betrayed him, like Judas, but without a kiss, even. I didn't put my arms around him and tell him everything would be okay.

Andrew says he'll be here for me, but I know how things change once you're facing death. Shawn died alone. Why should it be any different for me? It's what I deserve.

Sharon

I didn't think Travis would want to watch, but he turns on the TV without a word. Brian is over at Lettie's, where he's been for most of the week. Jess blasts music from her room. She won't talk to any of us—not even Lettie—because of the TV show. She may be the only person in Chester not watching.

I was hoping the producers would change their mind and not air the episode, but the theme music starts and Naomi comes out on stage and behind her runs a video of Chester: a rundown trailer park, the boarded-up IGA, a red barn, a field of clover and weeds, and Buckeye Creek curving around the hills. Then, downtown: our old church, the dentist office, the closed Ben Franklin where I used to buy school supplies for Brian and Jess. A small town, a broken town. It looks trashy and poor, and I feel embarrassed, seeing it on TV. This is where we come from, this is who we are.

Naomi asks, "What happens when a son comes back home, and he's sick with the most feared disease of our time?" A close-up on the empty swimming pool, the water so still, untouched.

Jittery, I light a cigarette. When the TV crew was in town, people were on their best behavior. There weren't as many prank calls, or people driving by yelling. Ever since Naomi left, things have been strangely quiet. The town holding a collected breath, waiting to see themselves on television.

The scene shifts to Lettie's kitchen.

"Good God," Travis says.

It's a shock to see Lettie sitting across from Naomi, her good china coffee cups in front of them. She's also put down the tablecloth that she only uses for special occasions—yellow, pink, blue flowers over a white weave.

"Well, I guess Mom got her chance to be on TV," Travis says. He still can't believe that he has lost control of the story, or that he never had control.

Lettie wears her favorite pink blouse with a white cardigan, and clip-on earrings. Her hair, newly dyed, shines in the sunlight. She went all the way to Madison to get her hair done. She's boycotting the beauty shop in town, the one she's been going to for thirty-some years, because she heard the owner was "spreading lies" about Brian.

Naomi, in a smart navy blazer, smiles at Lettie. She must use hot rollers every night because her brassy red hair is fluffy and airy, and held perfectly into place. Big silver shell-shaped earrings shimmer in the light, and her lips do too. She's wearing enough foundation and blush to hide the wrinkles, but I know she's no spring chicken. Naomi Cook was a newscaster before she had her own show, all through the '70s.

"Lettie, how did you feel when you found out Brian has AIDS?" Naomi asks in a hushed tone, as if it's impolite to say the word.

Lettie isn't wearing her glasses, too vain for that, and her eyes are clear and blue—she doesn't carry around the guilt or shame that makes a person look so old, tired, hurting. "Well, I already knew before they told me. I knew, but I didn't say anything."

"You're a religious woman. Do you accept homosexuality?"

Lettie looks surprised. She stutters, stops. "I love my grandson," she says.

"But, do you think it's wrong? I mean, many in this town have said that AIDS is a punishment—"

"Well, I don't believe that."

Naomi tilts her head, practiced concern. "But, do you accept homosexuality?"

Lettie fiddles with the cross on her necklace, and looks shockingly like she might cry. Naomi often makes her guests cry, but I didn't think she'd get to Lettie.

"Jesus loves everyone."

"But, do you think—"

Lettie cuts her off. She's composed herself. No tears fall.

"Who am I to judge?" Lettie looks directly into the camera. "Everyone in Chester must think they're God, by the way they're acting. Well. They maybe ought to stop talking about the speck in their neighbor's eyes and take care of that log in their own."

The faces on TV grow bigger and brighter, as if they will shatter the screen. Lettie and I have never talked about Brian's homosexuality. I've never talked to anyone about it, ever. Travis pops his knuckles. His gay son on TV—it's humiliating, it's shattering. I could go sit next to him, put my hand on his knee, make promises. But I bring the cigarette to my lips and watch Lettie, the only one in this family—other than my son—who is not afraid.

"Have you and your family thought about moving somewhere else that's more accepting?" Naomi asks. "Maybe to a city?"

"I've lived here all my life. I tell you what, this has shown me who my true friends are." Lettie lightly slaps the table. "I'm not going anywhere, and neither is my grandson."

During commercial break, Travis and I don't speak or move. From upstairs, Jess's music pounds through the walls. I'm waiting for the other shoe to drop—for a knock at the door, for something to come flying through the window. Sadie looks up and thumps her tail.

When the show comes back on, the scene has changed to Naomi standing with Wanda Spellman in front of the swimming pool. Looking sloppy in a T-shirt, shorts, and flip-flops, Wanda takes a long time telling the story, adding flourishes and lies. I squeeze the inside skin of my arms, relieved to feel physical pain.

"I tried to reason with him," she says. "But he wouldn't get out. I couldn't let him contaminate the swimming pool. I had to make a quick decision."

"She makes me sick," I say. Travis doesn't respond. We never talk about that day, but I think about it all the time. Everyone staring at our son. Wanda herding him out. The police. It stunned us into silence. Now, I think, it was a hot day. Why shouldn't he go for a swim?

The scene changes again. Wearing a business-style dress with a wide belt, Naomi walks briskly into Dot's. She talks to a handful of customers who promise they don't hate Brian, they just don't want him living here. Judy Dawson, our postmaster, who I've never seen wear a smidge of makeup, has dolled herself up with chartreuse green eye shadow and red lipstick, and she's let her hair down.

"He should have stayed in New York, where people are used to that kind of thing. His parents can't get him the care he needs here in Chester," she says. "They know better."

An old leather-faced man eating a stack of blueberry pancakes calls Naomi "ma'am" and listens carefully to her questions. He uses his knife and fork to cut the pancakes into impossibly tiny pieces. "The chickens are coming home to roost," he says. "You can't go against God."

The owner of Dot's Diner, Jack McCarthy, looks like he'd rather be anywhere else. He's standing next to the cash register, his hair slicked back, his shirt buttoned higher than he usually wears it. When Naomi asks him about kicking Brian out of the restaurant, he shakes his head. "No, ma'am, it didn't happen like that. I didn't kick him out."

"Didn't you make him leave?" Naomi raises her eyebrows.

"I don't have nothing against that boy, but customers were complaining. And, well, I know Lettie Jackson. She's a good woman, but she likes to stir things up. There wasn't no reason for her come in here with him. She wanted to get a rise."

Lettie will never step foot in Dot's again—none of us will. Lettie will do it out of loyalty to Brian, and Travis won't go because he's embarrassed. What is my reason? I take a long drag on the cigarette, wishing the electricity would cut out all across Chester. I want us to sit in the dark and hear nothing except our own breath.

Two young men appear on the screen and for a second I'm confused. I know them, don't I? Travis groans. Shocked, I watch my nephews, Matthew and Kyle. They're in a booth, wearing stiff, new shirts. Wayne didn't want Lettie to go on TV, but here is his son and Paul's son. They answer Naomi's questions with controlled, quiet voices. Yes, they're kin. Yes, they grew up together.

"I can't believe their nerve," I say.

Travis moves up to the edge of the couch, his hands balled in fists, the knuckles little white eggs.

"I wouldn't let my little girl get in that pool if I'd been there, I can tell you that," Kyle says.

"We just want people to know what he's done has nothing to do with us," Matthew explains. "I'm not saying I want anything bad to happen to Brian and I don't think people should be mean to him. But don't blame our family. It's not our fault."

My father used to say everything gets worse before it gets better. But things never got better for him after my mother died. He held onto God in a small, miserly way, and hid himself in a duplex in Columbus. He used to say that my mother swept him off his feet. Maybe what he mistook for love was only heartache.

Only Anita Brewer, the church pianist, says we shouldn't leave town. "I don't know much about AIDS. But we're all God's children," she says. "And, they're a good family, good people."

The camera cuts to our church. Reverend Clay and Josh, both wearing ties, sit side-by-side. "He knew exactly what he was doing," Josh says. "He wanted people to notice. It was like he wanted to shove everything in our face. He wanted us to react."

Reverend Clay has styled his hair in a new way. It's slicked back and shiny, as if he just stepped out of the shower, his bald spot expanding under the thinning strands.

"Homosexuality doesn't belong in a town like this," he says. "That's for big cities."

On commercial break, the phone rings. We don't pick up. Advertisement after advertisement for products that could make our lives better. Cars, laundry detergent, coffee, vegetable soup.

When the show comes back on, they've returned to Lettie's kitchen, but now it's Naomi and Brian at the table like old friends. My son wears a bright blue dress shirt that Lettie must have bought him, and it floats around his arms, exposing his thin neck, his gaunt face. The earring embarrasses me. Couldn't he have taken it out just this once?

He tells his version of that day at the pool, speaking with ease, more articulate than anyone else who's spoken, enunciating his words. The camera doesn't make him nervous. But his brown teeth and the dark gap in front make him look like he's from the hills. I feel a screw spiraling into my chest. I should have taken him in to see Dave. I know what people think. But he's not disgusting. My son is not a monster.

"I think people are more scared of me being gay than they are about me having AIDS," Brian says.

"What do you mean?" Naomi asks.

As they talk, pictures of Brian—taken from Lettie's photo album—appear in the corner of the screen. Brian as a two-year-old with his hands in his birthday cake. A sixteen-year-old, sunglasses on, slouched in a lawn chair, grinning. A picture of him playing baseball, holding a trophy, posing with his glove.

"They're homophobic," he says. "That's why the government isn't doing anything. It's gay men dying, and drug addicts, and black people. Reagan could care less—"

Naomi interrupts, gently but firmly steering him back to Chester, the pool, the gossip and prank phone calls and meanness. "Let's not get into politics," she says.

Brian suddenly looks tired. "I don't really care what they say about me," he says softly. "But it's not just me they're hurting. It's my whole family."

The camera closes in on Naomi—her teeth so straight, so white. She's got a whole staff to make her look pretty. Nothing out of place. Her eyes are pale green, intense, knowing. Her voice drops conspiratorially.

"Brian, are you scared of dying?"

I pinch the soft skin under my arms. Brian looks right at me. "Yeah," he says. "I'm scared."

Jess

The green second hand on my watch ticks by. It's past midnight. Nick is twenty minutes late. I sit on top of my duffle bag and change the tape in my Walkman. I'm practically shaking with adrenaline and excitement and fear, and I don't want the feeling to stop—because I know underneath the buzz, there is something big and still and sad, and it might just swallow me whole. Prince sings in my ears, and I think if he came to Chester, the town would explode in glitter. "Purple rain," he cries, "purple rain." I feel sorry for my brother, but I can't stay here.

My grandmother thought *On Location With Naomi* would make things better, but it only made everything a hundred times worse. Since the show aired, the phone calls won't stop. It's not just pranks, but other TV shows and newspapers calling to talk to my brother. We're famous, in a bad way. Last night, while we were all sleeping, someone spray-painted FAGGOT on the garage door. This morning, as I watched my father try to scrub the word away, I called Nick. "I can't wait anymore," I told him. My pockets burn with the one hundred and twenty dollars I stole—sixty from my grandmother's purse, forty slipped out of my father's billfold, and twenty from my mother's top dresser drawer.

I've already thought about what it will mean to be on the road with Nick. He'll want to have sex. I've always just accepted what my mother says, that you should wait until marriage. But what's marriage? I've never dreamed about it, not like Brandy White used to—she'd pour over catalogues, gush over wedding gowns. She already knew what kind of flowers she'd have (pink roses and purple tulips) and what color the bridesmaid dresses would be (lavender). I never cared about any of that and still don't. I want to be my own person. Josh Clay told us that pre-marital sex would lead to disgrace—we'd become sluts, or get pregnant, or kill our babies. We'd live on the streets selling ourselves.

I sling my duffle bag over my shoulder and walk up to the gas station on the corner, staying away from the road and close to the line of trees. I've never been to Nick's, and I'm not sure which trailer he lives in. Nobody drives by.

A big part of me regrets not meeting Naomi, a real celebrity. I could have shaken her hand and sat down with her at my grandmother's kitchen table. I could have told everyone what I was thinking. But nobody wants to know that. My grandmother taped the show, of course, but I haven't watched it yet. I don't think I ever will.

The dim, greenish light at the closed Shell station shines over four pumps. I dig a quarter out of my pocket and punch the numbers on the pay phone. I'm about to hang up when a deep voice says hello.

"Is Nick there?"

"Who is this?"

I don't answer.

"Is this that Jackson girl? Listen, he's gone back to his mom's. I don't want my son getting mixed up in—"

I hang up.

He's gone.

Moths fly toward the street lamps, burning their wings. I don't let myself cry. Maybe I knew all along I'd never go anywhere.

The strap of my duffle bag digs into my shoulder. I use my key to open the front door, trying to be quiet, but Brian hears me.

"Who's there?" he says in a hushed voice.

He is the last person I want to see, but I walk to the top of the stairs. In the basement, all of the lights are turned on and the room blazes like it's on fire. Brian looks up, holding onto the banister, an old crocheted afghan draped over his shoulders.

"Jess, it's you." He looks relieved, then confused. "You going somewhere?"

I remember my duffle bag. "No."

We're on the staircase, whispering. Brian's face shines with sweat, his hair matted down. I don't know what the disease is doing to him now or what it's going to do. I wish we could just walk back in time and start over. If I could, I would take away Naomi's show and the guy who threw the Coke and Wanda Spellman kicking him out of the pool and me telling Josh Clay, but most of all, I just want to take away this illness.

"Come here," Brian says.

I set down the bag and follow him downstairs. *Splash* is playing on TV. The volume is turned down too low to hear it, but I've seen it before. The mermaid, Daryl Hannah, crouches on a sidewalk in New York City, her long tailfin exposed, slapping sadly against the cement, while her boyfriend, Tom Hanks, stands back from her as reporters snap pictures. He refuses to help her—he's too devastated by her secret, her lie.

Brian pats a space next to him on the couch, but I stay standing. He's shivering, rocking back and forth, eyes wild like he just woke up from a nightmare.

"What's wrong?"

"Night sweats. They happen sometimes. It's okay."

He doesn't look okay. I ask if he wants another blanket, and he shakes his head.

"Hey, remember when you couldn't sleep, we'd listen to records? You always wanted to hear 'The Prettiest Star.' It was like your lullaby." He's smiling, hopeful.

"I don't remember," I say, a lie.

Brian's smile cracks, and he seems unsure what to say next. He stops rocking, but he's still shaking—his entire body, even his face jiggles. Sadie sits on the floor in front of him, leaning up against his legs. On

TV the mermaid is hooked to wires and stuck inside an aquarium, and scientists and government men in lab coats circle her, point and write things down.

"Jess, listen," Brian says. "I'm sorry."

"About what?"

"The pool. Just, all of it."

I know how the movie ends. If the mermaid stays too long on earth, she can't ever go back home. The government people and scientists and reporters will chase after her, and Tom Hanks, her love, tells her to save herself. So she dives into the ocean, and her legs transform into an iridescent tailfin. After a moment of hesitation, he plunges in after her—he gives up his life, his home, to be with her. They're free, but they'll never be the same.

"I'm the one who got you kicked out," I say. "It was me. I told Josh Clay you had AIDS."

Brian looks up, blue eyes burning, electric. It's like all the light in the room starts with him. His shivering has stopped. He is calm and cool. He speaks with kindness.

"People already knew, kiddo," he says. "It doesn't matter now."

He thinks I'm apologizing, but I'm not. I want to hurt him the way he has hurt our family. There is an ache behind my eyes.

"I wish you'd never come back," I say. "I wish you'd just leave."

Brian flinches, surprised. My heart beats wildly. I feel powerful and awful, like I just made the room go dark. I turn and walk away. My brother, except for Sadie at his feet and a beautiful mermaid on TV, is alone. He doesn't call me back.

Brian

Everything has changed.

I shouldn't have done the interview. Now the ugliness won't let up. I can't leave the house. People stare. They hate me because I'm gay. Because I'm sick. Because I'm here. The story isn't going away.

A few days ago, my mother lost her job. She says she quit voluntarily but I don't believe her. My little sister can't stand me. My grandmother hasn't said anything to me about friends she's lost, or how her own sons or grandchildren no longer come over. I'll never forget the look on her face when those fuckers threw that cup of soda.

There is no more hiding or pretending. It's coming for me. It's getting hard to eat. Sores sprouting inside my mouth. My joints ache, my legs. The pain emanates from my bones, my skin, my blood. I don't think I can even shoot much longer—holding the camera, even just setting it up on a tripod, takes too much out of me. There is so much more footage I wish I had gotten. Don't have any of my father. Not much of my mother either. She doesn't like to talk about the past. Most of it is just me, maybe too much.

Once you get sick, it's impossible to remember what it felt like in the Before. My body only knows what it feels now. I've spent the last few days just lying in bed. I can't sleep. Some days I flicker in and out of dreams. Remembering New York. Random things flash in my mind. A drag queen, kissing me. Shawn, on a dark stage, stepping into a spotlight. Masses of people trying to make it in a city that never sleeps. I can't wake up or I'm more awake than ever. I've thought about killing myself, but I don't know how—I don't have any pills, and maybe I'm too scared, too alive, too sad. I miss Shawn.

Last night changed everything. Last night showed me what I need to do, the only option.

I was on the couch, falling in and out of sleep, in and out of dreams. Then, a loud noise, like a crack of thunder, jolted me awake. Tires squealing. Sadie barking. Footsteps, doors opening, frightened voices. I hurried upstairs.

My father was running to the front door, holding his deer rifle, a look of pure panic on his face. My mother and Jess huddled together on the upstairs landing, my mother chanting, It's okay. Now Sadie was whining, pawing at the door. My father told us all to be quiet, to stay still. He cracked the door open, looked out. It's fine, he says. Nobody's here.

I followed him out to the front yard, and my mother and sister came outside too, all of us standing on the lawn in our pajamas in the dark. Across the street, the O'Malleys' light was on. They didn't open their door to come out.

Still holding his gun, my father walked over to his broken-down Chevy, its tail pointed toward the garage. He circled around to the front of the truck. My mother asked what was wrong. For a moment I couldn't get my breath.

Be careful, my father says. There might be glass.

Under the moonlight, I could see what he was looking at: a perfectly round bullet hole through the front windshield, a web of cracks blooming out from its center.

Someone shot it, I said, feeling a need to state the obvious.

My mother wanted to call the cops, but my father said not to bother. It's just stupid kids, he said. It would be worse to involve the police, and what can they do anyway?

The only way for my family to get their lives back is for me to go.

It's time.

I've packed, I'm ready. A few pairs of underwear, some clothes, toothbrush. My camera, of course. I don't need much. I'll come back for the tapes, maybe, or write a letter to make sure they get in Annie's hands. She can edit out if I said anything too mean or too personal. Or maybe not. I also shot short videos that are like letters. Goodbyes. All the things I can't say. One for Annie, one for Jess. One for Mamaw. One for my mother. One for my father. Those, I can't ever watch. But I spent the day reviewing a lot of what I've filmed since I've been here, all this documentation. Everything that ever was. What will be left? Who will watch? Maybe my family, or maybe strangers. Glimpses of a life. A death. Maybe one day, people will want to know. Maybe, you.

We live our lives not realizing which moments are special or which are ordinary—what will we remember, what memories will we try to grab onto, to hold close? All of these moments that make up a life.

I wish I could believe the way my grandmother does. Even Shawn, who did not believe in God, claimed to feel the energy of the dead. I want to see his ghost. I want him to talk to me. I want to tell him I'm sorry. Forgive me.

One more look back—no, everything will turn to salt. My chest burns. My bones hurt.

Infected waters. Infected blood.

I lost my lover. My friends.

I could have swam to the bottom. Could have drowned in the Hudson.

But I came back here. Why? Why does anyone go home? You come back to be seen, to be accepted, and to be loved.

Time to sign off, my friends.

Ciao.

All the
Young Dudes

Sharon

I stop outside his door, listening, wishing for the sound of a record playing, his voice, his cough, anything. The pain loops around my heart, tightens. What I should have said, or done.

When Brian told us he was moving to New York, we didn't believe he'd really go. Who went there, except for people on TV or in the movies? He'd been working at the IGA, stocking shelves, bagging groceries, saving money. Enough for a bus ticket. The first few weeks, months, he was gone, I couldn't sleep. All I could think about was my son out on the streets. Travis kept telling me, It'll be all right, he'll come back home.

This time, Brian didn't warn us. He went in the middle of the night. In the morning, I found a note, stuck underneath the butter dish, and my knees buckled.

Still, I wasn't surprised. The disgusting graffiti. Me losing my job—I knew it was coming. Patients told Dave they didn't feel safe around me, and he suggested I take some time off "until things settle down." I'll never go back. Like Lettie, I won't forget who was on our side. All of it was taking a toll on my son, but I didn't know how to fix things, how to make them better, how to reassure him. The last straw was the gunshot through Travis's windshield.

I'm sorry I brought this on you, he wrote.

I called Annie, but no, she promised, he wasn't in New York. He was still in Ohio. Staying with a friend, she said. That's all she would tell me—said she didn't know his name, or where he lived. She was lying. What friends does my son have?

"Tell me where he is," I demanded.

"He's fine, Sharon. I promise you, he's okay."

Lettie, who's watched too many made-for-TV movies, said we should file a missing person's report. Before we could, Brian called.

He spoke softly but firmly. "Don't worry, I'm just staying here for a little bit, until things calm down. Don't look for me." He added, "I'm fine, please, believe me."

The receiver burned in my hand. "Come back home," I said.

I listened to his even breaths, but I was too late. "Bye, Mom," then the brutal beeping dial tone assaulting my ear. He was gone. Again.

"Maybe we should think about moving," I say, though I'm not sure I mean it. We can't leave, not without Brian. But if he comes back? I'm thinking about fresh starts, about wiping the slate clean.

Travis looks up. "What?"

"I'm worried about Jess," I say.

Although I spoke to the principal and he assured me that he and the teachers would make Jess feel welcome, I know they can't, or won't, stop every kid from saying something stupid and mean. Jess hasn't said anything about school, or about Brian leaving. She won't talk to me. She hides under those headphones, pretending she can't hear me, or leaves the house, running, her legs taking her away from us.

"We can't just run away. Anyway, things are getting better," Travis says.

He truly believes things will turn around. Yesterday, he finally succeeded in getting rid of the graffiti on the garage door. The first time he tried painting over it, the red paint just bled through. Various cleaners didn't work. But this most recent coat of paint took care of it. "Good as new," Travis said, pleased. Clean slate.

"Listen," he says now, "I talked to Wayne. He's having a get together over at his house this weekend. He wants us to come."

"You're kidding."

"He does this every Labor Day."

"So everything's okay now?" I ask. "Between you and Wayne?"

Travis turns back to the TV. A player stands at the plate, bat pulled back in anticipation, knees bent, waiting. "He's my brother," he says.

The player swings and the ball flies through the air. I don't state the obvious: Yes, and Brian is your son. The words pierce my tongue like thin hooks, holding it still. After someone shot at our house, Travis said everything would be okay. He didn't believe anyone truly wanted to kill us. And he was right—not us, but Brian. They came to kill my son.

Travis would never say this aloud, but he's convinced himself that Brian is better off wherever he is, that he's getting the care he needs, that he did this for himself, not for us. He's telling himself an easier kind of story. Maybe Travis shouldn't have painted over the garage door at all—then every day we would have to look at that hideous word and remember what they think of us, what they think of our son. I don't want to start over, I realize. I just want Brian to come back.

Jess looks worried. "You're not coming?"

"No, I'm going to get some stuff done around the house." I make sure I smile. "You have fun, okay?"

"Let's go, kiddo," Travis says, his hand on her shoulder.

Maybe it is the right thing—let things get back to normal. Even Lettie is going to Wayne's cookout. To keep the peace, she told me. A few of Lettie's old friends, the ones who turned their backs on her, have been trying to make amends. With them, Lettie doesn't budge. When Edna Davis came over with a green bean casserole, a peace offering, Lettie refused it. "Some things you can't forget," she said, but family is different. Or maybe it's not.

After my father moved back to Columbus, he preached for a few years, and then retired to live out the rest of his life in that cramped, dark duplex. In the beginning, I visited every couple of months, then less as time went on. The kids didn't enjoy going. There was nothing for them to do, and they preferred Lettie over him. They didn't know him.

I didn't either. Without my mother to care for or a sermon to prepare, he was a stranger. He sat in that recliner, watching the news and game shows and westerns. Pictures of my beautiful mother all over the house. I had no idea what to say to him.

He died from a heart attack when Brian was a sophomore. Jess, a toddler, didn't go to the funeral, but Brian wore a tie and stood solemnly between me and Travis. The funeral was small and dismal. Church members in Columbus, and his sister, a shriveled raisin who I'd only ever seen a handful of times, stood in the back. My father left all his belongings to me. It wasn't much. I sold the duplex and almost everything in it. I kept his Bible, photographs, and my mother's thin gold necklace.

I went back to Chester with my husband and son, and closed the lid on that part of my life. I belonged to the Jacksons now, and I knew they would always be there. For so long I'd dreamed of the perfect life, and now I had it. I tried to forget my mother's sadness and my father's futile preoccupation with making her happy, and I held my family close, believing, foolishly, that we were protected from the strange, lonely grief that had taken such a heavy toll on my parents.

Where is my son?

I've driven all over Chester and Madison, searching. I wonder if Lettie has had any dreams or seen any signs, but I'm afraid to ask. The nights are rough—I toss and turn, and when I do close my eyes, I see him, not a dream, but actually him: standing there and glaring, arms crossed. I'm scared I've lost him forever.

I pick up a dust rag and wander the rooms, but there is nothing to do. The house is clean. The grass mowed. The garage door painted. Here I am, and my son is not. Across town, my family holds its annual cookout. The women congregate in the kitchen cooking and gossiping, and the men drink beer and tell the same old stories over the fire pit. Nieces and nephews, grandchildren and great-grandchildren, they'll all be there. No one will mention Brian, and, I realize, that's what I'm most scared of, that everything will be the same after all.

Jess

I dreaded going back to school, but at least it gets me away from our sad house, where every day my mother cries. No one sits with me at lunch, and when I'm walking down the hall, I hear kids cough "AIDS" or "faggot" behind me, then laugh. They make a big deal of me drinking at the water fountain, and one day in the bathroom I overheard a group of girls talking about my brother and how they heard he went to church and smeared his germs all over the pew, trying to give everyone AIDS. I don't tell any of this to my parents. When my mother asks how school went, I say "Fine." Mrs. Lansky, my English teacher, asked in a pitying voice, "Is everything okay?" I told her it's fine. Everything is fine, fine, fine.

Sometimes I see Josh Clay—Mr. Clay, now, the guidance counselor—in the hallways. He wears pleated pants and button-down shirts, and he high fives the students he likes. He wants me to come by his office to talk. "Tell me if anyone is mean to you—that won't be tolerated," he says. But I won't go to see him, not unless they make me. When he says hi, I keep walking, head down, my Trapper Keeper pressed to my chest. I like it best when I'm invisible, a ghost sliding through the hallways.

We don't go to church anymore, but one evening Reverend Clay came over to the house, and he and my father talked on the front porch as if they were friends. My mother busied herself in the kitchen and would not come out.

No one in the family comes by and we hardly ever see the neighbors, except one day Deb Dennison brought over store-bought doughnuts, and she and my mother talked for a few minutes on the porch. I don't know what they said. The doughnuts were stale.

Sometimes I miss Nick, and I think about how we should be living on the coast right now, watching whales migrate. He called a few times right after he left, but it's weird on the phone—we don't know what to say to each other. We go to different schools, we like different music. We don't talk about my brother. We don't talk about running away. A childish fantasy, a different life.

One good thing has happened. The track coach, Ms. Sizemore, saw me running through town this summer, and asked me to join the cross country team. I missed out on the summer training, but she said it's okay since I was training on my own—I just didn't know it at the time. It's the first time our high school has had a team. My teammates, all upperclassmen, mostly ignore me. It doesn't bother me. It's not like soft-ball where you have to work together. We run through town and the woods by the school and along the Buckeye. When I'm running, my thoughts are clearer than when I'm at school or at home. Sometimes I think about Brian and wonder where he is and if he's okay. Sorrow pushes out through my hot breath. My muscles burn with the truth. I miss my brother. I think about how one of the last things I ever said to him was that I wished he'd never come back.

On my walk home, a green hatchback, with windows rolled down and blasting John Cougar Mellencamp, pulls up to the curb. I keep my head down, annoyed at myself for not wearing my Walkman. The headphones block out taunts and threats, and make me feel invisible. Without them, I'm a target.

"Jess, hey Jess."

A girl's voice. I look up. Angie Ray leans out the window, and Brett Wilson, the one who embarrassed my brother at the pool, sits behind the wheel, wearing sunglasses with orange reflective glass. In the back-seat, Brandy White cuddles up to Mike Kirby and pretends not to see me.

"Is your brother dead yet?" Angie calls over the music. Their laughter tumbles out of the car. I see their open mouths, their joy. I keep walking. The skies are blue, the sun shining. Don't cry, don't cry.

"Are you gay?" Angie yells.

Then one of the guys, I don't know which: "Don't come back to school, faggot weirdo!"

Brett guns the engine and they take off, their laughter echoing all through me.

I get my Walkman out of my bag and slip the headphones over my burning ears and push play. I want to blame Brian for everything, but it's not that easy. What did he do that was wrong? I walk over the bridge and look down. Things could have gone differently. Now it's too late. The Buckeye looks muddy and still, like it's frozen in time, but I know it's moving. It runs from here into the Ohio River, which eventually spills into the Mississippi, which goes all the way to the Gulf of Mexico where there are over twenty-five species of whales and dolphins. I turn up the volume and Bowie sings in my ear. Love, you're not alone.

A couple of days later, when I get home from practice, my parents are still at work or out somewhere. I let Sadie out the back door, and pour a glass of OJ. Even when they're home, the house is weirdly quiet. Since Brian left, it's like we're nervous about making any noise, like we don't want anyone, even ourselves, to know we're still here.

I go downstairs and turn on the TV to distract myself, but all I can think about is practice. I couldn't find my rhythm today, and had a hard time breathing. Coach said not to worry, everybody has bad days. But I know who to blame—today, after the bell rang for lunch, Josh Clay stopped me in the hallway. "Jessie," he said. "I need to talk to you. Can you come after school?"

"I can't, I have practice."

He saw the brown lunch sack in my hand. "I brought mine too. Let's have lunch together." He smiled, showing me his big white teeth. "We can eat in my office."

I didn't want to go, but he put his hand on my shoulder and guided me down the hallway. I saw a few kids glance at us. His hand felt too heavy and soft at the same time. When we got to his office, he opened the door. I just stood there.

"Am I in trouble or something?"

Josh's face wrinkled in concern. "No, of course not. It's just, well, we haven't really got a chance to talk, since everything—"

"I have some homework to do," I say. "For English class. I gotta go."

"Jessie," he said. As he stood in front of me, he moved his hand from my shoulder to my chin, cupping it and tilting my face up. He held his eyes on me. "Listen, someone told me that some of the older students were bothering you. Do you want to tell me about it?"

"No," I said. "Nothing happened."

His eyes, which looked lighter than I remembered, studied my face. I hated how his hand felt under my chin, like he was holding me still, a dog hooked to a leash. He said he'd been worried about me. "I heard that Brian left," he said. He didn't look sorry, but like he wanted me to tell him it wasn't his fault.

"I have to go," I said.

"My door is always open," he called after me. I kept walking, didn't look back. All through practice, I couldn't stop thinking about that day at the pool, how everyone stared at Brian, and how Josh Clay just stood there, gloating.

There's nothing on TV, and after a few more minutes, I turn it off. I haven't gone into Brian's room since he left. It feels wrong, worse than trespassing, like if I walk through the door, it means he will never come back. I do it anyway.

Dust floats around in the last light of the day. I plop into the beanbag chair and pull over a crate of records. I wish we still had the record of whale songs Brian checked out from the library all those years ago. They were so strange and eerie, like thin, warped, high-pitched calls, and not at all like the deep, slow, sonorous sounds I was expecting. I decide not to listen to anything. My brother is gone. I sit in the silence, and I wish I knew how to call him back.

At least now I get my grandmother to myself again. But she's not the same. Brian has been gone for three and a half weeks, and him leaving broke something in her that can't be fixed. She sits around with the TV on, smoking. She doesn't go to the mall, or to Bingo, or out to see her friends. She stares out the window, waiting for him to walk through the door.

But today when I go over, she's different. She's baking a cake. Country music plays on the radio.

"Why aren't you in school?"

"Teachers meetings. We have the day off."

Sunlight floods the room and bounces off the glass bottles and jar of marbles on the window sills. The cake sits, perfect and round, on a milk glass cake stand.

"What kind of cake is that?"

"Carrot." She takes a quick puff off her cigarette, followed by a swig of coffee, probably cold. Mamaw brews a pot of coffee when she wakes up and drinks it all day long, doesn't matter if it's cold or room temperature.

"I was just about to leave, but I'm glad you're here. You can come with me. Here, want to lick the spatula?" She hands me the bowl of white frosting with the spatula sticking out of it. "I'm going to fix my makeup."

After I hear her upstairs, I sneak a puff off her cigarette. I don't smoke much anymore. I lick the spatula, then use my finger to wipe up the last of the icing clinging to the sides of the bowl. I'm not on a diet anymore either. Coach says I need to eat more, so that I burn calories and run for longer and build up my stamina.

Mamaw comes back in the kitchen with reapplied lipstick, the heady stink of Aqua Net wafting off her. She's changed out of her house slippers into navy blue tennis shoes. She picks up her rings off the counter and slides them on her fingers. Acting more like the grandmother I know.

"Where are we going?"

"It's a surprise," she says.

She puts on her tortoise-shell sunglasses and locks the door behind her just as Edna Davis is getting out of her Oldsmobile, carrying a sack of groceries.

"Come on," Mamaw says sharply.

Edna, wearing a purple velour jogging suit, marches up to her house without saying a word. My grandmother pulls out onto the road, her rose-pink lips pressed together in a hard line. I don't think they'll ever make up.

The days are getting a little cooler, and the light has changed, turning the sky a deeper blue. We drive past the empty drive-in, and I wonder if they'll ever tear down the screen or just let it stand there and rot. I haven't been back since Nick left.

When I change the station from country to rock, Mamaw doesn't even notice. She chews spearmint gum and smokes a menthol, and every so often she lifts up her shoulders like she's caught a chill. She seems excited and nervous, acting the way she did when Naomi came to town.

She takes several turns, and then we're out in the country, going down a gravel road. "Look for number 624," she says.

I can't imagine any kind of good surprise out here. We pass trailers, falling-down barns. A homely horse tied to a tree. A bunch of wild-looking kids, shirtless, chase each other with sticks. Everyone here is dirt-poor, trailer trash. My mother wouldn't like this, I think. She'd tell me to make sure my door is locked.

"Here we are."

My grandmother pulls into a dirt driveway that leads up to a trailer home, as if it's the most perfectly normal thing to do. According to my brother, Mamaw used to go all over the county, places most Avon ladies wouldn't venture. But I don't see any boxes of beauty products in the backseat.

"What are we doing here?"

She takes off her sunglasses and looks at me with those blue eyes that are just like Brian's, just like my dad's.

"We've come for your brother."

"He's here?"

My grandmother opens her purse and drops in the keys. Her hands are shaking. She fusses in the mirror.

"How do you know?"

Satisfied with her makeup, she turns toward me, smiling.

"I did some detective work. I called Annie and after some cajoling, she told me his friend's name. Then I remembered that fellow who works at Sears. So I went over there a couple of times, but he wasn't at work. Then, last night, this Andrew called *me*. A sign. God was working His wonders."

She opens the car door before I can stop her. Why didn't we talk about this first? I get out, my Keds grinding the dry dirt, and my legs tighten like they want to sprint down this gravel road. It's quiet and still out here, lonely. A jaybird squawks from a tree. I'm think of Brandy and her friends yelling at me from the car. The man in the pickup throwing a Coke in Brian's face. Someone shooting a gun at our house.

"Wait," I say. "Mamaw, wait."

She stops and looks back at me. "What is it?"

"What if I don't want him to come back?"

She pauses for just a second, her expression impossible to read. Then she turns and keeps walking toward the trailer. I run after her, up the half-dirt, half-grass walkway, past a family of plastic deer and two dirty white lawn chairs. When we get to the steps, she stops and turns, her sunglasses propped on her head. She's not smiling now. She speaks low—an almost whisper, an angry whisper.

"After all your brother has done for you," she says. "And this is how you act."

She gives three hard raps on the metal strip of the screen door before I can defend myself. Her accusation drills into my chest. She never scolds me. A cricket chirps from under the trailer like a cheap alarm. My grandmother doesn't understand what it's like at school, what people say.

"Yoo-hoo," she calls.

A woman comes to the door, the features of her face hidden by the mesh screen.

"I'm here to see Brian," Mamaw says, warmly. "I'm Lettie, his grandma. This is his sister, Jess."

The woman squints like maybe she's not used to coming into the light. "He's sleeping," she says.

"Mama, it's okay," a man says. "You can let them in."

The woman hesitates, then opens the door. She's probably around my mother's age but looks older, and she looks poor—you can just tell. Bad teeth, a few pimples scattered on her chin, a flat, expressionless face. She's not wearing any makeup, but she put time into her hair—the bangs are curled into a stiff ball, like a cupcake balanced on the tip of her forehead.

My grandmother walks in first, and I stand behind her. The trailer is dim and warm, and smells like fried eggs.

Then, a short, spry man with puffy hair steps out of the kitchenette. He's wearing black satiny pants and a bright, billowy pink shirt, looks like he's about to do a magic trick or break out into song. A gold chain hits the top of his chest.

"You didn't get lost?"

"No sir, you gave good directions." My grandmother reaches out her hand and he holds it, not like a handshake, but as if her hand is a precious stone. He introduces his mother, Janey, and then looks at me.

"You must be Jess. I'm Andrew."

He lisps when he talks and I know right away he's gay. I wonder if he has it too. Mamaw's eyes bear down on me.

"Hi," I say.

"He might still be sleeping. I didn't tell him you were coming."

"Don't wake him up," Mamaw says. "We'll wait."

"Let me go check."

Janey asks if we want anything to drink. "There's Coke or iced tea."

Mamaw says she'd love a Coke, but I shake my head—I just want to get out of here. I sit next to my grandmother on the brown and red plaid sofa, and Janey hands her a plastic cup. Then Janey nestles into a corduroy recliner, stretching out her thin legs and wiggling her bare toes. We gaze at the TV. *The Price is Right* is on. Bob Barker, in a gray suit, explains to a giddy, out-of-breath woman named Phyllis how to play a game where she has to guess which two products have the same price. A frozen steak dinner on a mini Ferris wheel rotates by, followed by a jar of peanut butter.

Behind the TV, on the wood-paneled wall, hang framed pictures of fashion models—Christy Brinkley, Brooke Shields, and Paulina Porizkova. The wall adjacent to the sofa is covered with pictures of Andrew—recent ones to baby pictures, and all the years in between.

"Honey, you like this show? Here, you can turn on whatever you want." Janey holds out the remote to me.

"This is fine."

Low voices sound from the hallway. One of them is my brother's. My grandmother won't look over at me. My muscles vibrate. Even my earlobes feel tense.

When he walks in, his flannel shirt unbuttoned, he's leaning on Andrew. I would gasp but I can't make a sound. Mamaw does it for me.

"Oh!" she exclaims.

Brian looks awful. You can see ribs, and his skin is ashy and gray. Beads of sweat cross his forehead. Dark circles under his eyes, and painful-looking blisters are scattered around his mouth like chicken pox. He's wearing sweatpants and old man slippers. His hair sticks up in the back like turkey feathers.

"What are you doing here?" he asks, his voice so faint I can barely hear him.

"I called her," Andrew says. "I had to."

I can't tell if Brian is pissed or scared or sad. His eyes are enormous. Mamaw goes over to him and wraps her arms around him. He disappears in her flesh.

"Oh, you're warm," she says. "You're burning up."

When she lets go, Brian asks her why she's here. On TV, the contestants spin to see who gets to be in the Showcase. The Big Wheel clicks. *Click, click, click.* The numbers slowly spin by, and the audience yells and Bob Barker watches solemnly as the wheel stops on sixty-five cents. Phyllis says she'll stay, and walks over to the red circle to wait.

"Honey, it's time for you to come on home," Mamaw says.

"I can't."

"Yes, my house. Come stay with me."

A woman with blond hair and dark eyebrows spins the wheel next and it goes ticking by. Fifty-five cents. She spins a second time, and lands on seventy-five cents, and the crowd groans because she went over a dollar. Bob Barker tells her goodbye. Phyllis, the winner, waves her arms in the air and yells, "Yee-haw," and Bob says they'll be right back.

Maybe he's too tired and weak to put up much of a fight, or maybe he really wants to come home. "Okay," Brian says.

Andrew says he'll get his things, but first he and my grandmother help Brian over to the sofa. I don't want to look at him again. But I can't help it. His busted-up mouth, bulging cow eyes. He breathes hard like he's been on a run.

As Andrew flits out of the room, my grandmother approaches Janey. "I'm grateful for you taking care of him. It's real nice of you."

"I can't turn no one away," she says, still sitting down, her thin chicken legs stretched out.

"No, no I can see that. You're a good woman."

Andrew comes back in with a suitcase, duffle bag, and my brother's silver camera case that looks like a big briefcase. He's also holding a cane. He crouches to help Brian stand, and Brian leans on the cane.

"I give him that." Janey kicks the footrest down. "It was my grandpa's."

"That's real nice of you," Mamaw says.

Shaken, I look at my brother, holding onto that cane like an old man. That's what he looks like, an old man in a nursing home.

"Jess, help get his things," Mamaw says.

I grab the suitcase, happy to have something to do. Maybe I made this happen—I'm the one who told him to leave. He doesn't even seem to notice I'm here. His eyes are glassy and unfocused.

Janey pats Brian softly on the back. "You take care of yourself, honey."

Andrew gives him a careful hug, cautious not to squeeze too hard. "I'll miss you."

Mamaw holds onto Brian's elbow, guiding him to the Queen's Ship, and Andrew and I put his things in the trunk. A blue jay screeches at us, lands in a tree.

"We need to get you to the doctor's," Mamaw says.

"No," Brian says. "Just take me home."

Brian's breathing gets slower and deeper, and I realize he's asleep. Mamaw goes what I think is the long way, so that she doesn't have to drive by the swimming pool, but then she misses the turn.

"Where are we going?"

"To get help," she says.

Sharon

The air is cooler in the mornings now, and the leaves are changing colors. Tiny black-capped chickadees buzz from branches. Autumn is here. As I set a sack of clean, folded sheets in the backseat of the Citation, a sharp pain pinches my lower back. I suck my breath, ignoring it, and go back in the house for another load of laundry. Staying busy is the only way I know how to stop the pain from taking over.

When I come back out, Deb Dennison walks up her driveway to retrieve the paper. She's wearing baby blue sweatpants, and when she bends over, her butt rises like a blue moon. As she stands, shoving the rolled newspaper under her armpit, she sees me.

"Sharon," she calls, not taking the cigarette out of her mouth. "How you doing?"

"I'm okay. How are you?"

She walks over, stops at the edge of her property, and I can't help but notice her fluffy Mickey Mouse slippers, the ridiculous smiling faces looking up at me, black round ears sticking up on either side like over-sized headphones.

"Hanging in there," she says in her gruff, scratchy smoker voice. "How's your boy?"

"He—he's getting better." The obvious lies are easier—for others to hear, for me to say.

"Well, good," she says. "I'm glad all that mess is over."

I nod, but I'm not sure what she means—the town's reaction, or his illness? Does she think it goes away, like the flu? Isn't that what all of us hope? Still, my eyes burn with gratitude. I had assumed Deb Dennison would be one of the first scrambling to get on camera to talk bad about my son, but she hasn't been anything but kind.

"You tell him I said everything's going to be all right," she says.

There are a handful of people who have stood by us, or at least not shunned us entirely. We still get the occasional prank call or nasty letter, but most of town just ignores us. _On Location With Naomi_ amplified all the hate and ugliness, but also changed a few minds. I like to think that when die-hard fans heard Naomi defend Brian, they started to rethink things. Sometimes the media still call the house—not Naomi or her people, but newspapers and news teams in Ohio. They want updates. They want to know if he's still alive. We do not speak to them.

Deb waves and I tap the horn. Then, as I've done every morning since Lettie brought Brian back, I head to her house. I go back and forth between my house and hers, washing, cooking, vacuuming. I'm never still. Whatever I can do to help out, and to stop the pain from paralyzing me. When Lettie called to tell me she'd found him, I wept. Then she told me she was calling from the hospital in Madison.

Brian stayed in the hospital for five days. His white blood cell count fell dangerously low, and he ran a fever of 103. He battled a painful outbreak of herpes in his mouth, and a fungus called thrush coated his tongue like a film of cottage cheese. I was terrified he would not live through it. Some of the nurses and aides refused to speak to us. They knew who we were. They wore latex gloves and masks over their mouths and gowns, and we had to do the same when we went into his room. As Lettie and I sat in the waiting room, the staff's hard, hateful stares and side glances made the air feel impossibly heavy. One day, his food tray was just sitting outside the door. I didn't complain to anyone.

I just carried it in, and helped him eat a few bites of Jell-O. Only one younger nurse, Tracy, didn't seem alarmed. Warm and gentle, she patted me on the arm as she walked by. She squeezed Brian's hands. There was only one doctor who would see him, who didn't look at Brian with disgust or judgment. Dr. Patel. He's from India. The first time he spoke, Lettie just stared at him, trying to follow his quick words. Then she thanked him over and over for saving her grandson. You have the kindest eyes, she told him.

The kitchen smells like coffee and burned toast. Sadie greets me at the door, wagging her tail, her nails clicking on the linoleum. After Brian got out of the hospital, he asked for her, and Jess said she didn't mind. "She's his dog," she said. It was decided without discussion that Brian would live at Lettie's.

"Anyone home?" I call, knowing of course they are—where else would they go? The days of Brian going on drives or to the shopping mall are long over. On the stovetop oatmeal hardens in a pot like clay. He hardly eats. Nothing tastes good, he says. It's like the food itself hurts. At least, for now, the sores in his mouth have retreated.

"In here," Lettie calls from the family room.

Sadie follows me, and jumps up on the sofa next to Lettie. Swallowed up by the recliner, Brian doesn't look up from the TV. It's turned up too loud, the way my father used to listen to it. One of Lettie's quilts drapes over him, hiding his frail bones. His gaunt grim face peeks out from the bright colors and geometric shapes like a shriveled-up weed in a field of wildflowers.

"How are you feeling?"

"Peachy keen," he says, glazed eyes glued to the TV. A heavily made-up woman in a shimmering dress and high heels talks about Jesus.

Brian has changed since the hospital—and not just physically. A low-burning rage hovers under all his words, except he's usually too tired to let loose. Sometimes the anger makes me feel better, like he's still got fight in him. Other times I hear the truth under his sharp words and snappy tone, and I know it's not anger but fear. His camera sits next to him, turned off. He's too weak to hold it.

"Can I get you anything?"

He shakes his head. He can't get around without a cane now—even then, if he walks further than about fifteen feet, he loses his breath, stumbles, and complains of the pain in his legs. The first time I saw him using the cane, I had to leave the room—I was shaking all over, trying to hold back my sobs. He lashes out because he cannot do the things he used to. Searing headaches make him weepy and fatigue drags him down. He constantly battles the unsettling, dizzying feeling that he might vomit at any moment. Diarrhea leaves him weak. My poor son. I don't know how to make him better. There are good days—when he keeps down the little food that he eats, when he's in better spirits—but they are rare.

"Did you eat breakfast?"

He doesn't answer.

"He ate a couple bites of oatmeal. I put another pot of coffee on. It should be ready in a few minutes," Lettie says. Lettie has received a few mean phone calls, but she doesn't avoid picking up. She yells, "You ought to be ashamed," and the caller always hangs up first.

She's still in her housecoat, and without makeup, her face looks naked and scared and small. There is something else. It takes me a moment to realize. Her hair. She's let her hair go. Strands of her natural gray web through the fading dye, which is now more of a dull brown. It's the first time I've seen Lettie without black hair.

"You need another cup?"

"Yes, thank you."

She hands me the mug, her hand shaking just slightly. She probably needs a cigarette. No more smoking in the house. We go out to the front porch or backyard, fill up ashtrays and coffee cans with our ashes, our sadness, our tears. Lettie still tries to live in her own world of pretend, believing Brian will get better, that he'll defy all the odds. I remember my mother, always in the hospital, or tucked away in her room, a body of bones. Too much suffering. I am not ready to let my son go. It is not fair—he came back to us, and now God is taking him away.

"Mamaw and I placed bets on how many times Tammy Faye will break into tears," Brian says, pointing at the TV.

"I'm winning," Lettie says.

"I always underestimate her crying." Brian looks at Lettie and they giggle. It's silly, but I feel a pang of rejection, like years ago when I'd walk in on the two of them fervently discussing actors and TV shows, and they'd look up and smile in a way that excluded me. There was no way to come between them. And, now, no matter what I do for Brian, I can't undo the truth: it was Lettie, not me, who found him and brought him back home.

While Lettie makes a trip to the grocery store, I take her place on the couch, keeping Brian company. He spends most of his time in the family room watching TV, and the living room serves as his bedroom because it's too difficult for him to go up and down the stairs. His first day back from the hospital, Lettie ordered Travis and Gus to move a twin bed out of one of the bedrooms. Brian lay on the couch while they did the moving, sleeping or pretending to sleep. Since Brian's been back, he and Travis have hardly spoken. Travis visited him in the hospital, but stayed in the waiting room most of the time, anxiously leafing through magazines. When he saw Brian, he was shocked by how frail he'd become, how sickly and strange. He stood stiffly, too far away from the bed, unable—or unwilling—to look his son in the eye.

Travis has only come over to Lettie's a few times. He asks Brian how he's feeling, and Brian says, "Fine," and then Travis will talk to me or Lettie or Jess, whoever is in the room, chattering about work or the weather or anything other than what he still hasn't faced. Travis doesn't talk to me about it either. After the hospital stay, one of the only things he asked me was about the bill. How would we ever pay for it? I explained Brian had disability from social security and Medicaid. So the government's paying, he said, shaking his head, and I wanted to slap him. Travis wants things to go back to the way they never were.

"Mom," Brian says.

"What?"

He doesn't respond.

"Is there something else you want to watch?" I ask.

"Whatever you want," he mumbles.

I turn on MTV for him. A scantily-clad woman dances around a pole. Then the video switches to men with long hair and tight pants screaming into microphones, one of them pounding drums, another holding a red guitar above his head.

"Oh, I hate this band, they're awful," Brian says. "Turn it, please."

I push buttons on the remote, and Brian tells me to stop on a nature show. Giraffes graze on tall trees, stretching out their long necks.

"Your mom, she had cancer, didn't she?" he asks.

I hesitate. "Yes."

"Painful death?"

My fingertips tingle. On TV the giraffes walk gracefully, as if they're gliding, across a golden plain. "I don't—yes, I think so."

Brian closes his eyes, then opens them wide. "When it started, nobody knew what was happening," he says. "We were all so scared."

Perched on the edge of the couch, I don't move or make a sound. It's rare that no one else is around. When it is just the two of us, he's usually sleeping. Or staring at me with large, furious, frightened eyes. My ears hum. I want to be a good audience. To listen.

"Guys were just getting so sick. And dying. Healthy guys. Friends." He makes a small sound like he's gasping, and it shakes me out of my stillness. I jump up from the couch, and lay my hand on his clammy forehead. "Lost too many. My friends. Shawn."

"I'm sorry." Then I say, "I wish I'd met him," I don't realize I mean the words until they leave my mouth. This man loved my son, he took care of him, he made him happy. Brian looks at me, and his sunken eyes seem huge.

"Mom. I'm scared."

I crouch next to him. "It's going to be okay." When I put my arm around him, I feel his bones. He's crying—a thin, weak weeping, his brittle body resting lightly against me. I clench my teeth and hold myself together. He shudders, his breath hot and ragged on my shoulder. "Don't be scared, honey," I say, holding back tears.

I stay there for a long time, even after he's fallen asleep, even as my arm aches. On TV, a cheetah flies across the land, a blur of gold and black, its muscles rippling, powerful paws pounding into the dirt—a dream creature, all beauty and strength, nothing I'll ever see in my life-time unless it's in a cage.

"Please," I whisper. "Please."

The noise of footsteps on the porch startles me. We don't get many vis-itors. One day Betty Russell brought over a Bundt cake and told Brian, "Don't you worry what anyone says, you just worry about getting bet-ter." When Gus came over, he stood at the bed and cracked his knuck-les, looking terrified. I tried to get him to stay longer, but he hemmed and hawed, diverting his eyes from Brian. He said he had to go, apol-ogizing on his way out. I don't know if he was telling Brian or me or himself that he was sorry. One day Liz and Paul brought a casserole and flowers but didn't stay long, both teary. Kyle and Matthew haven't showed up. They either don't want to see him or they're scared of facing Lettie. Wayne hasn't visited, of course, and I don't expect him to.

Brian told me he doesn't want to see family anymore anyway. "Why not?" I asked, and he shot me a look. "I'm not a side show," he said. I don't press him. I can't forget these last few months either, all the times they didn't come over to the house or avoided us in public. I'm furious at all of them.

It's not like when my mother was sick, when women from the church came every day. Nobody was scared of catching it. Nobody blamed her.

As I go to answer the front door, it creaks open.

"Hello?" A man's voice, falsetto, a bird's trill.

Andrew, of course. I open the door. He can hardly see over the Sears shopping bags in his arms. "We were having a big sale, plus my dis-count," he explains.

"He's sleeping," I say.

But Brian calls out that he's awake, and Andrew prances in. Everything he does is flamboyant and dramatic. "Look at all these goodies!" he says.

At first I just wanted Andrew to leave us alone. His flowery cologne and silky, bright shirts, his fluttering hands, overly expressive eyes—he's the type you can take one look at and know. But I've gotten used to him, and not only that, we rely on him. He comes over a couple of nights a week to cook dinner. He'll do women's work without a second thought—wash dishes, fold laundry. Twice he's brought his mother with him. A quiet, rough-around-the-edges woman, she sits beside Brian and rarely says a word to the rest of us.

Andrew goes right over to Brian and kisses his cheek, not afraid to touch him. Then he pulls the items out one by one like a magician, and Brian laughs.

"Here, we have a package of Hanes underwear—look at the elegant white cotton," he says dramatically. The only kinds of clothes Brian needs anymore are soft and styleless: pajamas, socks, T-shirts, sweatpants, sweatshirts.

"And this is for Lettie," Andrew announces, and spins around with a red blouse in his hands.

"Great, she can wear it to my funeral," Brian says, still laughing.

The word sucks all the air out of the room and hangs above us, a blade about to drop. "Brian—"

"Relax, Mom," he says, but he's looking at Andrew, not at me. Something passes between them. I'm not included. "It's nice, she'll like it," Brian adds.

Andrew twirls once more with the blouse up over his head like he's waving around a flag. He makes Brian laugh, and I wish I could too. But I feel like I'm alone in a snow drift, clawing at the sides that keep collapsing in on me, trying to find my way out. It's so cold and white and empty.

Andrew comes in the kitchen. "I need more coffee. You want any?"

"Sure."

"I'll make a fresh pot."

He reaches for the tin of Folgers and scoops it out into a filter, humming as he works. I turn on the faucet, squirt in dish soap, and watch the sink slowly fill with hot water.

"He seems like he's having a pretty good day," Andrew says.

"So far."

I plunge my hands under the sudsy water. The coffee maker gurgles and burps. Andrew picks up a dishtowel and stands next to me.

"Sharon," he says. "Have you thought about home health care?"

I've made calls, all of them humiliating. There is a hospice center in Madison, but they told me they can't accept him. They gave an excuse about the lack of beds, but I know if he had cancer, it would be a different story. I've called other agencies, trying to get a nurse or aide, somebody out here. They've all turned me down.

"I can't get anyone to come out."

Andrew dries a bowl carefully. "That's not right, they can't do that."

"Well, they are," I say.

We fall into silence. I hand him plate after plate. I wash, he dries. We're a team.

Then he says, "Sharon, you need to talk to him about what he wants."

"What do you mean?" I make the mistake of looking over, and his eyes lock on mine. Underwater, he reaches for my hand. The touch is a shock. I try to pull away but he holds on.

"Sharon, honey, it's not going to get any better. You need to face this. Lettie too."

He's standing too close, his eyes searching my face, and the sudden intense rage surprises me. I want to grab him and shake him, to attack. He senses it: his slippery, strong hand lets go of mine. Then, I'm alone again. Nothing to hold onto, just warm, greasy water lapping over my skin.

"I am facing it," I say. "Lettie's not, but I am."

"Then talk to him about things. About what he wants, you know, for his funeral."

That word again. I get back to work. I pick up the sponge and scrub furiously.

Andrew sets down a glass. "I'm planning on making supper tonight. Banana pancakes. Why don't you take the night off? You look like you need a break, honey."

I turn to read his expression, to see if he's mocking me. But he looks sincere, even worried. I don't want to leave, but I'm thinking of Jess and Travis. It's been a while since the three of us have eaten together.

"Thanks," I say.

"Nothing to thank me for." He holds the dishtowel by his fingertips, his wrist bent. "This is what I'm here for."

"You don't have to—" I start. "You've helped a lot. But don't feel obligated."

"What do you mean?"

"I don't want to put you out. You don't have to do this."

Andrew neatly folds the towel and drapes it over the counter. "Yes, I do. I have to, and so do you. It's the only option." He looks at me, serious and clear-eyed. "This is the only thing we have to do. Take care of him."

The house feels strange and unlived-in. Jess is at cross country practice, Travis at work. I hardly see him these days. Even at night, instead of going to our bed, I sleep in the guest room. I tell Travis it's because I don't want to keep him awake with my restless tossing and turning, which is true, but there is more to it. His body, his skin touching mine, unnerves me, quickens the rage and hurt inside me, and it is all I can do to just lie silently in the dark, hands clenched into tense fists.

I'm browning onions and hamburger in a frying pan when Jess walks in, sweaty and flushed. She usually goes over to Lettie's a few times a week. She and Brian watch TV or, if Brian is having a good day, play Go Fish. There isn't any tension between them, not anymore. I've asked Jess if the kids at school have said anything to her, but she just shrugs, her eyes guarded and open at once.

"What are you making?"

"Spaghetti. How was practice?"

"Good."

"How far did you run?"

"Two miles." She peels off her hooded sweatshirt and tosses it on the back of the chair. I've had many sleepless nights worrying about Jess, but being on the cross country team has lit a flame in her—she's more confident, growing stronger.

"I couldn't run a mile," I say.

"You could if you trained."

She rummages through the refrigerator. She's stopped the excessive dieting. She needs protein and carbs, she explains, for her long runs.

"How was school?"

"Fine." She bites into an apple. "I got an A on my geometry test."

"Good for you."

Jess surprised all of us, how good she is at running. I'm just happy she's doing something. Maybe she'll make friends.

By six, no Travis. Another hour goes by. "Let's just eat," I say.

We set up TV trays and watch *Jeopardy*. It's been a long time since we've spent any time together, just the two of us. Jess responds to Alex Trebek with questions, and sometimes they are right. She doesn't ask questions about Brian. She knows he's sick. She knows he's sick with AIDS. I should talk to her about death, but words elude me. And, if I don't speak them, then I won't make them come true. The doctor told us we had to prepare ourselves—a month or two at most, probably only weeks. Travis looked at his shoes. I held back sickening sobs. He wasn't certain, I told myself, nobody could predict the future.

"How do you feel about your meet this weekend?" I ask.

"Okay."

"I plan on being there. Your dad will be too."

When I reach over to touch the back of her neck, she surprises me by curling into me, something she hasn't done for at least a year or two. My arm grows numb, but I don't move it. And across town, Andrew helps Lettie take care of my son, the way, Brian has explained to me, they are all taking care of each other back in the city, men—*boys*—abandoned and shunned by their parents. They feed and wash and cook for each other, they take each other to the hospitals and they make funeral arrangements, and they fight doctors and politicians and drug companies. They take care of their living and their dead.

Sunday morning, I'm on my knees, pulling up and cutting back spent marigolds and petunias. Maybe one day I'll go back to church, but not to the one where I have spent so many Sundays of my life. The Dennisons burn trash and the smoky scent of the air makes me nostalgic. I want to bake cookies for my kids, carve pumpkins, make wreathes out of Indian corn.

My knees ache from crouching, and as I stand up, my hips burn. The caretaking has added new aches and pains to my body. Travis, wearing a flannel shirt and workpants, rakes the first of the fallen leaves into a pile. I remember Brian running across the yard, leaping high and falling spread-eagle into giant piles, laughing.

"Travis."

"Hm?"

He doesn't stop what he's doing to look at me, the rake scratching, leaves crunching and shushing.

"He needs to see you," I say.

He drags the line of leaves into a pile, then turns toward me. His hands in leather work gloves hold the rake still, like a flag pole.

"I just saw him. What do you mean?"

I don't know how to get through to him. "I think he needs to hear from you, that you don't blame him, that none of this is his fault."

Travis's face darkens, his jaw tightening, his mouth drawn in a frown. I feel him fade away from me, a disappearing light. Then, fuming, he works the rake quickly—violently—across the scattered leaves.

"He knows that," he says.

But he doesn't. Because Travis doesn't believe it. My husband is not a bad man, but he is terrified of letting go of this mask of normalcy—because then what will he be left with, what will he have to look at?

"Lettie said I can have the extra bedroom," I say. "I need to be with him."

He's looking at the hill of leaves he's building, not at me. His shoulders lift and fall, his back curves, his arms flex and expand. Shh, shh, shh go the leaves. Then he stops, faces me. The baseball hat hides his eyes.

"You're going to live with my mother? And, what, I just stay here?"

I nod.

"It's not right."

I brush off my knees and dead petals spill from the creases of my pants. "It's not like I'm leaving you," I say. Maybe this is a lie. In our grief, our love has turned in on itself, eating itself alive. "He needs me," I add, but I don't know if this is true or not.

Jess

When I was little, I traced pictures of ocean creatures from the Life Nature Library books. I liked the way the thin tracing paper felt and sounded, the delicate crinkles, like candy wrappers. I was careful, following the lines with the pointed tips of my colored pencils. Jellyfish, killer whales, dolphins, sea horses, starfish. I didn't know how to read yet, but I studied the pictures. At the end of the book, they changed to photographs of ships, men with weapons, slaughtered whales. Slabs of hacked-up flesh and blubber. Men standing in gigantic jawbones, like the arches to a church. Rivers of blood. My mother didn't want me to look. "They'll give you nightmares," she said. But I did anyway. I wanted to see everything.

At my grandmother's, Andrew and Brian are watching MTV. Sadie curls next to Brian on the sofa. She wants to be around him every second, and gets nervous if he's out of her sight.

"Hey, sis."

When Brian smiles, it looks creepy—his mouth too big for his face, his eyes bulging. He's all bone, except for his neck, which is swollen and soft. He sits on the couch under a bundle of afghans and Andrew sits on the edge of the reading chair, bopping his head.

"I love Whitney." Andrew shakes his shoulders with the song. "How will I know?" he asks in a high, girly voice, and twirls his hand in the air.

I don't know how to interact with Andrew, and I slide by him to sit on the couch next to my brother. I've never met anyone like him. He never stops talking, and doesn't try to hide his gayness at all. My mother calls him flamboyant. Mamaw says eccentric. I wonder if Andrew got beat up in high school.

"You have practice today?" Brian asks.

"Yeah."

Even though Coach likes us to run together, like soldiers in training, she never says anything to me when I splinter off and go on my own. I get away with it because of my brother. Grownups either ignore me or they act extra nice because they feel sorry for me. When I'm running, I'm so far inside my body, nobody else can see me. It's different at school—no matter how hard I try, I can't hide from the stares.

"We have a meet this weekend."

"So, what happens at one of those? You just run and run and run, and people watch?" Andrew asks.

I nod.

"Boring," he sings.

Brian stares at his own hands, head bent. Sometimes I don't know if he hears half of what is said. It's hard to read his expression, except when the pain gets too bad. Then his face turns white as bone and his eyes glaze over. He's in pain a lot. His legs hurt, his joints. He feels sick to his stomach.

"I want a popsicle," Andrew says. "Either of you want one?"

Brian shakes his head. I don't want one either. "Where's Mamaw?" I ask. "And Mom?"

"Shopping," Andrew says on his way out of the room.

"I told them to get out of here." Brian sounds grumpy. "They're driving me crazy. Everyone is."

There are days when I don't like to be around him, and this may be one of them—he yells at us, even Mamaw, or he's snippy. My mother tells me to be patient. "He doesn't mean to be like that," she told me one day after he made me cry. "He's just scared."

"They need a break from me too," Brian says.

My mother moved into my grandmother's so she wouldn't have to keep running back and forth between her house and ours. She promised nothing was wrong between her and my father, but I don't believe her. She still comes over to clean up or leave a casserole in the fridge, but doesn't stay long. She asked me if I want to move in to Mamaw's too, but I don't want to leave my father alone. And, I don't know if I can be around Brian every day.

Cyndi Lauper's new video comes on, her crazily teased orange hair like a giant sunflower bursting open. The scene changes to a sandy dune, maybe it's supposed to be Mars, and she's wearing a headpiece like a chandelier with gold chimes dangling like coins. In her hand she holds a giant pink shell and tells us to call her up if we're sad.

"Show me your true colors, Jess," Brian says, trying to be nice. Then, he grimaces, clutches his stomach. His face suddenly whitens, and the veins in his neck bulge. I don't know what to do.

"Are you okay?"

"Does it look like it?" he gasps. "Get Andrew." He bends at the waist, still holding his stomach, like he's trying to hide something. "Go!"

I'm too slow. As I stand up, the stench is sudden and awful and powerful. Brian looks up at me with horror in his eyes, and I remember the day at the mall with Annie, when he needed a bathroom.

"Brian," I start.

"Get the fuck out!"

Andrew comes running in. "What's wrong?"

There are tears in my brother's eyes. He holds his stomach, sweating, his skin a bluish white. He's shit his pants.

"Tell her to go," Brian croaks. "Get the fuck out of here!"

"Come on, honey," Andrew says. "It's just an accident, no big deal."

Shaking, I follow Andrew into the living room, where he gets out the supplies stored next to Brian's bed. He snaps on rubber gloves and grabs a box of wet wipes and a towel. I watch from the other room as he helps my brother up.

"Come on, hon. Let me get you to the toilet."

Then I'm running out the back door. I can't get my breath. I lean against a tree, gagging and shuddering, then press my cheek against the scratchy bark. I breathe in the clean scent of wood. The air is cool and crisp. Above me yellow leaves look like hundreds of birds, heads tucked into their wings, asleep.

When Brian was in the hospital, I was scared he'd never get to leave. I hated the sound of the machines, the sight of nurses wearing masks, the sharp scent of rubbing alcohol and medicine. I sat in the waiting room and stared at the polished linoleum floor and told myself if he didn't die, I'd be a better sister, I'd help take care of him, I wouldn't be ashamed.

I can't go back in. I still have my sweatshirt and shorts on from practice, so I just start running. I run along the Buckeye and through town and past the drive-in, which looks even more forgotten and sad. I run until my legs feel like they're going to burn off. I run until the sun sinks and the sky is a soft lilac. I run until the hurt disappears. I run until my mind goes quiet and it's just me inside my body: muscle, blood, bone, skin.

When I get home, the house is dark. My father usually gets home late. I don't see much of him anymore. Usually, I eat supper over at Mamaw's, or I'm in my room or watching TV by the time he gets home. I get the house key from under the flower pot and open the door. Underneath my sweatshirt my skin feels chilled and damp, and my legs are red and itchy, like they've been stuck with hundreds of thistles. It's the blood rushing through my body, my muscles and nerves wide awake.

I flip on the kitchen light, and yelp. A person sits at the table. He turns around—my father with a beer in his hand. He blinks a couple of times like he just woke up.

"Jess, sorry, didn't mean to scare you," he says. He sounds strange, like he's trying to hold back a bark of laughter. But his eyes look heavy and sad and dazed. I'd like to hear him laugh.

"I didn't know you were home," I say.

"I just walked in," he says quickly, in a way that makes me think he's lying. How long has he been sitting here staring into the dark? He's still wearing his work uniform, and his hair is messy like he's been pulling at it.

"There's some of that tuna casserole left," he says.

"You want some?"

He shakes his head no. I get the pan out of the refrigerator and spoon the cold, chunky noodles onto a plate. My father drums his fingers on the table.

"What did you do today?" he asks, and I realize what is weird about his voice—he's slurring his words, just a little. He's drunk.

"Just went on a long run," I say.

"You go over to Mom's?"

"For a few minutes."

He takes a drink of beer. The microwave beeps, and I take out the warmed casserole.

"How was Brian?" he asks.

"Fine."

He holds his eyes on me like he wants to have a serious talk. No thank you. The casserole isn't hot enough, but I eat it anyway, quickly shoveling it in. It's not just his gray hair making him look old anymore. My father looks frail and uncertain. He starts to say something, then his voice just peters out. I remember watching him with a bucket of water and a sponge, the word FAGGOT looming above him in blood-colored paint. My father, on his knees, scrubbing. He couldn't make the word go away.

On my way home from school, Gus pulls up in his pickup and rolls down the window. "Want a ride?"

I get in. The truck smells like my father's truck, like motor oil and mud. A picture of Pam and Allie is taped to the glove compartment, and Gus's leather tool belt, also like my father's, sits between us. An empty Coke can rolls next to my feet. I miss seeing Gus, and Pam and Allie.

"How you doing?" he asks, his giant fingers relaxed over the steering wheel.

"Fine."

"I heard you're doing real good in track."

"Cross country. Yeah, pretty good."

Gus turns onto our grandmother's street. I don't know if he hasn't come by to see Brian because he's so angry and disgusted, like Uncle Wayne, or if he's just scared. One day I overheard Brian ask our mother if he'd ever see Gus again, then he told her, "I don't care if I do or not." I don't believe him.

"Aren't you coming in?" I ask.

"I gotta get home. I'll come by another day."

"You should come in now," I say. "Brian wants to see you. He asks about you."

Gus hesitates. Then he turns the key, and the truck stops shaking. He follows me inside, walking slowly, dragging his big feet.

My grandmother and mother sit at the kitchen table, and they look up, surprised. "Look who it is," Mamaw says.

Gus holds his baseball hat in his hand, like he's come to pay his respects. "How y'all doing?"

"Don't worry about us," Mamaw says. "You get in there and talk to your cousin."

I walk with Gus into the family room. Brian sits in the recliner, an afghan over his lap, staring at the TV. When he sees Gus, his mouth opens but no sound comes out.

"Hey, cuz," Gus says, like everything is fine, but he can't even look at Brian. He's trying to find a place to put his eyes: his feet, the ball hat crumpled in his big hands, the TV screen.

Brian watches this eye-dance with amusement. "Well, what took you so long?" he asks.

"I've just been busy—" he stops. "I'm sorry."

Brian hands me the remote and tells me to watch what I want. I run through the channels, pretending to care what's on, but I'm watching the two of them.

"You still hang out with Josh Clay?"

Gus's face goes red. "No."

I stop on *The Brady Brunch*. I've seen all of the episodes about a hundred times. This is the one where the family goes to Hawaii, and Bobby finds an ancient idol that causes the family one bad incident after another.

"I didn't think you'd be like your dad," Brian accuses.

On TV, Greg, wearing the bad luck idol around his neck, surfs the

Pacific, and the family, on the beach, watch in horror as a wave takes him down. After a moment, his father, bare-chested and wearing only a tiny pair of blue Bermuda shorts, runs into the ocean to save his oldest son.

"It's not like that," Gus says, his voice thick with tears. "It's just—" He sputters his words. "It's not that you're, you know—"

"Gay?" Brian says.

I don't know if I've ever heard him say the word aloud. I can't even pretend to look at the TV now. I glance back and forth between them.

"I'm not like my dad. I just—it's hard to see you, like this," Gus says. "When we were kids, you were like my hero. You were so tough, and now…I'm sorry."

Gus wipes his eyes, and then he's crying into his hand. Brian and I look at each other. I've never seen a man as big as Gus cry.

"It's okay, shh," Brian says.

Gus sniffles and sucks in deep breaths, and uses the back of his hand to wipe snot from his nose.

"Why don't you sit down," Brian says. "Stay for a little bit."

And he does. The three of us watch TV, but I don't think any of us are really watching. It's just nice to be in the same room together. We relax, look at the screen. When the theme music comes on during the closing credits and all the Bradys and Alice smile at us and at each other, separate in their blue squares but always together, Gus says he better get going.

Brian reaches out his hand. "Thanks, Gus," he says. "Thank you for coming by."

I look over, searching for my mother or grandmother. Whoever isn't staying home with Brian this morning will come—they take turns. My father stands by himself, baseball hat on, hands in jacket pockets. Sparrows and snowbirds hop around in the weeds, pecking at the ground, and other birds sing from the edges of the woods. I always feel wound up before a meet.

I stretch, jog in place, bend down and touch my toes. It's a perfect autumn day. Rusty, golden, and red leaves burst from the trees. The air is brisk. My teammates stretch, a few of them talking quietly, still waking up. Today's meet is at Colby, which has one of the best cross county courses in the district, winding through the woods and fields. Parents linger a little ways out from the start line, a few with lawn chairs. As we run the 3.1 miles, they'll move to different spots along the way to cheer us on.

"How is everybody?" Coach Sizemore asks, coffee in hand. She wears gray sweats and a purple Eagles sweatshirt, baseball hat, sunglasses. Coach is tall and strong—big-boned, Mamaw says. Her shoulder-length dark hair is buzzed on the sides and she never wears makeup. Unmarried, she is rumored to be a lesbian. I like her, we all do. She tells us we're winners even when we're not and pushes us to go hard. We want to make her proud.

As she makes her way through the group, giving each of us a little individual pep talk, I'm surprised to see both my mother and grandmother leaving the parking lot. My mother pushes a wheelchair. For a few seconds, I'm confused. Maybe they've brought someone with them, one of Mamaw's friends, or some old relative I've forgotten about. Then I know.

"Hey, Jess, you okay?" Coach asks.

"What? Yeah."

"Listen, now remember to go steady. Keep your pace. You're good at the kick at the end, but you need to be steady." She touches my shoulder. "Jess?"

Then she notices them crossing the field. Her face loosens into an easy smile. "You've got fans, that's awesome. Right?"

"Yeah, I guess."

She bends down to my height, her face in front of mine. "Focus on your run, kiddo. Everything's going to be just fine. Okay?"

The girls run first. We line up, and Coach stands on the side, calling out instructions. "Okay, let's go, be ready now," she says. I stare straight ahead. The starter pistol cracks, and we're off. There are nine of us. Four from my team, five on Colby's. My grandmother and mother scream my name and Brian claps weakly from his wheelchair. Up ahead, my father stands alone, waving me on.

We cross the field and move like horses into the golden woods. There are a few girls behind me, and a girl from Colby's team far in the lead. Our feet hit the ground hard, leaves crunch. The rhythmic thudding is reassuring, like one giant heart beating. Birds call out and flutter from the trees. The air smells sweet like maple syrup and smoky like a woodstove. The trail winds through red maples and yellow sweetgum, and we leap one by one over a small stream.

I start to feel a slight cramp in my side and slow down just a touch. I can hear the others breathing all around me. We run through shadows and then come out into a cleared space blazing in light. Some of the crowd has moved, and they're waiting for us here, cheering. I catch sight of my grandmother, too dressed up for a cross country meet. As I try to pace myself, I hear Coach yelling for us to keep going, don't stop, let's go!

My legs burn, my chest expands. I watch the feet of the girl in front of me. It's not about winning, Coach tells us. I've never come in first place and don't expect to, but this morning the drive consumes me—I want to reach a point where my body can't go anymore. I want it to hurt.

We're down to the last half mile, and suddenly it's like I'm running in sand. My feet sink into the ground, and my legs won't go. My body feels heavy and thick, I can't find my breath. Then we turn into the woods again, and a switch turns on. My body lightens and speed shoots through me. This is the kick. I'm good at the kick.

My feet hit the ground, and I stretch my legs, my arms, and glide in front of the girl next to me, then catch up to the next one. I listen to my feet, my heart, my breath. The fans wait at the finish line, cheering louder, and I run harder, leaning forward, propelling myself.

Coach slaps our palms as we cross over the finish line. I come in behind a few girls, but I'm not last. I want to collapse, my legs turning to mush, all the heat dissipating from my body, but I keep moving. My grandmother, mother, and Brian hoot and holler, and then I see my father. He gives me a thumbs-up.

I come in third. Coach tells me it was my best time all season. "By the time you're a senior, you'll be unstoppable," she says.

Shivering, I pull on my sweatshirt and walk over to the sidelines.

Nobody seems to be giving my brother a second glance—they're all caught up in their own kids' performances. Maybe they don't know who he is, or maybe they just don't care.

"There she is!" Mamaw gives me a big hug. It's taken me a while to get used to her gray hair. She looks like any other grandmother now, except she's still bedazzled in her jewelry. Her rings and bracelets and a beaded necklace shine in the autumn light.

My mother congratulates me, and says she doesn't know where I get my stamina from as she stands behind Brian, ready to push him wherever he needs to go. Nobody mentions the wheelchair.

"Good job, sis," Brian says, almost a whisper.

Barely visible under all of the layers, he's bundled in a thick hunting jacket that Mamaw says used to belong to her husband. There is a black toboggan snug on his head, and a purpled checkered scarf that Andrew brought him wound around his neck. He also has on a pair of sunglasses that Annie sent from New York. The sparkling silver frames and mirrored lenses look goofy and too big for his skeleton-like face. Even though it doesn't seem like anyone's paying attention to us, I'm still on guard, waiting for someone to call him a name or yell something.

Coach comes over. "Didn't Jess do a great job?"

"Kicked ass," my brother says.

"You must be Brian."

"The one and only."

"Good to meet you," she says.

She shakes his hand like he's not sitting in a wheelchair, like she has no idea that he is the man with AIDS.

"Nice to meet you too," Brian says.

My father comes over and pats me on the back and tells me he's proud of me, but doesn't say anything to Brian or Mom, or Mamaw, just gives them a kind of sad smile, and I smell the beer and feel a stab of embarrassment. Then he stands back, hands in pockets, alone. Brian may be watching him, it's hard to tell because of the big sunglasses hiding his eyes. I wonder what he thinks, watching me run while he sits in that chair. He used to be the athlete of the family, but he'll never run again. He'll never do much of anything again.

※

The bell rings and I head to the cafeteria. My mother used to pack my lunch for me every morning, but since she's been staying at my grand-mother's, I fend for myself. I usually bring a peanut butter sandwich and eat it in the gym, sitting high up in the bleachers, as far away as I can get, but this morning I woke up late and didn't have time to make a lunch, so my father gave me a few dollars to buy one.

The cafeteria is crowded and smells like too many different kinds of foods cooking together in a gigantic microwave. I wait in the long à la carte line, keeping my head down. I should have just bought a pack of peanut butter crackers from the vending machine and gone to the gym. I don't know how to act around the other kids anymore. They all seem so young, like badly behaved children. I miss Nick—if he were here, we could hang out by the trees on the other side of the playground, smok-ing cigarettes and skipping class, growing up.

Wendy Rooper gets in line behind me. She smiles, showing dimples on either cheek like a baby doll's. "Did you study for our Spanish test?" she asks. Her voice is girly and high. I don't know if she's ever spoken to me before.

"Not really."

"Me either."

The line moves along. Up ahead, the cafeteria workers, old women in white polyester uniforms, stand behind the counter, serving pizza slices, hamburgers, or grilled cheese sandwiches. When we're closer, about five people from the front, Wendy and I each take a green plastic tray from the stack. Then I hear a low mooing. Wendy hears it too—her cheeks and neck flush, and she looks down at her pudgy hands, but she can't hide. Brett Wilson and Mike Kirby pass by the end of the long line, heading in our direction. They moo again, cracking themselves up.

"Hey, Wendy, thanks for letting us cut the line," Brett says, stepping in front of her, and Mike pats her on the butt, and they laugh again. Wendy doesn't look at either of them. She deals with this every day. Everyone pretends not to notice.

A blue hot flame grows in my throat. The tray feels heavy in my hands.

Brett elbows Mike. "Oh, look who it is. The faggot's sister," he says, but then he gets distracted by Angie Ray and Carrie Driggs coming over, laughing about something. "Hey, girls."

Angie and Carrie join Brett and Mike, think nothing of ditching us in line. I'm surprised Brandy White isn't with them. Carrie doesn't even glance at me. She's grown out her hair and wears it bigger now, the sculpted bangs held securely in place with layers of candy-scented hairspray. Over the summer, Carrie climbed her way up into the popular girl crowd, leaving Molly behind. But even Molly won't associate with me. Nobody speaks to me or sits with me. I don't care.

"We were just about to ask these girls out on dates," Brett says, and Angie glances at Wendy and me, and rolls her eyes.

"Please," she snorts, and they crack up.

As Carrie reaches for a tray, she pushes into me. "Hey, don't touch me," she says.

"I didn't."

"You shouldn't even be here," she says loudly. "You're going to get your germs all over the food. Are you trying to give us AIDS?"

Brett and Mike howl, and Carrie smiles, proud of herself. Wendy looks at the floor. She wants to disappear too, but she's too big. One of the cafeteria workers yells at us to keep the line moving.

"You can't catch it like that, you idiot," I say.

"What?" Carrie turns back around, and now they're all watching. My fingers curl around the edges of the plastic tray.

"I said, you can't catch it like that."

"Oh, right. You can only get it from butt sex."

Carrie opens her mouth and brays an ugly laugh, and Brett and Mike slap high fives. Wendy Rooper glances at me. She's taken years of this.

As Carrie turns toward the cooks, I drop my tray and it clatters to the floor. All the tautness lets loose, and power curls into my hands. Enraged, I grab Carrie. She shrieks, and then we're on the floor. She's trying to hit me, but I pin her down and slap her across her red face and she screams louder. The heat pulses in my head. I can't see anything, just a blur, but I sense the crowd growing around us—watching, hollering, making bets. Carrie struggles under me and then as someone pulls me off of her, I'm swinging my fists. "Calm down, calm down," Coach says in my ear. I close my eyes, and let myself be led.

As I wait in the principal's office, the secretary, Mrs. Taylor, keeps looking over the top of her glasses at me, nervous I'm going to bolt. Behind the closed door, the principal and Coach talk about me. Maybe I'll be expelled. It doesn't matter. Mrs. Taylor taps the typewriter keys. A kid comes in and hands her a doctor's note, and then writes his name on the sign-in sheet. My body twitches with the desire to run until my muscles give out.

When I'm called into the office, I don't hear most of what they say. Principal Gleason stands with crossed arms, and Coach pats me like she's comforting a wild animal. I hear the word "parents." I hear the word "control." I hear the word "apologize." I refuse to answer their questions.

Principal Gleason sends me to the guidance counselor.

"Jessie, come in." Josh Clay closes the door behind me. He motions for me to sit in one of the empty chairs, but I shake my head. There isn't much to look at. A desk covered with files, bookshelves. A globe of the world. Pictures of Josh and wife and baby. Fluorescent lighting. Boring beige walls.

Josh sits down in the chair behind his desk and looks up at me with a fake teacher smile. "Jessie, please, take a seat."

"I don't want to," I say.

He's wearing a white collar shirt under a maroon sweater and gray pleated slacks. He's grown his spiky hair out, and wears it parted to the side, like his father. His smile fades.

"Jessie, listen. I know things are hard right now. But you can't just go around beating people up."

"She started it!"

Josh picks up a pen and clicks it several times. He wants me to sit and chat with him, tell him all my problems, like other kids do, but it's different between us. I remember his hand on my knee. He tricked me into telling him about Brian.

"Are you going to suspend me or expel me or what?"

"No, no. Nothing like that. Principal Gleason understands this is a... unique situation."

When he stands up, the pleats fall out of his slacks. "I want you to talk to me. Stop carrying around all this pain."

There is a picture of Josh in high school, posed in his baseball uniform and holding a bat. Brian was the best player on the team. Now he's at my grandmother's, in a wheelchair, face slick with sweat and pain and fear.

"You're going to have to apologize to Carrie."

"No way."

He folds his arms. "Jessie."

"It's Jess," I correct him. "Can I go or what?"

"Listen," he softens his tone. "Have you thought about coming back to youth group? I think it would be good for you."

"This is a public school. You're not even supposed to be talking about church."

He starts to laugh, he thinks I'm joking, but then his expression changes—a hard crease appears in his forehead, his eyes flash. I don't know how I ever thought he was cute.

"You're lost, Jessie. But I pray you'll see the light again."

"Whatever, dickhead."

The door slams behind me, and he doesn't come after me. I feel invincible, not invisible. I walk past the long line of lockers. The bell clangs and everyone spills out into the hall. I hold my head up. Nobody yells anything, nobody says a word. But they all see me. I'm the killer whale gliding through the halls.

Sharon

I stand behind the wheelchair, waiting for Brian to come out of the bathroom. He's been in there a long time, refusing my help. He doesn't want me to see his tortured, emaciated body, prefers Andrew to help him with these kinds of things—getting dressed, bathing. But Andrew can't be here every day. Whenever Brian has to rely on me, his embarrassment and seething anger tighten around him like a lasso, making him difficult to reach.

When he finally comes out, he doesn't even glance at me. I help him back into the chair. Though I've done this often, I'm still surprised by how light he is. He's lost so much weight, down to 111 pounds. A husk. I want to massage fat back into him, to flesh out his face, to return the strong strings of muscle to his shriveled legs and arms.

I push the wheelchair into the living room, where his bed is. Lettie has hung some of Brian's pictures on the walls to make him feel more at home. The one of him and Shawn at the beach, arms around each other—best of friends, but more than that. What was it like to lose him, when they were both so young? Brian sometimes stares at the picture, says Shawn's name, a prayer. There's a picture of Annie looking like she's posing for the cover of some trashy magazine: unzipped leather jacket over a lacy bra-like shirt, hair teased, a cigarette between her lips. And, in a thick brass frame, Lettie's most prized photo: Lettie, Brian, and Naomi with their arms around each other, Naomi's famous signature in the corner.

"I don't want to lay down," Brian says.

"Do you want to watch TV?"

He nods. I take him into the family room, and help him get out of chair and into the recliner. Though he's shockingly weak, he's still clear-headed, and this is encouraging.

He squints at the television. "Sometimes it hurts my eyes to watch," he says. "Makes me dizzy."

It's a commercial for ketchup. The bottle tips, and thick, red blobs fall onto a sizzling hamburger patty.

"Do you want me to turn it off?" I ask.

"No. Leave it," he says.

The furnace kicks on with a thump. Already, I can barely breathe it's so stuffy in here, but Brian's always cold. Lettie keeps the heat turned high for him. He wears sweatpants and a sweatshirt, white cotton socks, and a heavy velour robe that Andrew gave him. I arrange a blanket over his legs and feet. I've been thinking about what Andrew said.

"Brian, honey."

He turns his giant blue eyes on me. The illness has changed the shape of his face—sunken, concave cheeks, and everything else too big: his nose, his mouth, his eyes, his protruding forehead. His once-pretty blond hair has grown thin and coarse and lackluster, the color of yard dirt.

"Is there anything I should know? About what you want?" I stroke his delicate hand lightly, don't want to cause any pain. He blinks several times. "I mean, if you go back into the hospital, is there anything—"

"DNR," he says.

The letters at first mean nothing, then I understand. Heat zips through my body like a current. Goddamn—I want to yell, to curse, but all I can do is nod.

"There's a tape," he says.

"What?"

"You'll see it. Next to my bed in my room. Watch it. Watch it after—"

He stops talking and a hoarse sob escapes my throat, and I'm embarrassed—crying when he is the one who must be terrified. What goes through his mind? Everything is slipping out of his grasp—strength, words, time—and I don't know what he needs. His father? Travis hasn't been over here in three or four days, and Brian hasn't asked for him.

"It's going to be okay," I tell him. "It'll be okay."

Later, while Lettie watches soaps and Brian sleeps, I go back to the house. It's the middle of the day, and Travis isn't home. Jess is at cross country practice. Thankfully, she wasn't suspended from the team after her squabble at school. "We're giving her another chance," her coach told me. "But she needs to talk to someone." Who? I thought, didn't ask. Both Travis and I went in to meet with the principal, the coach, and Josh Clay. It was the most time we've spent together in months. Side-by-side, pretending to be fine.

"I know how hard this is," Don Gleason, the principal, started.

I didn't want to hear his excuses. "You said you'd keep an eye out, to make sure kids aren't making fun of her."

"Sharon, we can't watch her every second," Josh Clay said, and I resented him calling me by my first name, just as I resented Travis reaching out and touching my arm, as if to silence me.

"We'll talk to her," Travis said.

We didn't. We got in separate vehicles, drove to separate places. When I saw Jess at Lettie's, I asked her if she wanted to stay home from school.

"They won't bother me anymore," she said, and that was the end of the discussion.

I open the door to Brian's room. A poster has fallen off the wall, and I unfurl it. I know the singer only because Brian used to be so obsessed. Wild makeup, over-the-top flamboyant clothes. I study his catlike face. He's handsome and pretty and strange. He stares back—one light blue eye and one brown—as if he's judging me, blaming me for the state of things. He's right, I think.

When I raise the blinds to let in the afternoon light, it shines over a layer of dust on the lamp and dresser and shelves. The baseball trophies are gone—I wonder what Brian did with them—but the photographs of his friends still hang on the wall next to the bed. Brian has told me stories about these men: they were fired from their jobs, evicted from apartments, abandoned by their families. I look at their faces, caught in time. *It's not your fault.* They look back at me. How many are dead? All of them.

I run upstairs and return with a roll of Scotch tape. Who cares if it strips the paint off the walls? Why did I ever worry about such stupid things? Taking my time, I carefully reattach the poster of David Bowie and smooth out the wrinkles.

I stop putting off what I came here for. The box of VHS tapes sits next to the bed waiting for me. One day, maybe I'll watch them all. Travis believed that Brian missed his chance for a better life by not pursuing baseball, but Lettie always knew he was born to do something else—something beautiful, artistic, imaginative. God's given him a gift, she said. I should have listened to her, should have encouraged him to follow his dreams.

The tape sits on top of the stack, impossible to miss. WATCH AFTER MY DEATH written on the label in red permanent marker. *After.* I should have done more, I think. If I'd been more accepting. If I'd visited him in New York. If, if, if. I sit on the edge of the bed, which I finally made the day Lettie called from the hospital. Before that, when I didn't know where Brian had gone or if I'd ever see him again, I'd left the bed as he had, a mess of covers and sheets that still smelled like him.

Chilled, I rub my arms. It's too cold and quiet—not just this room, but the house itself. I don't want to be here. I want to be back at Lettie's, to be around people, to be with my son.

The poster's edges start to curl. One side slides down from the wall, the rock star's face tilting, then upside down. As I watch him fall, my body explodes, and a scream shatters the silence.

I tear the comforter free and yank the sheets out from under the corners. It's a relief, a terrifying joy. I'm a wild woman making a mess—stripping the bed, throwing blankets on the floor, pounding the mattress with my fists. I hit it again and again. I hate everything in this room, everything in this house.

Exhausted, sobbing, I collapse, and as I reach for the wadded up blankets, hugging them to me and trying to hold onto something, to keep my son from leaving this terrible, beautiful world, the rock star looks up at me from the floor not with judgment but something else, understanding, or maybe, I hope, forgiveness.

Jess is on the phone. "It's Annie," she says. "She wants to visit."

"Oh, good," Lettie exclaims. "Tell her we have plenty of room."

"Mamaw said to tell you we have plenty of room," Jess says, then a minute later, she says goodbye and puts the phone back in the cradle.

"When is she coming?" I ask.

"A couple of days."

This will please Brian, but it makes me tired, thinking of her in this house. Jess turns on a sitcom that she, Brian, and Lettie like to watch about four old women living in Miami. Each episode focuses on a different dilemma, and after they argue and trade insults, they gather around the kitchen table late at night to eat cheesecake: problem solved, friends again, a family.

Brian coughs, moans, and goes back to sleep. One TV show blurs into the next, one perfect family after another. Lettie and I take turns checking on him. I put my hand on his forehead. Warm, but no fever. In the last couple of days, he's stopped eating any solid foods. Instead, he subsists on the diet of an invalid: Jell-O, popsicles, vanilla-flavored protein drinks.

Later, upstairs, I pull the door closed behind me. This is the room where Brian used to sleep whenever he stayed at Lettie's. It's a plain, simple room with a full-sized bed, dresser with a mirror, a book case. The wood floors creak under my weight. On the dresser, Lettie has arranged her collector Avon bottles—a glass horse, Little Bo Peep, a vintage car, and a unicorn with a gold horn. Nothing in here particularly reminds me of Brian, except that everything does.

My neck and back ache. Everyday helping him into the wheelchair or into bed, and all the nonstop chores, are taking a toll on my body. But what is a little pain compared to what he suffers?

I look awful. My hair hangs dismally around my face. Puffy eyes. Lines around my mouth. I haven't worn makeup in weeks. I'm ugly but it's okay—I want to look ugly. I want people to look at me and feel guilty about how they treated my son. I want them to see how I wear my own guilt.

I get in bed with no expectations of sleeping. I rarely do these days. On the other side of the wall, Lettie sleeps, or maybe she's awake too, fretting and worrying. These past few weeks she has hardly spoken to her sons or her other grandchildren. Everything is about Brian now, it has to be.

Lettie and I have not spoken about the future. She hovers and fusses, and jumps at Brian's every beck and call. I tried to tell her what Brian told me. *DNR.* I needed a witness. Lettie's face whitened. Then she began unloading the dishwasher. "Oh, he's going to get stronger," she said. "He's going to come back to us."

I could pray. Should pray. The words won't come. The house groans. My muscles burn. Last week, Reverend Clay came by, but Lettie wouldn't let him in. She told him Brian was sleeping. "Lettie, is he right with the Lord?" he asked urgently. Lettie said she wanted to spit in his face. Furious, she told him her grandson was more right with God than most people in Chester, including him and his son. I don't ask God to forgive Brian anymore. I ask him to forgive me, to forgive his father.

I hear her before I see her, and something in me sinks. Brian's sitting up in bed, pillows propped behind him. Annie, Jess, and Lettie gather around in chairs they've brought in from the dining room. For a second, I think about slipping out the door before they see me, but Lettie looks up.

"Well, come on in, Sharon, don't just stand there."

Annie gives me a big, confident smile, but her eyes look red and washed out. "We're doing makeovers."

"Mom, what do you think of my nails?" Brian sounds weak, but he's still here. He holds out his thin, delicate hands and wiggles his fingers, showing off pearly orange polished nails.

"They're nice," I say.

Lettie's nails are newly painted too, fire engine red. Jess waves hers at me, dark purple, and she's wearing lipstick and eye makeup, dolled up like a prostitute.

Annie rummages through bottles of fingernail polish cluttered on the end table. She holds one up. "I bet this color would look good on you, Sharon. It's called seashell."

I hesitate. All of them looking at me. It's Brian I want to please.

"Okay, I'll try it," I say.

I sit next to Annie and hold out my hands. She seems surprised. "You sure?"

"It's now or never."

"Okay." Annie takes my hand in hers, steadying it, and I suddenly feel hot tears in the corners of my eyes. I hold them back. Conversation goes on around me. I sit very still. Annie dips the tiny brush in the bottle and runs it over my thumbnail, turning it a glossy pink. "Pretty," she says.

"Can't sleep either?" Annie asks.

I shake my head. I'm trying to get used to her being here. She makes Brian happy, I tell myself. Still—it irks me, seeing her so comfortable in Lettie's kitchen, like she's here to take my place. I know Brian relies on her, trusts her more than me.

But when she offers to make me a cup of tea, I find myself nodding. She points to the chair, as if the house belongs to her. Of course he trusts her—Annie has never turned her back on him.

She busies herself with putting on the kettle. She wears a pair of very short shorts and a loose fitting sweatshirt torn at the neck. Her hair sticks up in all directions.

After the kettle whistles, she pours the hot water over a teabag. "All I could find was Lipton," she says. "Sure this won't keep you up?"

"Doesn't matter," I say. "I can't sleep." Then, trying to be nice, I share a memory with her about how Brian loved to drink hot tea when he was little. "The sweeter the better."

Annie snips a smile—there, then gone. "I know," she says. "He told me."

We sit across from each other under the glow of the stove light and sip our tea. I have no idea what else to say, and for a moment, I think she won't say anything either, a relief. We'll sit here peacefully. But then she opens her mouth, of course.

"I quit my job so I can stay here as long as Brian needs me. Patty— that's my girlfriend—told me to go. She said, if you don't go, you'll regret it."

Does she mean girlfriend like a friend, or something else? I don't ask.

"When Shawn died, it was so fast," Annie continues. "He went into the hospital, and then he was dead. They treated him terribly."

"What happened?"

"Well, first, he had to sit in the waiting room for hours because he didn't have insurance. By the time he was seen by a doctor, he was half out of his mind with fever. And, you know, the usual. Nobody coming in to touch him, the staff avoiding him. His parents didn't visit."

"That's horrible."

"Happens all the time," she says. "One guy I knew, his family, who hadn't talked to him in years, swooped in after he died to take over his apartment and claim all of his things. They wouldn't let his boyfriend have any of it."

"That doesn't seem right," I say, refusing to react to the word boyfriend. Annie wants to make me as uncomfortable as possible.

"That's how it goes. The lover isn't even allowed to go the funeral. This other guy I heard about, a friend of a friend, his mother wouldn't let anyone in his hospital room. Said she didn't want any faggots in her son's room."

"Oh," I exclaim.

"Lovely, isn't it?" Annie slurps her tea. "You know, I've got to tell you, I wasn't happy about Brian coming back here. I mean, New York was a hard place for him, especially after Shawn died. And I just thought, why come back to this place, and these people, who rejected you? But, he wanted to. He missed you."

She's not accusing me, not exactly, but she's not offering me forgiveness either. And why should she? I drink the tea she made for me. We don't have to like each other. All we have to do is show up and take care of Brian. Andrew was right. It's the only thing.

"And, now, he's here," Annie says. "He's still here."

✳

The next morning after Jess leaves for school, Brian wakes up moaning, then screaming. He's drenched in sweat, burning up.

"We should call an ambulance," Annie says.

"It'll take too long," I tell her.

Annie drives Lettie's car because Lettie is too nervous. She rides in the back with me, and we hold Brian. Cradled across our laps, he hardly weighs anything. We stroke his head, his chest, his face. He trembles and gnashes his teeth, and I think there can never be anything as bad as this, my son dying in my arms.

But he does not die.

At the hospital, Annie runs in for help, and it seems to take a long time, too long, before two EMTs come out with a cart. They're lifting him, they're taking him away. The automatic doors close.

A nurse hands me a stack of forms. "Fill these out," she says.

"DNR," I tell her. "That's what he wants. DNR."

Lettie breaks down in tears. Annie puts her arm around her, speaks to her in a soothing voice. Others in the waiting room look away. They don't know who we are, why we're here, not yet. But one of the nurses knows and she glares, irritated we've brought him back.

I go over to the pay phone. My hands shake as I stick a quarter in the slot, another one slick in my hand. I don't cry. I feel surprisingly numb. I punch the numbers I know by heart. First, I call Andrew. Then I call Travis.

I don't know how much time passes. I pace the waiting room like an anxious father waiting on the birth of his child. Then, Dr. Patel calls me in to his office. I invite Lettie to come in too, but she holds onto the arms of the chair as if it might launch her like a cannon. I don't even have to ask Annie—she leads me to the office. The doctor closes the door behind us. He's slim and neatly dressed, and his lab coat is immaculately bright.

"He's very, very sick," he says.

He's on fluids and oxygen, and pain medicine and antibiotics. He has an abscessed tooth. His teeth will have to come out, so that the infection doesn't spread—his immune system is terribly weak. Annie asks questions, and the doctor answers rapidly. I miss most of it. He's alive, is all I'm thinking. He's alive.

"He'll need to be here a few more days," Dr. Patel says. "Then he can go back home. But he must have home health care."

"They won't come."

"They'll come," he says matter-of-factly, and shows us out the door.

Travis stands in the waiting room, along with Wayne, Paul, and Gus, wearing their dirty, greasy uniforms. Their healthy, enormous bodies take up too much space.

"Is he okay?" Travis asks.

I walk past him and punch the button on the elevator. No, he's not. He'll never be okay. When I step in, I see Travis watching me, his hat crumpled in his hands. The doors close.

For the next five days, Annie, Lettie, Travis, and I make trips back and forth from the hospital and home. They won't let Jess see him yet—no one under eighteen—and we all have to wear gloves, gown, and mask when we go in. Annie complains about the hospital treating him *like a leper*, even now, in 1986, almost 1987. They should know better, she says. But we don't put up a fight. We're too tired, and every shred of our energy goes toward Brian, wishing him to stay alive.

As I sit by his bedside, he sleeps or stares at the wall. My beautiful boy. His missing teeth—it hurts to look at him. Brian sobbed when the doctor told him they had to come out—a braying, ugly sob—and I tried to reassure him it would be okay, but nothing I said would ease his angst.

"Where is everyone?" he asks.

"They were just here," I say. "Everybody's been coming to see you."

Which is not exactly a lie. Liz brought carnations. A few cousins came by. Gus, without Pam, stayed for a few hours, crying into his hands. I no longer care about who comes to see him and who doesn't. I wish everyone would leave us. I want to spread open my arms like giant wings and enfold my son, so it's just the two of us.

Travis never stays long. He stands too far away from the bed. He looks out the window at the parking lot. He fiddles with the remote. He couldn't look at Brian before because of his earring, but now he can't look at him because there is no more pretending. He is a creature with only the slightest resemblance to our son.

As Brian sleeps, Travis and I sit in chairs on either side of his bed, suited up in our masks and gloves and gowns. Mindless commercials flash on TV, the sound turned off. We watch without speaking. We don't have anything to say to each other.

"I guess I better go." As Travis stands, the yellow paper gown crinkles. Brian opens his eyes.

"Dad."

Travis stands at the edge of the bed, nervously, looking at me for guidance. Brian mutters something. His lips flap together like an old person's, then open to expose red gums and darkness. I could have stopped it from happening. I worked at a dentist office. I should have demanded it. Now, it's too late.

"What did you say, honey?" I lean in closer.

"Dad," he says faintly.

His lips are dry and chapped, and the hideous, painful herpes sores have returned. It hurts him to talk. He licks his lips, tries again. I motion for Travis to come closer.

"You think this my fault," Brian says.

"What? No," Travis says.

"Brian, he doesn't think that," I start, but before I can smooth things over, Brian continues—he's speaking quietly, but there is no mistaking his words.

"I'm queer, Dad."

Travis's face scrunches, like he's going to cry or yell. Because of the surgical mask, only his eyes and his forehead are visible. I hear him breathing through the paper.

"Don't say that word," Travis says sharply.

The hushed sound of the IV. Travis's face, what you can see of it, drained of all color. Brian closes his eyes.

"Just go," he says.

"Travis, wait," I call, but he's already heading toward the door, his work boots clicking loudly on the linoleum. His back fills the doorway, then he's gone. Moments later, a nurse, one of the nicer ones, pops her head in.

"Everything okay?"

"Fine," I say.

Brian's eyes are closed, but I'm not sure if he's sleeping. I want to crawl into bed with him and keep him warm.

"He loves you," I tell him. "Your father loves you, Brian, he's always loved you."

Annie joins me for a cigarette. We stand outside in an area designated for smokers and turn our backs to the wind. I'm wearing a flimsy jacket, and the sharp cold cuts through me. Oak leaves rattle. A crumpled McDonald's sack rolls by.

"I'm so tired," Annie says.

"Go back to Lettie's," I say. "Get some sleep."

"Not just tonight. I mean, tired. Tired of hospitals, tired of watching my friends die." Annie stops, and her voice catches. "It's hard, you know. All my friends. I mean, I seriously thought of not coming back here to see Brian. But, of course, I have to be here."

I don't know what to say. I shiver, stamp my feet, and put the cigarette between my lips. It's colder than I thought it would be, and I wish I had a scarf.

"Goddamn it," Annie says. "I hate this fucking disease."

I don't react to her language. It's just us tonight. I made Lettie go home and get some rest. Travis hasn't come back, he won't. I remember after the miscarriages, how I sunk deeper into some dark, quiet place, how easy it was to shut everyone out. But Travis stood by me. He cooked for me, took care of me, and coaxed me back into the land of the living.

"Sharon, listen, I have to tell you something," Annie says. She's wearing her hood up, loose around her small, pale face. She looks so young, she's just a child, I think. "I brought pills," she says.

"What? What do you mean?"

"Brian said he didn't want to suffer." She looks at me with urgency. "I've got enough."

I stare at her. I don't understand. And then I do.

"No," I say. I want to tear my fingers into the grass and the dirt and the weeds and the cement. I want to dig until my fingernails are bloody, until my hands stop working. "No, no, no."

Jess

rom bed, Brian stares out the window at the bare trees.
I put on David Bowie's *Aladdin Sane*. We try to keep music playing
for him around the clock. My mother, grandmother, and Annie
are in the kitchen. I move the needle to the "The Prettiest Star." Brian
used to play this song for me when I couldn't sleep. It's different from
the rest of the tracks—jaunty, upbeat, sweet, almost like a jazzy show
tune.

Even though we're inside and the heat is cranked, Brian wears the
hunting coat that belonged to our grandfather. He's always cold. The
evening sun coming through the window makes him look like he's glowing under an orange halo like a saint.

"Shawn, turn this up," he mumbles.

Brian got home from the hospital yesterday. He doesn't have any
teeth. At first, I felt embarrassed to look at him. I still haven't gotten
used to it, but I don't cringe anymore when he opens his mouth. His
top lip curls down, and whenever he smiles, which is rare, you just see
gums and tongue and a dark space. When he remembers, he covers his
mouth, mortified. "My teeth, they took my teeth," he cried.

"I wish you could have met him," Brian says, realizing now that Shawn isn't here. "You and Mamaw. You would have liked him."

My brother doesn't look young or pretty anymore, but I still can't think of him as ugly, even with his toothless mouth. His eyes are dim and cloudy. Sometimes it's like he's vacant, staring at nothing. Other times, he's looking at something nobody else can see.

In movies, in a situation like this, there would be a conversation about death, but nobody talks about it, even when it's happening right in front of you. When Annie came back, I knew. I thought my mother would want to have a talk, but she looks like a hunted animal. Scared, she goes outside to smoke. My grandmother still talks about Brian bouncing back, getting better. My father stays away.

The camcorder sits on the table. Brian hasn't used it in weeks. He told us to shoot footage, but Annie is the only one who does. Now I pick up the camera and turn it on. I look through the viewfinder and watch him, his eyes closed and the light around him dimming, and I tell myself he's going to die, remembering I already knew this the day he came back. But I still don't want to believe it. I want to believe that somewhere there is a door and when he walks through, the sickness will disappear, and he will be healthy again, like the kids on TV who have cancer but always go into remission and live long lives. The light outside darkens, changing to purple, and the halo disappears.

I cut algebra and go in the bathroom. I check under the stalls, but nobody else is here. Sometimes, sitting in class, I feel like my body is going to explode. Cross country season is over, and I miss running.

I lock the door and sit on the toilet. The door is covered in graffiti: hearts, girl names plus boy names. But it's not all love. There is a sloppy drawing of a penis. And: *Theresa Smith is a slut. Tina Marshall is a lez. Ian and Richard are fags.* I search for my name, but it's not here. I'm sure someone has written about me on one of the doors. Kids still give me looks, and sometimes I hear them talking. But nobody has yelled anything or written anything on my locker since my fight with Carrie Driggs. She avoids me.

The outside bathroom door opens, and I hear a purse opening and closing. Someone hums, the sound of the faucet. Paper towel crank. I wait until I hear the door close before I unlock the hook and step out of the stall.

But I'm not alone. Brandy White stands at the sink, reapplying lipstick. She watches me in the cracked, splotched mirror. I take a deep breath. I wash my hands. This morning, my mother told me I didn't have to go to school, but I can't stay at my grandmother's all the time—the suspended quiet is too much, all of us just waiting.

"I heard you beat up Carrie Driggs," Brandy says.

The pink liquid soap slides between my palms, and smells like my grandmother. I rinse them with water and reach for a paper towel.

"I'm glad you did. She's such a bitch."

Brandy offers me her lipstick. I stare at myself in the mirror and color my lips strawberry red.

"It looks good on you," she says.

"Thanks."

We look at each other in the mirror.

"I guess I'll see you later," Brandy says to my reflection.

"See you later," I say.

We walk out together, but in the hallway we turn and go in opposite directions.

After school, I go to my grandmother's. I'm staying here now with my mother and Annie. The nurse Mabel walks out just as I'm walking in. She's shriveled and old, with bright white hair and skinny goat-like legs, and never gets tired. She isn't bothered by Brian or AIDS. She doesn't wear a mask, or look at him funny. Yesterday a different nurse came by, covered from head to toe, and didn't say a word to Brian, just dropped off bedding and pads and other supplies. But Mabel talks to him, even when he doesn't respond.

"Hey, darling," she says. "He's awake."

Annie is with him, sitting at the foot of the bed, his socked feet in her hands. She's wearing a long cable-knit sweater over stretch pants, and she looks up and smiles. "Hey, kiddo."

It's good having Annie here. She knows what to do, and she talks to Brian all the time, even when he doesn't respond.

Brian sighs with pleasure as she massages his feet. Then he opens his eyes. You can see the blue veins under his pale skin. He doesn't do much anymore. He gets short of breath just trying to sit up.

"Sing to me," he says.

Annie opens her mouth and the hairs stand up on my arms. I don't even hear the words, it's just the sound of her voice that's like some kind of magical bird calling from the woods. Soon my grandmother comes in, followed by my mother, and then Andrew. Nobody touches each other, we just stand there around the bed, listening to Annie sing and looking at Brian, his upturned face peering above the nest of covers like a bird's egg.

Stars shine from the clear night sky. We stand apart, arms at our sides. I don't know if I should give him a hug. But he doesn't move toward me, so I don't either. Nick and I haven't talked for at least a month, but today he called and told me he was visiting his dad for the weekend.

"Hey," he says.

"Hey."

Most of the leaves have fallen off the trees, and the wind rushes through the naked branches. The cords that used to hook to the speakers dangle from the poles like broken IVs. When the wind blows, they whip around. The movie screen shivers.

Nick offers me a cigarette.

"I don't smoke anymore," I say.

"Oh, okay."

We walk over to the merry-go-round and our breaths make clouds in the dark. Nick talks about how much he hates school, and I tell him about my fight with Carrie Driggs, which impresses him.

He puts his arm around me, and leans into kiss me, but I turn away. The air is brisk, the ground cold. I'm trying not to shiver.

"I don't want to," I say.

"Okay."

I don't know if it's because of all the time that has passed, or just that we're different people now. It doesn't feel bad. Just different. We lie on our backs on the merry-go-round and look up at the stars.

"I think my brother's going to die soon," I say.

Nick doesn't know how to respond, but that doesn't matter—I just wanted to say the words. Last night Annie put her arm around me and said, "Jess, it won't be long." I went to sleep trying to recall my best memories of my brother, but I couldn't remember anything. I wish that he'd been with me when I went to SeaWorld. I would have liked to have had him there beside me when Shamu exploded from the water, for him to witness this massive creature magically leaping into the sky, beautiful and fearsome, the most magnificent thing I've ever seen.

Nick hops off the merry-go-round. "Hold on," he says.

At first, he can't get it going—too many weeds, too much rust. He grips one of the bars and heaves harder, leaning his entire body into it. The merry-go-round creaks, then starts to spin. I stay on my back, not holding onto anything, and look up at the starry sky. Nick runs faster, pushing as hard as he can, and then he hops on and lies down next to me. The merry-go-round goes around and around. I'm dizzy and light-headed, but I keep my eyes wide open, watching the sky like it's a movie. The stars twirl, like whales diving and breaching, a beautiful blur. I feel so small. Space goes on and on, and the world keeps spinning.

I was only eight years old when my brother left. He didn't tell me he was going until the morning of his trip. I remember it was still dark, but not night-time dark. A silvery-purple light fell over the room. I opened my eyes, and there was Brian was standing in my doorway. Why was he up so early? I must have known something was wrong—he was already dressed for the day, wearing jeans and a T-shirt, and a denim jacket, his long, scruffy hair hitting the collar.

"Morning, sleepyhead," he said, and walked into the shadowy light. He sat next to me, and then I could see his face clearly, the fuzz of his sideburns, his deep-set blue eyes, the familiar lips, nose, forehead. My brother, my hero.

"Are we going somewhere?" I asked. Maybe to the woods, or maybe he'd take me on a drive. My brother liked adventures.

He smiled, but it was a small smile, a little bit sad. "I'm going on a trip," he said.

"Where?"

His smile grew. "New York City."

A dream place, where people went to be free.

"When?"

"Now," he said.

"When will you be back?"

"I won't be gone long."

I wondered if our parents knew. Brian said they did. He told me he'd send me letters. I didn't understand. I was only eight years old. I remember feeling a tightening in my stomach, a pain, but I didn't cry. Brian told me he'd be back. He promised.

"Scoot over," he said.

Then he stretched out next to me, and we lay side-by-side. He slid one arm under my head, and I rested there, in the crook of his arm. I felt warm and safe. I remember he had on his brown leather boots, and thinking our mother would be irritated if she knew he was wearing them in bed. We stared at the ceiling. Brian pulled me closer. He smelled like cigarette smoke. He smelled like adventure.

"Let's pretend we're under the ocean," he said.

"Should we get under the blankets?"

"No, let's just close our eyes."

The light behind my eyelids was a dark blue. We were under the sea. Brian described what we saw. Look at the starfish, he said. Look at the coral, what color is it? Pink, I said. Green, blue. A school of silver tuna headed toward us. Dolphins played and laughed around us. And here came a giant blue whale. We climbed on its back. The whale carried us across the sea.

When I opened my eyes, the room was orange and bright, and my brother was gone. I thought maybe I'd dreamed it all. But when I went downstairs, I couldn't find him. I wouldn't see him again for six long years.

✳

I keep waiting for everyone to show up to say goodbye, so Mamaw's house will be loud and full, like it used to be. But there aren't many visitors, and they don't all come at once. A few relatives, and a couple of friends of my grandmother's. They file in quietly to speak to Brian. Most of the time, he's asleep. Nobody stays long. They talk in hushed tones. Most everyone stands back, spooked to touch him or get too close, but Coach Sizemore went right over to him and put her hand on his head.

My father doesn't come over. But a couple of days ago, I looked out the window and saw his pickup parked across the street, in front of Betty Russell's house. He was just sitting there. Then he lifted his hands to his face. His shoulders shuddered. It was so bizarre that at first I couldn't comprehend it. My father was crying. He sat there a few more minutes, then wiped his forearm across his face, adjusted his hat, and drove off. I didn't tell anyone.

Andrew comes every day. It's better when he's here. He and Annie never stop talking, and their chatter makes things feel more normal.

Today he and Annie went with Mamaw to pick up food from the Dairy Freeze—she refuses to ever step foot in Dot's again. The food is for us, not Brian, who only eats baby food or Jell-O. My mother is taking a nap, and I'm the only one in the room with him. The house feels big and empty.

Sometimes, when you talk to Brian, he just smiles and looks out past you. You can't always tell if he heard you or not. But he seems better right now, like he's actually here and not drifting into space.

"Jess."

"What?"

The dreamy, dopey, toothless grin doesn't leave his face.

"Help me sit up," he says.

"Are you sure?"

He nods. For the past month, I've watched him get smaller and smaller, but still I'm shocked by how little he weighs. I put my arms behind him. He winces, and I stop.

"It's okay," he mutters. "Keep going."

Carefully, I help him sit up. I know he's in pain. A sheen of cold sweat breaks out across his face. It takes all his energy. I'm stronger than him, I weigh more. I fluff the pillows behind him and adjust a blanket over his legs. He gets chilled easily.

"Open the window," he says, his voice strained, hardly a whisper.

The air is cool, and smells like fall. Brian stares at the indigo sky. He taught me there is more than one way of looking at the world.

Killer whales are the ancient ones. There are some Indian tribes who believed whales possessed spiritual powers, healing sickness and guiding humans to safety. If a person comes into contact with a whale, the person will be transformed. There were some who believed the first humans were actually killer whales who turned into humans when they reached land. Then the whale-human forgot how to get back to the sea. A whale spotted near the shore was said to be looking for his lost land family.

Others believed killer whales are the souls of humans. They believed killer whales live in a parallel world—as people, deep under the ocean. And when we die, we return to our true selves: we return to the sea. This makes more sense than a heaven in the sky. There is life in the ocean. It's where we originated, so maybe that's where we return.

Nothing transforms, there is no magic. Or, does everything transform? I hesitate, and then reach up and touch my brother's face. His skin is warm. I don't pray anymore, but sometimes I dream. Giant, enormous, beautiful bodies. All of us together in the ocean. We die and we swim. I hold my palm to my brother's cheek, and he looks quietly at something I cannot see.

Brian

Listen, I wasn't always sick or afraid of dying.

Before all of this, before I owned a camcorder even, before Shawn was sick, before we knew what was in our blood, before so many deaths, I was just living my life. We all were.

I remember, it was one of the first warm days of the new year, one of those perfect New York days when everyone shakes off the last of the gloomy winter and spills out of offices, apartments, the projects. Shawn met up with Annie and me at our favorite Chinese restaurant. He had just found out that he won a part in a play. Not the lead, but a major part. And, this wasn't one of the usual artsy, experimental, downtown plays. This was uptown. Not Broadway, but close. He would play a gang leader. Of course that's what they offer you, how predictably racist, Annie said, and Shawn just shook his finger at her. Girl, you think I don't know that? What, do you want me to just walk away? Shawn said at least he'd be doing what he loved, and he'd get paid for it. Listen, this is gonna be one complex gang leader, he said, and Annie laughed and said she didn't doubt it. I didn't either. When Shawn was on stage, he made people *feel*. He was good. He slipped into characters easily, shifting the way he stood, or the timbre of his voice, or the wrinkle in his brow. I loved to watch him. No matter what role he took on—gang leader, father, young boy—he never lost the essence of him, a glowing, silvery light that shined off of him.

We celebrated by ordering too much food. Annie's father and step-mother, who she despised, had given her birthday money the week before, and I had a good week waiting tables. We planned to spend it all. What the hell were we saving it for? We cracked open our fortune cookies and pulled out the slips of paper and read them aloud. Annie said we had to eat them in order for them to come true. We ate our fortunes. We would be wise and wealthy, we would hold our friends close, and we would follow our dreams.

When we left the restaurant and stepped into the warm city air, surrounded by noise and lights and strangers, we felt energized and alive, so alive.

Let's make a night of it, Shawn said.

Why not? Annie said.

Why not, indeed?

We started at a dive bar in the East Village where the drinks were strong and the music loud, a place frequented by punks and artists and transsexuals and fags, our people. We took a table near the front. Lou Reed on the jukebox. A woman in a sequenced shirt dancing by herself. Our cigarette smoke swirled, the ice in our drinks clinked. We made summer plans—Fire Island, concerts, a road trip. We talked about traveling. We'd save money, get our passports, see the world.

Italy!

France!

Iceland!

We laughed into our drinks. Iceland?

Shawn, his hand on my thigh, grinned around his cigarette. Think of it, he says, the three of us in some crazy snowy dreamscape, the Northern Lights dancing above us, like being on another planet.

Fine, fucking Iceland, Annie said. Don't forget Thailand.

And Costa Rica.

And Portugal.

There was another bar or two, maybe a party or two. Sometime after midnight, we hailed a cab, snorted some lines, and spilled out in front of a club, pupils dilated, bodies buzzing, noses twitching.

New York, the city of dreams.

Most of the night is a blur. What I remember: everything is loud and fast and thrilling. What I remember: the three of us dancing, jumping around and twisting our bodies with abandon. The reflections of the disco ball like a million pieces of colored glass. What I remember: Shawn coming up behind me, his sweaty skin sliding against mine, his voice low in my ear, *Baby*. What I remember: Annie, laughing, pulling me onto the dance floor and spinning me around like I was the girl. What I remember: feeling breathless and joyous and invincible. We loved the city, we loved each other.

By the time we leave, the sun is up, it's Sunday morning and people are going to church, and we're leaving ours. We walk back to our place. While Annie and I wait in bed, smoking cigarettes, rehashing the night, Shawn busies himself in the kitchen. We hear the pop of a cork. Then, he saunters in, in just his underwear—beautiful, sexy—carrying a tray of mimosas and waffles, the golden squares perfectly holding the warm syrup Shawn has drizzled over them. The windows are open, the pink curtains dance in the breeze. We eat and drink in bed like queens. At some point, we fall asleep, we dream.

This night, we thought then, was just one of many. This is what life was, and this is what our lives were supposed to be. I didn't do anything to cause this—none of us did. We were just living. We were young and happy and alive, and nothing could stop us.

Sharon

Here we are. Annie and Jess sit on the floor playing the board game Life. Andrew rubs Brian's feet and hands and never stops talking—stories about work mostly, or he jabbers about fashion and models. He used to make Brian laugh, but now Brian just struggles to breathe. Lettie shuffles around in the kitchen, Patsy Cline croons.

Mabel the hospice nurse has told us what to expect, but I still don't want to believe. For now, he sleeps. Shallow breaths, a body of bones. He's in a hospital bed that a friend of Lettie's gave us. Next to the bed, a table cluttered with Kleenex, a plastic cup of water, bendy straws.

Brian's bony hands twist like hooks in front of his chest. Yellow nails, and feathery fungus sprouting between his fingers. His face is no longer my son's but the face of the terminally ill, the dying. Giant forehead, hollow cheeks. I stroke his thin hair, dry as straw, falling out in my fingers. His jawline covered in whiskers. Glassy eyes. Loud, labored breaths. When I touch his slight chest, I feel the thud of his heart—the body holding on. He doesn't want to die, but he doesn't want to live like this. Annie has not said anything else to me about the pills.

Now he doesn't fight me. He has no fight left. I change his clothes, I wash his naked body. Sagging, bruised, delicate skin. Concave stomach, bony chest. So fragile. It's impossible, sickening, to think about—one day he will not be here on this earth. But, sometimes, on the hardest days, I wish for his death. It's a terrible feeling, to want that kind of peace and relief for him, for us. I've bathed him as I used to do when he was a boy. I've fed him. Changed his diapers. The hospice people bring pads and bedding, and I've thrown out sheets—the diarrhea, the blood. And it's not just me. Andrew and Annie and Lettie—we've become the nurses, the aides, the caretakers. Everything stinks like sickness and shit and death.

How cruel—that I sit here, breathing, healthy, alive. When my mother was dying, I was hardly around. Now, I stroke my son's hand, his face. Sometimes, he seems to sense other spirits in the room. I don't know what he's accepted or not. There are no profound words or secrets he tells me. His needs now are only concrete—*I'm cold, I'm in pain, I'm hot, I'm hurting, I'm scared.* I do what I can to make him comfortable. I press a washcloth to his brow. I tell him everything will be okay.

"Have you talked to Travis?" Lettie asks.

"I've called. He doesn't answer."

"He needs to get over here."

We stand outside smoking furtively. Lettie doesn't break down as often now. She looks harried and exhausted. We're waiting. We don't want the moment to come, we do.

Earlier, one of Brian's old teachers and a girl he went to high school with and one of Lettie's Bingo friends came by. The old woman from the gas station, Lucy Highsmith, brought cinnamon rolls. Turns out, she knew all along who I was, but never said a word. Relatives stand in the doorway, slouched with what I wish was remorse but is probably just discomfort and unease. Gus comes regularly. He doesn't say much, just holds Brian's hand. Wayne hasn't come and Lettie does not mention his name. When Kyle stopped by, Lettie scolded him—"You ought not have said that on TV." He apologized, but only to his grand-mother, not to Brian, not to me. People who didn't talk to him before now come out of duty. They stand far away, don't get too close. Most of the time it's just the five of us, and that is fine by me. Lettie, Annie, Jess, Andrew, and me—this strange family that Brain has built.

Annie holds the video camera. I hate it, but Brian insisted she record everything. He wants Annie to take the footage back to New York to do something with it—what? To show strangers what suffering looks like. To change their views about this disease, or homosexuals, or love. I want to believe there is a God and heaven and continual life. But all I see right now is the pain of the body.

I sit next to him. I hold his wrists, his hands, his face. The morphine Dr. Patel prescribed helps ease the pain, but it's not enough. He hurts. Sometimes he still says a word or two, but most of the time he's in another world: beyond the restraints of language, but still locked in a body. Or maybe he's found some other plane of existence, seeing what the rest of us can't—divine emotions and brilliant flashes of color and sound and tone, like being inside a song.

I unscrew the lid and dip the spoon in the orange mush. "Honey, here," I say. Carrots were always his favorite.

I bring the spoon to his dry lips. He opens his mouth, clamps down, swallows. Lettie, Jess, Andrew, and Annie gather around, watching this strange newborn eat. I feed my son from the jar of baby food just like I used to do when he was so new to this world.

"He's holding on," Mabel says. "Not ready to go yet."

I show up early in the morning, before he goes to work. A film of frost shines over the pale grass. Baskets still hang from the hooks in the porch ceiling, but the flowers are long dead—dried up, brown, shriveled. I stand in the middle of the kitchen and look around at the mess. Stacked plates with the remains of baloney sandwiches on the counter, empty cans of beer.

Travis walks in the kitchen, dressed for work, and doesn't seem sur-prised to see me. He's changed his hair—it's buzzed, and he's shaved his mustache and sideburns, revealing skin I haven't seen in years. Instead of making him look younger, his exposed face makes him more severe.

"What's wrong?" he asks.

I go to him, and he flinches like I'm going to hit him. But then, as I lean in, he puts his arms around me. We stand like that for a long time. I feel him shudder, trying not to cry.

"You need to see him," I say.

"I'll come after work."

"No. Now. Go see him now. Talk to him."

At Brian's bedside, Travis looks at me with accusation, as if I didn't do a good job preparing him, but it's impossible to describe how emaciated he's become. So light, you can lift him like a baby. He can't weigh more than a hundred pounds. Each day, hour, minute, he grows further away from this world, or closer to some other place that I can't see.

Brian wakes up. His eyes are open, cloudy, distant. He doesn't speak, but he's here.

"Talk to him," I say.

Travis can't. Or won't.

He reaches down to pat his shoulder, and then too soon he takes his hand away. "I'm going to be late. I'll come by later."

"You, Travis," Lettie calls after him, but he hurries out of the house, then I hear the rumble of his truck, the sound of leaving.

Brian no longer eats food. I hold ice chips to his lips. I suck water in a straw and then drop it into his mouth, like I'm feeding a baby bird. Sometimes, my son is air, sometimes he is fire. He opens his eyes, two blue pieces of glass. He sees me. He closes them. His lips move. I lean closer so that I can hear him.

"Where's Dad?" Brian asks.

"He's here," I say. "He's right beside you."

Sorrow

Travis

His pickup smells like motor oil, tools, and some darker, denser smell—his body, his fear. Finally got the Chevy to run, after all this time.

Bullet hole is still there. He should replace the glass, but he knows he won't. A clean circle hisses with the cold air. Fracture lines, a tiny web. He wants to look at it. To remember.

He drives away from town, toward frosted fields. The trees are bony antlers sticking up against the pewter-gray sky. He used to go hunting with his brothers, his nephews. Brian didn't like it. Never went with them.

"If I found out one of my boys was a faggot, I'd shoot him," Wayne said.

He overheard him talking at work. Their family's name, smeared all over the papers. The way people still look at him when he walks into a store or the bank. Judging him, blaming him.

On the baseball diamond, he was perfect—a beautiful sight. Quick, strong, agile. He understood the art of the sport in a way that was so natural. What went wrong?

Back in his day, it was something to stay hidden. You didn't admit it. You certainly didn't flaunt it. There was a boy in the army, a nice kid— but weak. One night, the other guys wrapped him in a wool blanket, and took turns punching and kicking him. Fairy. Queer. Travis didn't protect him. He watched in silence. Or maybe he hit him too.

It's Sunday.

They don't have a church to go to, but even if they did, he doesn't want to be inside a building, all those people feeling sorry for him. Or feeling superior about their own lives, their children.

He never remembers the nightmares—it's just a cold, black fear when he wakes up, a buzzing of dread under his chest. He once lived in the jungle. He couldn't talk about it, not to his wife or his mother, not to his brothers, certainly not to his children. He didn't know how to describe the endless rain and strange noises coming from the trees, or the fear that ate away at his insides as he waited for gunfire to suddenly light up the darkness. He watched his buddies get killed. The numbers kept rising. None of them knew what they were dying for. He killed men, he killed boys. None of it was in their control. It was just dumb luck that he survived.

Sharon sleeps in Brian's room now. He expects she'll leave him soon. He's been filling out job applications in other towns, places where nobody knows his name. Where is he going? He doesn't know. Away. Not far. But he can't stay in that house. His wife, crying in the basement, his daughter worried about the extinction of whales.

He pulls over on the side of the road and gets out. When he closes the door, although he does so gently, it sounds too loud, like a crack of gunfire. There is no one around—not even anyone driving by. It's just him, alone. He crosses the road and walks out into a golden field. His boots crunch the frosty grass. His breath blasts the cold air, shivers of smoke. Chilled, he keeps walking out toward a stand of trees.

His son. He looked like an old man, bones and thinning skin, a skeleton with cracked lips, giant scared eyes, no teeth. Young men dying of a disease that has no cure. He heard on the news a prediction that there could be 14,000 new cases this year. The number of infected could be anywhere from 500,000 to two million. Millions will die of the disease all across the world if they don't do something to stop it. Some deaths don't matter, that's what people think. There are people who are glad his son, and his kind, are dead. AIDS. Say the word. AIDS.

They used to play catch in the backyard, and they watched TV, side-by-side, his son snuggled up next to him on the sofa. His son, who moved to New York City, who was not afraid. His son, who saw what he couldn't. Who recorded memories. Who made things.

Sharon has watched some of Brian's tapes, and so has Lettie, Jess, and that Andrew. There is one marked FOR DAD, but he hasn't watched it. Not yet. He didn't watch any of the tapes until a few days ago, when no one else was home, and he chose one at random from the big box supposed to go to Annie. He pressed play. And there he was. His boy, talking, smiling, looking at him. Then, he wasn't smiling. He read the names of the dead. Don't forget. Say their names.

Three buzzards circle high. Clouds shift and the sun parts the gray sky and glistens on the naked trees wild with bird song. He walks toward the forest and stops at a stand of sycamores. Tall, with mottled skin, branches reaching like fingers to the sky. He saw and he did terrible things. Years later, after the war, the guilt and shame, along with the blasts of fear, came for him. He walks over to the biggest tree, touches it. It wasn't just that he was embarrassed—there was that, but it was more. He was scared. He didn't know how to protect his son, how to save him. That's what went wrong: he let him down. The things people said, the way they acted. They helped kill his son. His silence. He helped kill his son.

His son, his beautiful son. An artist. He rubs his hand against the rough bark, scraping the skin until beads of red blood rise. A scuffle from behind him. He turns and sees a doe, wide-eyed, ears pricked, tail up. She watches him. He can hear his heart. She is beautiful. The kind he's killed before. He'll never forget. He holds his breath, and she stares back at him—and then turns and runs and leaps into the sky.

Starman

The sky.

Golden fields at dawn, at dusk.

Your grandmother's strawberry shortcake, the strawberries soaked overnight in sugar, Cool Whip on top, syrupy sweetness.

Ocean waves, a shell pressed to your ear, a heartbeat.

The black, curled hairs on his chest.

You close your eyes and she sings to you and you're back in the pool, but it's empty, just you, floating, the water holding you up, lightness. Weightlessness.

Your mother dancing with a broom in the kitchen.

Lighter and lighter.

Now he's on a stage, wings sprouting from his back.

Pink sunsets, beautiful men. Green woman with her crown and torch.

Give me your tired, your poor.

Sportscaster voices. The car windows rolled down because it's summer time, the air smells sweet and hot. Your father takes the curves slow. It's dark now, reflectors like orange eyes on either side of the road, trees looming, blocking the stars.

Choke up on the bat.
Keep your eye on the ball.
Your grandmother bakes cookies for you. Sugar cookies, chocolate chip, oatmeal raisin.

Your sister turns into a beautiful blue whale.
Annie is a mermaid.
She squeezes your hands.
It's okay, honey, it's okay.

The movie stars glowing in the night, brighter than the stars in the sky.

Brian, Brian, wake up.
You pretend you're still sleeping, this is your favorite part.
I'll get him, Dad says. *Come on, buddy.*

You're outside playing, and you hear her voice through the treetops and the green grass and the dandelions and clover. Your mother calling you home.

Snowflakes caught in your boyfriend's eyelashes. His smile. His strong hands reaching for you.

Twirling in your grandmother's apron.
Applause.

Shimmering gown. Sparkling eye shadow. Red lips.

A giant sleek body raises up out of the water. Salty sea on your tongue.

Flock of birds, snowy wings.
Morning light, waking, your mouth finds his mouth.
New York, a city of dreams.
You stand in a field. The sky is blue and cloudless.

He picks you up. The crook of his arm sliding under your butt,
his palm pressed to your back, his whiskers tickling your cheek.
You rest your head on his shoulder, and your father—
he carries you in his arms.

Acknowledgements

I am immensely grateful to everyone who encouraged me to keep writing, and supported me over the years. PJ Mark, you are the best. Thank you. For believing in this book, for your brilliance and keen insight. And, thank you to Ian Bonaparte and to everyone at Janklow & Nesbit.

Thank you to the small but mighty dream team—Betsy Teter, Meg Reid, Kate McMullen, Ashley Sands—and everyone at Hub City Press for shepherding this book into the world with such enthusiasm and genuine care, for answering all my questions and emails, for your endless hard work. Thank you to my publicist Alyson Sinclair at Nectar Literary for your attention and support, and thank you Luke Bird for designing such a perfect, gorgeous cover.

Megan Kruse, you're a gem. Thank you for reading my work so closely, answering my many emails and calls, and giving me such excellent advice. Robert Gipe, I appreciate the helpful feedback, and for reading the manuscript in a day. Thank you Silas House for your generosity and support, your big heart. Thank you to De'Shawn Charles Winslow and E.R. Anderson for championing this novel. Thank you to my queer literary heroes and luminaries Paul Lisicky and Sarah Schulman. Lidia Yuknavitch—a million thank yous for your unwavering belief, and for inspiring me to be brave.

Thank you everyone in the Portland writing community, especially Tom Spanbauer and Michael Sage Ricci. To my Eastern Kentucky University colleagues: Lisa Day, Julie Hensley, Nancy Jensen, Bob Johnson, and Young Smith. For their friendship and wisdom, and for helping me navigate the complicated paths of employment, life, and writing: Miriam Abelson, Cara Blue Adams, Allison Amend, Katie Carter, Rebecca Gayle Howell, Liz Asch Greenhill, Chelsey Johnson, Karen Salyer McElmurray, Jessie van Eerden, and Toby Van Fleet.

Thank you to all my dear friends and family. Thank you to the editors who published my work, to professors who invited me into their classrooms, to the Hindman Settlement School, and to the low-residency MFA programs at West Virginia Wesleyan College and Eastern Oregon University. Thank you to all my teachers and mentors, and to all my students, who continue to teach me. Thank you dear independent bookstores, booksellers, and librarians.

The Regional Arts and Culture Council and Lambda Literary provided crucial financial support and recognition. For the gifts of time and space, I'm indebted to the Hambidge Center, the Sou'wester Lodge, the Virginia Center for the Creative Arts, Michael and Martha Hoeye, and Cecile Dixon and Eugene Durbin.

During my research, I consulted many remarkable books, articles, and documentaries. The following were particularly illuminating: *Surviving AIDS* by Michael Callen; "AIDS in the Heartland" by Jacqui Banaszynksi; *Borrowed Time: An AIDS Memoir* by Paul Monette; *Personal Dispatches: Writers Confront AIDS* edited by John Preston; *My American History: Lesbian and Gay Life During the Reagan/Bush Years* by Sarah Schulman; *And the Band Played On: Politics, People, and the AIDS Epidemic* by Randy Shilts; *My Own Country: A Doctor's Story* by Abraham Verghese; *Close to the Knives: A Memoir of Disintegration* by David Wojnarowicz; *Silverlake Life: The View From Here*, a documentary by Peter Friedman and Tom Joslin; *We Were Here*, a documentary directed by David Weissman; and the ACT UP Oral History Project coordinated by Jim Hubbard and Sarah Schulman. The music of David Bowie inspired me to write toward the starry cosmos. The seed of this novel was planted nearly thirty years ago in an episode of *The Oprah Winfrey Show* about Mike Sisco, a gay man living with AIDS in a small town, who decided, despite facing stunning prejudice, discrimination, and homophobia, to go for a swim—to live his life openly and courageously.

This book would not have been possible without all the queer writers, artists, and AIDS activists—those who came before me and those who are here now, all who make the world a better place. I especially write these words in honor of and with gratitude for the queer men and women whose lives were cut tragically short by AIDS, and who are not here to tell their stories.

And finally I want to thank José Cruz for his love, inspiration, and encouragement. He read multiple drafts, journeyed across the country for me (several times, along with sweet Roxy and Dolly), and always believed this was a story that must be told. This is for you.

The COLD MOUNTAIN *Fund*
S E R I E S

NATIONAL BOOK AWARD WINNER Charles Frazier generously supports publication of a series of Hub City Press books through the Cold Mountain Fund at the Community Foundation of Western North Carolina. Beginning in 2019, the Cold Mountain Series spotlights works of fiction by new and extraordinary writers from the American South.

Watershed • Mark Barr

The Magnetic Girl • Jessica Handler

PUBLISHING
New & Extraordinary
VOICES FROM THE
AMERICAN SOUTH

HUB CITY PRESS has emerged as the South's premier independent literary press. Focused on finding and spotlighting new and extraordinary voices from the American South, the press has published over eighty high-caliber literary works. Hub City is interested in books with a strong sense of place and is committed to introducing a diverse roster of lesser-heard Southern voices. We are funded by the National Endowment for the Arts, the South Carolina Arts Commission and hundreds of donors across the Carolinas.

RECENT HUB CITY PRESS TITLES

A Wild Eden • Scott Sharpe

Let Me Out Here • Emily W. Pease

What Luck, This Life • Kathryn Schwille

Baskerville
10.8 / 14.4

Mount Laurel Library
100 Walt Whitman Avenue
Mount Laurel, NJ 08054-9539
856-234-7319
www.mountlaurellibrary.org